Yours for a Song

Amy James

Sugar Branch Press

Editing by Jamie Chavez
Front cover image by Clay McLachlan
Cover design by Mumtaz Mustafa
Book Layout © 2016 BookDesignTemplates.com

Published by Sugar Branch Press, LLC
Columbia, MO, 65203

www.amyjamesbooks.com

For Jane

Claire never would have let the girl get away if it hadn't been the thirty-fourth hour of her shift. Or if the guy in the next bed hadn't been screaming, like some psych-ward opera singer, through his drug-induced existential crisis. Or if Anita hadn't come in at just that moment and told her there was a code blue in room four, and the O.R. was in use. Any E.R. doctor worth her scrubs knew a flight risk when she saw one. This was all Claire's fault.

The girl couldn't have weighed more than eighty pounds. Her henna-burgundy hair hung in limp dirty strings around her pale and petulant face. And God, please let that huge, hideous tattoo on her forearm be a fake. It was a dark-blue boat anchor, marring the downy skin above her knobby, too-prominent ulnar head and creeping onto her hand.

Claire had looked at the chart again. Age twelve.

"Zoe?"

The girl nodded.

"What seems to be the problem today?"

Zoe pointed at her left foot, which was bare and streaked with dirt, as though she'd tried to clean it with a muddy washrag.

"Mind if I take a look?"

She shrugged.

The cut was old, angry, and deep red. Claire's heart squeezed. It was bad. Really bad. Hadn't her parents noticed?

"Zoe, this looks infected. Do you know the date of your last tetanus shot? Can I call your doctor?"

Zoe shook her head.

"We need to find out about that. Where are your parents?

Maybe we could also have a chat with them about helping you remember to keep this clean? It's really important."

"No!" The word came out of the girl like a missile, and Claire involuntarily took a step backward in surprise.

"Okaaayy . . . So your parents are at work today? Or at home?"

"They had to work. Can't you just, like, give me some medicine?"

"Probably. Who drove you here?"

The girl thought for a minute. "My gramma doesn't drive and my mom's at work. I walked."

Claire hesitated, not believing her. She looked at the girl's foot, which had to have made for a painful walk to the hospital.

"You'll need both an oral and a topical antibiotic. I think I have some samples I can give you." Claire looked back at the chart. "Do you know if you have health insurance?"

The girl had shrugged again. She wouldn't meet Claire's eyes.

"I'll rustle up some samples. Zoe, look at me, hon."

The girl looked up begrudgingly, making sure to fully express her annoyance.

"It's very important that you follow all of the instructions on these medications, and use the whole bottle. Don't stop using them once things get a little better. You have to take them all."

Zoe nodded and looked back at the floor.

The man next to them let out blood-curdling howl. Zoe finally looked up at Claire, fear shining in her big brown eyes. Claire shrugged. "What're ya gonna do? We got a howler."

Zoe almost smiled, but then the fear dropped back over her face like a curtain.

"Hang tight, Zo." Claire patted the girl's knee. "I'll be back in one sec."

• • •

Claire poked her head under all the bathroom stalls, looking for dirty green Chuck Taylors and a noxious teenage attitude. She had to find her. If the girl didn't take some antibiotics, she could lose her foot. Or her leg. Or her life.

Claire pulled her hair back into its ponytail at the nape of her neck and straightened her glasses.

"Zoe?" She called into the men's room. No answer. She checked those stalls too.

She headed for the front desk. All was quiet now, the calm after the storm, and Anita sat, emery board at the ready, glaring at her fingernails.

"Anita, have you seen Zoe, the little girl with the dyed burgundy hair?"

"Foot with attitude?" Anita set down her nail file, held out her fingers and looked them over again without raising her eyes.

Claire sighed. "Yes, *foot with attitude.*"

"Thought she was still in admissions," Anita said.

"She was. When I left to get a Z-Pak and some Bactroban, I'm afraid she might've split."

Anita looked at her, waiting.

"May I see the forms she filled out?"

Anita handed her a clipboard then went back to fingernail-filing. Zoe's writing was a childish scrawl and Claire scowled at the form. She was just a little girl. Way too young to be filling out her own hospital forms unaccompanied by an adult.

Whatever she'd first written as her last name had been scratched out and replaced with Lopez. Claire thought of teen-girl idol Jennifer Lopez's beautiful light brown skin compared to this girl's ghostly pallor. Zoe looked about as much like a Lopez as she looked like a forty-year-old man. Claire struggled to read what was under the scribble of lines Zoe had drawn through her real last name. Andrews? Anderson? Anderton?

She looked at the address. 100 Pine Street. Pine Street was real enough, but 100 seemed a little too neat.

Claire thought for a moment. The girl couldn't go untreated, and now she was gone. Whatever happened outside the hospital doors was *technically* none of her business. But . . .

She needed the antibiotics. And what if she were neglected? It seemed a likely possibility. If Claire were lucky enough to have a daughter, she would never let her suffer with an infection like that.

The certainty that she was going to do some outside-the-job-description sleuthing settled in her chest before it reached her brain.

"What's up?" Anita asked, looking up at Claire with suspicion.

"Will you photocopy this for me? I'll need a CA/N form too," Claire said.

"Can?"

"Suspected child abuse/neglect."

"Right. Haven't seen one of those in a long time."

Anita took the clipboard back and swirled her chair around to face the large copier behind her desk.

"You oughta let Donna know about this, 'stead of going off on your own," she said, but she slapped the paper down on the copier screen.

Claire pictured the hospital social worker's perpetually overwhelmed facial expression and her mad-scientist hair, which usually housed two or more ballpoint pens protruding at odd angles. The hospital was trying to cut corners, and that meant paying as few salaries as possible. By the time Donna was able to get it on her calendar, it could be too late.

"Here you go, Nancy Drew," Anita said, handing her the papers.

Claire folded them in half. "Thank you, Anita." With any luck, Claire could be out of here in half an hour. She'd nap in her car, then head over to Pine Street.

"Oh," said Anita, resuming the nail filing. "I almost forgot. Dr. Nguyn's the latest with the norovirus. Fox sent him home. Quarantined. You're it 'til six."

CHAPTER 2

"My assistant *did* buy a seat for the guitar." Eli Archer was starting to sweat. If he didn't get out of New York today, he was going to seriously freak out.

"Sir, I'm sorry, I don't have any record of a second ticket." The face of the tight-haired woman behind the Skyview Airline counter was a practiced placid mask. "We can check the guitar for you. I assure you, we handle instruments through checked baggage every day. We have an excellent track record."

"It's a 1938 Martin D-18 Dreadnought. I'm not checking it." He'd even named the guitar—Bess. Of *course* he wasn't checking it.

"Perhaps we could check seat availability. Would you be willing to sit separately from your guitar, or do you need to ride together?" A hint of snideness cracked the mask just the tiniest bit.

His teeth clenched of their own accord. "Fine. Check seat availably. Separate is fine."

He took off his sport coat and draped it over the hard-shell guitar case. He'd worn a thick beard (real), long hair, black sunglasses, and well-worn Levis to the airport. He hoped he looked like any other jobless, aimless, thirtysomething musician with nowhere to be on a Tuesday. If he could hide his whole face in beard and hair right now, and just make himself invisible, he would. He *needed* to get on a plane today, to fly away from it all: the cameras, the tabloids, the overzealous fans, anyone who knew his name.

Tight-Hair began tapping on her keyboard with long red nails. Behind him, there was some kind of rustle, then the sounds of annoyed voices. He turned.

There was a camera in his face.

He cursed.

"Eli, what do you think of the rumors Coco has been spotted with John Mayer?" The paparazzo was in his mid-fifties and sporting a giant watermelon-belly over which his out-of-season short-sleeved shirt barely buttoned. He was sweating and his eyes held the hungry gleam of a coyote.

Eli held his hand up, silently warning him to back off. Acid adrenaline-sweat pierced his armpits.

"Are you and Coco still together?" the pap asked, coming closer.

"Back off, man." If Eli never heard the name Coco Skye again, it would be too soon. He held up both hands now, two stop signs. The guy came closer, and for a moment Eli imagined he could smell his devil breath. Eli's arm remained fully extended outward, and if this idiot had the sense of even a low-level street criminal, he'd back the hell off.

"Word on the street has her leaving John Mayer's apartment this morning in the same clothes she wore last night."

It was too much. The sleepless nights, the utter lack of privacy, the relentless attention, the public humiliation for his mother. His jaw was tight and his chest was bursting with an ominous slow drumbeat. He was ten minutes past his breaking point.

"Must've been some night for Coco," the pap said. He stepped forward, bumping Eli's outstretched hands.

Eli punched him in the face.

• • •

After he'd been fingerprinted, mug-shotted, paperworked, and relieved of his wallet and the suitcase he'd been carrying, Eli was told he could call someone to bail him out. Dread sloshed inside him like bad soup.

Of course this would make it to the tabloids. It'd be all over the Internet. The mainstream papers too. But he still had to make his best effort to prevent it. He thought of his mother, gentle and dignified Leah Archer—of her embarrassment, her disappointment—and felt even sicker.

He picked up the jail phone, held it a couple of inches from his face, and dialed.

"Eli, man, it's one in the morning. I was sleeping. Not. Alone."

Alec had been Eli's friend since high school. Once you found yourself famous, you prized the people who'd liked you pre-fame, teenage zits and all.

"I know it's late. I'm sorry. I was just hoping to keep this thing under wraps. Who else was I gonna call who wouldn't blab? Plus, you know, the whole lawyer thing."

"What are the charges?" Alec sighed.

"Battery."

The guard spiraled his right index finger in the air—wrap it up.

"He's telling me I have to get off the phone. Can you come?"

"Where are you?" Alec's annoyance was obvious, and for a fleeting moment Eli was tempted to remind him of the Mercedes incident. They'd been sophomores in college, and Alec had been nearly hyperventilating over the long and deep scratch he'd just put in his father's perfect, shiny car. Old Man McLellan had come down the driveway, pushing the big green garbage can, same as he did every Tuesday evening, and Eli had snatched the car keys from Alec and told the old man he'd been driving the car himself, and he was very, very sorry. And insured. McLellan wouldn't kill *him*. Going after Alec was another story. His mom's car insurance had gone up and he'd been in a moderate amount of hot water, but he'd never told a soul.

"Queens," Eli told him.

"Aw, man," Alec said.

"Sorry."

"You owe me. Big time," Alec said.

"Thanks. Really, thanks, man." Probably not a good time to bring up the Mercedes.

Alec growled, and Eli might've almost smiled if the guard

hadn't been looking down at him with psychopathic eyes and a too-short buzz cut.

After that, Eli was corralled to a holding cell, where about twenty other men were already in the room, seated on benches along the walls. In the middle of the room was a filthy metal toilet, the back of which was a metal column. Which was a drinking fountain. A retch pushed his stomach muscles upward.

A skinny man with light brown skin was rocking back and forth repeating "Oof, oof, oof, oof, oof."

"Shut the *fuck* up, man." An enormous blond guy who looked like Hulk Hogan in poor health started toward the little rocking guy.

Eli took a spot on a bench in the corner and tried to be invisible.

The Hispanic man next to him smelled like vomit, alcohol, and a chemical waste sewer. Eli tried not to breathe too deeply.

This was an unbelievable new low. This was pond-scum low. And who was he kidding? The news would be everywhere within days. His mug shot. Speculations about his temper. All the stories about Coco and wild nights would be dredged back up.

All he wanted was a normal life again. Maybe normal was a bit of a stretch, since for him that meant living half the year on a tour bus, but it was his life, and he wanted it back. At least he'd been able to walk into a grocery store and buy an apple and a six-pack.

A guard pushing a cart on casters swung the door open and entered the cell. "Dinner." He tossed boxes of Raisin Bran and cardboard half-pints of skim milk at the men. No spoons.

Eli's right hand shot into the air and caught his. He winced with the pain, and looked down at his hand, which was beginning to swell. Damn, he was an idiot. He looked down at the Raisin Bran. He couldn't imagine eating anything in this room.

Eli tried not to see the toilet in the middle of the room as the men around him poured cereal and milk into their mouths. The man two seats down from him leaned forward and addressed Eli. "*Vas a comer esto?*"

Eli could understand Spanish better than he could speak it, so he just handed the man the cereal and milk without answering.

"Hey, how come he giss it?" a voice from across the room called out.

Eli didn't want to say one single word, but not answering might make it worse. "He asked," he said through clenched teeth.

The voice got up and walked toward Eli. He was tall and thin, a light-skinned biracial man with a huge brown afro and bright blue eyes. He looked insane.

"I wanna sit next to him. Scoot over," he said to Eli's neighbor. Stinky looked up at him with dead eyes and didn't budge.

"I *said*, scoot over."

Stinky remained stubborn for a moment, then scooted.

Before he sat down, Eli got an unwelcome eyeful of the new guy's right butt cheek. A big round hole had been scissored out of the back of his jeans. His eyes were Adderall-wild.

Come on, Alec. Get me out of here.

"What're you in for?" Butt Cheek asked him.

Having a conversation with Butt Cheek was about the last thing in the world Eli wanted to do, but he didn't want to antagonize him with silence.

"Breaking a guy's nose with my knuckles." Possibly a slight exaggeration—it might be the knuckles that were broken, not the nose.

"Aw now, what you go and do that for?"

Eli shrugged and stared at the ceiling.

"Me, I got framed." The guy pointed at his own chest enthusiastically. "The pigs, they always out to get me."

Eli cut his eyes over to the guy.

"See. You know what I'm talking 'bout. You got the look

too."

Look?

The pain in his hand was increasing by the minute. He'd heard there were right and wrong ways to punch. His hand was nagging him—*wrong way, wrong way.*

"Yeah-ah, you got the look all right. Countercultural."

"*Mm.*"

"See, I provide a public service. Pot is *healthy* for you. People *need* the bud. I give 'em that." He pointed at his own chest again. "Well, maybe not *give.* I gotta make a living."

"True."

"Hey, you got a dealer?"

"No."

"We should hook up, man."

"I'm allergic."

"Frealz, man? You puttin' me on?"

A guard approached, keys clanking, and unlocked the door.

"*Shh, shh,*" Butt Cheek said. "Don't let 'em hear you."

"Eli Archer," the guard called.

Saved by the bail. Eli stood and joined the guard, a balding fiftysomething man with a beer gut and a clipboard.

"Word sure travels fast," the guard said, marking something on his clipboard. "Wife just texted me with your mug shot to ask if I'd met you. She's a fan. Saw it online. You think I could get an autograph for her?"

Eli nodded, and tried to push back against the rising dread in his chest. Word was already out.

"Facebook me!" Butt Cheek called. "It's Diggy Blunt!"

• • •

"You do not smell good," Alec said. His daytime look—Armani suit and two-hundred-dollar haircut—was missing, and in its place he wore plaid pajama bottoms and a Yale sweatshirt. "I can't believe I'm letting you in my car like this." They approached the BMW, which gave two short chirps when Alec unlocked it.

"Sorry." Eli opened the back seat to toss in his guitar and suitcase.

A blonde in a nightgown turned toward him from the front seat. "Hi. I'm Melinda." Her voice was sultry and suggestive, and her nightgown was nearly transparent. She'd skipped any kind of sweater or jacket on the chilly March night.

Eli raised his eyebrows at Alec.

"She saw your name on my phone." Alec shrugged. He took the driver's seat and Eli took the seat behind him. "What *is* that smell?" Alec asked. "Death?"

"Humanity."

"Oh, that."

"I'm *such* a huge fan," Melinda said. She flashed him a sexy little smile.

He looked away. "Thank you."

Alec pulled the car out of the jail and turned toward Manhattan.

"Actually, man, I don't want to go home," Eli said.

Alec braked on the deserted street and looked at Eli in the rearview mirror.

"I was trying to get out of town when it happened. Take me back to JFK?"

Alec shrugged and turned the car to make the block. "Where you going?"

"Away," Eli said.

"Is that a town in Alaska?" Alec asked.

"Not exactly, but that's the general idea."

"No women and butt-ass cold?"

Melinda giggled and put a hand on Alec's arm. She looked back at Eli and tossed her blonde hair over her shoulder, smiling at him again.

He turned away again. "Away from cameras and anyone who cares about them." Eli pointed at a Days Inn on the left side of the street. "Can you wait twenty minutes while I check in and take a shower and change these clothes? I can't get on an airplane smelling like this."

"You really can't." Alec whipped his car into the parking lot. "Hurry, man. I gotta be in court in the morning."

"I know. Sorry. Double my bill."

Alec pulled into the circular drive at the motel's entrance.

Eli grabbed his bag. "Be right back. Thanks, man." He opened the car door with his left hand and swung his legs out, only to see a feminine manicured hand waving behind Alec's seat. With a piece of paper in it. A phone number. Damn, that was brazen. He hoped Alec didn't actually like the girl. Eli pretended not to see the paper. "Fifteen minutes, max."

Alec shot a wave in the air without turning toward him.

An hour later, Eli was back in line at the Skyview Airlines counter.

• • •

Eli wielded Bess in front of him down the narrow airplane aisle. Seat 6B—the Asian kid sitting by the window barely looked up from his iPad as Eli strapped the guitar in.

"Sir, may I assist y—" The flight attendant stopped in her tracks when Eli looked up at her. "Oh. *Oh.* Sir. Mr. Archer, sir." She rubbed her pink-lipsticked lips together. "Mr. Archer, if there's anything, *anything*, I *personally*, can get for you . . ." She stood straighter, thrusting her C-cups forward.

"Thank you," Eli said tersely. He usually tried to handle such propositions with courtesy, but he was fresh out. He excused himself and tried to walk past her toward his own seat in 4A. She barely moved, forcing him to make full body contact as he moved past her.

"Anything at all!" she called after him.

He managed to sleep for a while, but the throbbing in his hand woke him. He opened his eyes and looked down at it. It didn't look quite right. Puffy and bruised. Damn. He'd have to get it checked out.

What had possessed him? He knew better than to hit a paparazzo. It was like hitting the tar baby. You just got yourself in deeper. If he'd had more than two hours of sleep at a stretch anytime in recent memory, he never would've snapped like that.

Finally, the plane shimmied to a stop and he sagged a little into the seat. Erin, his assistant, had made arrangements for a rental car, since there was no airport in the middle-of-cow-country town she'd chosen for him. She was a southern girl, grew up in Tennessee, and her family had vacationed at this place when she was a kid. She said it was "artsy." Whatever that meant. He pictured scarecrows with corncob pipes.

What exactly was he going to do if he'd screwed up his hand? At least it was his right one. He could still strum a guitar, since that didn't require dexterity. But everything else—cello, piano, trumpet, whatever else he needed to play . . . The inside of his skin pricked hot with shame and self-recrimination. All he wanted to do was check into a hotel and sleep for about three days. He'd feel so much better once he got to the house Erin had rented for him, then dead-bolted the door. Away from the world. Away from the cameras. Just him, a notebook, and the music.

He retrieved his guitar from seat 6B and made way for the rental car counter.

• • •

"Sir, are you talking about Haven Springs, *Missouri*? 'Cause you're in Arkansas right now." The woman in the Hertz uniform looked both offended and a little concerned for his safety and/or sanity. Her eyebrows were drawn with disapproval, but her dark chestnut-brown skin was unlined, despite being middle-aged.

He remembered it now. Erin had told him. He was flying into Arkansas, but he'd be living in Missouri—should be easy to remember because it sounded like Misery. "Yes, that's right," he said. "Missouri. Since I flew into Arkansas, you know . . ."

"You don't have Google on that phone?" She pointed to his iPhone on the counter and raised an eyebrow.

He looked down at his phone. "Dead. I like it that way."

"You're in Bentonville right now."

"So how far is Haven Springs?"

Now she was flat-out, not-bothering-to-hide-it, looking at him like there might be something wrong with him. She studied him with suspicion. "Sir? Would you like me to call you a taxi? Are you in proper condition to be operating a motor vehicle?"

"Just the car, please. Sober as a senator." He pushed the dark glasses up on top of his head to show her his drug-free eyes.

After a few more leery questions and not one, but two backup credit cards, reluctantly, she gave him the paperwork and the key.

The day was chilly, crisp, and sunny, holding the first hint of spring. Back in New York, there were still gray piles of snow at the curbs. He took a deep breath of clean air.

Eli located the gray Impala in the rental car lot, fitted his suitcase and Bess into the back seat. He slid into the plasticky-smelling beige interior and plugged in his phone, saying a silent prayer it would boot up with a screen empty of messages. No such luck. DMG wanted to talk about the contract, or lack thereof, for the next record; the P.R. lady wanted his body and to spend half an hour on the phone with him; and his mother had hung up without leaving a voice mail. He wished he could throw the thing out the window.

Instead, he pulled up GPS and typed in *Haven Springs, MO*. Sure enough, there, a little above the border of Missouri and Arkansas, was a small dot for Haven Springs. Very small. It was in the middle of some kind of mountain range. He zoomed the map out. The Ozarks. Cool, maybe they had fiddlers. Banjos. Harmonicas. He tossed the phone on the passenger seat and headed north on Highway 72.

By the time he was halfway to the tiny dot, he could no longer remain in denial about his hand. He hadn't slept in days, and he longed to crawl into a bed, any bed, but it was clear now that even if he tried, the pain would prevent him from sleeping.

He kept driving. First stop in Haven Springs: the E.R.

CHAPTER 3

Claire drove up and down Pine Street, hoping for some sign of Zoe. She slowed before each house with illuminated windows and tried to see inside. Her hair was piled into a Mizzou cap, and she tried to stay low in the seat to avoid being recognized.

This was so not on her list of things to do today—and she did have a list. Sleeping had been her primary goal, along with returning a call to a family friend with health worries, a phone call to her retirement account manager, and her biannual mattress rotation. She also had to get back for an E.R. shift starting at the dinner hour. She sighed, picked up her iPad, and moved her to-do list from today to tomorrow. She needed to pee, and she wondered how female private investigators handled such occasions.

It was getting near five o'clock now, and a minivan pulled into a driveway and deposited two boys in soccer uniforms. A petite blonde mother followed, and their house clicked on with yellow lights. Pine Street was on the east edge of town, and along it stood some of the more nondescript houses in a mountain resort town otherwise full of well-manicured Victorian architecture. In most of Haven Springs, artists had adorned their yards with sculptures and flowers and signs about saving the rivers, but on this street, everything seemed a little gray and droopy. A couple of patched-up trailers shared one lot, and a mangy dog roamed loose outside one of them.

In the hour she'd been circling the block, most of the houses on the street had gradually come alive with lights and flickering televisions and family dinners.

Except one house. One small house with dirty white vinyl siding remained dark and silent. She crawled her Honda toward it and parked in front of the house next door. A carpet of leaves lay rotting on the lawn, but autumn was long gone. The car in the driveway wore a coat of dirt and pollen half an inch thick.

This was the one. She could feel it.

Claire sat staring at the house, suspicion and fear crawling up her skin like bugs. Was she about to do something really stupid? But Zoe needed these antibiotics. Her hand flew to the Z-pack and tube of ointment on the passenger seat. Still there.

She looked back up at the house, and that's when she saw it. A very dim light flickered inside. Someone was in there. She couldn't tell if it was a flashlight or a candle, but the light had definitely moved.

Adrenaline shot through her.

What was she supposed to do now? Zoe's bony wrist and that awful tattoo came back to her. Zoe's frightened and guarded eyes. Claire had to do something.

A small movement darted across the front window, and Claire ducked low in her seat.

Should she call the police? Ask a friend, maybe Holly, to come back with her? Just go pound on the door and shout the name of a child who might or might not live there? She looked at the house number. 1012. This had to be it.

Bam bam bam bam!

Her car window rattled with impact, and her heart kicked into a thunderous rhythm. Her legs shook and the hair pricked up on her arms.

"What're you doing out here?" a male voice demanded. He was standing outside her car window, pounding on her window. It took her a moment to come back to earth. She cracked the window a quarter of an inch.

"I was just—"

"Wait a second! Dr. T? That you?"

"It's me." The adrenaline fog cleared and she realized it was Tony Rossi, one of Haven Springs's two mechanics, standing outside her window. She'd treated him for a broken metatarsal last year when his son had dropped a car battery on his foot.

In a town of two thousand, especially one tucked into a seven-square-mile mountain crevice, it was tough to remain anonymous while stalking a child's house.

"What'n the sam hill you doing out here?" Tony asked.

"Kind of a long story. Hey, Tony, can you tell me—does a little girl named Zoe live in that house?" Claire pointed at 1012.

He nodded. "Poor kid. Mom's an alkie. They're kinda new to town. Maybe a year and a half? My wife used to try to take 'em food and stuff, but the ol' hag told her not to come back. Cussed her out. Wife cried. Last year Zoe didn't have no coat, so my wife bought one of those pink puffer numbers and shoved it in the mailbox."

Claire imagined Zoe's reaction to a pink puffer coat and almost smiled. Then again, maybe Zoe'd been cold enough to wear it. Claire's heart cracked a hairline further.

"Why you askin' about Zoe? She in some kind of trouble?"

Claire got out of the car. "I think she might be."

Tony scratched his mostly bald head.

"Tony, do you think you could help me? To try to get someone to come to the door? And maybe go in if we have to?"

"*Go in*? That ol' witch don't let nobody in." He shook his head.

"Zoe needs medical treatment, and I'm afraid something really bad could happen if she doesn't get it."

He scratched his head again. He looked at Claire's face, then slowly nodded. "All right."

• • •

A moment later, Claire stood with Tony outside the aluminum door of the darkened house, waiting. On the other side of the door, there was silence.

"Zoe?" Claire called.

More silence.

Claire inched sideways toward the front window and tried to peer in without placing her body in front of the window.

"They don't go nowhere. That car ain't been moved in probly two years. Probly in there hidin'."

Claire couldn't see anything through the window. She stepped back. She needed to sit and think for a minute, but she didn't want her butt, or any other part of her body, touching the dingy chairs or steps. "What should we do?" she asked.

Tony shrugged.

Claire stepped back toward the window, and put just her face in front of it, cupping her hands to try to make out anything inside. Nothing. Whatever the dim flicker of light had been, it was gone now.

"I can't just leave her in there," she told Tony.

Tony shrugged again. "Police? Child Services?"

"There's not time to wait for her to go through the whole red-tape thing. She needs medical care now."

Tony nodded. They stood in silence for another moment.

"I got an idea," he said.

"Great. What?"

"Might be a tad illegal."

"A tad?"

He held his thumb and index finger apart by about an inch.

"On a scale of one to ten, how illegal are we talking?" Claire couldn't believe she was asking this question. She would never do anything that would risk her medical license. Felonies didn't go over well with the medical board. She'd never broken the law in her life, unless you counted setting the cruise control three miles over the speed limit on the expressway.

"A two," Tony said.

Claire thought for a moment. "I can live with a two."

"Get over there 'way from the window." He pointed to the left side of the door.

Claire moved past him to the other side of the door.

Then Tony pounded on it, his powerful fists against the door echoing into the night. "POLICE," he boomed, sounding every bit like the real thing. "Open up."

A loud crash came from somewhere inside the house, like a metal pot dropped on a tile floor.

"Someone's in there," Claire whispered.

Tony repeated his command and his banging.

Claire wondered if impersonating a police officer was a felony or a misdemeanor in Missouri. Then she remembered Zoe's foot and the angry red streaks shooting up Zoe's leg and decided to stop thinking about it.

Tony pounded again.

With a very slow and timid creak, the door opened an inch.

"Zoe!" Claire said, relief rushing through her, and stuck her Nike into the opening between door and doorjamb.

A face, round and pale as a china plate, peered up at her from underneath faded burgundy bangs.

Claire shoved the door open and resisted the urge to take the child into her arms.

Zoe's voice shook. "Is this about the hospital bill?" Poor kid looked like she might wet her pants.

Claire debated for a just a moment before answering. "Yes. Yes, Zoe, I'm afraid it is. You'll need to come with me."

• • •

Claire put Zoe into the steamy shower of an unoccupied hospital room.

Holly, Claire's closest friend and favorite nurse, held Zoe's dirty clothes far away from her petite frame between two gloved fingers. The clothes smelled like perfume, mildew, and foot odor. "I can have these through the wash and dry in just over an hour. Want to put her in a hospital gown until then, or get some old clothes from the stash?"

"Gown," Claire said. "I bet she likes her own clothes, and that'll buy me a little time with her before I go on duty. I want to wait outside the door, though. I don't want to take any chances she'll run again. Even naked."

Holly nodded. "I can't believe how *skinny* she is. I mean, Ryan's skinny, and he eats four times as much as I do, but she's . . . It doesn't look right."

"No, it doesn't. Don't tell Dan I'm breaking hospital—" Claire stopped. Dan was Holly's brother, a doctor at the hospital, and Claire didn't want him to think she was a flake. She actually wanted him to think she was date material, but—

Holly nodded. "Back in a flash with a clean gown."

When she returned a moment later, Zoe was still in the shower. "Wonder how long it's been since she's had one," Holly said.

A long time, was Claire's guess. Zoe's foot was probably infected due to sheer filth. Or . . . what if she didn't have enough to eat, and her body was too weak to fight infection? Claire shuddered. She needed some information—*truth*—about what was going on in that house. Earlier that night, at the dark and silent house, no one had checked on Zoe. Zoe had stood at the doorway talking to strangers—one of them supposedly a police officer, and no one had stirred.

Claire tried to tell herself she'd done her duty. She'd filed the required-by-law report on Zoe for possible neglect. She was making sure the girl was out of medical danger. Beyond that, this really wasn't her job.

"I'm going to get out of here so there isn't a gang outside her bathroom door when she comes out," Holly said. "Stick your head out and tell Anita if you need me."

"Thanks, Holl."

Holly gave a little salute, her dishwater blonde curls moving with her as she turned.

When Claire heard the shower turn off a couple of minutes later, she cracked open the bathroom and stuck her hand through the opening with the clean hospital gown. After a long moment, she felt the gown leave her hand.

"We're washing your clothes for you," Claire said through the door.

No answer.

A few minutes later, a wet and frightened child emerged in a too-big hospital gown. Claire was relieved to see the boat anchor tattoo had partially washed off, but the overall look was still of an unhappy Sphynx cat in a damp maroon wig.

"Now that you're clean, let's have a look at your foot."

"But . . . I can't . . . pay." The girl was trembling.

Claire's throat closed. *No crying, Claire. Absolutely* no *crying.* She was usually—always—able to keep her crying problem under control when she was on the job, but abused and neglected kids always got to her. She longed to be a mother so badly, it was impossible to comprehend this kind of parenting. Even more impossible to forgive.

"Don't worry about the money, babe," Claire said, tears successfully swallowed. "Hop up on the bed here and let me look at your foot."

"But I thought . . . you said . . . they were bringing me in to pay."

"I lied."

Zoe looked up at her with disbelief, and Claire made a funny face.

"You . . . you *lied*?"

"Sorry about that. Hop on the bed, Zo. This is really important. I won't go into the gory details of what could happen if you don't get medicine, but I promise I'm telling the truth about this—you would *not* like it."

Zoe got on the bed, never taking her eyes off Claire. "So I'm not in trouble?"

"No. No, of course not." Claire put a hand on Zoe's shoulder, intending to comfort her. Zoe flinched and shrank backward. Abuse? Claire surreptitiously looked the girl over for bruises. None were visible on first glance, so that was a relief.

But the girl's foot was worse. "You're not in trouble, Zo, but your foot is."

"It hurts." It was the first voluntary statement Zoe had made since they'd met, which Claire took to mean it must hurt pretty darn bad.

"It's fixable. But I can't stress to you enough that you have to take this medicine. Can I trust you to do that?" Claire held up the antibiotics in her hand.

Zoe nodded.

"I want to come by your house and check on you tomorrow. By the time you take your third dose, you should already be seeing improvement, and I want to make sure that's happening."

Panic flashed over Zoe's face. "I won't be home tomorrow."

"Why not?"

"Cheerleading practice runs late on Wednesdays."

Claire held back a snort. The girl was quick on her feet, she had to give her that. But although Claire had probably outweighed Zoe by a *few* pounds in high school, she knew all too well, from personal experience—girls with nicknames like "chicken legs" did not make the Haven Springs cheer squad.

"Where's your mom tonight?"

"Home."

"I didn't see her there."

"She hasn't been feeling well."

"Anything I can help with?"

"No!" Zoe looked a little wild-eyed, and Claire backed off. She took a swab from the sterile tray and put the topical antibiotic on the wound.

"We'll need to go to the cafeteria to get you some food. You can't take these on an empty stomach." Claire rattled the Z-Pak.

Zoe looked at the floor and said nothing.

"We'll wait here for your clothes, first."

Anita appeared in the doorway, her body round and plump in magenta scrubs, her presence announced, as always, by the clop of her floral Danskos.

Anita looked at Zoe, then at Claire. Her eyebrows raised in two perfectly plucked arcs.

Claire gave her a warning look. *Don't butt in here.*

"Fox says he needs you for a VIP."

Fox could kiss her shoe. "I'm not on yet," Claire said, putting her hand on Zoe's shoulder.

Zoe flinched a little again, but Claire kept her hand there, protective.

"Fox says you gotta. Everybody else is tied up, and this guy's some kinda big deal. Famous. Fox don't wanna get sued."

"I can't right now." She kept her hand on Zoe's shoulder. "I'm busy. And not on duty."

Anita's eyebrows ascended again. She put her hand on her hip. "*That's* what you want me to tell the Chief of Ass?"

Anita had her there. Fox was like a human pressure cooker lately, trying to get them all to bill for the maximum number of procedures, making sure the hospital eked every dollar it could out of every citizen's pocket. That included the doctors themselves, whose salaries were well below the national average for E.R. work. "Oh *all right*," Claire said, sounding pissy even to her own ears. "You're coming with me, kid," she said gently but firmly to Zoe.

Zoe looked up at her from under her cherry bangs. She looked down at her hospital gown.

"Anita, grab me a robe from the stash?"

"Yup," she said, shaking her head.

• • •

A few minutes later, just down the hall, an annoyed Claire headed toward exam room three with her arm around Zoe and her eyes on the chart.

This guy's injury wasn't even that serious. Was it really worth making her come on duty early after she'd just finished a three-day shift and half the staff was down with stomach flu? Who was this guy, some kind of delicate little prima donna?

Zoe gasped and her body went rigid under Claire's arm.

Claire looked up.

Her Nikes squeaked to a halt.

He was seated on the third exam table, across the room, the room-dividing curtain open.

This man was not your everyday sight in Haven Springs, Missouri. In fact, he probably wasn't your everyday sight anywhere, except maybe at a Tarzan movie audition. His long, espresso-dark hair hung in messy waves, and his dark brown beard was thick as boxwood. Claire's general opinion of beards—unsanitary and unsightly—remained unchanged, but this guy was so smoldering hot he could radiate sex appeal from . . . well, from an E.R. bed under a buzzing fluorescent light. And he was doing just that.

Bright brown eyes stared right at her, round and soulful and heavily lashed. Prominent cheekbones. Ever-so-slightly too-large nose. Nose breaks: one. Skin tone: healthy. Shoes: expensive.

The man nodded at her, then at Zoe, who seemed to be paralyzed, and was staring at him with eyes like ping-pong balls.

"Wait here, Zo. You can sit in this chair." Claire pulled the curtain divider between exam areas, which would meet privacy laws without giving Zoe a chance to hit the road in her bathrobe.

Claire walked back toward the man. This must be that thing they called star quality. His chest, beneath an open sport coat and fitted T-shirt, was muscular, but not so bulky as to be vulgar. Her stomach did an unwelcome somersault, and she averted her eyes so as not to stare. Women probably stared at him all the time. No sense giving his undoubtedly enormous ego any more fodder. Zoe was doing just fine on that.

The squeak of sneakers on waxed linoleum heralded Holly's arrival.

She took her place next to Claire, eyes shining, hands folded behind her back, her face a pent-up Elvis-concert squeal. Yup, let the ego feeding begin.

Claire shot her a look.

Holly elbowed her, and continued to stand there as though her presence was protocol rather than prurience.

Fine. She might need help with Zoe, anyway. Claire didn't make a habit of taking twelve-year-old girls on patient assessments—HIPPAA would not approve. Who *was* this guy? She looked back down at the chart. Eli Archer. No bells rang. Thirty-six years old. Nonsmoker. Normal body weight. He looked like a hipster Grizzly Adams.

"Mr. Archer." Claire approached him. She turned back and indicated with a tilt of her head that Holly should watch Zoe. Holly was staring at the patient like he was a chocolate cake.

"Holl?"

Holly snapped to attention.

"You two stick together." Claire waved a finger between Holly and the curtain.

Holly nodded, already returning to staring at the cake.

Claire rolled her eyes. "I see here we have an injury to the right dorsal, possible broken metacarpals?" The boxer's fracture. Self-inflicted. Short-sighted. Reckless.

"I took that note," Holly said dreamily.

No answer from the cake.

Claire looked back up at him. His eyes were . . . well, they were too intense, like they were boring right into her. She commanded her stomach to stop its gymnastics floor routine. He wasn't going to turn *her* into a star-struck idiot, no matter who he was.

So who was he? Stop that, Claire. He's a patient and a special-treatment inconvenience, that's who he is.

He nodded. His eyes were still trying to penetrate her, so she focused on his beard, instead. How would you keep such a thing clean? And why would you cover up a face like that? His lips were a little on the thin side, a perfect masculine combination with his strong jaw. Excellent genes.

She looked down at his hand and gently lifted it. "I see we have some swelling."

He made a guttural noise.

"Sore to the touch?"

Silence.

She looked up. His face was only a few inches from hers, and she met his eyes again. She snapped her eyes back to his hand. "Sore to the touch?" she asked again.

She saw in her peripheral vision that he nodded. He smelled

spicy, like cloves and pine and musk.

She gently lifted each of his fingers. "Can you move these?" she asked, gently lifting the last two fingers.

Another grunt.

"Can you *speak*?" He was famous, but maybe he'd been raised by wolves—though his clothes were awfully stylish for that. Her eyes traveled from his hand to his well-worn, faded T-shirt, which pictured . . . a ghost. A ghost playing a French horn.

"I can speak." His voice was deep and melodic, and when she heard it, everything else around her went still and silent.

She cleared her throat and tried to clear her head. "So, uh, can you tell me what happened?"

He looked at her electronic clipboard. "Can you just type 'he's an idiot' and leave it at that?"

Her mouth dropped open a little at the long string of words. His voice resonated in her body, sonorous, vibrating her chest.

"Injury," she said, typing rapidly with her stylus. Suddenly she was conscious of her street clothes, which she'd not yet changed since she wasn't yet on duty. Her navy fleece hoodie was nearly as old as Zoe. "We'll need some x-rays."

He nodded again.

"Follow me."

He rose, and Holly and Zoe fell into place behind him like he was some kind of emergency room pied piper.

Heads poked out of doors to watch as the four of them made their way to x-ray. Nurses whispered and giggled. Sheesh, was his whole life like this? She'd go nuts.

• • •

"Good news, Mr. Archer," Claire said, slapping his film up on the light box.

He waited, watching her.

She cleared her throat, willing his gaze to be less disconcerting. He was just an ordinary patient, and patients looked at her all day every day.

"Often, with this, ah, uh . . . *type* of injury, we see the box-er's fracture—hairline fracture to the fourth and fifth metacarpal bone. But you don't have that."

He waited.

"Heavy bruising, though, so I can imagine it's painful. You did the right thing coming in."

He looked at the films now. "So everything's okay? I'll be able to play my guitar?"

Ah. A musician. That explained the hair. "Today, no. Edema and bruising will limit mobility for the time being. Within a couple of weeks, you'll be fine."

"Let's make sure you get a precautionary follow-up to make sure it's healing properly. Just to be on the safe side, since, I take it, you're a musician. I'll have the nurse fill out a referral card for you."

"Thank you," he said, his voice quiet, deep, and melodic.

"Out the door and to your left," Claire said, pointing. She followed him into the hall, where Holly and Zoe waited for her. Their heads turned as though attached to him by strings, and they watched him walk down the hall.

"Yo, groupies. Snap out of it. Let's get our girl dressed."

• • •

"Oh. My. Good golly. Almighty," Holly sighed.

They walked toward the laundry for Zoe's clothes.

"Who was he, anyway?" Claire asked.

Two astonished faces turned toward her. They stopped in unison and stared at her.

"What, do you live under a rock?" Holly said.

Claire shrugged. "Probably. Sort of. Yes."

"He's like, the critical darling of the music world. Well, un-til his last couple of albums, which sucked. He's won, like, a gazillion Grammies."

"What kind of music?"

Holly shrugged. "It's kind of weird. Not the stuff the kids make me play on the radio for carpool, that's for sure. More like . . . modern folk, I guess? But kind of funky? I'm not sure how to describe it. But that's not how he got so famous, obviously."

"Obviously," Claire said, rolling her eyes. "Wait. What?"

"He was dating Coco Skye."

Claire paused. "*Coco Skye*?" She definitely knew who that was. People in remote Amazon jungles probably knew who that was.

Holly pressed her lips together to suppress a squeal and nodded vigorously. "*Mmm hmm.*"

Coco Skye was a zillion-foot tall Scandinavian with cheekbones you could rest a dinner plate on. Her white-blonde hair looked, and probably was, freakishly natural, and her huge round eyes were an arresting shade of alien light blue. Hers was a famous story, so famous it had trickled down to even a non–celebrity-follower like Claire. Coco, or whatever her real name was, had been a biochem student at Columbia when an Elite modeling scout had spotted her studying at Max Caffe' wearing coke-bottle glasses and a baggy sweatshirt.

From there it was nearly instant supermodel status, and the rest was history—especially the cocaine binges, the hundreds of thousands of dollars in designer clothing, the shoplifting of a tin of Altoids when she didn't feel like waiting in line, and the bar fights. She was probably the most commonly featured face on the cover of every magazine in the supermarket—both the fashion magazines and the tabloids.

"That's not her real name," Zoe said quietly, and Claire and Holly turned to her in surprise. It was only the second thing Zoe'd said voluntarily, and this one could almost be considered conversational.

"Oh, yeah? What is?" Holly asked.

"Petrolilla Vilhjalmsson." Zoe pronounced it with ease then spelled it out as fluidly as if she were spelling her own name. "That's why she changed it."

Both women stood in astonished silence. Holly recovered first. "And . . . how do you know that, sweetheart?"

Zoe shrugged. "YouTube." She chewed a nail.

The women continued to look at her with mouths hanging open.

Two nurses sped by in the hall, arm in arm, leaving behind a trail of squeals and the words *Eli Archer*.

CHAPTER 4

Driving the rental Impala on the streets of Haven Springs was like floating a pontoon boat up a roller coaster track. These streets were insane. They were all crooked, every last one of them. And steep. Really steep. Eli hadn't driven in years—no reason to in Manhattan—but he was pretty sure these streets would challenge Dale Earnhardt.

He pivoted the long car slowly and carefully around the hairpin turns.

The town was cute, he had to give Erin credit for that, and he made a mental note to give her a bonus. All shapes and sizes and colors of Victorian houses, lots of them with yard art or colorful wind chimes hanging from the front porch. A variety of signs peppered the yards—Save our Rivers! Social Justice Warrior—and one front porch was home to a mannequin dressed as Princess Di, her hand posed in the famous wave. A pair of pug dogs behind a white picket fence went wild at his passing, running alongside the car and yapping their hearts out. The whole place looked like a gingerbread Easter village, only real and lived-in, and much, much weirder.

Crescent Drive. There it was, number 907. It was a squat, gray bungalow in the midst of taller, brighter, more decorative Victorians. Yep, this was going to do just fine. Perfectly nondescript. Anonymous. He pulled the boat into park and got out.

The sun was just beginning to pinken and sink in the sky. Mature trees were everywhere, giving the whole street the feel of being surrounded by a forest. Birdsong mixed with the *wa-wa* of crickets all around him. Everything else was quiet. Then, somewhere in the distance, a baby cried. He turned, but he couldn't see anyone. Then he heard the distant hum of a brief conversation. The trees were so thick, and the street so steep, he realized he could hear his neighbors, but couldn't see them.

Perfect—be heard but not seen. If only he could live his whole life that way.

He pulled Bess out of the back seat with his left hand and tried to shimmy his suitcase onto his other shoulder without the use of his right hand. He wasn't going to allow himself one single recklessness when it came to this hand. If he had to tie it behind his back to make sure it healed, he would.

He was pretty sure he'd scared the hot doc at the hospital. She looked easily shockable. She looked . . . wholesome. And very, very clean.

Whatever effect he'd had on her, it wasn't his usual with women. She wasn't trying to get his attention. In fact, she seemed to be trying to avoid looking at him. Lately, everybody else wouldn't *stop* looking at him.

She was a pretty one. Lilting Southern accent. Skin and bones, but a beautiful heart-shaped face and sharp-as-a-whip perceptive blue eyes behind her not-so-fashionable tortoise-shell glasses. He usually liked some curves on a woman, but there was something about this one . . . and her hair was like a caramel-colored satin negligee.

Hot Doc was probably just uncomfortable around him because his face had been all over the tabloids, and none of it good news. He was particularly embarrassed by the picture the paparazzi had caught of him looking drugged, slouched half-passed out in a booth surrounded by half a dozen scantily clad models. And now the new one—the mug shot. He shuddered.

The heavy oak front door swung open to reveal a living room decorated by Little Bo Peep. It smelled like potpourri, and there were ruffles—lots of ruffles. Everything with a soft surface, from the chairs to the curtains, was floral. And pink. He closed his eyes for a moment, hoping it would go away. When it didn't, he walked through the rest of the house. Two bedrooms, a tiny, yellow-and-black-tiled fifties bathroom, and a decent little kitchen with plenty of pots and pans and plates and so forth.

Three months. He'd rented the place for three months. By the time it was over he'd have written a record, slept three months of normal sleep, and Coco's tabloid headlines would feature some other new guy—Eli would be a distant memory.

He tossed his single suitcase on the spare bed, put Bess next to it, then went into the other bedroom and slept like the dead for the next ten hours.

• • •

Eli got up the next morning, made a pot of coffee, and listened to the barrage of voice mails from the DMG Records people. Silence from his mother, which was worse than voice mail. He'd deal with all of it later in the day. For now, he needed a music store. He needed a piano, if he really wanted to make this record good.

Once he got outside and got another look at the size of the rental Impala, he decided to walk the mile downhill to downtown.

The sun was shining, and the birds sounded like a Nature Company CD, except they were real. They were everywhere. One of them, hidden by trees, cawed angrily and insistently as he passed.

He breathed deeper as he realized he was able to walk the streets in peace. No paparazzi. No cell phone selfies. It was everything he'd hoped, only better. People in their yards nodded at him as he walked by, but if anyone recognized him, he saw no indication of it.

The residential houses began to turn commercial—one of them a decent-looking breakfast restaurant with mismatched tables on a gracious front porch; another a house turned art gallery, with bright abstract outdoor paintings affixed to the wood siding. Eli entered the historic downtown by way of a stone staircase that descended onto a crooked brick street lined with restaurants and shops.

Once he was downtown, he got a few stares, but no one approached him, and there were enough Harley-Davidson tourists milling the streets that his current excess of hair wasn't even out of place. Erin had told him Haven Springs was a big draw for the Harley crowd because the winding roads surrounding the town were so much fun to ride on.

It was a pretty town. Sort of a New Orleans vibe to the buildings—upper level balconies hung out over the sidewalks. Ferns hung in front of a shop advertising metaphysical healing and tarot readings. Expensive-looking linen garments flapped in the breeze in front of another shop. There was already a good bit of foot traffic, even though most of the shops were just opening. Merchants set display signs out on the street and propped their doors open. Stone staircases connected the streets, which slanted up and down steeply at odd intersections.

There was an actual bookstore, with paper books in the window, and next door to that, gay pride flags flew next to a display of leather motorcycle jackets. Next to that was a crystal and bead shop, its wares glinting in the sunlit front window.

Five more minutes until the music store opened. He walked back up the block.

His phone dinged. Damn. Could he throw the thing away? He eyed it warily. Another message from Heather, his A&R rep at DMG. Already her third one of the morning. As annoying as it was, he *was* relieved it wasn't Coco. Sort of. He hadn't heard from her, and he was starting to get a little nervous. Coco was not accustomed to being denied anything she took a fancy to, and that included humans. He knew he'd broken things off too abruptly, but he'd felt this visceral need to get away. It was like he'd been trying to swim out of a tar pit in a life-stakes panic. For as long as he'd hung around with her ever-present entourage of models and assorted starlets, not one genuine word had been spoken. There was this constant feeling of competition, game-playing, and undercutting. And now his face was part of all that. He couldn't even go to Malt House for a beer anymore. Everyone knew his face.

Before Coco, he'd been more of a musician's musician. The

critics were kind to him, but his stuff tended to be far from the type of Britney Spears mass appeal that made one's face or name instantly recognizable.

Until he'd been stupid enough to let himself get dragged into Coco's scene. Now, his face was a public commodity.

Far up the street, Eli could see a man unlocking the music store, and he turned and headed back that way.

There were two kinds of music-store owners. One type would know who he was; the other wouldn't, and wouldn't want to. Eli hoped for the latter, but he hadn't gotten a good look at the guy. Those in the first type were true music geeks. Always male, often of a similar hairstyle (thin on top, long and fuzzy in the back), and passionate lovers of every musical instrument and the magic the instruments could make in the right hands. Lots of enthusiastic talking about said instruments.

The other type were the retired middle school band directors. Wire-rimmed glasses. Body thin and taut. Face tight as a facelift. All about the technique; none about the spirit of the thing. Those were the ones who would never've heard the name Eli Archer. They'd never moved past Brahms. Eli wouldn't dream of telling one of those guys he'd done three years at Juilliard. The old fart'd like it way too much.

He swung the glass door in by its metal handle and a bell jangled against it.

"Holy shit," a thirtysomething guy said.

First type.

"Man, I am just a huge, huge, fan." The guy came forward and extended his hand.

Eli held up his puffy blue hand to show the guy. "Out of commission."

"Oh, man, what *happened*?" He sounded genuinely concerned.

So far, Eli pretty much despised being famous, but this was a little different. This guy was obviously a musician—he had it written all over him. That meant he was Eli's people. He was wearing an ancient Metallica T-shirt over a beer paunch, and a small silver guitar dangled from one ear, and of course he had The Hair. But he had a nice face. Open and kind and friendly. Unpretentious.

"Oh, just a little accident."

"Like, what in the hell are you *doing* here, man?"

"I need a piano."

"Cool, cool." The guy paused. "But seriously. What are you doing here? Haven Springs, Missouri? Don't get me wrong or anything, I love it here, but, you know . . ."

"Just a quiet little vacation."

The guy wasn't buying it, but he was gracious enough to accept the answer. "I'm Dave," he said.

"Eli."

"I know, man. I *know*. So cool." He shook his head.

Eli had checked out most of the one-room shop room during this exchange, and he inclined his head toward the only piano in the room. "Got anything else?"

"Yeah, I hear you. That won't work. Listen, though, I got a neighbor here in town. Old lady. She's got a Bechstein she's been wanting to sell me forever, but I don't get much call for anything over five hundred bucks. You know, everybody just wants something for Little Johnny to practice on between lessons. So I never would buy it from her. It's a good one, though."

"I'll take it."

"For real, man?"

"Sure. It's in good condition?"

"Perfect."

Eli nodded. "You need a deposit?"

"Nah, man. Where you staying?" Something seemed to be dawning on him now. "Wait. Are you, like, staying? I take it you're not having a piano delivered to a hotel room at the Grand?"

"I rented a little house."

"Cool! Cool. Man, this is so cool. You want me to call you after I talk to her?"

"Yeah. You got a card? I'll text you my number."

He went over to the front counter and took a card from a holder. Dave Campbell. Dave's Music Store.

"You need anything else? Guitar picks, anything? I know you play practically everything."

"I might have a look at that cello. I didn't bring mine. Kinda regretting that, but it's a beast to fly with."

Dave practically hopped over to the two cellos in the shop. They stood on stands in front of the violins, which hung in neat rows on one wall. One of the cellos was a shiny new number, made in China, but the other one . . . his heart gave a telltale little "her" squeeze. An old Rugeri copy. Beat-up looking, but he had a feeling.

Dave followed his gaze. "Yeah. Cosmetics, you know. What're you gonna do? But I got a deal on her, and she sounds good."

Eli motioned to a case under the violins for a bow, and Dave handed him one. His right hand protested the grip of the bow, but eventually he found a comfortable modified hold. He sat on the stool and let out the end pin, then pulled the cello between his legs, plucking each string and giving the fine tuners a few twists. Then he drew the bow. Mellow sound. He pulled it again. Deep and soft. Sounded good. Real good.

He played all the major scales, and Dave managed not to have an orgasm right there on the spot.

"I'll take it."

"I can cut you kind of a deal on that. I know it's scuffed. And did you see this little repair here?"

"That's all right. The price is fair." Eli pulled out a small stack of hundred-dollar bills. "Keep the change toward the Bechstein."

"Thanks, man. Thanks. So, hey. Would you want to, like, jam, while you're here?" Dave was the deep pink of radish, and looking at the floor.

What could Eli say? "Maybe so. Sure." So much for keeping to himself.

• • •

Coco Skye was pissed. She couldn't believe the jerk had left without even saying good-bye. She looked in the mirror at the pale purple bags under her eyes and cursed him for it. An unfamiliar sensation was tugging inside her chest. Was this. . . heartbreak?

When Eli had dumped her two weeks ago, she'd been shocked. It had seared her chest beyond what she could've imagined. Plus it was just so *embarrassing*. Coco Skye, dumped? That had *never* happened before.

Then, after a while, she felt better. He'd be back. He didn't really mean it. How could he? He'd been so taken with her beauty. They all were. How many times had she been told no man could resist? Usually by some married jerk. But Eli . . . Eli had been different. So deep and mysterious. So all-man. The first guy who hadn't bored her. Ever.

Her chest amped up with the weird aching feeling.

She wanted to call him. She wanted to bawl him out. But if she did that, she'd blow it. If she just sat on her hands long enough, he'd eventually start to miss her. He'd be back. She just had to make him feel it. First, she wouldn't contact him. At all. She'd get super-silent on Twitter and Instagram. Then, when he finally called her, she'd make him try a couple of times before she returned his call. Play hard to get. For a while.

It was just going to take some patience.

And maybe a public appearance or two with stars who were bigger and brighter than Eli Archer.

CHAPTER 5

Claire sometimes wondered if buying a house whose backyard abutted her mother's—even if it was her dream house, the most beautiful house in Haven Springs, and possibly the world—was worth it. This was one of those moments. She looked up at the mustard-colored stained-glass panes in the top of the dining nook window. The thick antique glass cast a beautiful warbly light over her dining room table. She looked at the beautiful Victorian crown molding. She looked at her freshly remodeled kitchen. Then she looked back down at her mother, who was, of course, talking.

"If you'd just wear a little lipstick and some mascara, maybe a little rouge, he might ask you out. Oh, and contacts. You really need to show off your eyes, and your glasses are *not* helping." Joyce Taylor set a casserole dish of chicken enchiladas in the center of Claire's distressed farm table.

Claire's ever-present to-do list was open on her iPad, and she tapped in *Start cooking my own meals*, then shut it off and pushed it aside. "I kinda need my glasses, you know, to *see*. And Dan isn't like that. He's practical." It was one of the things Claire admired most about Dan. That, and he was one of the only single professional men left in Haven Springs.

"Honey, *all* men are like that." Joyce's gray-blonde bangs bobbed in agreement with her words. She slid a spatula into the enchilada dish. "But if you won't wear makeup, can you at least wear something other than scrubs?"

"Mom, it's the E.R. We have to wear scrubs. Picture blood and snot, and then picture something even less glamorous than that. A cocktail dress won't work."

"Well, at least he's a *doc-tor*, like you, so he can understand these things." Joyce always said the word doctor with special em-PHA-sis, so no one missed it. "I was thinking," she said, waving her fork at Claire. "Men *do* like to think they're getting the prom queen. Even though *we* know Dan is the right one for you, maybe you should—you know—let it be *known* that you're dating someone else. He might get jealous." The last word was delivered with singsong triumph.

Claire's mother was going to drive her to an early grave at the age of thirty-five. The obituary headline: Claire Marie Taylor, M.D., Old Maid.

"Maybe you could even date two or three other men. Make Dan think you're really in demand."

"Mom, what other men? Haven is a small town. Dan's *it*. He'll come around eventually. It's not like single professional women are all that plentiful here, either."

"He might not want professional. He might want sweet and housewifey. Like Cliff did."

"He doesn't want that. I've known Dan since we were in junior high. He doesn't want that. He just needs to see me as more than a friend."

Claire wished men were more like medical school: make a list of goals, then work through them. Accomplish them. Not easy, but straightforward. Something that could be written on a three-by-five index card. Or, now that the iPad had come into her life, entered into a list on the HandleIt app.

Sometimes she thought about just walking up to Dan and asking him out for a drink. And why *not*? It was the twenty-first century, after all. But she couldn't. Because maybe her mother was right. Maybe Cliff had dumped her two days before they mailed out their wedding invitations because Claire had been the one to make the first move in the relationship. She'd not given him the chance to *pursue*, Joyce said.

The week after the broken engagement, Joyce had left a copy of *The Rules* on Claire's bedside table while she was at work. Claire had thrown it away, the first book she'd ever put in an actual trash can. She didn't know much about men, but she knew she wanted something a lot more authentic than *that*.

Yes, she wanted to be married, and she wanted a family, but she didn't want to get it by pretending to be someone she wasn't.

"Lucas Mendell," Joyce announced, then took a bite of enchilada.

It took Claire a moment to realize what her mom meant. "Mom, *what*? I am not going out with Lucas Mendell." She tried to take a bite of enchilada, then put her fork down, staring at her mother in disbelief.

"And why not?" Joyce sat up straight and noble.

"He picks his nose! In *church*!"

Her mother waved a dismissive hand in her direction.

Oh my word, the woman was serious. "Would *you* go out with Lucas Mendell?"

"You know perfectly well I have terrible taste in men. This is why I don't date. I chose your father, after all." Joyce sniffed.

"*Mom*," Claire warned.

"Sorry." Joyce reddened and re-tossed the salad with two wooden spoons. "Anyway, his mother says he's very marriage-minded. Wants kids."

Claire felt the familiar ache of her childlessness. It was like a poorly healed bone fracture, always with her, always achy. "No. And that's a final answer. When I have kids, I want them to stop picking their noses by the age of ten. At the oldest. And also to be in the ballpark of average height and intelligence. Lucas Mendell is out of the question."

Joyce heaved a long-suffering sigh. "I'll never have grandchildren."

Claire's muscles tensed, even the ones in her toes. She stood. "Well, I need to get to work. Thanks again for dinner."

"But—" Joyce stood, her fork still in her hand.

Claire took an apple from the counter, tied it in a cloth napkin, and dropped it in her purse. "Sorry, Mom. I really need to get going."

"I'm making lasagna for tomorrow," Joyce said, her tone sulky. "Check your fridge when you get home."

Operation Grow Boobs for Dan. Joyce, who, even at the age of fifty-seven, was almost as rail-thin as her daughter, liked to quote Sophia Loren—*all that you see I owe to spaghetti.* Claire had, several times, pointed out that this was less than self-esteem building, given her thirty-four–inch barely Bs, but Joyce was never deterred.

It was April now, but the southern mountain air could still sometimes hold a bit of nip, and Claire pulled a navy fleece jacket from the coat closet. "Bye!" she called. "I'm out. Lock up when you go?"

Joyce followed her into the entry hall, waving an oven mitt. "Have a good night at work!"

"Thanks." Claire put her hand on the doorknob, but her mother stood by, vibrating with something more to say.

"There's just one more thing," Joyce said.

And there it was. Claire stopped. "What's that?"

"I already told Glenda Mendell you'd go out with Lucas."

"*Mom!*"

"Oh, it'll be fine."

"No."

"Have a good night!"

"Mom. I mean it. En. Oh. No."

The yellow floral oven mitt waved. "Oh, honey."

• • •

Claire was supposed to be home in time for breakfast, but that turned into lunch, then dinner. The E.R. hadn't been slammed, but they were short-staffed and it had been too steady-busy for a nap.

She walked up the steep mountain slope of Crescent Drive, her eyes trained on her rose-colored Victorian, its fresh white trim and its familiar heavy oak front door. Bed. Soon she would be in bed. Cool crisp sheets, pulling the cotton blanket over herself, her own pillow—heaven.

That's when she spotted the figure sitting on her front porch swing, and her mother's head turned at just that moment. "Where have you *been*?" Joyce leapt to her feet, wring-ing her hands.

"Work, Mom. I've been at work. Is everything okay? Why are you just sitting on my front porch?"

"I tried to call you! I tried to call you every five minutes since lunch!"

"Mom? What is it? Are you ill? I've told you—you have to page me if you need me while I'm working."

"Well, I couldn't do *that*."

Claire suppressed a sigh. They'd had this conversation sev-en hundred and thirty-two times. "What's up?"

"Your date! He'll be here in ten minutes!"

"I'm sorry. What did you say? My *date*?" Claire stepped onto the brick path in front of her mother.

"*Lucas!*"

"*Mom!*"

"Your hair!"

"*Mom*! I told you *no*!"

Joyce's hands flapped. Her yellow Chico's rhinestone track-suit quivered over her slender frame. Joyce did not own, other than underwear, one single piece of clothing that had not come from the Chico's catalog. She was very proud of this. Claire wanted to strangle her mother with the yellow Chico's track-suit. *Hello, boundaries?* Had she not been perfectly plain about Lucas Mendell? Now she'd have to hurt his feelings. Lucas was shy, and probably scored a two out of ten for self-esteem. He so did not need this. Maybe she'd *bury* her mother in the yellow rhinestone tracksuit.

Car tires approached on the quiet of Crescent Drive. Claire hated to even turn her head, afraid she would see that it was too late to call and cancel the date, but her pricked-up nerves told her that was exactly the case. Mrs. Mendell's white Buick inched up the street. Well, she'd just have to tell Lucas she'd worked much longer than expected and wasn't available this evening. Or for the rest of her natural life.

The Buick pulled to a stop in front of them. Wait, there

were two people in the car. Claire peered. Lucas and . . . Mrs. Mendell. Oh, for crying out loud. She couldn't reject him in front of his own mother. But really, who brought their mother on a date? And his mother actually *came*? Car doors opened.

Lucas's dress shirt was tucked too tightly into his pleated dress khakis, and he carried a bouquet of garishly dyed supermarket flowers. *Oh, Mom, how could you?* The flowers. Those flowers were so sad. She shot her mother a venomous glare. Joyce averted her eyes beneath her curled-under blonde bangs.

"Run in and see if you can do something about your hair. I'll stall them," Joyce whispered. "Oh, and wear your red dress!"

Claire looked at her mother in open disbelief, then turned toward their guests. "Hello!" Claire called, hoping she didn't sound too phony through her clenched teeth. "Mrs. Mendell. Lucas."

"Claire!" Mrs. Mendell called back. She and Lucas approached on the brick entry path. "You certainly are . . . sporty . . . this evening." Mrs. Mendell looked Claire up and down.

Claire looked down at her navy fleece hoodie and yoga pants. She looked back up at Lucas. He looked dressed for Sunday school. He also looked like he was sweating kittens. She looked down at the flowers. *Damn. Those damn sad flowers.*

He handed them to her.

Claire took the flowers and tried to look appreciative rather than pitying. "Thank you, Lucas. I'll be right back. Just let me put these in some water and get changed."

"I thought your mother and I could just chat while you two kids were out."

Kids. She was right about that. It appeared they were back in high school.

Claire controlled her steps to keep herself from stomping into her house. Once inside, she splashed cold water on her face and looked in the bathroom mirror. How had it come to this? She was thirty-five. She had a good career. She was moderately interesting and fun. She wasn't dog-butt ugly, and if she put a little effort into it, she could be decent-enough looking. How was she coming home to find a psycho-yenta Chico's poster girl waiting on her front porch with Lucas Mendell as the most promising candidate?

She thought back to the rock star she'd treated two days ago in the E.R. *His* life was probably all glamour, all the time. Parties and movie stars and sleeping in with no alarm clock. She'd never met anyone famous before, and she had to admit there was something to it, the whole charisma thing. He was different from other humans. Exactly the kind of guy she wanted to avoid—too good-looking for his own good, always being chased by women, a wild lifestyle, and an unstable career.

She blotted her face dry. Dan. Dan was the kind of man she would marry. A surgeon. Clean-cut. Dad material. Solid and stable and good. And God, please let it be tomorrow. At least one ovum was lost by cell death every hour of every day. That was roughly nine thousand eggs a year—*at a minimum.*

She went to her bedroom and took a simple gray dress from her closet. It flattered her blue eyes and her light chestnut hair, and had a little stretch to it, but it wasn't too sexy. The last thing she needed to do was catch Lucas's real interest.

She pulled the dress on over her head, slicked on some lip balm, put her glasses back on, and checked herself in the mirror. Her hair was tireder than usual after a long night and day at work, but it was still glossy, wavy, and thick—the saving grace of her appearance. She ran a quick brush through it and tucked it behind her ears. It would have to do.

Two hours. Two hours was a perfectly adequate length for a first date. She could stand anything for two hours.

• • •

Claire got into Lucas Mendell's mother's Buick. She clasped the heavy, old-timey metal seat belt. She waited.

In the minute it took Lucas to close her door and walk around to the driver's seat, Claire's exhaustion had turned aggressive, and she still had to check on Zoe. She'd planned to sleep a couple of hours first.

Lucas shut the driver's side door and slapped his palms to his khakis.

"Well." He laughed a short, nervous laugh. "Where would you like to go?"

"Actually, Lucas, I have an odd answer for that."

"Uh-oh." Lucas laughed again, this time sounding flat-out terrified, rather than just nervous.

"Nothing too scary," she assured him, raising her hands in innocence. "I just need to check on a patient. Sort of like a quick house call."

"Oh! Yes, of course. That's *fine*."

What did he think she was going to suggest? A quickie on his mother's back seat? "Great." Claire smiled at him. "I really appreciate it. 1012 Pine Street."

The drive to Pine Street passed in four minutes of uncomfortable silence.

When they pulled up in front of Zoe's house, the afternoon was beginning to grow dusky, but the house was dark inside. Again. Claire was now certain the utilities were shut off.

She got out of the car and approached the house. The vinyl siding was dingier than she'd noticed before, and had holes in several places, with mildew creeping around them. She knocked on the door.

Silence greeted her in response.

She knocked again. "Zoe!"

More silence.

"Zoe! It's Dr. Taylor. I'm going to stand out here until you answer!" After waiting another couple of minutes, Claire rapped on the window, rattling it. "Zoe," she shouted through the glass, "not kidding! Not going away." She glanced back at Lucas. He was looking toward the sky, slightly slack-jawed. She turned back to the window.

A light flickered from deep inside the house, like a penlight or a small flashlight. Claire slapped her hands against the glass. "Zoe! I can see you. Come to the door!"

Finally, Claire heard a shuffling sound and the door inched open.

Big brown eyes questioned Claire from beneath too-long bangs the color of dusty wilting beets.

Claire snuck her ballet flat into the six-inch door opening, chancing it that Zoe wouldn't try too hard to close it on her. "How's your foot?"

"Fine." Zoe chewed a fingernail.

"Hmm. Can I see it?"

Zoe shrugged.

Well, it wasn't a no. "May I come in?"

Zoe shook her head.

"Want me to look at it out here?"

Zoe paused, sizing up Claire out as though they'd never met, and finally emerged onto the porch, closing the door behind her.

"Have a seat here on the step, then." Claire looked up at Lucas. He smiled and waved. She raised a quick palm in return.

Zoe's gaze followed hers to the car. "Who's that?"

"My date."

Zoe looked at Lucas again, then back at Claire with disbelief.

Claire stifled a laugh. "My mother fixed me up," Claire said, peeling back the bandage on Zoe's foot just enough to peek under it. "Speaking of mothers, I'd like to meet yours." She eyed Zoe's face for a reaction. "Is she home?"

"No." Zoe looked away.

"Oh? Where is she?"

Zoe hesitated. "PTA meeting."

Yeah, right. "Oh! That's nice. I see her car's here. We could pick her up at the school, give her a ride home? That would be a nice thing to do, and she and I could go over your medications on the way home."

Zoe froze. "That's not a good idea."

"Oh yeah?" Claire kept a light lilt in her voice. Zoe was like an injured baby animal—if Claire moved too fast Zoe would run off and find somewhere to hide and die. "How come?"

Zoe glanced back at the house. "I forgot. They changed the PTA meeting. And Mom was sick. So she stayed home."

Claire paused. "If she's sick, maybe I can help?"

Zoe seemed to actually consider it this time. Then she pulled her knees up and laid her forehead against them, but didn't answer.

"You okay, Zo?"

Zoe didn't speak for a long moment. "A little dizzy," came a weak voice from under the hair.

Claire was pretty sure Zoe was just trying to avoid the mother conversation. Or . . . wait. Could she be . . . hungry? The guilt-spot in Claire's chest contracted in horror. She'd been so intent on the medication, how had she overlooked food? What if Zoe hadn't eaten since the meal Claire had bought her in the cafeteria two days before? "Well, we don't have to talk about your mom right now. But I could use a favor."

Zoe looked up at her, still suspicious.

"Rescue me from my date?" Claire nudged her, hoping for a smile.

"I don't know how to do that." Zoe, all earnestness, bit her fingernail again.

Claire tried not to cringe at the bacteria landing on Zoe's tongue right now, but she didn't say anything. "Come to dinner with us? Maybe we could get cheeseburgers?"

The girl's eyes lit up.

Damn. She's hungry. How long had it been since she'd eaten? Tears needled Claire's throat and eyes. *No crying. Absolutely no crying.*

"C'mon. You can wear those." Claire pointed at a pair of old flip-flops on the front porch. She didn't want to let Zoe out of her sight long enough to send her inside for different shoes.

Zoe nodded, her eyes never leaving Claire's. Claire considered this. The normal reaction would be to look back toward her house, or to tell her mother, or to at least worry that her mother would notice her absence. It didn't appear to have crossed Zoe's mind. Was it possible the girl was living here alone? It was starting to seem not just possible, but likely. Was she still going to school? A little detective work was in order.

Claire opened the back door of the Buick and waved Zoe inside.

Lucas turned around in surprise. Then he stared. For a long time.

"We'll have a little company at dinner tonight, *Lucas*." She emphasized his name, a little loudly, to snap him out of staring.

Zoe's eyes had fallen to her lap in discomfort.

"Lucas!" Claire snapped a finger. "This is my good friend Zoe."

His head shot upward, following her voice. "Oh." He cleared his throat. "It's a pleasure to meet you, Zoe."

"How d'y'do," Zoe said, deadpan, turning to look out the car window.

Claire smiled, raising a hand to her mouth to cover it. She wouldn't have thought Zoe had any smartassery left in her, but she was glad to see it. Her spirit wasn't totally broken.

"Where should we go?" Lucas asked. He looked at Claire.

Great. The man'd had ten minutes to do nothing but sit here and think of a dinner restaurant, and he hadn't done it.

"Capers?" Claire said. It was the old standby for locals—good food, full bar, not too expensive, and kid-tolerant.

"Capers," Lucas said, and pulled the old-school gear wand down into reverse.

A few minutes later, Lucas guided the Buick into one of the downtown street spots outside Capers. A handwritten poster was taped in the window with the daily special: Philly cheesesteak. Lucas held the door open for them, and they entered to a small line at the hostess stand. The restaurant was crowded with families and couples at tables, singles at the bar, and a smattering of Harley tourists.

A few steps ahead of them in line, Holly stood chatting with Ryan, her thirteen-year-old son.

"Holl," Claire called.

Holly turned around, smiled, waved, and took a few steps toward Claire.

"*Join us*," Claire said, inclining her head toward her little motley crew of a dinner date.

Holly's eyes moved slowly, disbelievingly, from Claire, to Lucas, then to Zoe. Then she looked back at Claire. A slow smile spread across her face. "Oh, no. I wouldn't want to *intrude*." She smiled a devil's smile. "Hi, Zoe."

"*Nonsense*," Claire said, gripping Holly's arm.

"Ouch!"

One of the waitresses, Darla, approached. "Hi y'all. How many?"

"Three," said Lucas.

"Two," said Holly.

"Five," said Claire.

Darla looked from face to face.

"*Five*," Claire repeated.

Darla nodded to Claire, indicating she was the winner, then retreated to the hostess stand.

"Zoe, this is my son, Ryan." Holly gave Ryan a light elbow to the ribs, and his hand shot out to shake Zoe's.

"Nice to meet you, Zoe," he said, looking to his mom for approval.

Holly smiled and nodded at him.

"Nice to meet you," Zoe said, barely audible. She stared at the floor.

Ryan stared at Zoe while she stared at the floor.

"Follow me," Darla said, beckoning.

Once at the table, the preteens stalked around it like a musical chair game, each trying to appear disinterested in where the other sat. When Zoe made a move toward a chair, Ryan made a move to sit next to her, then Zoe moved to the opposite end of the table, then Ryan followed. Zoe won the match, scoring a seat on the end next to Claire. Ryan peered at her over the menu he was pretending to read.

"So you two don't know each other from school?" Claire asked. "Get whatever you want," she whispered to Zoe, pointing at the menu.

"I've seen you around," Ryan said.

"Yeah," Zoe said.

"But not lately," Ryan said. "You're in sixth?"

Zoe nodded.

"Seventh," Ryan said. "I'm at the junior high now."

Zoe nodded. She stared down at her menu.

"So, how did this little . . . *grouping* come to be?" Holly asked, waving her hand to indicate Claire, Lucas, and Holly. She didn't bother to hide her amusement.

"My mother, she's a champion matchmaker," Claire said brightly, not wanting to hurt Lucas's feelings. He was studying the menu like it was a treasure map. Claire pretty much had it memorized.

"Ah, Joyce. Her powers continue to shock and awe."

Darla came back to the table carrying a cocktail they hadn't ordered. It was a short glass of amber liquid with a few cubes of ice and an orange slice.

"For Dr. T. An old-fashioned? The bartender had to look that one up, so I don't know how old-fashioned it really is."

"But I haven't ordered anything yet," Claire said.

Darla pointed at the bar. "It's from him."

Claire's eyes followed Darla's finger. She stopped breathing for a moment and her heart gave a forceful *thwomp.* Long wavy dark hair, piercing eyes, and a tall lean body. He nodded and gave the barest of waves. It was the rock star. Eli Archer. Claire's uterus did a slow somersault. *Not him,* she told it. *Definitely not him.*

"Oh my angels, devils, and sex gods," Holly said.

"*Mom,*" Alec said, appalled, eyeing Zoe. But Zoe was having an intense relationship with the menu and didn't notice.

"*Eli Archer* just sent you a drink. This is getting *good,*" Holly said. "Really, really good. I'm so glad we didn't stay home for leftover meat loaf tonight."

"Shhh." Claire took the drink from Darla's outstretched hand and reluctantly raised it toward the bar in thanks. "Thank you, Darla," she said.

Eli nodded at Claire in response to the raised glass.

"Invite him to come join us," Holly said to Darla.

"NO," Claire said. "*No*. Darla, no. En. Oh."

Holly nodded at Darla conspiratorially and Darla winked at her. She turned on her heel and walked away over Claire's protests.

And then Darla was talking to Eli Archer.

Eli looked back at Claire's table and appeared to be considering what Darla had said to him.

Say no. Say no. Please say no.

They were five at a table for six, and there was one open seat across from Zoe, catty-corner across from Claire. Claire held her breath. *Say no.* She looked at Lucas, seated next to her, who was attempting to pick his nose with a finger covered by thick cloth napkin. Claire groaned to herself. All humiliation, all the time.

She looked back to Eli, who was nodding at Darla and pulling a black sport coat from the back of his barstool. He slid it on, then picked up his plate of food and a pilsner glass half-full of beer. Her breath was too much for her chest. He was coming toward her.

In an eternity of slow motion, he approached the table. He was somehow both lanky and muscular, with a loose-limbed, graceful walk she imagined male models spent years trying to achieve. His hair hung damp and clean over his collar, and his jeans looked so perfectly well-worn, Claire suspected they'd been artfully broken in by a designer. His eyes were on hers as he approached, and the room went silent. The world went silent. Everything was still around her. *Not him, Claire. Completely unsuitable. Be bigger than your hormones.* But her squeezed-tight heart was beating a primal drumbeat, and the heat of her face was spreading all over her body.

Holly squealed through ventriloquist-pinched lips.

"*Shhh*," Claire shushed without looking at her, breaking the surreal bubble she'd shared with Eli as he crossed the room.

He arrived at the table, his eyes still locked with Claire's.

"Hi," he said. He set his plate and beer down at the empty seat.

"Hi." She tore her eyes away from his. If they didn't stop staring at each other, they were going to melt the table. Or their clothes. Her glance landed on Zoe, who was staring at Eli's plate of food like a dog chained three feet from a raw rib eye. Claire glanced around for Darla.

"*Helloooo*," Holly said, tossing her curls behind her shoulder.

Ryan groaned with the embarrassment of it all.

Lucas stood up and thrust his hand forward. His chair rocked a little, threatening to topple, and Claire's left hand shot out and caught it. "Lucas Mendell," he said.

Eli took his hand and shook. "Eli Archer."

He took his seat and looked back at Claire. "I was just saying thank you." He displayed his injured hand.

"It's my job," Claire said.

She looked back at Zoe. Zoe was still focused on Eli's plate, staring at it with open longing. Claire once again looked around the restaurant for Darla.

And then her mouth fell open, as she realized the rock star was sliding his plate across the table. The plate came to a stop in front of Zoe: two BBQ sliders and most of an order of sweet-potato fries. "I got full," he whispered to Zoe with a wink.

Zoe's eyes fell on the food with open gratitude.

Eli's arm lifted and he flagged Darla, who was emerging from the kitchen with two plates of pasta. "May we please have some appetizers?" he said. "One of each of whatever you have?"

Lucas made a strangled sound next to her, and Claire looked over at him. He was tap-tap-tapping his delicate hands on the table in a rhythmic motion, and his face was a mask of anxiety.

The bill. He was nervous about the bill. She thought of the supermarket flowers and the fact that they'd ridden here in a car borrowed from his mother. "My treat," Claire said to Darla.

"No." Eli's voice was low and deep, quicksand. There was no arguing with a voice like that. "Mine," he said.

The way Darla was looking at Eli, she probably wasn't inclined to argue anyway. She nodded as though under a hypnotic spell, her eyes fixed on him.

"I'm not sure I'm supposed to let another man pay on my date," Lucas said, raising a finger in the air. "But could we have separate checks?" He motioned the finger between Claire and himself. "We're together."

Claire felt the telltale tingling in her cheeks, and she knew she was blushing. She bit back the urge to refute Lucas's words.

"I'm paying," Eli said again.

Claire's insides did another somersault. So stupid, because he was sure to be a player. Weren't all those big stars womanizers? And on drugs? And how *was* it possible that his voice reverberated inside her like a physical thing?

Darla nodded to Eli, still hypnotized, and headed toward the kitchen.

Zoe was having a lovemaking session with one of the sliders from Eli's plate. She shoved some fries in her mouth on top of the unswallowed bite.

Claire and Eli watched her for a moment, then their eyes met. His held a question, but she didn't know how to answer. How *had* this happened? How had she wound up bringing a starving child on a ridiculously unsuitable date and then wound up sitting with a world-famous musician who gave away his food? *He gave away his food.*

Claire had spent most of her life trying to squash any superstitions that told her things were "meant to be," but it was hard to imagine how else tonight could have happened, if not some demented fate with a wicked sense of humor. As Eli's eyes held hers, she felt he could read her mind, like he knew, in minute detail, exactly what she was thinking. But of course that was ridiculous. He was probably thinking about baseball.

She snapped her gaze away from his and looked at Holly, who was taking it all in with unabashed glee. "This was a good coincidence." She smiled and turned to Eli. "Claire doesn't get out enough."

"But she does have a date tonight," he said.

"So she does!"

Oh, the humiliation.

"Claire and I know each other from church," Lucas said.

"*Hmm*," Eli said.

"Do you go to church?" Ryan asked Eli. His voice cracked on the word *church*.

"No," Eli said. He looked so darn cool sitting there. There was a striking stillness about him in the midst of the crowded and noisy restaurant. Poise.

But he didn't go to church. Of course he didn't. He was probably too cool. And children needed to be raised in church. Eli, as kind as he'd been to Zoe, was like an anti-dad.

"Ours is very open-minded," Holly said. "All Hearts Church. All religions are welcome. It's very *Haven Springs*."

"Is it?" Eli asked, polite.

"My mom goes to the Metafizzies," Ryan volunteered.

"She goes to the what?" Eli asked, his eyebrows raised.

"Metafizzies," Ryan repeated. "They meditate and gong bells and stuff."

"Ah. I think we have that in New York."

"New York must be so exciting," Holly said.

Eli shrugged. "Boredom can be underrated." He took one fry back from Zoe's plate and winked at her when she looked up at him, startled. He popped it in his mouth and gave her a sly smile.

Claire needed to get out of here. He was . . . too much. Too intense. Too beautiful. Too famous. Too dangerous.

Darla arrived with half a dozen appetizers and set them around the table.

"How come you don't go to church?" Ryan asked Eli, and popped something small and fried into his mouth. He waved his hand in front of his mouth. "H-h-hot."

"Mother working on converting to Judaism, Dad an atheist, grandfather Jewish, other side of the family staunch Baptist. I'm a religious mutt," he shrugged. "So I just try to stay out of it."

"Well, I go every Sunday," Lucas said, a little righteously.

Claire was feeling less and less sorry for him. "How about a change of subject?" she suggested.

"Yes," Holly said. "I want to hear about Eli's rock-star life-style. We can talk about Haven Springs anytime."

Eli shrugged, and a curtain of sadness fell over his face. In a split second he rearranged it back into a neutral expression. "Not as glamorous as one might think." He winked again at Zoe. She gazed at him, slightly dazed by the food and by—whatever that thing was Eli radiated—star quality?

"Oh, I doubt that. I bet it's glamorous compared to Haven Springs."

"Think five bickering guys living on a bus with smelly socks and delusions of grandeur, and you're closer to the truth."

A few minutes later, the waitress returned and Eli rattled off an order while Holly excused herself to the ladies' room. A minute later, Claire's phone buzzed in her purse. She snuck a glance under the table.

He is SOOOO into you!

Claire wanted to text back—*NO, he isn't*. But it was odd. He *was* looking at her like, like . . . well, she couldn't be sure how, but she knew she hadn't experienced it before. Cliff had certainly never looked at her like that, and they'd been engaged. It was like she was . . . beautiful. The most desirable woman in the room. But Eli was probably a player, and he'd probably practiced this in the mirror to melt the pants off the most hard-to-get movie stars and models. Claire crossed her legs more tightly.

Darla approached and set food and drinks on the table in front of them.

Holly slid back into her seat, announcing, "This looks good!" She loaded her fork with a bite of salad, then turned to Eli without putting it in her mouth. "So I liked your Grammies speech. The one where you said that thing about your mom and how you'd still get a real job with the symphony if the rock-and-roll didn't work out."

"Yeah, we have your first record at home," Ryan said.

"Thank you," Eli said. "How about you, Doc?"

Claire looked up from the meal she'd lost all interest in. "Sorry, I—"

"You're much more likely to hear the *Science Channel* at Claire's house."

Eli looked at Claire.

"What?" She shrugged. "It's good for your brain . . . Science."

Everyone applied themselves to their plates for a moment, before Holly took up the conversation again. Claire was surprised to feel herself relaxing a little; Eli wasn't quite as rock-starrish as she'd thought.

A brief lull descended, then Darla came back. Her always-sunny face was a shade darker than usual. "Dr. T?" she said, flushing deeper. "Can I show you something real quick?"

Claire knew from experience this meant a body part, so she excused herself from the table. But everyone watched her anyway.

One eczema diagnosis later, she returned to the table.

"See?" Holly said. "Rock stars aren't the only ones who get shown female body parts in public."

Eli's eyebrows raised, his mouth turned up, and his eyes landed on Claire's.

Is he flirting with me? He couldn't be. Definitely not. Still . . .

"Well," Claire said, slapping her thigh more forcefully than she intended. "We'd better get Zoe home." She turned to Zoe. "You ready?"

"OK." Zoe chewed a fingernail.

Eli stood when Claire did.

"Thank you for dinner," Claire said.

Eli's eyes stayed on Claire's, unwavering.

"Thanks again," Claire said, clearing her throat.

Eli just looked at her and nodded, saying nothing.

His silence left her with an odd premonition that there was more to say, and more would be said. But of course she believed in science, not premonitions.

CHAPTER 6

Claire had been parked at Zoe's house for nearly half an hour—a half hour punctuated by checking her watch and fruitless knocks on the front door—when a gray Ford Escort pulled up in front of the house.

A man and woman, people Claire had never seen before, got out of the car in unison. Claire, parked in front of them them, was caught spying on the house, and they looked her over in a not-too-subtle way.

"Do you live here?" the woman asked. The man was broad and alcoholic-ruddy, with fleshy lips through which he was breathing. Since Claire didn't recognize either of them, it meant they probably weren't local.

She said nothing.

"Do you live here?" the woman repeated. She was beige-haired and plump in black slacks, low pumps, and a polyester office blouse. Not your typical Haven Springs attire, which tended toward hippie, intellectual, or hiking gear, with an occasional full-body gay pride rainbow outfit.

"Have we met?" Claire asked.

"Social Services. Children's Division." She flashed a badge. "Barbara Thomas."

Just then, a police car pulled up and parked behind the Ford. Officer Kevin Dunavin got out. Claire nodded to him, and he to her.

Claire's eyes traveled toward the house. She'd come by to check that Zoe was really going to school. Now she didn't know if she hoped Zoe was at school or not. Just what would they find inside that house?

Officer Dunavin joined the group.

"Dr. T," he said, nodding to Claire.

"Hey, Kev. Are you a part of this too?"

He nodded.

"Can I come? I've been treating Zoe for an infection."

Kevin looked to the social worker, who hesitated. "She knows you?" she asked Claire.

"Yes."

"I can vouch for the doc," Kevin said.

The woman paused again. "All right."

Claire followed the group up to the front porch and waited behind them as they knocked.

Not surprisingly, there was no answer.

The oversized guy stepped forward and pounded his ruddy ham-fist on the door.

Claire thought she detected a whisper of movement beyond the living room curtains, but she couldn't be sure.

"Mrs. Anderton? Mrs. Joanne Anderton!" he bellowed. "Open up." He pounded again.

Definite movement. Someone was home.

They all waited.

Kevin tried next. "Mrs. Anderton? Zoe Anderton? Police. Kevin Dunavin, Haven Springs P.D." He paused. "Somebody's gotta come to the door now." He sounded apologetic.

Finally, the door inched open. Four feet ten inches of trembling, terrified little girl stood before them, and Claire wanted to rush forward and fold her in her arms, but she knew it wasn't appropriate at the moment.

Zoe held a crumpled tissue to her nose and her huge dark eyes were bright with terror. Her hair looked even dirtier than it had the day before.

Claire's throat gave a telltale ache—the tears were coming unless she put all her effort into stopping them, and for the thousandth time, she cursed her slutty, slutty tear ducts.

The beige-haired Barbara stepped forward, and Zoe stepped backward, stumbling slightly.

That was when Zoe spotted Claire. "Claire! What's going on?" The relief in her voice was palpable, and Claire felt the tears come. She swiped at her eyes furiously, before anyone could see, and quickly and stepped forward. "They're here to help, Zo."

"We're here to make sure you're safe," Barbara said.

"I'm safe. I just have a cold."

"That's why you're not in school today?" Barbara asked.

Zoe nodded.

"May we come in?" Barbara asked.

Zoe shook her head. "Not today. My mom's sick too. She's sleeping."

"We're going to need to come in anyway." The woman's voice was kind but firm.

Zoe looked to Claire.

"I don't think they're really asking, kiddo. I think they're telling," Claire said.

The beefy guy laughed. Claire shot him a murderous look and he snapped his mouth closed.

Zoe reluctantly moved aside, allowing them access.

Claire stepped forward and put her arm around the girl. "When did you get sick?"

"Last night."

Claire touched Zoe's forehead and chest, which were hot, but not dangerously so. "Drink plenty of water."

Zoe nodded.

"I want to check your Z-Pak too."

"I haven't missed any."

"That's my girl."

They all stepped inside the house.

Claire looked around, her eyes adjusting to the gloom of the living room. It was neat enough, but very dusty, and the carpet was filthy. A vacuum cleaner sat in one corner, eviscerated with an open zipper and exploding bag.

A small dog slept on the worn nubby fabric of an old brown recliner. Against the grimy fabric, the dog's fur was cottony white, calicoed by irregular light brown tufts.

"Aw! Is that your dog, Zo? I didn't know you had a dog.

Very cute!" Claire said.

Zoe walked over to the chair and patted the dog, looking nervously at Kevin and Barbara and Barbara's sidekick.

The dog began to open its eyes. Wait, eye? And then something odd happened.

When it saw the strange adults standing there, it sprang into the air like a turbo spring-loaded jack-in-the-box, reared back its head, and began emitting a series of high-pitched, soul-harrowing, cacophonous barks.

"Pippa, *shhh*," Zoe said.

The dog continued its maniacal, ear-splitting barking. The silky white hair on its neck stood up like a ridge of cotton cacti. Claire watched, agape.

"Pippa! *Shhhhh!*" Zoe said.

Devil-dog ignored her.

The barking abraded Claire's already frayed nerves. "*Shhh!*" She found herself echoing Zoe.

"Pippa, *shhh*," Zoe said. "Pippa!" She turned toward Kevin and Barbara. "Sorry—she's a very good dog. She's just surprised to see everyone because she doesn't hear very well."

They all stared at the creature, awed, appearing not to hear Zoe.

Once the barking paroxysm ceased, the dog stood on the recliner, hackles raised and out of breath, staring at them. Its eyes were wide, round, crazed with surprise and alarm, and . . . two different colors? One was brown and one was a pale, eerie blue—heterochromia.

Zoe picked up the dog, who immediately settled into her arms with the relaxed, entitled grace of a reigning queen borne up on her mobile throne, as though it hadn't just thrown a fit of crazy. From Zoe's arms, it surveyed the visitors with hooded, sleepy eyes.

"*Well*," Barbara said, straightening her blouse and eyeing the dog. "Let's proceed."

She and her sidekick began wandering through the house,

presumably looking for adult presence.

Claire had a bad feeling they weren't going to find any.

Kevin stood near the front door, rocking from foot to foot, looking like he wished to be elsewhere.

"Do they usually bring the police to things like this?" Claire asked him.

"Not for assessments. But I guess they tried to come by a few times and never could find anyone living here, so it turned into an investigation. That's when the police get involved."

"I can't believe the dog didn't bark," Claire said.

"She's deaf," Zoe said.

"Completely?" Claire pulled a factoid from the recesses of her mind, that deafness sometimes accompanied heterochromia in dogs.

"Sleeps through thunderstorms." Zoe shrugged. "And yelling. And stuff." The dog had fallen asleep in Zoe's arms now.

"I'm not finding your mother, dear," Barbara said, returning to the living room.

Everyone stood silent for a moment.

"Any idea where she is?" Barbara asked.

As steadily and suddenly as water poured through a leaky cup, tears began to streak down Zoe's face.

"Zoe? Where is your mother?" the woman asked. Her tone was kind, but in its own understated way, demanded a straightforward answer.

Zoe gave the tiniest shrug, and that shrug sank Claire's heart like the *Titanic*.

"She's gone?" Barbara asked.

Zoe nodded, a barely perceptible nod.

The woman started scribbling furiously on her clipboard and Claire wanted to clock her, but she knew that was irrational. She put her arm around Zoe, who did not resist.

"How long have you been on your own here?"

Zoe shrugged.

"We do need an answer, sweetheart."

Zoe chewed a nail and shrugged again. She mumbled something indecipherable.

"What was that?"

"About three months?" Zoe whispered.

Claire tried to wipe the tears from her face before Zoe could see them, but they were coming too fast.

• • •

Zoe looked at Claire, her eyes frantic. "Foster care? I don't want to go to foster care."

"We'll find you a real nice family. I noticed you don't have water or lights here. You're going to be better off," Barbara said, still writing on her clipboard.

"My friend Kayla said no one will adopt a twelve-year-old. I'm too old."

Claire had a momentary urge to murder Kayla.

"Now, that is just not true," Barbara said.

"Can I stay with you?" Zoe's face turned up toward Claire's, hopeful and hopeless, all at once.

Claire had managed to get control over her tears, but barely. Now, looking at Zoe's hopeful face, she wanted to wave some kind of magic wand and make the whole world different. "I wish I could, Zoe, but I can't. I have to work. So much."

Zoe nodded. Then, her face began to change, as though she were just realizing something. She looked at Claire accusingly. "Did you *tell*?"

"No, Zoe. I mean, it wasn't like that. But I am required to file a hospital report. And I don't even know if that's why they're here." Claire paused. "But I do think it's for the best. This will be better for you."

"You *told*!" Zoe's voice shook with tears and fury.

Barbara spoke up. "Now, now. We aren't at liberty to disclose the source of complaints. It could have been anyone. One of your neighbors or teachers, a friend."

Zoe's eyes hopped from adult to adult. They settled on Kevin. "Maybe the police could find my mom? She said she was just going to Branson to the casino for a few days. She had a new boyfriend. She was going to meet him. Maybe something happened, like an accident, and she's in the hospital, and she was trying to call, but the phone wasn't working?"

Barbara paused and set her clipboard down. "The thing is, Zoe, you're too young to be left alone, even for a few days, so even if we do find your mom, which we will make every effort to do, you'll still need to come with us."

Zoe, eyes desperate, looked to Claire again.

Claire approached her with her arms outstretched, to take Zoe into a hug.

Zoe recoiled and stiffened.

"Oh, babe, I'm so sorry." Claire settled for patting Zoe on the shoulder.

"Yeah." Zoe stared at the floor, shoving her shoe into the carpet. She blew her nose and put the tissue into her pocket.

"We'll give you some time to pack your things," Barbara said.

"Like what things?"

"Clothes, toothbrush, school books."

"What about Pippa?" Zoe asked, her voice trembling.

Barbara exchanged a look with the man she'd brought with her.

"I'm not leaving her!" Zoe said, her voice louder and shakier.

"Do you have a friend who could keep her?" Barbara asked, and Claire thought the social worker sounded a little like she was talking someone down from a ledge, and that this did not bode well for Pippa.

Then Claire realized they were all looking at her.

"But I . . . can't." She really couldn't. She'd always wanted a dog. Not that Pippa was exactly a . . . dog. But Claire worked too much. It wouldn't be fair to the dog. The poor thing would be alone all the time. Sometimes for a couple of days on end. She couldn't. "Pippa would be so lonely and unhappy living with me. The long shifts at the hospital . . ."

Zoe's eyes didn't meet Claire's again. She petted Pippa's

head, gazing down at her sleeping head.

Barbara paused for a long moment, then let out a sigh that sounded like it came from the soles of her feet. "We'll take her with us for now. Maybe we can work something out," she said.

Claire held her breath. Zoe was losing her home. The last thing she needed was to lose her dog too.

"Your medication," Claire said. She turned to Barbara. "Will I be able to find out where Zoe is? I need to follow through on her treatment."

"That should be fine."

"I'll come help you pack, Zo," Claire said.

"That's okay," Zoe said, her face a locked gate.

"I don't mind," Claire said.

Zoe turned to her, and this time looked her right in the eye. "No," she said.

• • •

Claire stared at the text from her mother: Lucas had nice time.

She willed her head not to explode, and wondered, not for the first time, what life would be like if her mother couldn't traverse their adjoining backyards in twenty-two seconds flat. Even if Joyce just had to walk all the way up her own block, and back down Claire's . . .

The sound of knuckles striking her front door preceded the familiar "Yoo-hoo!" in her mother's falsetto. "So, Lucas?" Joyce trilled from the kitchen doorway.

Claire looked up and sighed. "Mom, don't. "This is too much. I told you *no*."

Joyce paused. "I . . . I was trying do something *nice* for you."

Claire's mouth opened and hung there. "I need to run some errands." It was all she could think of to say, so she wouldn't say bad things. She reached for her keys and purse.

"How long will you be gone?"

Long enough to see a man about a fence, Claire thought.

• • •

The evening was fully dark now, and she opened a window so she could hear the cricket chorus.

But it wasn't crickets she heard. Classical music played from someone's open window. This was an inevitability in Haven Springs—neighbors could hear each other. There were no airplanes or trains, and very few diesel engines or police sirens, so you could hear a snippet of conversation when the wind was right, or someone singing Madonna in the shower if they left their bathroom window open.

But on this night, the music sparked Claire's curiosity. For the last few days, there'd been a car parked in front of the house next door to her. This wasn't unusual—the owner rented the house out to tourists—but it was a little early in the year for that. Tourist season didn't enter full swing until May. Also, the lights had been on at odd hours over there, almost like E.R. hours. Claire couldn't help but be a little curious to see who was staying there.

She stepped into the backyard, listening to the music. It was low and sweet, some kind of stringed instrument. The instrument played unaccompanied, like it was singing *a cappella*, but the sound was deeper and more plaintive than a human voice.

The house next door was only about fifteen feet from hers, and, upon reaching the back corner of her own house, she saw a light on next door. It transformed the porch into a glowing box in the otherwise dark April evening.

Inside that spotlight sat Eli Archer, his wavy brown hair falling around his shoulders, his eyes closed as though he were in some otherworldly place, drawing a long smooth note from the large cello before him.

He didn't see her. He just kept playing, eyes closed, arms poised, filling the night with a song so beautiful Claire found herself holding her breath.

Then Eli's eyes flew open and his bow paused mid-stroke. He turned. He looked straight at Claire.

Damn, how did he know I was here? Heat scorched her cheeks and chest, but she forced herself to make a polite nod.

Another awkward moment with Eli Archer. She was going to have a collection.

He rose. Then, slow motion, with that long-limbed lanky grace, walked toward her. "We meet again." His eyes on hers pierced her in the same odd way they had the night before. "Are you following me?"

"*No*," Claire said. She smoothed her hair and pulled her shoulders straighter, suddenly conscious of the yellow flannel pajamas she was wearing. "Of course I'm not *following* you. I live here."

"That house?" He pointed.

"Yes."

He nodded slowly, maintaining eye contact. "Then we're neighbors."

Slow and liquid, a strange new heat soaked through Claire. "Neighbors?" Her voice came out as a croak.

He nodded.

She pointed at the house next to hers. "You're staying there?"

"For the next three months."

"I see." She looked down at her pajamas. "Well, uh. Sorry to disturb you."

"You didn't disturb me," he said, and the words seized her. She looked back up at him, and his eyes were dark and hypnotic.

Her insides did the slow somersault again. She tried to tear her eyes away. His gaze should have been unnerving, and in some small way, it was, but more than that, it was . . . sexy. Claire drew her thighs closer together. Every woman in the Western world, and then some, thought Eli Archer was sexy. She did not need to join the masses. Why couldn't she have felt attracted to Cliff this way? Or her very nice college boyfriend, Jonathan? Or that nice man from Berryville who'd said he would be willing to relocate for the right relationship? Why did it have to be *this* guy?

"But you're not staying? I mean, it's only for three months," she said.

"Not staying. Touring. Life on the road."

And that was exactly her point.

CHAPTER 7

The next day, Claire sat in Holly's big, high-ceilinged kitchen watching Holly get Ryan ready for school. The smell of bacon filled the air, and Ryan was talking eagerly about a new chess strategy, while Holly made agreeable, if distracted, noises.

Holly was a single mom, though not because she wanted to be. She'd been devastated when she found her husband was a serial cheater, and the resulting divorce had been hard to watch. But Holly had made it through, and now she had a close relationship with Ryan to show for it. She even managed to make motherhood look easy, most of the time.

Not long after her divorce, Holly's parents had moved to Springfield, and she'd bought the house she now lived in, her childhood home, from them for much less than it was worth. But the house was big, too big for two people, too big for Holly to afford the upkeep on her own—so she took in roommates. She'd had three over the years.

"Claire, Mom says you might adopt that Zoe girl. I like her."

"Ryan Maxwell Jackson!" Holly gasped.

"Well, you *did* . . . "

"*What?*" Claire asked, puzzled. "No, of course I'm not adopting Zoe." She looked at Holly questioningly.

"I just thought . . . I'm sorry. I shouldn't have said that to Ryan. And *you*, y'little twerp, four minutes until the bus gets here." She shot Ryan a mock-angry look.

"Um. What was that?" Claire asked.

Holly paused. "It's just . . . Zoe seems like a pretty awesome kid. And y'all click. And she *needs* someone. And I know how much you want to be a mother."

The old, familiar ache kicked in with its usual twist in Claire's chest, but she had plenty of practice ignoring it. She smiled crookedly. "It's not going to happen like this. My child will weigh eight pounds, not eighty, and I'll have at least ten years to prepare before she develops a bad attitude and armpit hair." She glanced at Ryan. "Sorry."

He shrugged.

"Lunch, backpack, homework," Holly said to him.

Ryan slung the backpack over his shoulder and leaned down from his lanky height to kiss his mom on the cheek. "Love you, Mom."

"Love you, babe." Holly turned to Claire. "See. The teen years can be good too."

Holly was being ridiculous. Claire, a foster parent? Working forty-eight hour shifts at the hospital? Starting out with a troubled preteen when she had zero parenting experience? Never gonna happen. "Tea." Claire pointed at the kettle, which had begun to boil.

Holly took a mug from the cabinet and poured a cup. "You won't even think about the Zoe thing?" She slid the mug to Claire.

"Always the matchmaker." Claire smiled. "But seriously, do you have a screw loose this morning? *No.* No, I won't think about it. I can't do that. Who would watch her while I was at work? Plus a whole lot of other reasons."

"What reasons?"

"I know nothing about raising a troubled teen!"

"We don't know she's troubled."

"How could she not be?"

Holly busied herself with breakfast dishes, but Claire could sense her forcing herself to keep her mouth shut.

"Greetings." Holly's roommate, Marla, entered the kitchen in a fuzzy olive-green bathrobe that looked like it was a third-generation hand-me-down from the male half of her family. She put on a kettle and leaned against the counter.

They all three stood in awkward silence.

"How're you doing this morning?" Holly finally spoke, her voice a chirp of false cheer.

Marla shrugged and looked down at her oversized ceramic mug. "He didn't call."

"Oh, babe." Holly's hand shot out to pat Marla's green-clad arm.

"Maybe today he will," Marla said. "I left him several voice mails."

"Marla's having man trouble."

"I'm sorry," said Claire.

"Edwin and I broke up."

"Do I know Edwin?"

"He lives in Fayetteville. It's a long-distance relationship. He's an ecologist with the Department of Conservation."

"That sounds interesting."

"Very. It's extremely important work."

"That's good."

The silence stretched.

Holly and her newest roommate rarely socialized together, due to only having two things in common: their address and breathing oxygen. But over time Holly would change that, Claire knew. Holly was an irresistible force.

"How long had y'all been going out? Two months?" Holly asked.

"Nine weeks."

Claire and Holly exchanged a look.

"I have a good idea. Let's get our mind off things. Let's google Eli."

"Who's Eli?" Marla asked.

"That's not a good idea," Claire said. "That's a bad idea."

"Eli Archer is living in Haven Springs," Holly told Marla. "At least for now. You know who he is, right?"

"I heard about this. He's a big deal musician?"

"Yup."

"Let's do something else," Claire said. "Let's make a frittata. Or floss our teeth. Or do jumping jacks!"

"This'll be fun," Holly said. She opened her laptop on the kitchen island, and Claire watched as the screen filled with pictures.

Eli on stage.

Eli looking drugged out, surrounded by supermodels.

A mug shot.

A ridiculous stab of disappointment pierced her. But of course this was exactly what she should have expected. He was a rock star. Weren't drugs and women just part of the package? And apparently arrests too?

Except he'd seemed more decent than that. Claire remembered their dinner, how he'd quietly slid his plate across the table toward Zoe.

"A mug shot." Marla pointed at the screen.

There were some younger pictures of Eli too. He looked newly successful, sharp, happy. Short-haired, bright-eyed, and wearing a suit—he'd been impossibly handsome. And then there were the later pictures—long-haired and wearing the blackest of sunglasses even indoors—in which he looked unhappy and more than a little crazy.

Holly clicked a link for a YouTube video, and music filled the kitchen.

An unusual seesaw of guitar noise immediately captured Claire's full attention, and a modulated, throaty baritone layered over the repetitive backdrop of the guitar in skillful broad vocal swoops.

"I love this song," Holly said.

"I'm unfamiliar," Marla said.

Come on back
To the one who sees through you like a diamond
Come on back
Let me cloak you in Orion
Fly you around the living room

His soulful voice pierced her. Claire's heart cramped with the beauty of it, and also with . . . she couldn't be sure what the feeling was, but hearing Eli sing that way . . . He must have written this song for a woman, and hearing Eli sing that way to another woman created an unwelcome hotness inside her skin, prickly and uncomfortable, something that felt very much like . . . jealousy.

The song was over too soon, leaving Claire aching for more.

"He's so dreamy," Holly said, sighing.

"All right," Claire said, slapping her hands to her thighs. "That was fun."

"Let's listen to one more," Holly said.

"So." Claire turned to Marla. "How are you liking Haven so far?"

"I like it. It's interesting." She shrugged. "I hadn't planned to stay, but now that Edwin and I have broken up, I think I might."

"It's a good town," Claire said.

"We should have a party," Holly said, snapping her laptop closed. "Introduce Marla to more locals. Claire, are you in? We haven't had one of our parties in a while."

"Parties aren't my thing," Marla said.

"I know, I know," Holly said. "But think of it like one of your vitamin supplements. You get it over with, and then you're glad you did it."

"Not sure I understand," Marla said.

"This isn't just any party. Think of it like your debutante ball. Your coming out in Haven Springs." Holly grinned.

Marla looked down at her olive-green robe, then back up at Holly, dubious.

"You really can't stand in Holly's way when she has a plan," Claire said.

"It'll be fun," Holly said.

"I guess," Marla said.

• • •

"Mom, I'm glad to hear from you, but this is *not* a good time," Claire whispered. She willed her body to completely disappear behind the column of her front porch. Why oh why did today—after all these weeks of waiting for her new sofa—have to be the delivery day?

She waited what felt like an eternity as the furniture deliveryman scrolled through paperwork with a stylus on his electronic pad.

"Can we do this inside?" she asked the uniformed man.

Without lifting his eyes from the pad, he held up one finger, indicating that she should wait. That would have been fine on any other day, but on this day, Eli Archer stood in the front yard next door. He was shirtless, sweat-soaked, and stretching, his long and lean muscles visible even across the yard.

Two years she'd budgeted and waited for the right sofa. Four weeks she'd waited for said sofa to arrive. And delivery day was the day Eli was standing half naked, practically in her front yard, fifteen feet away from the delivery truck?

For that matter, why—of all the houses in Haven—did he have to rent the one right next to hers? It was just wrong.

She slunk around the side of the house, cell phone still cradled atop her shoulder.

"Did you get the package?" Joyce asked, and Claire turned her attention back to her phone call.

"Package?"

"From Amazon," Joyce said.

"Ma'am?" the delivery man called to Claire. She poked her head out from behind the side of the house and pointed at the front door. "No, no package. Mom. I've really got to go."

"It's just a few things to help with the Dan situation."

Claire took a long breath, trying to inhale a little patience. "Thank you for thinking of me. I'll watch for it." She paused. "Mom, there's something I've been needing to talk to you about. About my backyard—"

"Ma'am! I still need your signature," the deliveryman called.

Claire peeked out and held up one finger. The man's shout had caught Eli's attention. *Damn.* She took two steps backward to completely hide herself behind her house.

"Mom, listen—"

"Okay, okay. Just wait one second, though. I have the perfect man for you."

Oh good. Maybe Lucas has a cousin.

"Danny Sparks!" Joyce sounded triumphant.

"*Mom!*"

"It's perfect."

"He's *eighty!*"

"Fifty-six, but he's still very handsome, don't you think? And we know his sperm work because he has three kids with Marylee."

"Yes, he is handsome, and yes, I am sure his sperm still work—"

"*Herrhem.*"

The noise startled Claire into dropping her phone.

She looked down at the phone on the ground. Fluorescent blue Nikes were planted in the grass in front of her own camel flats. Her eyes traveled upward. Legs—medium hairy, lean, and muscular. Shorts—freshly cutoff khakis. Abdomen—don't look. No shirt. *Just try not to look.* Sweat slicked every inch of his naked and muscular chest. She finally landed on his face—square jaw, thin lips, high cheekbones—the face of a ludicrously attractive rock star. His sweat-soaked hair was pulled back from his face. His beard was thick and long and a not a little savage.

"Sorry for interrupting," he said, not bothering to hide his amusement.

Interrupting? Oh! Phone! Mom! The phone, in the grass, was making a faint squawking sound. She bent to pick it up, averting her eyes on the way back up to detour around the naked legs and chest.

"Ma'am?" The deliveryman's head appeared around the corner of the house. "Is everything all right? You're not turning down the delivery, are you? Because that would be . . . It's a big sofa."

"Gotta go, Mom!" Click. "No, of course not!" Claire cleared her throat and stood straight and tried to look sane-ish. "You said you had something for me to sign?"

He held out a digital pad and stylus.

Claire signed, shaking her hair back, holding out her chin.

He eyed her signature. "Where you want it?"

She took the iPad from her purse and pulled up the furniture graph she'd made. "In front of the west window in the living room, twenty-two inches closer to north wall than the south. Thank you."

Eli looked at the iPad, then at her face. He looked incredulous.

"*What?*" she asked.

"Oh, nothing. I've just never seen that software." He whistled a low little whistle, like she was the crazy one. *He* was the one with his mug shot on Google.

"It's an app. Moving Day. It organizes everything you need for a smooth moving day. Not that I'm moving, exactly. But, you know, getting a new sofa."

"Ah. Of course." He clearly didn't see the beauty of Moving Day, but he was a musician. He probably wrote his bank account number on scraps of paper then lost them. He probably didn't even have a five-year plan.

"Drink tonight?" he asked, and she almost dropped her phone again.

She looked up at him. His face, oh, his face. A man should not be blessed with looks that good. It was against nature. An unfamiliar flame licked the inside of her belly. "Uh . . . Uh . . . I . . ."

Eli waited.

"Think that's a bad idea."

"Really?" he was looking at her with frank curiosity.

"I have to do laundry. I really, really, have a lot of laundry."

"I see." He rubbed his beard.

A breeze kicked up and she caught a whiff of his plentiful sweat. The clean muskiness of it, the sex of it, nearly sent her over the edge.

"All done here," the deliveryman shouted.

"Thanks," she yelled back.

Her phone started ringing again, and she looked down at it.

Joyce again. Oh, how she would love to let it go to voice mail, but since she'd basically hung up on her a few minutes earlier, she knew she had to answer.

"Excuse me," she said to Eli.

"Mom, hi."

"What is going on over there?"

"Nothing, Mom."

"I heard a man."

Claire looked up at the man. "Just a neighbor, seeing if he could help."

"Neighbor? Which neighbor? Bruce Jenkins? Joe?"

"Mom, I really have to go. I'll call you later."

"Is he single?"

Claire hung up. She'd text later and say her phone had died.

"He is single," Eli said. "He also knows no one in town. A drink some other night?"

Claire nodded stupidly. Her best excuse had been laundry. It would only be downhill from there. This would buy her some time to come up with better excuses.

CHAPTER 8

Eli hadn't been running in a few months, not since the whole Coco thing started, and he hadn't counted on how hot the new beard would be. He had to get this thing off his face, and pronto.

He took the single brass key from his pocket and unlocked his new front door. The landlady had insisted no one in Haven Springs locked their doors, but he couldn't even imagine walking away from home and leaving an unlocked door with his guitar inside.

The tepid shower brought immediate relief as the water washed over him and cooled him. Still, the urge to get the hair off his face was strong, and he stepped out of the shower, wrapped a towel around his waist, and did the deed.

Fifteen minutes later, the sink looked like he'd given a haircut to a bear.

He looked at his face in the mirror.

Hey, I remember you. You're not a druggie or a publicity whore. You're not the arm candy of Coco Skye. You're not those last two damn records they talked you into making. And you're not your father, sleeping with every groupie who flashed a tit. You're Eli Archer, who promised himself and his mother he'd live an honorable and creative life.

What if he didn't re-sign with DMG Records? What then? Could he make it on his own? He was thirty-six years old, and the kids who were trying to make it started lying about their ages when they were a day past twenty-five.

Money wasn't an issue, thanks to an inheritance from his grandfather, which had skipped a generation, Eli's father having been deemed ungrateful and already too solvent for his own good.

Money aside, Eli had to have a career as a musician. It was

who he was. It was his identity, both external and internal. He would be nothing without it.

DMG had made it clear they thought it would be a career death sentence to go out on his own, but what else were they gonna say? They were right about one thing—no other record label was gonna touch him. The critics were right. His last two records had sucked, and sucked hard. Even though DMG had pressured him into making them the way they wanted, they'd lost a lot of money on it, some of which Eli had been required to pay back.

He got out his travel case in search of aftershave, then splashed it on his face. He came back up to the mirror. He needed some advice. As abhorrent as the thought was, he had one person to call. The only person he knew who'd been around the record business for forty years, and had played the game and won it. His father.

That would be "Gage" Archer, né Solomon Rosenblatt. Even though Gage had legally changed his name, Eli's mother probably would have figured out some way to get Rosenblatt on Eli's birth certificate, but good ol' Gage hadn't introduced her to his family until Eli was learning to walk and Gage was walking out the door.

His mother had been devastated by Gage's leaving. God only knew why she'd loved that man like she did, but it never really went away. Eli could see it on her anytime Gage dropped in for a paternal visit. About once a year. Sometimes once every two years.

But Gage knew the music business. He was king of it.

Was it too early for a beer?

"Son." Gage answered on the fourth ring, his voice raspy with years of cigarettes and vocal punishment. The tinkle and buzz of a party murmured behind him. It was eleven o'clock in the morning. Who was having a cocktail party at eleven o' clock in the morning?

"Where are you?"

"London."

"Ah."

"What's up?"

"Bad time?"

"Nah." A female voice said something in the background. "Sweetheart, I'll be with you in a minute. I'm on the phone."

"I'll make it quick." Eli outlined his situation with DMG.

"So you're not under contract?"

"Not as of last month."

"Cut the suckers loose. Or at least put 'em off. They're the ones who talked you into those last two crap records, right?" Gage took a long draw from a cigarette and exhaled. "Don't sign shit."

Eli didn't bother to defend the last two crap records. "But I want to work. I have to work." Never mind the fact that he *couldn't* work. He eyed the blank songwriting notebook on the coffee table. Well, it wasn't entirely blank. There was more crap record type stuff, scribbled out with copious and furious hatch marks.

"Then work," Gage said, pulling on the cigarette again.

"What am I supposed to do? Put a hat on the sidewalk and sing Neil Young covers?"

"Nah, man. It starts in your living room. It always starts in your living room."

Eli thought about that. Gage was a shitty father and an even shittier husband, but he was good at music.

The female voice said something else. "Listen man, I gotta go." His father took another puff and exhaled into the phone.

"Thanks, Gage."

"Anytime, man. Anytime."

Eli figured he should go on and call his mother while he was at it, but ever since the arrest, he hadn't been able to force himself. He'd left a couple of voice mails at times he knew the symphony was rehearsing, assuring her that he was okay and he missed her. He just didn't want to hear her voice. Her disappointed voice—profoundly disappointed—in him. She would try to hide it, but she wouldn't be able to. He knew her too well.

It was, in fact, too early for a beer. Eli eyed the clock. Eleven eleven. He'd been going a little stir-crazy in Haven Springs. In New York, he had friends. He had DMG or songwriter meetings. He had dinners to go to, and parties. The Strand, with its eighteen miles of books. Incredible restaurants. Good films, documentaries.

And women. There were always the women. Trying to pass their panties to him at shows, asking for his autograph in cafés, needling his cell phone number out of the receptionist at DMG if they were famous enough.

The total opposite of Claire Taylor. Hot Doc wanted nothing to do with him. She looked like she wanted to squirm right out of her skin just to get away from him.

That was probably why he found her so absurdly tempting. What *was* it about that woman? She wasn't the most gorgeous. She wasn't the most mysterious—her thoughts passed over her face like the stock market ticker board. He smiled at the memory. She wasn't the curviest or the friendliest or the sweetest—though she had been merciful to that outrageous dweeb she'd somehow been out on a date with the other night. But there was something . . . he'd now had two dreams in which he'd schooled her in the ways of multiple orgasms, and woken up in an aroused hard sweat.

Well, it would be easy to get over. Because she didn't like him, and he was leaving in eighty-one days.

He glanced at the clock again. Eleven twelve. Well, whether Gage was right or not, Eli didn't have much other choice. It was time to start in the living room.

He picked up Bess, went to the kitchen for a notebook and pencil, and headed for the floral sofa. He had to start in the living room.

CHAPTER 9

Claire's house was the most beautiful place on earth, she was sure of it. She'd moved in two years ago, and it still wasn't completely furnished . . . but it was her sanctuary. Well, except when her mother walked through the backyard without calling first. But Claire was working her way up to that fence. She had money in the budget for it now. It was just a matter of breaking the news to Joyce.

Her kitchen and laundry room remodel were complete, and now she had a sofa, like a real grown-up. Once she learned to cook, she'd be all set.

She ran her hand over the new sofa. It was perfect. Now all her furniture was coordinating in creams and beiges, combined with distressed and natural wood surfaces.

All she needed now were groupings of black-and-white family photos on the walls. She just had to get the family.

She hadn't actually *lied* to Eli with that lame excuse about laundry, she'd just made an idiot of herself. She grabbed the laundromat bag she'd been using during the remodel from near the front door.

Claire's new laundry room was to die for—spotless white Formica countertop, gleaming white porcelain laundry sink, the high-gloss shine of the brand-new white washer and dryer. The laundry room even smelled new, like glue and rubber and paint. She tossed in a load of scrubs and headed for the kitchen.

Claire knew how to make three foods: spaghetti, scrambled eggs, and turkey sandwiches—sort of. The sandwiches always came out a little bit dry and she was thinking they didn't count as actual cooking.

But the day she'd given the contractor the go-ahead on her new kitchen, she'd started a new category in her monthly to-do's on HandleIt. *Learn to cook.*

At the bookshop downtown, she'd ordered cookbooks, and the pristine hardcovers now stood sentinel over her virgin countertop: *Mastering the Art of French Cooking*, *The Culinary Institute of America Cookbook*, *The French Laundry Cookbook*. She'd decided to start with the best. When Claire had presented her list to the bookshop owner, the woman had gently suggested Claire start with something a little less challenging, but Claire had insisted she wanted to learn the right way. Now she was thinking she should have thrown a *Cooking for Dummies* into the mix.

Claire eyed her "dinner" on the counter, then the cookbooks. The man at the fish counter had said the whole trouts were selling out as fast as they could get them in, so Claire had bought one. The dead gray fish didn't look much like dinner yet, and Claire hadn't eaten anything since breakfast. The man had said to just sauté it in a little olive oil, as though this were obvious and easy. Then Joyce had called to tell her about a new haircut she'd seen in a magazine, and Claire had forgotten to buy the olive oil. She also hadn't had time to wash any of her new pots and pans yet. She eyed the microwave.

Salad dressing had olive oil in it, right? She put the fish on a plate, pulled a bottle of vinaigrette from the fridge, shook it, and poured some on the fish. She set it in the microwave. *Hmm.* The buttons said baked potato, popcorn, dinner plate, beverage. *Hmm.* The fish was on a plate. It was dinner. Dinner plate. She clicked the door shut and pressed the button, then waited.

After just a few seconds, the fish began to make popping noises. Maybe that was how it sounded when it cooked? She'd just keep an eye on it. Through the dotted glass door, it still looked like a dead fish, spinning around in slow circles. Slowly, a different noise permeated her consciousness, a hissing noise. Was that . . . water?

She whipped her head around, trying to figure out where the noise was coming from.

The washing machine.

She ran.

At the door of the laundry room, her mouth fell open in horror. Water was flying around the room like a spray park for kids. The washing machine hoses whipped in wild circular motions.

She ran toward the gushing snakes and tried to turn the machine off, but she was unfamiliar with the buttons and water was spraying her in the face. Frantically, she punched the buttons more forcefully, but the water kept coming. When she tried to move the machine, it didn't budge, not even the slightest movement, like it was affixed to the wall. All the water lines were behind it. *Water shutoff. She needed the water shutoff.* Where was that thing? Why didn't she know this? Must remember to put it on the to-do list as soon as the crisis was over. She checked under the cabinet, but everything looked like ordinary plumbing.

Would a neighbor know where the water shutoff was? She ran into the yard.

"Help!" she called lamely. No one was in sight.

A plumber. Did she have time to wait for a plumber? Did she have a choice?

"Help!" she shouted more loudly, then ran back in for her phone. *Plumbing . . . plumbing Haven Springs*, she typed into Google with shaking fingers. Who had her mom used for a plumber? Claire had always been at work, while her mom had handled things like plumbers.

But she didn't have time to wait for a plumber—her floors would be ruined. She had to figure out how to make it stop. She ran back into the laundry room and put her hands back on the buttons, averting her face from the spray. Surely if she just kept pressing, something would eventually happen.

That's when she felt arms around her.

An unanticipated scream, a horror movie scream, escaped her before she had time to realize what was happening.

And then the water stopped.

She slowly turned around, the arms still loosely around her. Eli Archer stood on the other end of the arms, looking drenched and different and . . . clean.

And wet.

"Thank you," she managed. What was different about him? His beard. His beard was gone. *But wait! The floors! The oak floors! Save the floors!*

She broke loose from him and started grabbing the towels that were stacked in front of the washer, ready to be washed, and began to mop, skating around with a towel beneath each foot. She was vaguely aware Eli was doing the same.

After a few minutes and a dozen very wet towels thrown into the bathtub, the floors were dry enough.

"Thank you," she said, breathless.

He bowed.

"How did you make it stop?"

"I unplugged it."

"How?"

"Yanked the anchor out of the wall."

"Thank you," she repeated, meaning it.

They stood there in awkward silence for a moment.

"Now can I get you that drink?" he asked.

She found herself nodding.

• • •

Fifteen minutes later, they both stood in her kitchen in dry clothes and damp hair.

"Red or white?" He'd returned to her house with two bottles, one of each color. "White," she said. "Please."

She stealth-shot her hand over to the iPad on the counter and swiped open the HandleIt shopping list. *Paper towels. Lots more Lysol.*

Eli eyed the iPad, looking like he was about to say something, but instead he nodded and picked up the white wine bottle. Even the way he opened wine was fluid and graceful, his hands square and brown, his arms long and muscular. He was probably a good dancer. And a good . . . An image flashed into her mind. An image of him above her in bed, that hair hanging down, those eyes reading her soul. A slow and wicked heat spread through her, searing her thighs. She looked away. Ridiculous. She hated long hair on a man.

She shook her head to clear her mind, and her eyes landed on the microwave. *The fish!* She'd left it in there when the washing machine had started leaking.

She pressed the door release button, holding her breath.

What was inside didn't really resemble what she'd put in there to begin with. Not only that, but the microwave walls were covered with splattered, burned-on vinaigrette and dead fish particles.

She pulled the plate out and set it on the counter.

She and Eli both stood looking at it. It looked like a toad. That had been exploded. Then petrified. Or petrified then exploded. What it did not look like was food.

"Dinner?" Eli asked.

She glared at him.

"No, wait. Science experiment?"

"Maybe," she sniffed.

He chuckled, then turned back to the counter for their wine glasses. When he handed her the glass, he let his hand rest on hers for longer than was necessary, and his eyes, those ridiculously sexy eyes, flickered when they met hers.

He was reading her mind. She was sure of it.

"New laundry room and kitchen?" he asked.

"Oh, yeah. I bought the place two years ago, but it's taken me a while to get everything together. I sort of moved out of my old place at the last minute, so I couldn't really plan in advance the way I wanted to. You know. Just kind of . . ." She was blathering.

"What was it, a bad roommate or a bad boyfriend?"

"What do you mean?"

"That made you move last minute."

She paused and took a sip of wine. It was good. Really good.

Crisp, dry, and cold. "Bad roommate, I guess."

"You guess?"

"It's a long story."

"I've got time." He inclined his head toward the living room and started walking, and she found herself following. When he took a seat on the sofa, she chose an armchair at a safe distance.

She set the wine glass down on the distressed-finish walnut coffee table and contemplated how to get him out of there.

He was just entirely too good-looking. It was embarrassing to look at him. A guy like that would *know* you were thinking about how good-looking he was. His prominent cheekbones with the slightest hint of a hollow beneath them, his round eyes, the deepest most luminous brown, and fringed with even darker lashes. His nearly perfect nose, which wasn't too perfect, thanks to the hint of dent under the bridge. Then there was his wild thick hair, lush and wild and perfectly suited for running her hands—

She shook her head. She hated long hair on a man! It was just so . . . so rebel without a clue. Plus the whole soul-searing eyes business. He had to go.

She stood up. "Well, thanks for the drink!" she chirped, sounding deranged even to her own ears. "I should be getting to sleep now."

He stood too. He was looking at her like she was crazy, which she was thinking might be correct. "Are you serious?"

She tried to look innocent and sane.

"Did I say something wrong?" he asked. "Wait. I wasn't saying anything."

"No, no." She shook her head.

"You're about to turn into a pumpkin?"

"No . . ."

"The sight of my hideous face makes you sick."

She felt her blood soak her face in what she knew was a deep red blush. "No."

"I know. Let's try charades. You can act it out while I guess."

"No."

"Spoilsport." He pointed at the chair behind her. "Sit."

She sat. Erect on the edge of the seat.

"Okay, we're going to try something new. I'm going to set my watch"—he held up a finger while he set it—"and every thirty seconds, I'm going to give you a signal, and you're going to move one inch closer to the back of the chair. Starting . . . now." He dropped his hand and the slightest hint of a smile played at the corners of his mouth.

She found herself smiling back at him. Against her will.

"Now, while we're waiting for the thirty seconds, I'd like for you to try to take a sip of wine." He pointed at her glass. "If that's not too scary." He looked down at his watch, then held up both hands, making a zero with his left hand, and holding up three fingers, two of them splinted, with his right.

She rolled her eyes a little to keep herself from laughing.

"We're moving on the next part of the evening now." His voice was low and melodious and held the slightest hint of rasp.

"Oh, I don't know—"

"A game. Twenty questions. I get ten and you get ten."

"No. No, no, no, no."

"You have two other choices. You can go all weird on me again and kick me out and then feel awkward about it tomorrow and have to come apologize, or you can sit there looking like you died an anxiety-ridden death and you're in the middle stages of rigor mortis."

"Actually rigor mortis—"

"Oh no. No medical talk." He held up his hand. "I have a weak stomach."

"No you don't." It was only a guess, but she'd put money on it. He didn't have a weak anything.

"Maybe not, but I still want to talk about something other than dead bodies."

"Fine. What do you want to talk about?"

"Okay," he said, leaning back into the sofa and putting his feet up on the ottoman. He put his hands behind his head. "First question."

Claire waited, said nothing.

"Was your roommate a man or a woman?"

"Why are you so interested in my roommate?"

"Is that how you want to use one of your ten questions—why I'm interested in your roommate?"

She shrugged.

"Fine. Here's my answer." He paused and looked at her. "*You know why*," he said. "That's my answer."

Her eyes flew back up to his face. And there was the answer, written there. His frank gaze was unmistakable. He wanted to know if there was a man in her life, one she'd been living with. He wanted to know because he wanted her. Hot desire slid through her body like an avalanche.

He just sat very still, watching her.

Her lips parted . . .

And then she snapped out of it. The rascal was doing this on purpose! He thought she was just like any other groupie who was going to fall for some silent-but-deadly seduction trick.

"No, you don't," she said, setting down her wine glass and wagging her finger at him.

"What?"

She circled the finger, indicating his face. "That. Whatever that thing is you're doing. With your face. Don't do that."

"I have no idea what you're talking about."

"You know exactly what I'm talking about, and I have no intention of becoming Dr. Groupie. Now. Proceed with your next question."

"Did you say *Dr. Groupie*?"

"You know what I mean."

"Yes. Yes, I do. And trust me. If I ever meet anyone less likely to become a groupie, anywhere in the world, I will drop everything and call to tell you about it."

• • •

A glass of wine later, they'd learned they were both only children raised by single mothers, and both despised horror movies.

Eli splashed more white wine into her glass, and she felt herself ease back into her new beige canvas club chair, her back finally fully meeting the back of the chair. She probably should've eaten dinner, but she didn't care anymore.

"Okay, here's my question," she said.

He sat back and waited, his eyes liquid sex.

"What's it like to have a dad who's, well—a legend?"

He let out a puff of a sigh. "You've been researching."

"I googled you. Well, I didn't. Holly did. Against my will."

"Against your will, huh?"

"You know."

His eyes crinkled a little at the edges in amusement. "I do."

"So?"

"It was a lot like not having a dad."

"Oh. Yeah. I read that book."

"Did your dad leave?" Eli asked.

"Yes. Well, first he left. Then he died."

"Oh. Wow. I'm sorry."

Claire shrugged. "He left because he found a girlfriend he liked better than his wife. Then one night, apparently, he decided to take the woman for a spin after they'd been drinking. Car accident. They were both killed."

"How old were you?"

"Three."

Eli nodded, and they both sat silently for a minute, which Claire found oddly comforting. She was glad he wasn't trying to say the usual stuff people said about how maybe she was better off without a cheating, alcoholic father.

Claire knew Eli's father was a whole different story. Gage Archer was kind of like . . . the reigning king of sex, drugs, and rock and roll, even at his age. He'd held the position for multiple decades. His face was now like a large, craggy, masculine version of one of those shrunken apple dolls, but it didn't seem to be hurting his career any. "I guess you've been dealing with fame your whole life," she said.

Eli sighed, shrugged. "Yeah. In a way."

"Was it like seventh grade sycophants trying to get to your dad through you?"

"Some of the moms, when I first started a new school. I didn't understand what they were doing until later. But pretty soon everyone realized I had no more access to him than they did, so it wasn't so bad."

"What's your mom like?"

"Quiet. Religious. A cellist with the New York Philharmonic. We did all right."

"Yeah. You do what you've got to do. I guess we did all right, too, in a way. But I won't be repeating that pattern—the whole single mom thing is not for me. Children who grow up in single-parent homes are more likely to commit suicide, need psychiatric care by the age of twenty-two, or be treated for drugs or alcohol. Oh, also more likely to witness domestic violence or drop out of school."

"Seriously?"

"It's true."

"No. I meant, seriously, you just happen to know all of that?"

"I like to read studies." She sipped her wine, realizing she'd just exposed herself as a giant nerd. "And *Psychology Today*, and, you know, stuff." *Psychology Today* sounded normal, right? They sold it in supermarkets, after all.

"I see."

"You see what?" she asked. *Everything. He saw everything.*

"Nothing. Nothing at all." He looked amused. "What about your mother?"

"Best we not talk about that right now."

"Yeah?"

"We're having some boundary issues. She lives right behind

you."

"Behind me?"

"Yup. Which means catty-corner behind me. You might have noticed the lack of fence. She feels free to come over whenever she wants. She also knows how my life is really supposed to be, down to the lipstick I should be wearing. Her ideas do not resemble the life I'm actually living."

"Sounds like fun."

"Yeah. Let's talk about something else."

"So, no boyfriend?"

Claire choked on her wine.

"Hey, haven't you already had your ten questions?"

"I quit counting at four," he said.

"I'm pretty sure this is eleven."

"You were counting?" His mouth twitched. He looked up at her bookcase, where she'd organized her favorite books and movies by size and color, then turned back to her. "I'll take your word for it."

Of course she'd been counting. Who wouldn't have been counting? It was called twenty questions, after all. But counting was probably uncool, and from the way he was looking at her bookshelves, those were uncool too. Claire could do an emergency tracheostomy, but she couldn't do cool. And cool was the only word for Eli Archer. She squirmed in her seat.

He looked away from the bookshelves and back at her. The man could make eye contact better than most men could make love. Not that she knew very much about that, but she was pretty sure it was true.

Heat zinged through her, and she found herself holding his gaze.

"I should get going," he said, standing.

The suddenness of it pricked Claire's mood like a pin to a beach ball. But that was stupid, because of course she *wanted* him to go.

She stood, and they were facing each other, and an odd ache traveled through her.

He watched her face, and for a moment, just a moment, she thought he might . . . kiss her. But instead he took a step backward.

CHAPTER 10

Holly called to Claire from the hallway. "How do your sheets *look* like this?"

"Like what?" Claire followed her into the hall, wiping her hands on her apron.

Holly stood in front of Claire's open linen closet. "Like Martha Stewart folded them herself."

"Don't everyone's sheets look like that?"

"No. No, they do not."

"Just grab me a hand towel and quit staring at my bedding."

"Mom? Can I play chess on my iPad?" Ryan appeared in the hall doorway, hands resting on the top of the doorjamb.

"Have you finished your homework?"

"All but social studies, and it's only like twenty minutes."

"If it's only twenty minutes, finish it up, then play chess. Just take in the living room while Claire and I get ready for dinner."

Ryan let out a long-suffering sigh.

Holly watched him go, then turned to Claire. "Any word on Zoe?"

"Yeah, yesterday. I called the social worker to check in."
"And?"

"You know Mrs. Stamper, from church?"

"Carolyn Stamper? Brian and Emily's mother? Didn't Emily move to Little Rock?"

"Yes and yes. Zoe's with her. Mrs. Stamper is Zoe's foster mother, that is. And Zoe's foot is healing, and everything's fine. Mrs. Stamper even took in the devil dog for Zoe."

"Oh," said Holly, crestfallen.

Claire swatted her. "What are you talking about? Mrs. Stamper is perfect."

"She is. Of course she is."

Claire opened her mouth to speak, then closed it again. She didn't want to hear what Holly might say. They stood in awkward silence for a few seconds.

"The new kitchen is really great," Holly said, regaining her composure. "The laundry room too."

"Thanks! Yeah, I'm in love," Claire said. *With the house. Of course she meant with the house.*

Claire had woken that morning from a dream in which Eli was doing things to her body no man in real life had ever done. She'd woken with her T-shirt soaked with sweat and her flesh aching for his touch.

And that was when she'd known she had to do it. She had to ask Holly to set her up with Dan. Immediately, if not sooner. It was a fix-up emergency. She'd always wanted to ask Holly to do this, but she hadn't let herself go there, because she hadn't wanted Holly to feel awkward. But who was she kidding? Holly loved nothing better than fixing people up, and she was very good at it. If things worked out—which, why wouldn't they?—she and Holly would be both best friends *and* sisters-in-law. Claire could be Ryan's aunt. Ryan would have cousins, once Claire and Dan had children. They would all be one big happy family.

Still, Claire found herself hesitating, dreading speaking the actual words. Shouldn't these things—romance, dating, marriage—happen a little more easily? More naturally?

Claire poured them each a glass of red wine, handed one to Holly, and stirred a jar of Ragu into the ground turkey. She flipped on the burner to boil the water for pasta.

"So Pete hasn't called me back. It's been three days." Holly said, leaning against the counter and watching Claire work.

"Oh, Holl. I'm sorry. Maybe he's busy?"

"Meh. Probably for the best."

"Why do you say that?"

"Have you *seen* his ex-wife?"

"Brandy? Yeah. She's scrappy." Claire grinned. "You

wouldn't want to meet *her* in a dark alley. She might put a Virginia Slim out on you."

Holly took a sip of wine and nodded. "Good wine. You know, being divorced just sucks. The pickings go from slim to anorexic."

Claire couldn't even imagine trying to date as a single mother. It was hard enough as just a plain old single woman. Holly had done the right thing getting out of her marriage, though. The first time Holly had caught Sean cheating, she'd forgiven him, even after he'd lied to try to cover it up. The second time, she'd gone to an attorney.

Claire didn't ever want to experience that. She desperately wanted her children to grow up in a two-parent household, nothing like what she'd had. She wanted to choose someone foolproof. Someone totally, one hundred percent, *safe.* Like Dan.

"But you kind of liked Pete, right?" Claire asked.

"Oh, kinda. I don't know," Holly said. "It was only a couple of dates. Want to hear something weird?"

"Always."

"He smelled funny."

Claire snorted red wine and coughed out a laugh. "What do you mean by 'funny'?"

"I don't know. I mean, he was clean . . . Well, he looked clean. And he would brush his teeth and shower and show up at my house—at least he appeared to be doing all of those things, and he looked nice, and all—but then he would come toward me and hug me and I would think, Ew. *You do not smell good, dude.*"

"What did he smell like?"

"Squash."

Claire threw her head back and let a full-body belly laugh take over. "*Squash?*"

Holly shrugged. "Crazy, I know. Must have been a pheromone thing."

Claire snapped her fingers, remembering something. "Oh,

yes! Of course you're right. Do you know about the Sweaty T-Shirt Study?"

"No, you freaky brainiac, I do *not* know about the Sweaty T-Shirt Study."

"So, listen, this is a real thing. This Swiss scientist took a bunch of men's sweaty T-shirts and then he had women sniff them. Without the men in them, of course. The women had to pick the most attractive sweat smell."

"Oh my word. Sweat smell? Seriously?"

"I know. It's cool, right? The best part is, the results were consistent. The women liked the sweat of the men whose MHC genes were most different from theirs. Pretty much every time." Claire set her wine glass down on the counter. "You and Pete were genetically incompatible!"

"But I don't *need* compatible genes," Holly said, and it sounded a little like a wail. "I don't even want to reproduce. I just don't want to sleep alone for the rest of my life. Or keep paying one hundred percent of the health insurance bill forever and ever amen. A family auto-insurance discount would be nice too. Plus, you know, I'm tired. Parenting alone—it starts to wear you down." Holly picked a carrot off one of the salads and popped it in her mouth.

"I couldn't do it." She was so glad Zoe had such a great place to be, with Mrs. Stamper.

"Sure you could. I mean, it's not ideal. Of course it's not. If I could go back and marry a non-cheater, of course that's what I'd do. But I wouldn't have Ryan, so actually I wouldn't change anything. You find the strength once you're in the situation."

"*You* find the strength. I'm not sure I could."

They were quiet for a minute.

"Do you have anyone lined up, now that Pete bit the dust?" Claire asked.

"Not a soul. Maybe I should have let Pete kiss me when he tried. Maybe I would have gotten over the smell thing."

"Sounds like you did the right thing. If you have a small

amount of chemistry, I think you can work with it, sort of fan the flames, you know, but zero chemistry won't work. I think squash smells are irrecoverable."

"You're probably right. It would have been different if it had been peaches or strawberries."

Claire raised her glass to that.

Oh, chemistry. She thought of Eli's gaze on her the night before. His arms around her when he'd stopped the washing machine. The scent of him, mint and musk. She took a sip of wine and looked toward the dining room window at Eli's house. His lights were on.

"Wait. What's going on with you?" Holly asked, tipping her wine glass toward Claire, following her eyes toward the window. "I smell something other than sweaty T-shirts."

"Can everyone read my mind lately?"

"*What?*" Holly asked, suspicious. "Who else is reading your mind?"

"Nothing, nothing. No one," Claire said.

"So something *is* going on? Is it the rock star?"

"*No*, it's not the *rock star*. Of course it's not the rock star. Trust me, my dating life is less interesting than Ryan's."

"Wha?" Ryan called from his iPad chess match in the living room. "Did someone say my name?"

"No, honey," Holly shouted toward the living room. "Finish your game and we'll call you to dinner in ten minutes. Clean hands, please!"

"Okay, Mom."

"You're such a good mom," Claire said. It was true. Ryan was a great kid, and Holly moved heaven and earth to make sure her hospital schedule allowed as much time with him as possible.

There was that familiar pang, the one that reminded Claire of her own childlessness. It was like sciatic pain, sparking at inconvenient moments, taking over everything when it did. She breathed through it. It was just further proof it was time to do what she needed to do—ask Holly about Dan.

"Speaking of my dating life." Claire took a swig of wine. "I have sort of an embarrassing question."

"Oh, please. It's me. I just told you my last date smelled like zucchini. There are no embarrassing questions."

"Fix me up with Dan?" Claire let the words somersault over each other, getting them out of her mouth as quickly as possible.

Holly didn't look surprised. "I will." She hesitated. "Of course I will. If that's really what you want me to do."

"What do you mean? You think it's a bad idea?"

"I love my brother. You know I do. It's just . . . are you sure he could make you happy?" Holly looked skeptical.

"Maybe? That's what dating is for, right? To find out?"

"So they tell me."

"What's your misgiving about it?"

"Dan is . . . he's just . . . Dan is—"

"A dweeb," Ryan announced, coming into the kitchen, his hands grasping the doorframe above his head.

"Ryan!" Holly looked horrified.

"Well?" He shrugged. "He is."

"Okay, okay, so maybe that's not so far off." She shot Ryan a look even as she was agreeing with him. "Dan can be a little . . . rigid."

"Reliable," Claire said.

"Humorless," Holly said.

"Sensible," Claire said.

Holly sighed, and Claire watched her face as she considered it. "Maybe you're right. I'm the one who wound up divorced, after all."

"You're the best, Holl. It won't be too weird?" Claire asked.

Holly shrugged. "Not weird for me, and I think Dan is impervious to weird. I'll ask him for you. I'll make it sound like my idea."

"Thank you," Claire said, meaning it.

"Here's to tall blond genius babies." Holly raised her glass.

Claire clinked her glass against Holly's, crossed her eyes, and made Holly's favorite duck lips.

"That." Holly pointed. "That's my concern."

"What, my duck lips?"

"You're *fun*! I mean, you're freakishly well-organized and your list-making borders on mania, but you're fun."

"Oh, now. Dan's fun."

Holly and Ryan looked at her. Neither said anything. "Let's eat," Holly said. "I'm starving." She pointed at Ryan, whose Adam's apple bobbed like a golf ball in his pale, slender neck. "The growing man-child ate everything in our refrigerator, and then part of the refrigerator too."

Claire set her new hemstitch linen napkins on the reclaimed wood dining table and surveyed the sight. Her first dinner guests in her new kitchen. Soon she'd be setting a rack of lamb in the middle of the table with . . . some kind of fancy vegetables. She'd get great at being wifely, so she'd be ready. And soon, thanks to Holly, her love life would be in order. She looked up and smiled at Holly, who was delivering the salads from the kitchen island. "Ready?"

"Ready," Holly said, putting a salad at one of the places. "Ryan, why don't you sit here?"

The doorbell startled all three of them. A salad plate paused midair as Holly looked up. "Joyce?"

Claire sighed. "She didn't call, but of course that doesn't mean anything. Be right back. Go ahead and start without me."

• • •

Eli Archer stood on her front porch holding a magnificent bouquet of a dozen Stargazer lilies.

He was clean-shaven, wearing a beige T-shirt that was just fitted enough to show off his muscular chest, and sporting his trademark soulful gaze.

Damn him. Why did he have to be so . . . so Eli?

"For last night," he said, handing her the flowers.

"Last night?"

"I left abruptly."

"Oh. That. Probably for the best."

"I don't know anymore, but that was why I left."

"What was why?"

"I wanted to tear your clothes to shreds with my bare hands."

Claire stopped dead. Had he really just said that? Out loud? To her? Her whole body throbbed with his words. Her lips parted and hung there.

He watched her. Their eyes locked and held, electric with heat and energy.

She snapped her mouth closed, closed her eyes, and gave her head a brisk shake, forcing herself to return to earth.

Eli handed her the flowers.

"Claire?" Holly stopped in the doorway, and her eyes traveled from Claire to Eli and back again.

"Oh!" Eli said. "I didn't see a car. Didn't realize you had company."

"We walked," Holly said. She pried the flowers from Claire's frozen grip. "Let me just put these in water. Come in, *come in*." She waved Eli toward the kitchen. "Forgive Claire for leaving you standing in the doorway. She's socially challenged."

"He doesn't want to come in," Claire said.

"I don't?"

"No."

"Of *course* he does."

Claire shot Holly a look.

Holly grinned and shrugged. She led Eli into the kitchen and got out a glass for him, and Claire listened with resignation to the *glug-glug* of wine pouring.

"Spaghetti?" Holly offered.

Eli had the decency to look at Claire, a question in his eyes. She was positive she could have an hour-long conversation with this man without one audible word. She shrugged—*how can I say no?*

"Maybe I'll just have a couple of sips of wine, then let the

Haven Springs natives get back to dinner. Thanks, though," Eli said.

"Nonsense," Holly said, and began spooning spaghetti onto a plate. "Sit," she commanded, and pointed at the empty seat.

Eli looked at Claire again. She nodded her consent. There was no fighting Holly once she'd made her mind up.

"So. How much money do famous people make?" Ryan asked, setting down his fork and giving Eli his full, bright-eyed, cowlicked-head attention.

"*Ryan!*" Holly said.

"*What?* It's career research."

"You can't just decide to be famous like you can decide to be a schoolteacher," Holly said.

"How come?" Ryan asked. He shoveled a big bite of noodles and sauce into his mouth and waited, chewing.

"Because . . . because . . . There's a lot of luck involved," Holly said. "With being famous. Or something like that."

Eli laughed a good-natured laugh, and it reverberated through Claire's body with a warm buzz.

"I don't mean, I didn't mean . . ." Holly flushed azalea pink and shook her dark blonde curls.

"It's all right," Eli said. "Good spaghetti, by the way." He nodded at Claire, managing to scorch her with just a split second of eye contact.

"Your mom's right," he continued. "A lot of talented musicians work hard without ever making it."

"Work hard?" Claire said, a little skeptical.

He set his fork down and looked at her, leaning back in his chair. After a moment he said, "Yes. To make good music is hard work."

"Do tell," Holly said, putting her chin in her hands and her elbows on either side of her placemat.

"Well, your work is never really done if you're doing it right. And when you're making a record, it's grueling. Long hours and more intimate contact with four other men than I would ever wish for. And they all have a different—and fanatical—idea of how things are supposed to be done. Everyone goes a little nuts. They fight. A lot. But I *am* lucky to do what I do. It's the only thing I love. No whining on the yacht."

"Sounds cool," Ryan said, nodding.

"It is, if you can handle being famous," Eli said. "Famous isn't for everyone."

"What do you *mean?* Being famous must totally rock."

"It has its moments. There's a privacy downgrade. On a continuum. I somehow got to the bad end of that continuum. Lately."

Claire thought he sounded like he was talking to a thirty-year-old, but Ryan was nodding as though he understood every word.

"I bet a lot of girls like you."

Holly let loose her musical laugh.

Eli's eyes traveled to Claire's, lighted there, and lingered. This time, she looked away. She didn't care how many women liked him, he wasn't going to be adding her name to that roster.

He shrugged. "I don't think much about it."

"*I'd* sure think about it," Ryan said.

"The less you focus on it, the more they like you." Eli winked at Ryan.

Ryan nodded slowly, contemplating Eli's words. Then he switched gears to his upcoming chess tournament.

The rest of the dinner passed amiably enough, with Ryan chattering on about chess, and the adults politely listening.

Claire started clearing the table, taking plates and utensils back to the counter.

"Well, I hate to eat and run, but Ryan has homework," Holly announced. Holly had the worst poker face ever.

"Aww, Mom, I hardly have any homework!"

"See, *Mom,* he hardly has any homework. You don't have to go," Claire said, giving Holly a slight poke in the back.

Holly grinned at her. "I'm *so* sorry we have to go. We'll just be getting our jackets." She walked toward the hall closet. "Eli," she nodded. "Claire, thank you for dinner."

Eli gave Holly a small salute. "Ryan, my man." He held out his hand for a fist bump.

Holly pulled on her windbreaker. "Well. Good night, you two. Don't do anything I wouldn't do."

Claire groaned.

The front door closed behind them, leaving a *whoosh* of cool evening air behind them.

That left Eli and Claire alone in the entry hall.

"Well. Thank you for the flowers. And good night," Claire said.

He stepped toward her in one easy stride, closing the gap between them, his face looking down into hers, close enough to touch.

They stood that way for a long moment, eyes resting on each other. Claire's breath caught. The way he was looking at her, she thought he might kiss her, but he just stood, watching her, not moving, and the whole world seemed to go still and silent.

And then she felt his hands on her arms, both of his hands on both of her arms, making a slow journey from shoulder to fingertip. She stared at him, mesmerized. She felt him everywhere. And somehow Eli touching her arms was R-rated, like they were doing something incredibly intimate, something erotic and powerful.

By the time his hands reached her fingertips, she no longer remembered that she wanted him to leave. She just wanted him. She wanted his lips on hers, she wanted to press her body against his and feel the strength of him against her.

Stopping at her fingertips, he slid his arms around her waist, pulled her body close to his, and pressed his lips, gentle, slow, and firm, against hers. He took his time, first taking her top lip between his, then her bottom lip.

He kissed her like he had all the time in the world. By the time his tongue found hers, she was desperate for him.

Reflexively, she pressed the lower half of her body harder

into his, and what she felt there sent waves of liquid heat through her.

Outside, a band of kids ran by, whooping into the night.

Claire and Eli pulled back from each other, quickly, as though burned.

Claire cleared her throat.

Eli smoothed his hair back from his face and straightened his shoulders.

They looked at each other, the knowledge of what might happen next hanging in the air between them.

"I should probably get going," he said.

"Yup," Claire said.

• • •

Claire went back to the kitchen for her phone and texted Holly.

Need to go out with Dan right away. Please help.

The phone rang in her hand.

"Why?" Holly asked, before Claire even had a chance to say hello.

"Because I'm attracted to Eli Archer," Claire wailed.

"Well, duh. But why is this a bad thing? He is so obviously into you. I'd be jealous if it weren't so obviously some kind of freaky kismet."

"Freaky kismet?"

"Yeah, you know. Destiny. Fate. Just maybe not in the package you were thinking it would come in."

"Eli Archer is *not* my destiny."

"*Mmm hmm.*"

"Don't say that!"

"I didn't say anything."

"Don't *not* say it, then."

"Fine, fine, fine. You really want me to go through with this Dan thing?"

"Yes. It's a very sensible plan."

"Fine," Holly grumbled. "I'll call him. If he answers, I'll call you back."

"Thanks."

They hung up, and Claire eyed the clock.

The phone rang in her hand again, and she answered.

"You're not out?" Joyce's voice held an unsubtle whiff of reproach.

"Not out," Claire said cheerfully, her teeth clenched.

"I made some casseroles for your freezer. I'll bring them by tomorrow while you're at work."

Claire thought about her new kitchen and her resolve for culinary independence. It would also be nice to be able to leave her underwear on the floor without worrying about her mother letting herself in. Not that Claire ever would leave her underwear on the floor (who *did* that?) but what if she had a moment of passion with Eli—no, wait, make that Dan—and her mother found the evidence? Or walked in during the moment of passion? Would Claire ever be old enough to deserve privacy?

Not until you're old enough to ask for it. "Mom, listen, I—"

"I also have some catalogues for you. Cute stuff. Date-type stuff. I'll leave them on your coffee table."

Claire squeezed her eyelids with her free hand.

"I'll just leave them when I come by tomorrow."

"Mom—"

The phone beeped the signal of another call coming in. Claire pulled the phone away from her face and looked at the screen. Holly.

But Claire knew if she didn't get this over with, telling her mother about the fence, she could keep putting it off forever. And the bottom line was, they needed that fence.

"Mom," she said, trying to keep the tremor of nerves out of her voice. "You know I've been working toward fixing up the house—the kitchen and laundry room, and furniture, and, you know, just getting it all finished."

"The kitchen looks great."

"Thank you." She paused. "The next thing on the list is a

fence. For the backyard. A privacy fence."

"But then I won't be able to cut through the backyard. I would have to walk all the way up the block and back again. That would be, what? Probably ten minutes!" Her mother sounded horrified, and also like she was certain Claire just hadn't thought of this before.

Claire took a deep breath. "I know, I just . . . I . . . think it's time."

"What do you mean, time?"

Claire paused, unsure of what to say.

"I have to say, this seems pretty ungrateful."

"I don't mean to be ungrateful, Mom. I appreciate your cooking. You should have seen my last attempt to do it myself. But this is something I need to do."

"I could call first."

That would last about four days. "Mom, you won't call first."

"I could work on it."

"I feel this is the right thing."

There was a long pause. "Fine." Joyce spit the word out, then hung up.

• • •

When Claire regained her equilibrium, she called Holly back.

"So, I'm the best friend ever," Holly said.

"I know. What happened?"

"Well, I told Dan I'd been thinking about all those rumors he was gay, and I thought he should start dating you to help out with that. If, in fact, he wanted to dispel them."

"Holly!"

"Just kidding. I told him the two of you would make a really great pair. He made some grunting noises but I stayed on him, and he finally said he'd call you tomorrow."

"I'm . . . underwhelmed."

"You can't take it personally. That's just Dan."

This was the thing she liked about Dan—not too emotional.

Always predictable. Stable. He was the most stable man in the state of Missouri, she was sure of it. He would never get swept away by his emotions and run off with a younger woman. He wouldn't become an alcoholic or a gambler or a race-car driver. He wouldn't get on Facebook two months before their wedding and get back together with his girlfriend from college. *He wouldn't gaze at her like they were having sex with their eyes, get her heart all in a knot, then go back to his rock star life in New York.* Dan would drive to Little League games and go to church every Sunday and make sure the retirement account was properly funded and they both had disability insurance. He was husband material, and Claire wanted a family. A real family. Not just her, Joyce, and Thanksgiving turkey that went to the neighborhood cats because the leftovers were more than two people could eat.

"Thanks for doing it, Holly. I hope it wasn't too awkward."

"Nah. I didn't sweat it. Now for the important stuff. *What happened with Eli?* It must have been good if the Dan thing suddenly became a dating emergency."

"Nothing happened."

"Liar."

"Eli kissed me."

Over Holly's shrieks and squeals, Claire spoke loudly. "But I can't talk about it, really."

"Why *not?* I want to hear *everything.*"

"It was . . . I don't know. Hard to put into words."

"Oh boy."

"What?"

"You two are so going to fall in love."

"You said Dan's calling tomorrow, right?"

"I'm going to Walmart tomorrow to buy a popcorn maker."

"*What?* Holly, that was your biggest non sequitur ever."

"Nope. Totally relevant to the conversation. I'm going to need lots of popcorn for watching all this go down."

CHAPTER 11

Eli's heart pounded with adrenalin overdose.

He wanted to take the reporter's camera and make the wormy little guy eat it, but he was already on the books for his last paparazzo assault, and he couldn't afford to go again. Not that he made a habit of going around hitting people, even scum-of-the-earth paparazzi. The jerk at the airport had actually been the first guy he'd ever hit. He rubbed his still-healing hand.

Eli didn't want to hit this guy, not really. He just wanted to grab him and make sure the photograph of his rental house, of him in the front doorway, shirtless, with the house number right above his head in shiny brass numerals, didn't see the light of day. If he could just have a couple more months of privacy . . . Haven Springs had been good to him that way, so far. People recognized him, but mostly, they didn't make a big deal of it. He could grocery shop in peace. He could hang at the music store for a few minutes, chatting with Dave. No one had videoed him, and not one person had asked him to sign a breast or butt cheek.

Eli took a moment to grab his shirt and put it on before he took off after the guy, but he still caught up with him in less than five long strides. "Give. Me. The. Camera."

The guy was trying to speed-walk away, but Eli's legs were longer, and he kept pace easily.

"Sorry, man, that picture'll pay for a year of my kid's college."

"*I'll* pay for your kid's college. Just give me the camera."

"Sorry, man." The guy broke into a trot.

Eli walked beside him. The guy's pale beige shirt collar, a foot below Eli's gaze, was begging to be grabbed, but Eli knew he couldn't touch it without making things worse for himself.

Just then, Claire's white Honda pulled up on Crescent Drive. Eli raised a hand in greeting, still striding alongside the weasel.

The car turned toward him, pulling perpendicular on Crescent Drive, blocking them, and the window slid down.

"What have we here?" she asked, looking amused.

The guy started to walk around the car, but when he saw Claire, he stopped.

"Oh." His gaze lowered to the sidewalk. "Dr T." *Now* he had the decency to look a little chagrinned.

"Byron," she said. She got out of the car, wearing her usual ultraconservative getup—a navy cardigan and loose khakis—and Eli marveled again that she managed to look so damn sexy in something that should have looked more off-duty nun than bombshell.

"Just hoping to keep my address under wraps for another twenty minutes," Eli said.

One perfect beige eyebrow arched, librarian-style. She turned it on Byron.

He looked at the pavement.

"What's going on?" she asked him.

"I'm a journalist."

"I know that."

"I gotta make a living."

"I know that too."

"They'll pay. A lot." He pointed at Eli without looking up. "For him."

She waited until Byron finally looked up at her, and the eyebrow inched higher.

"Damn," he said, shoulders sagging with defeat.

"Give me the camera, Byron."

He toed the asphalt, and he hesitated, but he handed her the camera.

She made quick work of deleting the pictures and handed the camera back to him. "And I can trust you're not going to walk away and call a tabloid?"

"I won't," he said, petulant.

She paused. "I believe you," she said finally, sounding matronly.

Eli looked at her in disbelief. "*I don't*," he said.

The guy looked at Eli, surprised. "Dr. T told me not to," he said, as though that were equivalent to Moses carving it into stone.

"You always do what she says?"

"Well, yeah. Everybody does. She's Dr. T."

Eli hadn't realized an M.D. was equivalent to reigning queen in Haven Springs. He eyed the navy cardigan. She looked so . . . demure. He should be vigilant to remember she could melt people into submission with one arch of an eyebrow.

"Besides, if the address leaks, Byron knows we'll be asking him first," Claire said. "The accountability of small-town life."

"Can I go now?" Byron asked.

"Yup," Claire said.

Looking relieved, Byron hurried down the street, clutching his Nikon.

Eli and Claire watched him go.

"It's hopeless," Eli said. "If it's not him, it'll be somebody else."

"Maybe not," Claire said.

"How do you figure?"

"Hang on, let me park my car."

"Give me a ride back to the driveway?"

She looked at the thirty feet between her car and her driveway and smiled. "Sure."

He folded his long body into the small Honda. Even though it was only a four-second drive to the driveway, Claire clicked her seat belt shut, which made him smile. The car was old, but it was immaculate, not a speck of dust on the dash, not a soda can or a water bottle in sight. The car-related papers clipped to the visor were folded in origami-perfect rectangles.

"Nice car," he said.

"There was an Australian study that said white cars are ten percent less likely to have an accident in the daytime. Which is weird, you know, because you'd think white would show up more at night. Did you read that statistic?"

"Uh, no." He looked back at the origami car insurance papers and found himself wondering if she folded her underwear that neatly. And there it was again, the image he couldn't shake: Claire, head thrown back, having an earth-shattering orgasm—provided by him.

He snapped out of it when she turned the key in the ignition and the radio started. A sappy pop song, a Stephanie Kelly song, one that always got stuck in his head if he had the misfortune of hearing it, filled the car. He reached over and pushed in the power knob, silencing the radio.

"Hey!"

"You can't like that," he said.

"I *do* like that."

"It's not allowed."

"Sorry, *Dad*. I'm thirty-five." She pressed the power knob back in, and the saccharine chorus started up and assaulted his ears—something about how the singer was so sexy all the men in the club needed to bow to her.

"This is the worst music in the world."

"It's in the top forty!"

He groaned with the pain of it.

She pulled the car into the driveway and he snapped the glove compartment open. "Don't you have at least a Radiohead CD in here?"

"Radiohead?" She looked confused.

"You're kidding, right?" He stared at her, incredulous.

"It's a band?"

He groaned again.

She shut the car off, mercifully silencing the music, if you could call it music.

"Radiohead is probably the most important band since the

Beatles."

"Oh."

"*OK Computer, Hail to the Thief, The Bends, Amnesiac*? Any of that ringing a bell?"

"Sounds kind of depressing. And how can you not like Stephanie Kelly?" she asked.

He covered his eyes with his hand.

"Well, *I* like her. And most of the country agrees with me."

"Most of the country is wrong." Someday, he'd like to play her something really good.

"Anyway, I was saying, about the newspaper thing. Most people here aren't like Byron. I've known him since kindergarten, and he's always been a twerp."

"Does everyone always obey you like that?"

She shrugged, smoothed her hair, reddened, nodded.

She was crazy sexy, librarian sexy, with her flushed cheeks and those tortoise-shell glasses, and he wanted to kiss her again. "I'll take that as a yes," he said instead.

"Well, I did help Byron out with a little bit of a . . . private problem, so he might be more inclined to do what I ask him."

"Private problem?"

She eyed him. "Which remains private."

"Ah."

She reddened deeper. "Also, it's kind of . . . a thing."

"What kind of a thing?"

"Oh, people just have this weird thing. About, you know, doctors. They might've changed your diapers in the church nursery, but you come home with an M.D., and suddenly people get a little . . ."

"What?"

"Obsequious? I thought you might understand."

"Ah." Yes, he did know a thing or two about that.

"It's not everyone. It's just . . . a lot of people."

He nodded. "Sometimes you just want to go back to people being real with you."

She glanced at him, and their eyes locked in understanding

and held there for a moment.

"Anyway," she said in a rush. "Don't worry too much about the address getting out. It's Haven Springs."

He shrugged. "It's just a matter of time. I knew that. It's my life. I'm lucky. I'd be a spoiled brat to complain about it." Only, he did want to complain about it. He fucking hated it.

"Do you ever just want to put a bag over your head?"

"It's occurred to me."

Claire laughed. "But Haven Springs is different. You might've noticed it already."

"I wasn't expecting so many gay pride flags in a town of two thousand in the Ozark Mountains, that's for sure."

"Haven's a place where people come to run away. To reinvent themselves. Some people even change their names when they move here. Sure, there are a few second- and third-generation locals—I'm a local. But two-thirds of the people who live here, at least, came here to get away from something. We honor privacy here. And being a misfit. It's kind of a code. I wouldn't live anywhere else."

He looked at her. Her eyes were glowing with what she was saying.

She was beautiful.

"You don't look like much of a misfit." He eyed the glasses and the cardigan. The sweater was a deceptive piece of clothing. Navy and plain and modest, resolutely unsexy—and yet—the tiny white buttons. Those damn buttons. He could just—open one. Two. Three. What would spill out? What would she look like?

"At least I know I can be if I want to be."

"Be what?" He pulled his eyes away from the buttons.

"A misfit."

"Oh. Right. And how would that look?"

"Oh, you know. Pizza. Netflix. If I were feeling really wild and crazy I might have a beer."

He laughed.

"I guess your life is a lot more interesting," she said.

"I'll take some boring."

She eyed him, and silence fell.

He remembered their kiss. And her wet T-shirt after the washing machine leak. And what she'd said about not being Dr. Groupie. That kiss—how she'd melted against him—trusting, soft.

And now, like she was thinking the same thing, her eyes grew larger and softer. Did she want it too? All he could think about was doing it again. To kiss her lips, to kiss her neck, to kiss her everywhere. It filled up the car, stealing all the air.

He reached out for her, and his hand grazed her thigh. She looked up at him, all liquid heat and desire and sweetness. God, she was sweet.

Her lips, pink and lipstickless, waited for him, still parted.

And then the sound of pinging chimes nearly jolted him out of his body. It took him a moment to realize it was his phone. It was ringtone he'd never heard before.

Coming to, he fumbled with the phone, trying to make it stop. Once his eyes registered what was on the screen, he cursed.

Large pink nipples on balloon-shaped breasts stared back at him from the phone screen.

A woman in Coco's model crowd—he wouldn't have even remembered her name if he weren't looking at it on the screen right now—had grabbed his phone and taken a picture of herself with it, one night when they were all out in a club. She'd programmed her phone number to go with the picture. And there was that picture now, with the word Ashlee over the forehead. And two bare nipples on the tip of two round breasts, displayed proudly above the neck of the dress she'd pulled down to showcase them. He'd forgotten all about it, or he would have deleted it.

"Shit. It's not . . ."

Claire was looking down at the phone, and her face had changed.

Then it changed again, like she was watching things happen on a movie screen.

It wasn't good.

Usually, he could read her like a billboard, but right now, he couldn't tell exactly what she was thinking. He could guess. Hell, he knew what *he'd* be thinking if he were her.

"Well. Gotta go," she said.

"Claire." He reached out, took her arm.

She looked down at the hand on her arm, then back up at him.

She looked . . . disappointed. Maybe even a little hurt. Maybe disgusted.

Damn.

He'd known this about her. She wasn't casual about this kind of thing. She was more of a where's-my-engagement-ring type than a here-are-my-nipples-selfie type.

And her face, her face right at this very moment, was proof: he couldn't go screwing around with her, no matter how much he wanted her. She wasn't his to take, and she deserved better.

"What?" she asked, sighing.

He dropped her arm. "Nothing," he said. "See you around the front yard."

• • •

Claire hurried inside and shut the front door, sinking against it.

Her hands were shaking.

She was *such* an idiot. She'd almost let him kiss her. *Again.* And if they kept kissing, or worse, did even more than kissing, she was going to put her heart at risk. She'd *known* he had to be a player. Weren't all men like that players? Surrounded by groupies. Partying all the time. Perpetually playing the field.

He just seemed so nice. So . . . decent. He'd given his food to Zoe. Claire's heart, which she had supposedly guarded up until now, gave a ridiculous little ache. Pitiful.

She was an idiot. This guy seriously did something to her

hormones, something that turned her brain into scrambled eggs. Her, and no doubt every other woman in North America and on several other continents, as well.

She went into the living room, flopped on the sofa, pulled her iPad out of her handbag, and opened HandleIt. She scrolled through her list of things to do today, checking them off, one item at a time, her finger tap tapping next to each item. She was counting on the usual dopamine release provided by list checking, but today, it wasn't working. No dopamine rush. Just an odd feeling of restlessness. Hollowness.

She called the social worker to ask about Zoe, but got voice mail.

She looked back down the list of all her other files. Insurance policies. Calendar. Reminders. Her five-year plan.

Her five-year plan—the one she'd made when she finished her residency—three years ago.

Married by thirty. Thirty-two at the latest. Start trying for a baby after one year. Six weeks of maternity leave per child—ideally three children in all, two boys and one girl. Or two girls and one boy. But definitely one of each. Reduction to part-time work until the children were in kindergarten.

She was running seriously late.

She tossed the iPad on the neighboring club chair and let out a big sigh.

The image of the naked breasts, proudly displayed, on Eli's ringing phone, came back to her, and she groaned. It was a good thing it had happened, though. It was just the reminder she needed.

She pulled herself up from the couch to get ready for work. Nothing like a thirty-hour shift to distract you from misplaced lust.

• • •

Anita appeared in the doctor's lounge doorway in her magenta scrubs and floral Danskos. "So much for the slow night," she said.

Claire could hear Jimmy Beasley through the open door behind Anita. His bellows, same as always, carried throughout the hospital.

Claire got up, clicking her iPad off and tossing it back on the vinyl sofa. "Coming."

She followed Anita into the hall.

"He was gonna, hewashgonna—" Jimmy's words were a combination adult slur and toddler whine.

His twentyish and very pregnant daughter stood in the hallway wearing a strapless maxi dress and drinking a twenty-ounce soda. "Dad, *nobody wants to fight you!*" She turned to Claire. "You remember us."

Claire nodded. "Miss, ah—"

"Missus!" the young woman announced proudly, showing off the ringed hand holding the soda bottle. "Mrs. Lewis."

"Okay, Mrs. Lewis," Claire said, drawing in a patient breath. "I know we've spoken about this before, but I want to encourage you again to seek help for your father."

"He won't do that."

"I understand, but—"

"You mean like against his will?"

A particularly loud slurred bellow, nearly unintelligible, with only the words "he was" clear, interrupted their conversation.

"Dad, *nobody* wants to fight you!" Mrs. Lewis bellowed back.

Claire sighed, a sigh that came from someplace so deep and tired, it seemed like the soles of her shoes must have exhaled. She walked into the room where Jimmy Beasley's face was a mask of bright red anguish. How could anyone this drunk still be walking around and speaking? The stench of sweated-out alcohol was so strong it nearly made her take a step back, but she didn't.

"And then, then, my mom died," he wailed to the ceiling, not yet aware of Claire's presence. He pounded his chest but his fists mostly missed the mark. His face and head were round and florid and too large for the width of his shoulders, which led to a massive distended belly, barely covered by a dirty white T-shirt.

"Mr. Beasley," Claire said.

He lurched himself into a sitting position and then fell back down to the bed.

Anita appeared in the doorway. "You got a tourist pain pill scammer in Room 5. And Fox wants to see you."

• • •

By the time Claire found herself in Fox's office, she was seriously not in the mood.

Fox had a stack of files in front of him, and he motioned for Claire to sit down in the chair across from him. His office was small and grim and lit with fluorescents, hardly anything to lord it over people about, but he managed.

"Dr. Taylor."

Claire waited.

"I've been going over everyone's files—"

Jimmy's bellowing came closer to them. That could only mean he was mobile—as in, out of his bed and traveling. With or without his IV? That was the question.

"—and we really want to make sure we are coding each patient accurately and optimally."

"Dad! Nobody wants to fight you!"

Definitely traveling.

Fox looked unperturbed by the ruckus. "Take this, for instance." He opened the top file. "This particular patient could have been eligible for three more ICD-10 codes."

He pushed it toward her.

"That's Mrs. Hayes. She doesn't even have insurance."

Fox shrugged. "She'd still be obligated to pay the bill." His eyes blinked like a lizard's.

Claire hated him at that moment.

"And this one." He opened another file. "Why wasn't a CAT scan done?"

"We already had a diagnosis. It wasn't necessary," Claire said, like she was talking to a second-grader. She didn't care how she sounded. This was just ridiculous. And unscrupulous.

A crash sounded in the hall, followed by Jimmy Beasley's wails.

Claire sat forward in her seat a little, ready to make a run for it.

"Sit down, please."

She stilled, rage coiling in her. Further sounds of commotion followed in the hallway, all punctuated by Jimmy's crying.

"The thing is, if we can't get compliance, here, on this issue," he waved over the files, "I'll need to start checking all your files. Daily."

Another loud crash, this one metallic, came from the hallway.

Fox remained still, blinking his lizard eyes at her. "Well?"

"Well? Do you mean, am I going to check out what's happening in the hall to make sure everyone is safe? Yes, I would like to do that right now."

"Is that sarcasm? We *will* make sure all staff physicians are taking this seriously. That does include you, Dr. Taylor."

Claire sat, incredulous, and waited.

"Well?" he repeated.

I quit.

She thought it. She didn't say it. She wanted to say it—oh how she wanted to—but of course she couldn't. It was everything she'd worked for. She had student loans, a mortgage, bills.

She tried to force her mouth into speaking the words *Yes, sir*. Or at least *Okay*.

But she was saved.

But Jimmy Beasley chose that moment to do (possibly the first) noble thing of his life. He appeared in the doorway of Fox's office, completely naked, and vomited.

CHAPTER 12

When Claire got home from work, there was an Amazon box on her doorstep. She shoved it aside with her toe, then went inside to strip off the hospital and put her scrubs in the hottest wash allowed by modern luxury—and herself in the hottest shower she could stand.

Once she felt human again, she went back to the porch for the box. A box that turned out to contain, in addition to a mother/daughter relationship self-help book—one set of false eyelashes, one set of fake breasts in the form of a foam bra that could make a ten-year-old boy look buxom, frosty pink lipstick, hooker shoes, and a barely-there silk blouse. Ah, Joyce. Ever the subtle touch. Claire felt a little pang of guilt about the fence, but she knew she had to stay strong.

She eyed the contents of the box. She *was* a *little* curious. In front of the full-length mirror on the back of the bathroom door, she tried on the tall black patent-leather pumps. She pointed her toe toward the mirror. Her unpolished toenails showed through the peep toe, but she had to admit, they made her calves look fantastic. Still, she couldn't wear something like that in public.

What would Eli think of these shoes? *I don't care. Yes, I do. No, I don't.*

She eyed the contents of the package, the lacy pink push-up bra. What harm could it do to try it on?

Va-va-voom. She was Marilyn Monroe! And all it took was two little pieces of foam. She could store medical instruments in this cleavage! The bra was cut low in the center, creating a deep crevice she hadn't known her breasts were capable of.

Was she brave enough to wear the new bra on her date with Dan tonight? He was picking her up at seven. She tingled a little at the thought. Surely any man would notice curves like *this*.

She pulled the wispy silk blouse over the bra. The bow in the front weighted the V-neck of the blouse enough to show a good inch of her newly discovered cleavage.

She wobbled back to the bathroom mirror and surveyed the full package—heels, jeans, the blouse, and the new bosoms.

Was her mother right? Would she be married if she went around like this? But she wanted a man who liked her for her mind, didn't she? Eli seemed to notice things other than her mind, and it felt pretty darn good . . .

She shook her head and glanced at the eyelashes and lipstick. What the heck, she might as well finish the job so she could take a picture for Joyce. At least she'd have her mother off her back about *one* thing.

She carefully glued the eyelashes to her upper lids, only nearly blinding herself once. She slicked on the frosty pink lipstick.

She stared at herself in the mirror for a long time. Was it possible, just a little bit, that her mother was right? She looked . . . sexy. Claire had never, not once, in her entire life, thought of herself as sexy. Apparently Cliff hadn't either, since he'd told her he no longer felt that spark between them, and the feelings he had for the woman he actually intended to marry were, quote—*electric, irrevocable.* Yes, he'd actually said both of those words to her, about someone else, while breaking up with her. Those two words were burned in her brain forever. Those were the kinds of feelings she didn't inspire in men, and apparently, they were the kinds of feelings that made men want to get married.

The doorbell rang, startling her out of her mirror admiration. She looked at the boobs and eyelashes and felt like she'd been caught picking her nose, or worse.

She eyed her phone. Damn. It was later than she thought. 6:40 already. Could Dan be this early? What had she been thinking—*gluing objects to her eyelids* half an hour before an important date?

For the third time in as many days, she made a mental note to call a handyman about a peephole in her front door. As it was, she just had to open it blindly.

"Oh my God," Eli said. For the first time in the short time she'd known him, his mouth hung open.

"What?"

"*What?*" he said, incredulous.

She put a fist on her hip and poked her hip out defiantly.

"You look . . ."

She waited, tapping the black hooker pump.

"Like a different person."

"What does that mean?" Her heart gave a traitorous little leap of hope, and Claire tried to call to mind the image of breasts on his phone, but she couldn't quite muster anger at him.

He cleared his throat. He seemed to be speechless. Finally, he said, "I'm pretty sure you'd look good in sackcloth."

She felt her face grow hot. "What, um, what's going on? I mean what are you doing here?"

He held up his phone. "I asked you over for dinner."

She'd meant to answer him. Then she'd gotten sidetracked with the whole Fox situation. Besides. She was doing what she needed to do—the responsible thing—going out with Dan.

"Oh. Yes. That. I was about to answer you." She bit her lip, still unsure of what to say. The lipstick tasted like a scented wax candle.

"Is, ah, this . . . this"—he waved his hand up and down over her outfit—"what you're wearing to my house?"

She chewed more candle residue off her bottom lip. She watched the realization dawn on his face, the realization she wasn't saying yes.

"I see," he said.

"I'm sorry."

He shrugged. "It's fine. I see you're busy getting ready for a costume party, anyway."

"I have other dinner plans. Oh!" She remembered the time

and her clothes. "I have fifteen minutes to change for dinner."

"So you just hang around the house wearing this?"

"It was . . . it was a . . . an experiment."

The sound of car tires approaching on the street drew Claire's glance, and with a sinking stomach she saw Dan's navy BMW pulling up. She looked down at her clothes. He was early.

The BMW pulled in behind her faded Honda.

Eli turned and looked at the car, then turned back to her, eyebrow raised.

"Your dinner date?"

She nodded.

They both watched as Dan emerged from the car—tall, blond, and gorgeous. A Ken Doll to Eli's Tarzan. Dan wore a white button-down so perfectly starched it looked like it could conduct business on its own, and dark indigo fitted jeans that were almost black.

"Spiffy," Eli said, turning back to Claire. Amusement glinted in his eyes.

Claire glared at him.

"First date?"

She ignored him, trying to clear her face in preparation to smile for Dan.

"You can go out with him as many times as you want."

Her head whipped to Eli's face. "Gee, thanks. I was waiting for your *permission*."

"Hello, Claire." Dan smelled like soap and aftershave and hair product. He smelled really good. Clean, professional. Not like Eli's earthy, spicy, man smell.

Claire nodded, trying to smile. Her lips felt rubberized and uncooperative.

Eli extended a hand and Dan stood halfway. "Eli Archer."

"Dan Jenkins," Dan said, taking his hand.

"Doctor Jenkins?" Eli asked him.

"Yes. Have we met?"

"Lucky guess."

"I'm a fan," Dan said.

"Thank you."

Everyone stood silent for a long beat.

"Well," Dan said, turning to Claire. "Ready?"

Eli eyed the outfit.

She looked down at her wonderboobs and hooker shoes. She could make an excuse and run inside to put on normal clothes. But no—she wasn't going to give Eli the satisfaction. Or leave him alone with Dan. No way was she leaving him alone with Dan.

"Ready," she said brightly, and finally succeeded in pasting on her biggest toothpaste smile.

• • •

Claire tried to pull her jacket completely over the revealing pink silk blouse and cursed her mother. Though of course it wasn't really her mother's fault Claire had actually worn this getup *in public*. She tried to press the left eyelash, now half-on and half-off, back onto her eyelid.

It was important to look on the bright side. Maybe the outfit would get Dan's attention. It had certainly gotten Darla's. Darla had done a double take when she saw Claire waiting at the hostess stand of Capers, and it had taken her a full twenty seconds to regain her composure.

Now Darla returned to their table with two glasses of water. "I'll give you two a minute."

Claire eyed Dan over the menu. His jaw was unbelievably square and perfect. The muscles in it were so strong and taut they sometimes twitched, even while he was still. He had very good teeth, too—square and white, and not caps, the real thing. Sturdy-looking. No excessive orthodontia necessary for this guy's offspring. He was a near-perfect male specimen. Ears well-placed, not too low. Hair and nails thick, strong, and glossy. Symmetrical features. No pallor or grayness to his complexion. Perfect health, it appeared.

Plus they already knew each other. They knew each other's families. That could prove a serious advantage in getting caught up on her marriage-and-children schedule. If it worked out, they could almost just get married already. Then babies and barbecues and birthday parties wouldn't be far behind.

Yes. Dan would do nicely. Dan Jenkins, M.D. Blond of hair, blue of eye, square of jaw, cardboard of personality. Claire knew that last bit might sound like a negative to some people, but she *liked* this about him. He was completely predictable and safe, exactly what she wanted for the father of her children. He was kind. He was extremely intelligent. A wee bit boring was a positive quality in a husband.

She'd given so many of her prime dating years to the wrong man, to Cliff. She wouldn't be making that mistake again. This time, she was going with a safe bet.

"What looks good to you?" Dan asked.

Claire had been alternately sneaking glances at Dan and staring at the menu, but not reading it. She shook her head to try to force her eyes back into focus. "The salmon?"

"I was thinking the same thing." He set his menu down and they smiled a timid smile at each other.

The smile held none of the heat she'd been experiencing with Eli, but this was a good thing. Lasting attraction grew slowly—it built up its heat—it didn't just ignite.

"So," she said. A minute passed.

Silence.

Another minute passed.

"So," he said. A pause. "How's your mother?"

"Driving me a little crazy. But I uh, got a bid for a fence to be built in the backyard. She's not happy with me, but I think it's going to be a good thing for our relationship in the long run. She'll have to call now. Or risk a walk around the block to find I'm not home. And you know how steep that hill is on Crescent Drive . . ." Oh, but she was already rambling, and he was already looking bored. "Have you seen Holly lately?" she asked.

"Yesterday, at the hospital," he answered.

Claire nodded. She tried to think of something else to say,

but nothing came, and an anxious little flutter flitted around her heart.

Dan's phone lit up and Lou Reed sang, *Take a Walk on the Wild Side*, and he looked down at it. "I'll let it go to voice mail," he said.

The awkward silence returned.

"So you were saying?" he asked.

"I was?" she said.

"About your mother?"

"Oh, yes, about Joyce."

His phone trilled a voice mail alert, and he glanced at it.

"Do you need to get that?"

"Oh. No. No, it's okay."

"Well, hello," an unmistakable baritone said from above their table.

Claire felt that voice in her bones. She pulled her jacket over her blouse, and willed herself not to look up. But, of course, she did. *My word, he is beautiful.* Clay and dirt and flesh to Dan's plastic. She brushed the thought away.

"Dr. Jenkins," Eli said, nodding. "Claire." He smiled a wicked little smile at her.

Claire glared at him, then put her full attention back on the menu. "Hi," she muttered to the menu.

"Good to see you again," Dan said, extending a hand. "What a coincidence."

"Yright," Claire said under breath.

"Join us?" Dan offered.

"Love to," Eli said.

"No, he doesn't love to. He definitely doesn't love to. He's very famous. And busy. And he doesn't want to have dinner with boring old us."

"Oh, but I do."

Dan shrugged. "I think he does."

Eli slid into the booth next to Claire, and she could feel the heat of him, just an inch away from her, igniting the whole left side of her body in flames. She felt sweat seeping through the pink silk fabric of her ridiculous blouse, and she wished she could shrug out of her jacket without displaying her new wonderbosoms.

"Has the waitress been by?" Eli asked.

"She's coming right back," Dan said. He pushed his menu toward Eli. "So, there's been a good bit of volatility in the music business over the last decade, yes?"

"Changing times," Eli said, glancing at the menu.

Dan's phone rang again, this time singing, "Relax, Don't Do It."

"Excuse me for just a moment." Dan picked up his phone and slid out of the booth. He put his hand over the phone. "Pinot noir, please," he said to Claire.

"You *followed* us?" Claire hissed.

"No, I—"

Darla appeared at the table again. "I see you two are together a`gain," she said, and winked at Claire.

Claire groaned. "Could you *please* move to the other side of the booth?" she said Eli.

He ignored her and gave Darla a killer smile.

Claire turned back to Darla. "Pinot noir for Dan. Please. And I need a real drink. Whatever's strongest. Maybe a martini?" Claire paused. "A sweet one, though."

"Chocolate, pink, appletini . . .?" Darla asked.

"Pink, please."

"Draft IPA," Eli said. "Thanks."

"I still can't believe you followed us."

"Coincidence," he said, raising his hands in innocence. "I needed food. I'd been here before, and liked it. Don't the locals know some other restaurants?"

She snorted. "I so do not believe you."

"Dr. Jenkins is very good-looking." Eli looked smug, and Claire wanted to swat the look off his face with her menu.

"I'll be sure to pass that along," she muttered. Teeth tight, she looked back down at her menu.

"Listen, Claire. About that phone call. In the car."

She didn't look up. "I don't want to know."

"It wasn't what it looked like."

"I'm pretty sure it looked like a phone call from naked breasts. I wonder if Dan wants an appetizer?"

"Claire, I don't even know that woman's last name. Before yesterday, I couldn't have told you her first name. I don't even know her at all. She just took my phone off me one night in a club, and I forgot to delete it. I don't accept those kinds of offers."

Claire felt herself soften a tiny bit. But she shouldn't. She needed to keep her guard up. Besides, she was out with Dan, so what did she care what Eli did or didn't plan to do with the phone breasts?

"Well, hello!" Another male voice said from above the table.

Claire looked up to see music store Dave. Dave's eyes were alight and trained on Eli like he was . . . a star. Which, of course, he was.

The faintest hint of annoyance at the interruption flashed over Eli's face, so fast she almost missed it, but he put a kind smile on his face and greeted Dave. That. That right there was the thing that made it so hard to keep her guard up. He was *nice*. Down to earth. Somehow, strangely, not really rock-starrish at all.

"Hi, Dave," Claire said.

Dave reluctantly tore his eyes away from Eli. "Hi, Claire." Dave's eyes widened at the sight of Claire's chest, and he cleared his throat and snapped his glance away. "You look . . . nice."

"Thank you," Claire said, resigned.

"Claire's on a date. With Dan," Eli said, obviously enjoying himself. "Dan—what's his last name again?"

"Jenkins. You just called him that," Claire said through her teeth.

"Ah yes. Doctor Dan Jenkins," Eli said. He leaned back and somehow managed to give the impression he was grinning, even though he really wasn't.

Dave looked confused.

"He's in the bathroom," Claire said. Where *was* Dan? She'd only wanted a date with him for a year, and now she was out with him, and he'd been in the bathroom for a month.

"Hi, Dave." Oh. There he was.

"Hey, man."

Dan slid into the booth across from Claire.

"Wow, so this is, like, a group thing? Mind if I join?" Dave asked.

Eli held an open palm toward the seat across from him, next to Dan.

Claire sighed to herself. There was no point in protesting. At this point, they might as well invite the whole town on her date.

"Hi, y'all!" Holly's cheery voice called.

And now, the whole town *was* on their date.

"Hi, sis," Dan said.

"Hey, Holl," Dave said.

Holly took in the grouping and grinned, exposing a dimple. "Well, well. I guess I'll just pull up a chair, then."

Claire repeated Eli's motion, indicating the empty spot at the end of the booth. Holly pulled a chair from a nearby table and sat between Eli and Dave.

Darla returned with three drinks. "You grew," she said.

"Oooh, I'll have one of those," Holly said, pointing at Claire's pink martini.

Dave ordered a beer and resumed staring adoringly at Eli.

Holly surveyed Claire's appearance and her eyebrows rose in a question mark.

"Joyce," Claire said. "It was an accident."

"Ah."

"So, man, you went to Juilliard, right?" Dave asked. He and Eli were alone in the room, as far as Dave was concerned.

Claire's attention pricked despite herself. Eli went to *Juil-*

liard?

"Just three years. College dropout."

Dave seemed to think this was extremely funny. "Yeah, you're hurting." He laughed his quiet honk of a laugh. "Were you already making it, was that why you dropped out?"

Eli chuckled. "Hardly. I moved to Paris and played street music. The lean years."

Dave snapped his fingers. "Yeah, man, yeah! I forgot about that! I've seen footage of that! You were all playing garbage cans and shit!"

"Playing garbage cans?" Claire asked. *Garbage cans?* No wonder he didn't like Stephanie Kelly.

"Yeah!" Dave said. "So, like, somebody started filming. It was like street art. Eli was all skinny—so funny, man—sorry, sorry, but even back then, his voice would just slay you, and he's walking down a Paris street with this accordion-playing dude, and he's singing, no mic or anything, but it doesn't even matter, and people start to follow him, and then he gets to a whole huge gang of people with all these instruments. They're all out there on the street, waiting for him. So many instruments—horns and strings and percussion—and it looks like it's gonna be a big mess, but Eli stops in front of them and raises his arms like he's the freakin' maestro. And then they all start playing, and everybody's *good*. Like, *really* good. And Eli's like this street conductor, singing, and motioning to everybody what to do at the same time. And the percussionist! He's banging on trash cans. And then the trumpets blaze in. Beautiful man, just beautiful. It's a famous video, right?"

Eli shrugged. "Not sure," he said quietly.

"Well, it is," Dave said. "Famous. Big cult following."

"Garbage cans," Claire repeated. "How long did you live in Paris?"

"A couple of years."

"So you speak French?"

He nodded, but no French was forthcoming.

Everyone else at the table had gotten quiet, looking at Eli

and Claire.

Claire cleared her throat. "I speak Spanish," she volunteered.

Holly snorted. "So, Dave." She turned toward Dave just as Darla came back with her drink. She thanked Darla and took a sip, still eyeing Dave. "Are you seeing anyone?"

Dave reddened. For a split second his glance returned to Claire's wonderbosoms, then nervously back to Holly. "Uh, not at the moment, no."

"Good. Claire and I are having a party. Well, I'm having a party; Claire's paying the caterer. You're invited. There's someone I want you to meet."

Dave cleared his throat. "*Uhh . . .*"

"In a town of two thousand, how many of the people do you already know?" Eli asked.

"*Everyone,*" Holly said. "It's so annoying. But this is my *new* roommate. Fresh meat. She just moved here from Little Rock to manage her cousin's shop." She turned to Dave. "You know, Elaine Bascomb's place? Just up the street from you."

"The bead shop?" asked Dave.

"Yup."

"I think I've seen a new person going in and out of that place."

"You're going to be so good for her," Holly said. "Oh, and she's pretty! And a jewelry artist!"

"You're invited, too, of course," she said to Eli.

Claire laughed, took a sip of martini, and shot Holly a look—*don't.*

Holly assumed a look of angelic innocence and shrugged.

"Well, I've got an early day tomorrow," Dan said. Looking at Claire he said, "Shall we head out?"

"Oh!" Claire said, shocked by the suddenness of it. She looked down at her half-finished drink. They hadn't even ordered dinner. "Sure. Of course." Claire wrapped her jacket around herself more tightly and nudged Eli to let her out of the booth.

"If you've got an early day, I'll be glad to walk Claire home," Eli said.

Claire wanted to say that she wasn't a poodle and didn't need walking, but she was curious to see what Dan would say, so she bit back the words.

Dan hesitated. "You don't mind?" he asked Eli.

"Not a bit." There was that grin again, which wasn't really a grin. A ghost grin. You knew it was there even though it was invisible.

"Thanks, man." Dan nodded.

Claire wanted to sink into the floor with mortification. Her date was basically standing her up, while they were actually on the date, in front of half of Haven Springs. She glared at Eli. Now he had a *real* grin on his face, a visible one. A big, fat, pie-eating grin.

• • •

Back on her front porch, which was dark other than the light of the half moon, Claire realized she was feeling her nearly two martinis. Her stomach was mostly empty. She circled her hand through her purse, looking for her keys. They were *always* hooked to the key latch on the side—always—but somehow, not tonight. She'd forgotten to hook her keys in their spot; she'd forgotten to leave her porch light on. She wasn't even dating Eli Archer and he was somehow managing to mess with her head.

She could feel him watching her, and she looked up at him.

And then she stilled, their eyes locked, and they stood that way, motionless, in the dim light for several frozen seconds. And they fell onto each other's mouths like they'd been waiting to do it all night. She couldn't have even said who kissed whom. It was like water pressure that had been building and building and building, and finally, the dam broke. His body felt so wonderful against hers, it was like relief. Until it wasn't. Until her body started letting her know it needed more.

But she couldn't keep letting this happen. They needed to

stop. With effort, she broke away. They stood, breathless, facing each other, eyes locked and heated.

"I need to find my keys." She put her hand back in the abyss of her handbag. "And come to my senses."

"Want to come to my house, where there's some light?"

His house. His house. There were a hundred reasons she should say no, but right now, she was having trouble thinking of a single one of them.

He unlocked his front door quickly, and just as quickly, her body was pressed against the wall of his entry hall. Their mouths, making contact, were hot and wet and perfect together, and before she knew it, she'd wrapped her legs around him. He held her there, legs wrapped around him like she was weightless, and he pressed himself against her until she was desperate with wanting him.

"Claire, come here." He gently lowered her and set her down, then gestured toward the living room. Claire straightened her blouse and tried to look dignified. Then she took in her surroundings, and tried to wrap her mind around the pink floral sofa, pink floral everything—what the heck?—but she was too shaken by their kiss to form words to comment.

"Sit," he said.

She did.

He knelt before her, and his left hand, square and brown, rested on the front of her pink silk blouse, and pulled the bow untied.

Desire shot through her as the air hit her breasts, bare down the middle in her alien bra. He pushed the lace cups aside, and something big began to swell inside her, something new and mysterious, and *oh my word*, he was touching her now. And then his mouth was on her breast, and it was almost unbearable, it was so intense.

And then he was touching her everywhere. An electric tidal wave of pleasure soaked her entire body as his hand moved against her, opened her jeans, found her. She cried out in shock at the intense pleasure, and a small, ugly voice told her she should be embarrassed, but then she looked at his face, and she knew she shouldn't be, couldn't be. He was looking at her like she was . . . everything. Like she was sexy, desirable—like she was the only woman on earth.

It was the best thing she'd ever felt.

Still watching her face, he moved his hand more insistently, and Claire felt herself about to break open with the pleasure of it. She hadn't known, hadn't known it could feel like this. How could she not have known? The waves took her over like possession, and her body went rigid with the shock of it, and then she became aware of a noise, and then of the fact she was the one making the noise, that it was her own voice crying out.

Eli slowed his touch, still watching her, and finally rested his hand softly against her while she recovered.

She stared at him in shock. What had he just done to her? They hadn't even undressed, for crying out loud. Still watching her face, he withdrew his hand and slowly, deliberately, put it to his lips. His finger disappeared inside his mouth, and he tasted her. Her body cramped again with arousal and astonishment. Had he really just done that? He was so . . . naughty. So . . . earthy. So unexpected. She was pretty sure he was some kind of sex god, and they hadn't even had sex.

"I'll walk you home," he said.

Her mouth hung, pre-word, unable to speak. He wasn't going to pressure her? She could see his arousal through his jeans. Wasn't she supposed to . . . return the favor? He took her hand and lifted her from the sofa.

"Come on, Doc."

• • •

Watching Claire have her first orgasm was the sexiest damn thing he had ever seen in his entire life. The surprise on her face, the total lack of artifice. He'd never seen anything even half as sexy. That included his first peek at a *Playboy* magazine at the age of fifteen, the real-life naked and spectacular figure of a supermodel, and any number of other things he'd ever seen—all of which he could now just forget, because anything would pale in comparison to watching Claire give herself over to him, inhibitions down, face alight with ecstasy.

The thing that made it beyond-the-pale erotic was that she wasn't doing it on purpose. She wasn't performing for him. She wasn't thinking about his response at all. The last thing in the world Claire Taylor cared about was impressing him, and somehow that was the most potent aphrodisiac he'd ever tasted. And he could still taste her . . . musky and sweet and clean. He groaned.

But he knew he was playing with fire. He'd gone through too many breakups not to be able to see this one coming a mile away.

Claire was the farthest thing from a casual-sex kind of woman he could imagine.

And that was all he had to offer her. Three months of sex.

It would be the hottest sex of his life, of that he was now certain—not that he hadn't been certain already—but that kind of intensity would just make the breakup worse. Women had a way of taking sex seriously, and he bet that went double for Claire.

There would be tears. There would be hatred. And he didn't want that with the doc. He liked her. Hell, he respected her. He needed to rein it in. He needed to rein it in yesterday.

One cold shower and a cup of coffee later, Eli went back to his living room to get back to work.

He had to make a good record. He had to make a stupendous record. Not that designed-by-committee bullshit DMG had forced him to make for his last two records. He had to make something Rolling Stone could sink their teeth into and name Record of the Year. He wanted his reputation back. He didn't want to be the male version of Stephanie Kelly.

And the last two records really had been that bad. He was so ashamed of them, it was a sit-up-in-the-night, cursing, sweating, three-in-the-morning kind of humiliation that felt nearly unbearable.

He needed to make something beautiful. Something powerful. Something he was proud to put his name on. Something that made the world just a little bit better. If you couldn't make the world a little better, what did your life even mean?

Also, he wanted to go back to New York with his head held high. Or at least not staring down at the sidewalk, avoiding eye contact, wearing maximal facial hair and mirror shades.

But he'd barely been able to even think about that, because he had the big black secret to deal with. It was a hell of a secret. He hadn't even told Alec, his oldest friend. He definitely hadn't told his mom. Because, the secret was this: he hadn't written anything during his last six months in New York. Not one single line. To his horror, he'd found he *couldn't* write anything. He would just sit there, and all he could think was *oh baby*, or *na na na*. It was every songwriter's worst nightmare. For a while, he'd really thought his career was over.

He'd once written a song with Arcade Fire, dammit. But now, Eli knew, for absolute certain, that no decent songwriter would touch him. He'd made a public fool of himself. He'd released a truckload of radio-ready manure with his name stamped on it.

And somehow it stuck around, spinning through his head, preventing him from moving past it, every time he'd tried to write something.

Eli looked at the three sheets of paper on the coffee table in front of him.

Songs. Whole ones. Good ones. Three of them. Those three pieces of paper, lined up there, looked better to him than three ten-carat diamonds.

He could write again. And he was pretty sure these songs weren't just good. He was pretty sure they were excellent. Actually, he was certain.

And all three of these songs had happened after hanging around with Doc. He'd written them easily, in that magical kind of fever that so rarely happens, but when it does, produces gold. Perhaps even literal gold, if he got a gold record out of it.

There was something about Claire. He thought about her; he dreamed about her; he stared out his window, looking for her. Pitiful. He was turning into some kind of obsessed teenage boy. But . . . a productive obsessed teenage boy.

He looked back at the three pieces of paper, and they looked like the whole world on his coffee table. They *were* the whole world on his coffee table. They were three pieces of paper, but they were also him getting his life back.

He looked out the window toward Doc's house. She was . . . decent. Wholesome. Funny. Down-to-earth. Kind.

And now, he'd really done it. He'd touched her, and she'd let herself go with him. It wasn't something he'd be able to forget, even if he wanted to.

She was . . . irresistible.

She was . . .

He grabbed his pen and notebook and started to write, trying to find any words that could begin to describe her, and what he'd felt tonight.

⋅ ⋅ ⋅

Claire woke the next morning, her body remembering what had happened before her mind was fully awake. She was sweaty with sleep-arousal.

Holy smokes. What was *that?* And why hadn't she ever experienced anything like it? Not even a little like it? Wasn't she too old to have her first real . . .

But of course she'd had . . . Claire flushed. Of course she'd had . . . an . . . *orgasm* before. She almost whispered the word in her own mind. But she was thirty-five! Of course she had! Hadn't she? But if she had, why had last night been so different? The difference between looking at chocolate and eating it.

He'd probably just had a superhuman amount of practice. She needed to remember that. He was an international playboy who dated supermodels and had naked breasts ringing in on his phone.

But while she was waiting for Mr. Right to kneel with a ring, would it be so bad to let Mr. Wrong touch her again? Her body was already aching to experience it again. Could she let Eli be Mr. Right Now? Maybe her mom was onto something—if Claire seemed more like the homecoming queen, with lots of men competing for her, she would be more likely to find the right one? The right one, like Dan—if he learned enough manners to stay for dinner next time. At any rate, someone stable and family-oriented, and with good genes.

But of course, playing around with Eli in the meantime was dangerous territory. Eli was a whole continent of dangerous territory.

She rolled out of bed and headed for the electric kettle, next to which her phone was plugged in. She pressed the *on* button, and the screen lit up with a text message. Eli. From the night before.

When I am an old man and nearly blind, I will still be able to picture your face. That was the sexiest thing I have ever seen.

She stopped breathing and her heart lurched erratically. She pushed the phone away, still staring at the message. He probably had a whole arsenal of lines like this ready for unsuspecting women, after he gave them earth-shattering orgasms. She forced herself to look away. Yes, probably a premade line—the poeticism was definitely suspect.

Except . . . she knew that wasn't true. It seemed like it would be true, given his status, profession, and unbelievable sexual magnetism, but she thought of his kind eyes, and the patient way he listened to her, the gentle way he'd touched her, the way he was kind to everyone—the way he gave his food away to a hungry child—and she *knew* he was a good man. Eli wasn't a womanizer. Which, come to think of it, maybe meant she *could* let herself have a little fling with him—*maybe just, you know, for practice?*

Because really, now that she'd experienced it, and he was right there, a hundred feet away from her, there was no way she could live without feeling Eli's touch just one more time.

• • •

"I need help," Claire said. She'd waited an hour to call Holly, watching until the clock struck seven a.m.

"Well, we knew *that*," Holly said. A metal utensil clinked against something in Holly's kitchen.

"Seriously," Claire said, imploring.

"What happened?"

"Eli and I . . . we, uh, fooled around. Last night."

"Good!"

"No," Claire wailed. "Not good!"

"Okay. Hold on. Just let me get Ryan off to school. One minute. Don't go anywhere."

Claire listened to the sounds of Holly telling Ryan good-bye, and then the phone rustled.

"Okay. Spill," Holly said.

"I want more."

"More what?"

"More of . . . whatever that was last night with Eli."

"And this is a problem *because* . . .?"

"Four reasons. One. He is leaving in three months. Less than three months now. Second. He's not husband material. Third. I need to be dating Dan or at least a close Dan approximation or at least someone with a steady job. Four. Now I can't think about anything else but having sex with *Eli*." The last word came out as a howl.

"I repeat, I do not see the problem here."

"*Holly!*"

"Well? It's true. You could stand a little fun in your life."

"Heartbreaks are not fun. I'm *old*. My eggs are dying by the thousands. Upon thousands."

"True. But can't you just, you know, use him for his body? Just for a little while?"

"I want to. I thought about it. I planned to. But, the truth is, I don't know."

"You don't know what?"

"Whether I can *just* use him. Or let him use me. Or whatever. Without it getting . . . complicated."

Holly paused. "I see."

"Yeah." Claire let out a deep breath. "It's like that."

"In a way, how could it not be? I mean, have you *seen* that guy? Plus, he's, you know . . ."

"Nice," Claire said.

"That's the one," Holly said.

"And it gets worse. It's like we can talk without speaking. He's so . . . soulful. And his voice. And his eyes."

"Oh, lordy." Holly sighed. "You're a goner."

"Not completely."

"Well, there's no point talking about this anymore."

"What do you mean?"

"It's an inevitability."

"What is?"

"Sex. Love. You know, the whole big mess."

Claire started to argue, but only a small bark of a sound came out.

Was it an inevitability? She could still think of some way out of this, right? But it was like she hadn't eaten in three days, and Eli was beef stew and fresh-baked bread. It was impossible to think of anything else. She could smell it, she could taste it, it was right across the lawn from her bedroom, and it was waiting for her.

• • •

Later that day, back in the E.R., the hum of fluorescent lights mingled with the sounds of squeaking sneakers on the linoleum.

Claire stood in front of Anita, looking over a chart. Anita, as ever, was working on her nails.

Which reminded Claire of the last time she'd stood in front of Anita while Anita filed her nails. She set down the chart. "Hey, Anita? Remember the kid, Zoe, the one with the dyed hair?"

Anita's manicure clicked away on her keyboard. "Sure."

"Did her bill go to collections?"

"No . . ." Anita looked up from the emery board. She looked surprised that Claire had asked the question.

"What happened?" Claire asked.

"Didn't you hear?"

"Hear what?"

"That musician fella, the famous one, Ezekiel, or whatever his name was."

Claire's heart lurched. "What about him?"

"That day. That day they were both here. Ezekiel overheard me talking to Fox about the kid and the bill. Of course Fox was freaking out about it. Micromanager." She said this as though it were a complete explanation.

"*And?*"

"And Ezekiel paid the bill. Requested anonymity, but I figure since you're staff, he didn't mean you."

Claire was pretty sure he had meant exactly her, and her throat gave its telltale ache. She hurried to the bathroom so the tears could spring in private. *Eli had paid Zoe's bill?* How could she resist a man who would do that? She looked at herself in the mirror and swiped her tears away in frustration.

This was all getting out of hand. Eli was too much. She was heading ninety miles an hour toward a heartbreak.

She needed to avoid him. From now on. Despite how his touch had made her feel . . . *because* of how his touch had made her feel.

She wet her fingertips with cold water and squeezed the water onto her eyelids. *Focus. Focus on your goals, not on a distraction that will only hinder them.* She should do a fresh goals list in HandleIt as soon as she had some downtime.

She straightened herself up, double-checked the mirror, and exited the restroom toward a staph infection in Room 3, where she nearly collided with Dan.

"Hi," he said.

"Hi."

They stood awkwardly for a moment.

"Thank you for last night," Claire finally said.

"Anytime, anytime." Dan tapped the sides of his thighs with stretched-flat fingers.

"Really?" she asked.

"Really what?"

Oh, this was so not going well. She was about to pull a Cliff all over again, where she had to make the first move, or nothing would happen. But she needed to give this a little nudge. If she had a boyfriend who was husband material, she could quit lusting for Eli. She could just put the whole thing out of her mind until Eli was safely back in New York.

"You said anytime. For dinner? Or whatever," she said, feeling like an idiot.

"Oh!" Dan said. "Sure." He actually looked at her and smiled like he meant it.

"Great." She smiled expectantly.

She waited. Nothing happened.

And so she forced herself to say it. "When?"

"Oh," he said. "When? Okay. Yes, when. The party? I could drive you to the party?"

"Party?" Claire was momentarily perplexed. "Oh! Holly's party. This weekend! That sounds good."

"Great," he said.

"Great," she said. She smiled to herself as she continued down the hall. See? Everything was under control.

CHAPTER 13

Claire needed food. She needed food two hours ago, which was roughly when she'd planned to leave the hospital.

But the hospital was jam-packed with the two dozen people, more or less, who'd been browsing or working at the Haven Springs Public Library that morning when the fire broke out.

Smoke inhalation were the two words on everyone's lips.

By the time Claire got to room six, she was seriously shaky from lack of calories.

She stopped in her tracks in the doorway.

Zoe. It was Zoe.

For a moment, Claire's heart clenched in dread. But Zoe wasn't *in* the hospital bed, she was beside it. She stood over the bed looking distressed and slightly sooty, holding the hand of Carolyn Stamper.

Claire didn't know Mrs. Stamper well, but she'd been acquainted with her all her life, and her kids had been a few years ahead of Claire in high school. Most Sundays, Mrs. Stamper sat two rows in front of Claire and Joyce at church, but Claire hadn't been to church in recent months due to her schedule.

She approached the bed. "Hi, Mrs. Stamper. Hi, Zoe. How y'all doing?" she asked.

"Oh, you know. Just another day at the library," Mrs. Stamper said.

Zoe turned toward her, and Claire saw that she'd been crying. There were dried sooty rivulets streaking her cheeks.

"Aww, babe." Claire put her arm around Zoe, who, thankfully, didn't protest, even though she'd been angry with Claire the last time they'd seen each other.

Claire looked down at Mrs. Stamper's chart. "How are you feeling?"

"Oh, fine, fine. Just took me a minute to get out of there.

That fire alarm was like a rocket launch in my ear, and I got all confused and got tangled up in my handbag straps on the back of the chair."

"Let's have a look at you."

Claire checked Mrs. Stamper's pupils and listened to her chest. She made a note in the chart, *audible rhonchi*. The wheeze was more pronounced than Claire would've liked, and accompanied by diminished breath sounds, but not enough to cause serious alarm.

"Cough?" Claire asked.

"Oh, it was something awful," Mrs. Stamper answered. "Lawd, it hurt. But I haven't had another spell in maybe half an hour. About like that, Zoe?"

Zoe nodded.

"Okay, and I'm going to ask you some silly questions, just to make sure you didn't get hypoxic. Do you know where you are?"

"Haven Springs Hospital."

"Very good. Do you remember what happened this morning?"

"We were at the library, and there was a fire."

"Your address?"

"819 Haven Street."

"How's she doing on her answers, Zoe?" Claire winked at her.

"She got them right."

Claire withdrew the stethoscope and stood straight.

"Your lips are good and pink. We don't want blue, which would mean your lungs weren't getting enough oxygen."

Mrs. Stamper made a kissing pucker and gave Zoe an air kiss.

"How about you, Zoe? You weren't admitted. How long were you in the building?"

"I was near the door, so I went outside as soon as I heard the alarm and saw people running out there."

"That must have been scary."

"Lawd, it was," Mrs. Stamper said. "I like to never got myself untangled and out of there."

"So, you're Zoe's foster mom now?"

Mrs. Stamper nodded and patted Zoe's hand.

"That girl reads more than anything I ever saw. We were there for more of them Lord of the Rings books. It's her fourth"—she looked at Zoe questioningly—"time through the series?"

"Fifth."

"I told her we could buy one, but it was a nice morning to walk to the library and the bookstore wasn't open yet."

"You got a little more than you bargained for at the library."

"Lawdy, we did. People running to and fro. It was so smoky, I couldn't see Zoe for nothin'."

"Do they know what happened?"

"Not yet," Mrs. Stamper said. "Half the fire boys were there, seemed like. Chris and Bert and Daniel, and lawd, I don't know who all. Oh, Sam. And Robert Maxwell."

Zoe looked up at Claire, her eyes dark with fear, "Is Ms. Carolyn going to be okay?"

"Oh, now child, don't worry your head. I'm just fine," Mrs. Stamper said in soothing tones, patting Zoe's hand.

"She looks pretty good to me, Zo. She's not confused or blue or coughing too much. Try not to worry. Mrs. Stamper might need your help for the next few days. She may be a little tired. Now. Can I ask you for a favor?"

Zoe nodded.

Claire reached in her sock and pulled out a twenty-dollar bill. "Run to the cafeteria and get me something to eat? Get something for yourself too." Claire was running on empty, but really she wanted a chance to talk to Mrs. Stamper alone. "Are you hungry, Mrs. Stamper?"

"Lawd, no. I couldn't eat right now. My stomach's still a ball of nerves."

"What should I get?" Zoe asked.

"Anything you want," Claire said.

"For you," Zoe said.

"Oh. Um, anything hot that I can shovel into my mouth as quickly as possible." Claire winked.

Once Zoe was safely into the hall, Claire turned back to Mrs. Stamper. "I'm so sorry this happened."

"Oh, honey, it's just one of those things."

Claire hesitated. "How's Zoe?"

"A little better every day. Seems like she's gained a few pounds. Never seen anybody so happy to wash her hair, poor little thing. I guess she hadn't had water in weeks, other than the sinks at school. I had to tell her she could only wash it once a day or there wouldn't be enough hot water to clean the dishes. She *needs* to wash that crazy little dog. That thing smells bad enough to gag a maggot. But Zoe says Pippa don't like the water, and if you think about it, it's pretty amazing she kept the little thing alive."

"How did she do it?"

"Well, now," Mrs. Stamper said, and patted Claire's hand. "Don't you tell her I told you, but she had to steal a bag of Kibble from the SuperFoods. I told her I didn't think God would mind, given the circumstances. Zoe was right worried about it, couldn't sleep one night, got up out of bed to tell me about it."

A lump rose in Claire's throat, and she swallowed it. "It was kind of you to take in Pippa too."

"I told the social worker it didn't bother me. We both thought it didn't seem right for a girl to lose her dog after all she'd been through. In that house all by herself. No electricity. No water. No money for food." Mrs. Stamper gave a little shudder.

Claire let out a pent-up breath. Knowing Zoe was safe and well fed and clean with someone as gentle and kind as Carolyn Stamper was an immense relief. Mrs. Stamper'd been the one who got everyone at the church calmed down after the Great Bingo Argument of 2012, and she was famous for changing the subject if anyone tried to gossip around her. Claire knew this because that last quality infuriated her mother to no end.

"Thank you," Claire said, her voice cracking, "for taking care of Zoe."

Mrs. Stamper's hand shot out and held Claire's. "She's a special little thing. I see it too."

Claire nodded, unable to speak, throat aching with held-back tears.

"Well, I'll be glad to have Zoe as long as they let me."

"Let you?"

"Sure, sure. I'm like a foster parent, whattayacallit? Like a foster kid clearinghouse. Kids stay with me while they're waiting for a permanent family. Or to go back to their birth family. When they go back to their troubles, sometimes I see 'em again, after while."

"So you're not going to adopt Zoe?"

"Lawd, honey, no. I'm seventy-one years old. I'd be doing her a disservice. And I got my own brood to care for. Five grandbabies now," she said, a wistful smile on her face. "Three of 'em in Little Rock."

Claire nodded. "So what will happen to her?"

"Too soon to say. The social worker and all them, they're still looking for her mother, trying to figure out what to do, I reckon."

• • •

Claire woke on top of her bedspread, still in her scrubs, her hair glued to the side of her face.

She came to slowly. It was dusk, and the light was changing in pulses outside her window, and something was vibrating under her leg.

Her phone. It was sticking out the top of her handbag, which had somehow migrated underneath her left thigh.

She fumbled for her glasses and put them on her face.

A text from Holly.

Where ARE you? Party meeting an hour ago. I made margaritas!

There were eight other messages from Holly. Claire must have slept like the dead.

She hopped up and washed her face, slicking her hair back with the cold water.

She hated to be late, but she couldn't bring herself to rush out in her scrubs without putting on something clean first. Back in the bedroom, she opened her T-shirt drawer, then slid the window open to let in some fresh air.

Through the window came the haunting sweet sound of a cello, stopping Claire still and alert. Her heart contracted, feeling pronounced in her chest, a new thing that seemed to happen whenever she let herself think about Eli, which was too often.

Her eyes closed and Eli's touch was happening to her all over again, right that very minute. His touch, his eyes, his voice. She gave her head a furious shake and threw off her scrub top. "No!" she told herself, loudly.

The cello stopped.

Damn. Of all the houses in Haven Springs, did he have to rent *that* one? She backed away from the window, hiding herself around the corner, and hurriedly put on her jeans.

"Everything okay in there?" It was the baritone. *The* baritone. It was close. Too close.

"Fine," she said, covering her bra with her arms, even though she knew he couldn't see her.

She waited to hear his retreating footsteps, but she heard nothing. Waited more . . . still nothing. She could feel him standing there. "Are you going to stand out there all night?" she snapped.

"I was thinking about it."

She sighed. They were screwed. She came out of hiding and in front of the window, which put her at eye level with Eli, standing in the yard. She kept her arms over her chest and tried to glare at him, but he seemed unfazed. How had she let herself get all tied up in a knot over someone she stood no chance of building a relationship with?

"Hi," he said. In the dark, framed by the window, in a ratty T-shirt, he was still clearly beautiful. Damn him.

"Going for a new career as a peeping Tom?"

"If I get to see you in nothing but jeans and a bra, yes." His eyes traveled downward admiringly. "But actually, I knocked earlier, and didn't get an answer, so when I heard you shout, I thought I should check things out. Make sure the marauding bands of Haven Springs criminals weren't on the loose again."

"Funny."

"I try. You're getting dressed?"

"Yes."

"Another hot date?"

"Maybe."

"Dan?"

She shrugged.

"Ah." His eyes were now unabashedly resting on her breasts, which were definitely not at their pushed-up best in the white cotton number she'd had the misfortune of choosing today. But he didn't seem to mind. She tightened her arms around herself, but seeing the look in his eyes was like lighting a match to her own desire.

But Holly was waiting. And she *needed* to nip this whole thing in the bud.

"Hey," she whistled, and pointed at her face. "Up here, Casanova."

His eyes remained on her breasts for a long moment, while a slow, wide smile spreading across his face. By the time his eyes traveled to hers, she found herself a little out of breath.

"We could make your date nights a traditional thing."

"Traditional?"

"Yes. You go out on a date, then you come over to my house afterward and let me entertain you. A tradition."

"Entertain . . ." Her body started up like it was a marching band and he was the drum major who'd just given the signal. *Just one more time? I could just let him touch me one more time . .*

"No," she said with more force than she felt.

He watched her face. "Knock if you change your mind. I'll be up late writing." He gave her a small salute and turned to go.

"Eli?"

He turned around.

She didn't want to ask, but she had to know. And if she was going to avoid him from now on, this was her last chance to ask. "Didn't it bother you?"

"What?"

She felt herself flush hot and red. Still, she had to know the answer. "Bother you, I mean. The other night. That it was, just . . . me. That we didn't do more. Go all the way, or whatever." Her cheeks were getting second-degree sunburn.

He smiled a hint of a smile, accentuating his square jaw and the slightest bit of five o'clock shadow. "Babe, I could do that with you for a month before I got frustrated."

"What would happen after a month?"

"Now *that* I would love to find out." He disappeared into the dark, and a moment later, the cello resumed.

Claire pulled the T-shirt on over her head, snapping back to reality when her phone started to ring.

"Claire! Where are you?"

"I'm so sorry. I'm on my way."

"Your margarita is melting."

"Stick it in the freezer. I'm walking out the door right now, I promise."

Eli's offer was throbbing through her—he would be up late. She could just go over. She could just . . . let him touch her like that. Just one more time. He was right there. Willing. Next door. Fifty feet away. Waiting for her. All she had to do was go to him. Her body was practically screaming at her to go to him. But she knew that was stupid, for all the reasons she gave herself all the time: want kids, need husband, not Eli, running late. The other reason, the deeper reason, was that she was feeling all kinds of things she didn't want to be feeling. For a famous person. Who did not live here. Who was a rock and roller and probably had tattoos. And a harem. She was feeling the kinds of things that didn't go away easily. The kinds of things that could level a person.

It was like he'd given her was some kind of dark-chocolate-sex-heroin, and she was hooked.

Okay. Here was the plan. She'd go to Holly's house. While she was there, she'd figure out some way to forget about him and/or avoid him. If she could just forget and/or avoid him until he left Haven Springs, she'd be home free. It was only two and a half more months. She could mark it on a calendar. It was a tangible, achievable goal.

• • •

"Finally!" Holly said, taking Claire's umbrella.

The rain had started on Claire's three-block walk over, and she kicked off her wet shoes just inside the kitchen door.

"Come in, come in. I started a preliminary guest list, but I want you to look it over."

Claire hung up her coat, and a strawberry margarita floated in front of her face.

"Here. Drink up and let's talk food and music."

Claire smiled and entered Holly's warm, cheerful, ramshackle kitchen. Jars of canned peaches sat next to open cookbooks sat next to Ryan's report card sat next to a half-drunk mug of tea. Battered ecru cabinets referenced years of family memories and meals. The kitchen table held stacks of checked napkins and mismatched paisley and plaid placemats. Claire sat, sighing with relief. It felt good to be here.

"So here's my grand scheme," Holly said, her huge brown eyes alight.

"Oh, good. I was hoping there'd be a grand scheme."

"Dave and Marla," Holly announced.

"Dave . . . Dave . . . *Campbell?* Music store Dave?"

"Yes, Dave *Campbell*. Don't you see it?"

"No. No, I do not," Claire said.

"Oh, open your mind. It's going to be *perfect*."

"Please explain. Apparently I haven't had enough to drink to understand." She took a long pull of strawberry margarita.

"Well, you *see*," Holly said, drawing out the last word dramatically. "What Marla needs . . ." She paused. "Is a good bonking."

Claire spewed strawberry margarita.

Holly picked up a cloth napkin and started wiping up margarita without looking at what she was doing. "I'm *serious!* Her dweeb of an ex-boyfriend has her all uptight, thinking she wasn't virtuous enough for him and his savior-of-the-earth ego. Or fun enough. Both, really, though they seem a little contradictory to me. Anyway. She needs Dave."

"But Holly, *you* dated Dave."

Holly waved a hand. "Oh, whatever. That was high school. Well, it was the summer after senior year."

"Won't that bother you? Won't it bother Dave? He shows up to pick up his girlfriend . . . your *roommate*?"

"Nah. It's ancient history. But I can tell you one thing." Holly set down her margarita and the cloth napkin. "He was my first, so I didn't appreciate it at the time, but having been with some real duds in the sack since then, I can tell you—Dave was ahead of his time at eighteen. I bet at thirty he is *quite* the catch. You know, orgasmically speaking."

"Orgasmically speaking."

Holly put the pink straw back in her mouth and nodded.

"This is twisted," Claire said.

"No, it's not! Dave's gentle, kind, never judgy. The total opposite of Marla."

"Lucky Dave." Claire took another drink.

"He will be lucky. See, Dave's a man-boy."

"A man-boy?"

"Oh, you know what I mean—a *man-boy*. He has that long fuzzy hair and those rock concert T-shirts and zero responsibilities in life outside of his music store. He thinks he's busy if he has to go to the grocery and wash his car in the same week. He's never lived with a woman or had a relationship longer than year or two. Missy Shrader said Dave was too passive for her, and I can totally see that. But *Marla*, see, she's sort of a man-woman."

"A man-woman?"

"Yeah. She's like, a pants-wearer. Figuratively speaking."

"Not following, and, is she home right now?" Claire looked around.

"No, she's out. And also bossy and controlling."

"Oh. That."

"But not *too* bossy and controlling, see. And I am fully convinced. I mean, *fully* convinced, Dave can tame her with good sex. And that he might like a woman with a little bit of dominatrix in her."

Holly was looking at her expectantly.

"This really is a grand scheme."

"I know, right? And Marla can give him structure. Finally get him down the aisle. He'd make a great dad. You know, the fun dad, who actually likes playing Darth Vader in the backyard."

"I'm just going to go ahead and start calling you God."

"I'm just giving them a helpful nudge, that's all."

"You missed your calling when you became a nurse."

"What do you mean?"

"You should have run a matchmaking agency."

"Oh, I *know*."

"Really?" Claire asked, surprised.

"Well, if the electric bill never came and I had my dream job . . ."

Claire thought about it. "You're really good at it, Holl. Actual marriages have happened because of you."

"Yeah." Holly smiled. "Three. Wait, no. Four."

"That's a lot. Especially in a town of two thousand."

Holly shrugged. "Yeah. But back to reality. And the party. We need some ambient music to start, and then we want to get dancier as the night goes on. With, of course, plenty of Eli Archer thrown in."

"And why do we, of course, need to throw in plenty of Eli Archer?" Claire shook her head no.

Holly rolled her eyes—*duh*. "Be*cause*, he'll be here, and everyone will think it's very cool to be able to see the person whose music is playing over the speakers."

Claire set down her margarita. "We don't need to invite him. I mean, I guess he heard us talking about it at the restaurant, but I'm sure he won't remember. And even if he did remember, I'm sure he wouldn't be offended not to be invited. It's not like he lives here or anything. Not really."

"I anticipated this response," Holly said.

"Good."

"I anticipated this response so I already had Dave make sure he was coming."

"Holly!"

Holly grinned. "He's totally crazy about you. Anyone can see it."

"He is not."

Holly kept grinning.

"I'm coming to the party with Dan," Claire said.

Holly's mouth dropped a little, then she grinned. "I definitely did not buy enough popcorn."

CHAPTER 14

Claire cast a longing glance at the house next door as she marched up her own walkway an hour later. *No, Claire. Don't be stupid. Go home. Stay home.*

Once safely inside, she made herself a cup of herbal tea, and took it, along with her iPad, to the bathtub. After she'd soaked for a few minutes, she would work on renewing and fine-tuning her goals list. It was a much smarter use of her time than the one Eli had suggested, and infinitely *safer.*

The water was hot and scented and she sank in with a deep sigh of relief. With her one dry hand, she pressed the play button of her usual music station on her iPad. Soft music filled the bathroom, and Claire sank back against the tub with a long sigh.

She tried to relax.

This was very relaxing.

She was in her own home in her deep bathtub with clean hot water and bath salts. How could she *not* be relaxed? Only a seriously uptight person would not be relaxed right now.

Her hand began to itch for the iPad, as a thought nagged at her, just under the surface. *With just a few taps on the iPad, she could be listening to Eli's music instead.* But of course that was the last thing in the world she needed to do. She might as well just go ahead and start on real heroin—or maybe crack—just for kicks.

Her wet hand found a towel and wiped itself off. Against her will, she found herself entering his name and listening.

Like it had the day at Holly's house, his music sounded like nothing else she'd ever heard. What sounded like multiple cellos made short low, repetitive bursts, backed by intricate and relentless drumming. The instruments quieted for a dramatic moment, then, after the pause, Eli's powerful voice, rich, low, and majestic, began to sing.

Wrap me in your dress of crumbs
Fly me through the super void
Until the birds get free from gravity
And remind us
Until the birds remind us
We're waiting to be pecked apart . . .

Well, that was cheery. A) The lyrics were pretty depressing. B) What was he even talking about?

Claire tried to force herself to think snarky, but it wouldn't stick. The song had ahold of her heart and it was squeezing—hard. She couldn't have stopped listening if she'd tried. The cellos picked back up again, staccato and smooth at the same time.

Hold onto my coat, love
The tarmac glows in the dark
It's that house you remember
The one
Where the birds sleep
The one
Where you fed me an apple

What? Was it nonsense? But it wasn't. Not the way he sang it. She *wanted* to dismiss it, but in truth, the music pierced her. It was soulful and plaintive and his voice was more beautiful than any instrument. Maybe he'd visit her tonight, knock on her door, even though she'd turned him down? Then she wouldn't be responsible for it.

She tossed a wet washrag over her face and groaned. So maybe he was a guy who paid hospital bills for neglected children, and maybe he was thoroughly decent all-around, and maybe he gave her an orgasm unlike anything she'd ever experienced without even taking clothing off, but Eli Archer didn't even live in the same kind of world as she did. He was passing through, an alien.

But the logic couldn't, wouldn't, make a dent in her desire to be with him again. The longing was so powerful inside her, there was no talking herself out of it with mere logic.

She stood, slaking the soapy water from her arms and legs with her palms, and still wet, put on her ivory knit bathrobe and made for the door.

Skulking through the front yard, half-naked, she cursed the clear, bright-moon night, and looked around for neighbors.

Eli's door was closed and solid and heavy brown wood, and it was her chance to get ahold of herself and go home.

She stared at it.

Then she knocked.

The door swung open, and Eli stared at her, open-mouthed. "You look . . ."

Claire arched an eyebrow.

"Unbelievably sexy," he finished.

"Let me in before the neighbors see."

"By all means." He moved to the side of his front door, letting her into the entryway.

She stepped in, and his eyes traveled back down to the wet robe, which, she'd realized on the way over, was completely glued to her skin. She watched as his hands traveled toward her, reaching her, touching her with reverence. Lust shot through every cell of her body.

He made a low, soft groan. "You're so beautiful."

And then her robe was open, and then he was kneeling before her, and his mouth was all over her.

He pushed her backward until she was seated in a small wooden chair in the entry hall. And then his mouth found her . . . there, and she looked down at his head, shocked. He was . . . he had his mouth . . . *there*. Should she feel embarrassed right now? Tell him to stop? Was she clean enough? She'd just had a bath, but . . . After a few more moments, she could no longer think at all. It was beyond anything she'd ever thought to imagine. She must have shouted, probably loudly, when her body went rigid with the intensity of it, but she couldn't be sure, because she was trapped in an earthquake of pleasure. Finally, she sank back into the chair, spent.

Afterward, his head rested on her thigh, and she found herself stroking his hair, which seemed incongruous, since she knew all they were doing was messing around, purely sexual, nothing more.

He looked up at her, his head still resting there.

"First time?"

"No. Of course not," she said, indignant. *Yes.*

He pulled back and studied her, smiling.

"*Fine.* Yes. First time."

"How can that *be*?" He shook his head.

She shrugged. "Cliff thought it was unsanitary. My college boyfriend . . . I guess they hadn't taught him that yet in sex ed."

"I want to do it again."

"I feel weird . . . that we're not . . . you know . . . doing anything for you. And I feel weird saying it. And, I don't know, I just feel weird in general."

"Well, you are a little weird. But I like it. And we are."

"Are what?"

"Doing something for me."

"What?"

He paused, then sat back on the floor in front of her, his arms propped behind him. "Well, see. From the minute I met you, I thought—I want to show that woman what a mind-blowing orgasm can be like. I even dreamed it. It kind of . . . took hold of me, wanting to do it."

"You thought that right away?" she asked. For a moment she felt a flush of pleasure, that he'd been attracted to her right away, but then, what he'd said sank in. She sat forward. "Wait. You mean, you knew I'd never had one, just by looking at me?"

"Um, well . . . sorta."

"*Sorta?*"

He looked her in the eyes. "Yes. I knew."

She sat back again, letting out a gust of breath. This was awful. "Wow. I must come across like a total prude. Is there a Japanese symbol for prude? Or for frigid? Maybe I could have it tattooed on my face." She pointed at her cheek.

"No." He took her chin and pointed it toward him. "Claire, no. That's not what I meant."

"What did you mean, then?"

"Oh, hell." He ran his hand over the stubble on his face. "I don't know how I knew. I just knew. It was just a weird intuition. Please don't feel insecure about it."

Claire wrapped her robe more tightly around her body. She felt insecure about it.

"Claire, you're incredibly beautiful and sexy. I thought so from the first time I saw you. It's just that . . . you acted differently around me than any woman has in a long time, or maybe ever."

"What's that supposed to mean?"

"Well, we had an immediate spark, right?"

"Maybe . . ."

He eyed her, eyebrow arched. "Definitely. But you wanted to avoid that spark, rather than encourage it."

"Because I'm *smart*."

"Well, obviously. But that wasn't why."

She continued clutching the robe. "Do tell."

"It seemed more like cautiousness."

"Same thing as smart. Exact same thing."

"Maybe. Or at least there's overlap. But here's the thing. It was obvious within five minutes we would have explosive, once-in-a-lifetime sex. Yet you didn't even feel the least bit tempted by that. You wanted to get as far away from it as you could."

"So? Like I said, careful."

"Right. But if you'd ever had good sex—I mean, *really* good sex—you wouldn't have been able to avoid at least being tempted."

She paused and tried to take in his words. They made a weird kind of sense. "Do you still think that?" she asked.

"Think what?"

"We'd have . . . that kind of sex?"

"I know it."

She thought it over for a minute. Quietly, she said, "I think I want to try it."

CHAPTER 15

Claire stomped around her kitchen, making tea and toast and grudges.

The morning birds were entirely too cheerful, and the men building the fence in her backyard were just entirely too noisy for this hour.

He'd *turned her down.*

For the hundredth time, her face grew hot with rage and humiliation.

She violently scraped the butter knife against her toast, then realized there was no butter on the knife. Jerk had probably slept with half the women in North America and he'd turned *her* down?

She slammed the butter on the counter.

It was so *condescending.* She could very well decide for herself whether they needed to slow down a little. She did not need some misguided long-hair thinking he was some kind of father figure. Hadn't he ever heard of women's lib? Women's choices? She'd *chosen* to have sex with him. He had *not* chosen to say yes. She got out a fork and beat two eggs like they were Eli's stupid face. Stupid gorgeous face.

Well, it didn't matter.

She began to calm. It really didn't matter. Now that Eli had opened her Pandora's Box, so to speak, she knew what she really wanted. This was good, to finally know what she really wanted in a husband—a commitment, kids, backyard barbecues, *and* great sex. Just imagine, a whole lifetime of feeling like that, anytime you wanted it. Eli was only good for the sex part, and apparently, only halfway on that one, so it was time to get serious. Tomorrow night was Holly's party and her date with Dan. Things were about to start *happening.* She was going to make sure of it.

She was thirty-five and tired of waiting for her real life to start. So really, she should thank Eli. The jerk had helped her to get motivated. Very, very motivated.

• • •

Eli took his fourth cold shower in twelve hours. How he had found the strength to turn that woman down, with her robe open and her big blue eyes and her innocence and her asking for him—well, it defied an answer. It was a superhuman act he hadn't even known he was capable of. He deserved a medal. He deserved Buddha status. He was officially the most virtuous man on earth.

It *sucked*.

But he knew how it would end if he and Claire got any closer. He'd been through it too many times—the tears, the guilt, the heartbreak.

That was how he'd been stupid enough to get mixed up with Coco Skye. With her placid, flawless face and her always-cool demeanor, she'd seemed like she would be impervious to real feelings. She'd seemed more android prototype for the perfect female form than human. Or at least not a woman who would be secretly scrolling through the Tiffany ring selection after their third date, same as it ever was. He'd been an idiot.

Eli was always honest with anyone he went out with: he was not a man who could make a commitment. He'd already made his commitment, and it was to the musician's life. The two were completely, undeniably, irrevocably, mutually exclusive. It was one of the few useful things his father had taught him. You can't do both.

Still, it seemed like once Eli dated someone for a while, something always happened. It was always the same. He'd be going along, thinking things were perfect, and then he'd discover something was up. Whoever he was dating would decide she was the one—the one who would change his mind about commitment. They never understood that it wasn't even a good option—he'd make a lousy long-term bet. And he didn't suffer any delusion that these marriage dreams had anything to do with himself. They were some mix of the headiness of fame, money, sex endorphins, and a guy who was decent to them.

His girlfriend before Coco had been a keeper—good-natured, hilarious, and easygoing—he could've kept up their casual relationship for years, if she'd stayed cool about it, like she promised. She hadn't. Their breakup had included a decidedly not cool, not easygoing Sarah yelling the words *commitmentphobe* and *asshole* in front of half of his Greenwich Village condo board, which was a drama-averse group, to make an understatement. He'd had to endure a talking-to by Mrs. Snooty-Schiff the next day.

He didn't want things to go down that way with Claire. He liked her too much. Hell, he respected her too much.

He never should have kissed Claire in the first place. Never should have touched her, not even a little bit. It was just that . . . he felt for her. He liked her. Maybe he more than liked her. He might even be a tiny bit in love with her. When he was around her, he felt . . . happy. Clean. Decent. For the first time since his picture had started regularly appearing in the tabloids, he felt . . . normal.

And whenever he saw her, his heart did this weird little clutch. She was . . . irresistible. Impossible to stay away from. There was something about her, something so wholesome and decent and down-to-earth. He had to have it. She was real with him. No pretense, no acting. He didn't have to wonder what she really thought. Mostly because it was broadcast over her face, but also, because she was authentic. She was smart and strong and he bet once they got to know each other more and she relaxed a little, she'd be feisty as a hellcat. He'd already seen glimpses of it. Fun to fight with, fun to make love with. No simpering porn-star act from this woman. One hundred percent the real thing. Plus, his fame meant nothing to her, other than maybe as an annoyance.

But here was the real clincher. The biggest factor of all. The biggest thing of his *life*. Claire had broken the spell. Whatever that awful spell he'd been under, where he couldn't string more than three words of a song together on a piece of paper. It was like she was some kind of muse for him. He had four songs now. All because of her. If he kept hanging around with her, maybe he could keep doing it.

But he knew the truth about himself. He'd known it since he was fifteen years old. At least, that was when he'd first articulated it in his mind. But he'd known it long before then, really: *Eli Archer was just like his dad.* He was a leaver, a musician, a man destined for life on the road. Not a family man.

Eli would never do to a wife and son what Gage Archer had done, so he would never *have* a wife and son. He'd hated growing up without a father, and there was no way in hell he'd inflict that on another Archer generation.

In his younger years, when his friends were still guileless and buck-toothed, and they'd found out who Eli's father was, they'd eagerly asked Eli everything about the old man. Only to discover, much to Eli's embarrassment, that Eli himself knew almost nothing. Eli mainly knew the same things anyone else did—what he could learn on *Entertainment News Daily* or *Stargazer Magazine*. What Eli did learn from the news was never good: More groupies. More fights with bandmates. More drugs and damaged hotel rooms. Lawsuits.

Eli knew he wanted to move through the world with a hell of a lot more dignity than *that*. It was one of the only things his dad had ever given him—an example of how *not* to do life. You had to pick—musician or father. Gage had proven it. And Eli had made his choice, and he was content with it. It was bone-deep for him, being a musician, and he couldn't change it. Didn't want to.

And Claire. Claire had fat dancing babies in her eyeballs. He would bet his right pinky she already had baby names and china patterns picked out. She probably had the model number of the backyard swing set with the highest safety ratings programmed into her iPad.

Whoever the guy was who married her, he'd be lucky.

Eli wanted to go to her right then. To make her laugh, to find out what scientific study she'd cite next, to see her face wracked with pleasure. To bury himself in her, to feel her, to feel right in his own skin again.

He slammed down his coffee cup and picked up Bess.

The new song he was working on, the one he'd half-finished, was all about frustration.

Virtue blew.

• • •

Claire tied her hair up, straightened her scrubs, and shoved her bag in her locker.

She was at work, and while she was at work, she was going to think about work, not about Eli Know-It-All Archer.

Anita appeared in the doorway of the locker room. "You know how you told me to tell you if Carolyn Stamper or that Zoe kid ever came back?"

Claire straightened. "Yes?"

"Both of 'em." Anita tossed her head to one side, indicating the north wing.

Damn.

"Room?"

"Twelve."

Claire hurried to room twelve, shoes slipping, stopping along the way to pull her neon shoelaces tight with their toggles.

"Zoe?" she whispered, entering the room. Mrs. Stamper appeared to be sound asleep, but ashen and dusky, with shallow rapid breathing—definitely not right.

Zoe's face was pale, resigned, forlorn.

"What happened?"

"She's been getting worse."

"How so?"

"That other doctor said it's pneumonia."

Claire's stomach sank. She pulled the chart.

"They said she has to stay here," Zoe said.

Claire nodded slowly, looking over the chart. A cold dread penetrated to her bones, like a ghost brushing past.

"They're calling my caseworker," Zoe said.

Claire sat down. Suddenly she was very, very tired. It was not a fair world that left Zoe without anyone to look out for her.

"What did they say they thought would happen next?" Claire asked, though she was pretty sure she knew the answer.

Zoe chewed a nail and shrugged. "Some other foster home. I'm too old to get adopted."

"Oh, Zo. Of course you're not. Anyone would want you. But what about your mother? Aren't they trying to find her, make sure she gets help, or whatever needs to happen?"

Zoe nodded, eyes vacant. Hopelessness was plain on her face.

Claire squeezed Zoe's shoulders. She wanted to take her in her arms and rock her like a baby, make it all go away.

Donna Wilson, the hospital staff social worker, appeared in the doorway, hair floating around her head like a fuzzy brown cloud.

Mrs. Stamper still slept.

"Dr. Taylor," Donna nodded.

Claire nodded in return.

"I'm afraid your next foster family is currently out of town. Since we don't have that many in the region, I'm not going to be able to get you placed today."

Zoe chewed.

Claire stood. "What's she supposed to do?"

"She should not leave the care of her current foster parent," Donna said, sounding like she was reciting something from a manual.

Mrs. Stamper slept on.

"Uh . . ." Claire waved her arm at Mrs. Stamper, then gave Donna an incredulous look. "How do you propose Zoe work that out?"

"Well, those chairs do fold out into single beds," Donna said.

Claire gaped at her. "Are you serious?"

"I know it's not ideal, but it's an overburdened system. And she would be safe here."

"You want Zoe to live in the hospital?"

"Not *live* here. Just stay. For a little while. It's only temporary," Donna said, sounding like she was trying to calm an irrational person.

Maybe Claire was feeling a little irrational, but how could she not be? She looked at Zoe's hollowed-out face.

"She's staying with me," Claire announced, then wondered how in the heck she was going to work that out.

Donna was speechless for a moment, her mouth a perfect O. "That's not legal."

"I'm her friend. I'm inviting her over for a slumber party. As my friend. With Mrs. Stamper's permission. Isn't Zoe allowed to have friends?"

"Well, I . . . Yes."

"I'm allowed to have friends," Zoe said quietly, still chewing, but looking much less zombielike. A faint flicker of hope lit her eyes.

"Okaaay," Donna said. "This is a little unorthodox, but under the circumstances . . ."

"Great," Claire said, sounding much more confident than she felt.

Anita appeared in the doorway. "Fox wants you. Something about billing. Again."

"*Great,*" Claire said.

She turned to Zoe. "I have to work until seven. Sorry, kid, you're going to be here for a while. But I'm off tomorrow. We'll do something fun. Do you have enough books or homework or whatever to keep you entertained until I get off work today?"

Zoe nodded and pulled a hardcover library book from her backpack. It was thick.

"Whoa. What's that?"

Zoe showed her—*The Book Thief.*

"Try not to get into any trouble with that thing."

Zoe looked up at her, confused, then realized Claire was joking. She almost smiled. A little bit.

What in the heck was she going to do with a twelve-year-old? She knew nothing about twelve-year-olds. And tomorrow was the party and Dan and then back to her ongoing ridiculous work schedule. But maybe Mrs. Stamper would be better by then. Claire looked at the sleeping woman and knew it wasn't true.

• • •

Claire put her breakfast dishes in the dishwasher and eyed the clock. It was 10:47 a.m., and Zoe still hadn't stirred. Should she check on her? Let her sleep? She pushed her iPad aside and rose to make another cup of tea. She couldn't focus on reading the news anyway.

Pippa sat next to her food bowl expectantly, even though she'd just eaten twice her weight in Canine Complete Kibble.

"You're not barfing on my hardwood floors," Claire informed her.

Pippa just looked at her, her body shimmying a little at Claire's attention, hopeful for more food.

Claire went back to the kettle and started the water. She hadn't heard one peep from Eli. Not one little, tiny, stupid, peep. Almost two whole days. Which was for the best. But it hurt. She dunked the tea bag up and down, sighing.

"Hi," Zoe said.

Claire turned. Zoe looked so young and fragile in the too-big pajamas Claire had loaned her. They'd both been too exhausted to pack up anything more than Pippa by the time Claire's shift had finally wrapped up at the E.R. last night.

"Hi," Claire said, resisting the urge to hug, smother. "Hungry?"

Zoe shrugged. She walked over to Pippa and picked her up,

settling into one of the dining chairs. Once in her rightful place in Zoe's arms, Pippa went to sleep almost instantly.

Hmm . . . how to interpret the shrug, which seemed to be the preteen version of an applies-to-everything answer?

Claire pulled some eggs and milk from the fridge and got to work.

"I was thinking maybe we could go to Branson to the mall this morning. If we hurry, we could still make it there and be back in time for the party. You might need some new clothes, right? Have you and Mrs. Stamper bought much yet?"

• • •

A little over an hour later, they were at the mall in Branson. They stood before the map of the mall, staring.

"Which stores do you like? Justice? That says it's for children, and I think I remember seeing some cute things in the window."

Zoe looked afraid to answer, but it was obvious Claire's suggestion had missed the mark. She gave Zoe a gentle elbow in the ribs. "If you tell me, we can *go* there."

"Charlotte Russe?"

"Oh! *Oh.* Okay, sure. That's not too . . . adult for you? I mean, big. It's not too big for you?"

"Kayla, at my school, she can wear the extra-smalls."

"Kayla. Extra-smalls. Okay, Charlotte Russe it is." Claire had a mental image of leaving the mall with the fashion equivalent of a twelve-year-old streetwalker, but once they were in the store, Zoe showed good taste and even some fashion flair.

She emerged from the dressing room in jeans and an asymmetrical T-shirt in a pale-blue slub cotton. The top was definitely her color. Her face was lit up, and she looked beautiful.

"Keeper!" Claire said, giving her a thumbs-up, and Zoe smiled the first real smile Claire had ever seen on her.

She ran her hands over the top, admiring herself in the mirror.

"Next," Claire said.

There were a couple of fails, but they left with a sundress, two pairs of jeans, and three tops. Zoe was beaming.

"Oh! We should get our hair done for the party!" Claire said.

Zoe looked dubious.

"I won't make you do anything you don't want to do. It's your head, your hair." Claire held up two, then three, then two fingers. "Girl Scouts' honor?"

Zoe held up three fingers.

Claire laughed and did the same. "Girl Scouts' honor."

"Maybe . . ." Zoe fingered her faded burgundy locks.

They walked a few doors down to the hair salon, where a twentysomething young woman with a pierced nose and jet-black dreadlocks sat in a hairdresser's chair, adjusting a long piece of hair while studying herself in the mirror. Around her, several older hairdressers were busy rolling perms, blowing dry perms, and setting perms.

The younger hairdresser looked up at Claire and Zoe when they entered, hopped off the seat, and sauntered toward them. The chains on her boots made a clicking noise as she approached. As she drew closer, Claire saw that she had a spray of blue stars tattooed from her ear, down her neck, and into her shirt.

"Help you?"

"We're going to a party. We were hoping for, uh . . . party hair?"

The girl walked up to Zoe and began ruthlessly inspecting Zoe's scalp. "There's ombré, and then there's roots. This is roots. Pale roots. It would be one thing if they were dark. This won't do."

Zoe stared up at the girl, her face slack with awe.

"Do you want to commit to the pink, or try to match your roots?"

"We could do that?" Zoe asked, hopeful. "The roots thing?"

"Sure."

"How long would that take?" Claire asked.

"Let's see, for a solid color, no weave, about an hour from start to finish."

"Okay. We have an hour."

"And you"—she pointed at Claire's head—"you need highlights and some layers."

Claire looked at herself in the mirror. Then she looked at the time on her phone and shook her head. "Next time?" she said. *Maybe? No.*

"Suit yourself," the stylist said. "I'm Storm, by the way."

Storm? Should she let a woman who called herself Storm near Zoe?

But Zoe was staring at the tattooed, pierced badass of a twentysomething with unabashed worship, like she was preparing for ascension.

"Hop up." Storm pointed at Zoe. She turned to Claire. "Grab a magazine, but the selection bites."

By the time they left, Zoe was transformed. She looked . . . sweet. Like the little girl she was.

Clarie paid for the hairdo and left Storm a thirty percent tip.

Storm looked at the tip. "Come back," she said.

"We will," Claire said.

Zoe's hand smoothed her new hair, and her smile had taken over and stayed.

• • •

An hour later, they were back in Claire's bedroom, sorting through her clothes.

"I like the red sweater," Zoe said.

"Really? It's not too much?"

"It's beautiful," Zoe said. She was wearing her new jeans and a turquoise sweatshirt with an ivory crochet detail at the top of the back. Her hair was beautiful, clean and trimmed, a light nutmeg brown, not dissimilar to Claire's own color.

Claire eyed Zoe with satisfaction. "You look fantastic, kiddo."

Zoe smiled, and Claire eyed the red sweater. It was a soft

red, fine-knit, and it clung in all the right places, even without the help of Joyce's architectural bra. The bias cut made it swing attractively over her jeans. She slipped it on.

Claire thought of Eli. *What would Eli . . .?* She shook her head harder. She hadn't heard from him since the night he turned her down, and it was for the best. The little ache in her chest—the one that wouldn't go away only—would have been worse if she'd really gotten involved with him. Right?

When Dan rang the doorbell a few minutes later, the girls were ready.

"You look nice," Dan said to Claire, then, to Zoe, "Hi."

They arrived a few minutes early to help Holly set up. Dan parked just behind the caterer's van, which was actually a station wagon with the back windows whited out, then hand-lettered: A Moveable Feast.

Zoe looked up at Holly's house hesitantly.

Claire reached toward the back seat and placed a hand over Zoe's. "Ready, kiddo?"

"I was thinking about reading in the car for a while."

"Bring your book with you, but stick with me, and I promise it won't be too scary." Claire made a face.

Zoe nodded, still staring up at the house.

Claire looked too. It really was a beautiful house—two and a half stories, white clapboard, and very old. Most of the houses in Haven Springs were similar—old and Victorian, but this was one of the oldest in town.

How would it go tonight? Claire barely had time to wonder before Holly threw open the front door.

"Y'all," she said, "look amazing! Come in! Dan, can you start the grill? We're doing hot dogs for the kids."

"Sure," Dan said. He slid his phone in his pocket. "Backyard?"

As soon as he was out of earshot, Holly turned to Claire. "Eli is going to *die* when he sees you in that sweater. You really look beautiful, Claire."

"Thank you, but it's definitely not for Eli. I'm here with *your brother.*"

"Oh." She paused. "Right. Right. How are things going?"

Claire shrugged, and Holly gave her a sympathetic look.

"Well, anyhoo, we're all set for operation Marla and Dave."

"Yeah?"

"I have a plan," Holly said, rubbing her hands together. "*Mwa ha ha ha.*"

"Let's hear it," Claire said.

"It's a good one. Are you ready?"

"Let me get a drink."

Holly laughed and pulled her into the kitchen. She took a bottle of rosé out of the fridge. "Hostess stash. Okay, remember that creepy room on the third floor?" Holly looked toward the ceiling.

"The madwoman in the attic room? Who could forget?"

"The very one," Holly grinned.

The bedroom on the third floor had odd markings on the floor, deep enough that the floor refinisher had not been able to remove them entirely. But odder than the deep scratches on the floor was the lock—a slide-rod lock. On the *outside* of the door. Holly's parents had thought it added to the history of the place, so they'd never taken it off, and then Holly hadn't either. Now the room housed a white cast-iron guest bed with a cheery floral coverlet, but it kept its name, along with its creepy lock and scratches.

"We're going to use that for the coat room. Eli will be bringing Dave at 7:14—"

"Wait a second." Claire held up her hand like a stop sign and tried not to choke on the wine that was halfway down her esophagus.

"Did you just say Eli will be here at *seven fourteen*?"

"Yes. With Dave. It's only a little chilly, so not everyone will be wearing jackets, but Eli will, and he's going to—"

"When did you talk to Eli?" Claire tried to squelch the red-hot poker of jealousy and embarrassment she felt right now.

Holly had talked to Eli, and she *hadn't* talked to Eli, after what they'd . . . done together?

"Yesterday. I called him. So, *anyway*—geez, will you listen up?—Eli will be here with Dave at 7:14. He will ask Marla to show them to the coatroom. I will be upstairs, waiting for Dave and Marla to go into the madwoman room, and then, drumroll . . . locking them in the coat room together."

"Holly! You can't *lock* them in a room."

"With a bottle of champagne. And a guitar."

"*Holly!*"

"What? It's brilliant!"

"It's probably illegal!"

"Oh, pish. Details."

"Oh my word." Claire squeezed her temples.

"Unfortunately, since there's no bathroom attached, we'll have to let them out in about an hour."

"Yes, that is the unfortunate part."

"Ryan will sit on the steps and play chess and redirect people to the downstairs office if they need a place to set their things."

"You're making your child a criminal accessory?"

"Of course not. I'm telling him there's a leak in the ceiling up there. Zoe can sit with him. He can teach her chess."

"Oh, good. Social services will be so pleased. Zoe as kidnapping accessory."

"You are being seriously no fun. What bug got up your butt?"

Claire sighed. "I know. I'm sure Dave and Marla will thank you at their wedding. For *imprisoning* them. But Eli and I . . ."

Holly perked up. "Eli and you?"

"We fooled around again the other night."

Holly swiveled her body in a twist dance, a huge grin on her face. "Yesssssss."

"It's not good," Claire said, dejected.

"It's good, Claire! It's good!"

"No. I want a husband, not a hookup." She paused. "And also . . . because he never called."

"Oh." Holly froze mid-dance. "He didn't?"

Claire shook her head miserably. "I honestly haven't had time to think about it, with Zoe staying with me and work and all that, but now that I know I'm about to see him, I'm . . . embarrassed."

"Embarrassed?"

"I sort of . . . let myself go. With him. In a different way."

"Let yourself go?"

"You know." Her skin heated and she was sure she was bright red. "Sexually," she whispered. "And I haven't heard from him since."

Zoe came back into the kitchen with the empty plastic ice bag, Ryan at her heels.

"We need to talk more about this," Holly said, pointing at Claire.

"Okay, kids. I need your help with the condiment station for the hot dogs. People should be arriving," she looked at her watch, "really any minute now."

Ryan followed Zoe outside with the hot dog fixings.

"It's like Zoe has a new pet," Holly said.

Claire smiled, watching after them.

"Let's talk more about Eli—but wait, before I forget—" Holly put her hands on the ice bucket of champagne and two glasses on the kitchen countertop. "This goes to the madwoman room for Operation Dave and Marla. Will you run it up there?"

• • •

Eli was a little hazy on Holly's so-called grand scheme, but he figured it was all in good fun, anyway. Holly'd been hyped up when she'd called him, and it had taken him a moment to figure out A) who she was, and B) what the hell she was talking about. Also, he'd been on the other line with Alec going over contract possibilities, so he'd been eager to get off the phone.

Now Eli stood on Holly's doorstep with Dave, as instructed, wondering if Claire was there yet, and carrying a bottle of red wine and a heavy load of Dave's musical enthusiasm.

Dave rang the doorbell. "This is so cool, man. We're like, hanging out. Just a couple of guys."

Eli rang the bell a second time, and Ryan answered.

They exchanged greetings, and Ryan, eyes wide and Adam's apple bobbing, said, "Come on in."

"Take your jacket, man?" Eli said to Dave.

"That's all right," Dave said cheerfully, and put his hands in his pockets.

"I'm *supposed* to take your jacket," Eli said.

Dave looked confused.

"I don't know man," Eli sighed, still holding out his hand for the jacket. "I'm just trying to keep the women happy."

"Oh, *that*. Here, then, have a jacket, I guess." Dave handed it to him.

Eli took the windbreaker and turned to Ryan. "Third floor?"

Ryan nodded and pointed toward the staircase. "I'll take you up there."

• • •

Holly arrived on the third floor of her house to find Ryan standing outside the madwoman in the attic room. The door was closed behind him.

"Hey, kid. What are you doing up here? Where's Zoe?"

"I was just bringing the musician up here. With his coat, like you told me."

Holly looked at her watch. "He's early!"

Ryan shrugged.

She looked up at the closed but still unlocked door.

"He's in there?"

Ryan nodded.

"And Marla?"

"Marla?"

"Yes, Marla's supposed to be in there with him."

"Mom, are you crazy? Claire was in there, fiddling with some ice bucket and weird skinny glasses."

"Dave and *Claire* are in there?"

"No, Mom!" he said, exasperated. "Claire and Eli Archer— the *musician*—are in there!"

Holly gasped. Her hand slapped over her mouth involuntarily.

"Claire and Eli?"

"Mom, is your hearing okay? Do you have Alzheimer's? And can I go now?"

"Yes, yes," she said. "Run along, naughty child."

Holly stared at the closed door of the madwoman room. She figured she had about ten seconds to make a decision before a red-sweatered, red-faced Claire came bolting out of there.

She closed the distance to the slide-rod lock in three large steps. The lock slid into place with a satisfying little click. A huge smile spread across her face.

• • •

Claire smoothed the front of her sweater and straightened herself. "Hi."

Eli tossed a jacket on the bed. "Hi. You look great."

They stood for a long moment, and Claire knew her cheeks were approaching the color of her sweater.

"I didn't call," he finally said.

She shrugged.

"You're mad?"

"Of course not," Claire said. "Of course I'm not *mad*. I didn't even notice."

"You're serving champagne in the coatroom?"

"Following orders."

"Funny. Me too."

"What were yours?"

"Something about somebody who got dumped and a coat," he shrugged. "It all sounded a little silly, but I cooperated."

They stood in silence for another long and awkward moment.

"Well, I should get back to my date," Claire said.

"Another date?"

Claire shrugged. "I'm single. Why not?"

He looked at her with those all-knowing eyes.

Her heart did its Eli thing, and she cursed it. "Well, see you later." She brushed past him.

His hand flew out and gripped her arm. She looked down at it, then back up at his face. His intense brown eyes pierced her.

"I didn't call because I wanted to call."

She rolled her eyes. "Is that the new thing you're telling women? It needs some work."

"Claire—"

"Listen. I really do have to go," she said. "Plus it was no big deal. Plus my date is waiting for me downstairs." She remembered his hands on her, his tongue on her, and her face felt like it might burst into flames. She reached out the arm not currently in Eli's grip and reached for the doorknob.

"It was a big deal," he said.

She turned her burning cheeks away from him, but his hand continued to circle her arm.

"Let's talk about this later tonight," he said. "I don't want things to be awkward."

She shrugged, a handy method of communication she was learning from Zoe. "No need. Nothing's awkward," she said.

"You built a fence in your backyard."

"Oh, get over yourself. That was for my mother, not for you."

She reached her free arm out toward the door, and turned the doorknob to the right. Then to left. She tugged. *She had a grand exit to make, for crying out loud.*

But the door wouldn't budge.

CHAPTER 16

"Here, let me try."

His body was behind hers, making light contact with her back. Every electron and proton inside her was at full attention.

Her mind, through the fog of embarrassment and lust, tried to make sense of what was happening. It was just barely out of her reach . . .

Wait, no, there it was. They were locked in.

"It's no use," she said. She ducked out from under him and leaned against the bed, sighing. "We're locked in."

"Locked . . . what? How is that possible?" He pulled at the doorknob again.

"It won't budge. The lock is on the outside," she said.

"Dare I ask *why*?"

"It wasn't supposed to be us. In here."

"Oh, well, then. That explains it." He raised his eyebrows and looked at her like she was insane.

"It was supposed to be Dave and Marla," she said miserably.

She watched as Eli's eyes traveled to the champagne flutes and guitar and understanding dawned.

"The grand scheme," he said.

"Holly has sort of a thing for matchmaking."

"I see." His eyes on her were liquid sex.

Claire's skin soaked with pleasure at the lust in his gaze. She cleared her throat. "Stop looking at me like that."

"I need my sunglasses," he said.

"Just," she waved her hand around, pointing at the guitar. "Look at that. Or make yourself useful with the champagne." She averted her eyes.

He stood still for a moment, then went to the dresser where she'd set up the bucket and glasses. The cork popped a moment later. Claire was pretty sure she heard footsteps retreating outside the room at that point, but she knew it was hopeless to shout. She'd just have to kill Holly later.

"We're not scheduled to be let out for urination for an hour, so we should probably minimize the champagne intake."

"You say the sexiest things."

"I try."

The champagne sizzled its way into the glasses.

He handed her a flute, and the bubbles hit her nose with a light burn.

"To imprisonment," he said.

"To escape," she said.

They took a sip.

"So you're supposed to woo me with the guitar now."

"A parlor guitar," Eli said, looking at it. "Not a bad one. The kid's?"

"Yeah, Ryan's, I guess. Holly doesn't play."

"It'll do."

He sat on the bed next to her and began to tune the guitar. "Not bad at all." He looked it over again, then strummed a few chords.

Claire waited. "That's all you've got?" she said.

"No," he said, then set the guitar between his legs.

She was about to smart off again, but he was looking at her with his soulful gaze, and no words came. She wondered if he made every woman feel like that—like he was making love to her just by looking at her. She'd love to dismiss it that easily, but somehow she didn't think it was true. Eli, whatever else he was, seemed real.

"I didn't call or come by because I didn't want things to get any messier," he said.

"Don't worry about it." Her voice was quiet and her eyes trained on the champagne flute in her hand.

"But now that I see you again, I *want* to get messy. I want to get as messy as it takes."

She didn't dare look at him.

He took her hand.

For a long moment, they sat, holding hands, saying nothing.

"My lease here ends in June, and then I have to go back to real life. My job. New York."

She nodded, still looking down at his square brown hand around her small fair one.

"I could fall for you. I have about an inch and a half to fall," Eli said.

Her head snapped up. His words were headier than the champagne.

"And you don't seem like a detached, meaningless sex, one-night-stand kind of woman."

"I've never had a one-night-stand," she admitted.

He groaned.

"What? That's not a bad thing. They're disgusting and dangerous. Plus, it affects women differently than it does men. Women's hormones are different. In England, they did a study—"

He held up a hand. "I don't need the study to know it effects women differently. I believe I've witnessed it up close and personal."

"I bet."

"That was a long time ago, Claire. I'm not like that. And it's not a bad thing you've never had casual sex. It just makes me want to show you the world. The whole world. In bed. Or maybe on a kitchen table."

"And you don't think we could handle it for two and a half months? We'd already know not to get too involved. It has a set end date. We could, just, you know, live a little, temporarily. That's what Holly's always telling me to do."

"Holly's advice is now suspect." He pointed at the door.

"She knows me pretty well."

Eli looked at her. "Woman, don't tempt me like this."

"It's just that . . . I've never . . ."

He waited, his eyes alert with full attention.

"I've never had that before."

"Had what?"

"That kind of . . . that kind of . . . orgasm."

A low moan escaped his lips.

"But you knew that."

"I knew. But when you say that, I want to take you right here on top of Dave's coat."

"We can't give Holly the satisfaction. She could open the door early, and I have to kill her when she does."

"True," he said.

"But since I've never had it before, I kind of keep thinking about . . . having it again. Like, a lot. A lot of thinking about it." She cleared her throat and took a swig of champagne.

"And you think we could both stay neutral?"

"I think I can," she said. *Liar.*

"I think I can't, but I think I'm not caring right now," he said.

"Does that mean we have a deal?" she asked, more hopeful and far less cool than she wanted to be.

"A deal?"

"Yeah. You know, a no-strings thing until June?"

She waited.

"How can I say no to you? All I can think about is being with you."

"Really?" she whispered, sounding like a small girl on her birthday, even to her own ears. A big smile worked its way across her face.

"I write about you."

"You *do?*"

He nodded. "This is not very neutral. Already. And we haven't even gotten started."

No one had ever written a song about her. She'd never been that kind of girl. She put her hand on his thigh, rested it there. "It'll be okay," she told him. "We know it's doomed. We know it ends in June."

He pulled her into his lap and kissed her, a long and slow kiss that heated every nerve in her body, like sitting by a fire on a cold day.

She could kiss him like that forever.

His hands began to travel over her, over the smooth knit of her sweater, into the thickness of her hair. He pulled back and looked her in the eyes, cupping her chin in his hands, and he was right, it wasn't neutral. Not at all.

There was a noise outside the door, and they both pulled back, waited.

Then they heard the sound of tiptoeing footsteps moving away from the door.

"I guess our hour's not up," Eli said.

"She could leave us in here longer. It's Holly. You really never know what will happen with Holly." She slapped her hand to her mouth. "Dan!"

"Dan?"

"I forgot about Dan!"

"What about him?"

"I can't make this arrangement with you. I'm on a *date!* With Dan!"

"Dan won't mind."

Claire sniffed and held her chin out. "He might."

"He won't."

"Hey," she put her hands on her hips. "Other men find me attractive."

"I'm sure every heterosexual male who's ever laid eyes on you finds you attractive. Dan just happens not to be one."

"One what?"

"A heterosexual man."

"Oh, whatever. That is not true."

Eli shook his head.

"Dan is husband material. If things go well with him tonight, the deal is off. I want to get married, and I want to have kids. That goes for anyone who's husband material. The whole deal is off if anyone husband-ish comes along. I have to keep my eye on the goal. In her late thirties, a woman's fertile eggs are dying by the thousands."

He raised his eyebrows. "Husband-ish?"

"Well?"

"Fine." Eli smiled a little to himself and picked the guitar back up.

He strummed a few melodic notes, then began to sing. His voice was even more incredible in person than it had been recorded—deep and sure and true.

He seemed lost in the song, his eyes closed and his expression rapt. After a moment, his eyes opened. "Something I've been working on."

"It was nice."

"Arrggh." He sighed. "Nice?"

"It didn't rhyme."

"It's not supposed to *rhyme*."

"Most of the singers I like rhyme. You know, like Stephanie Kelly." She knew she was baiting him, but the look of suffering on his face was so funny she couldn't help herself.

He groaned.

"She's very popular," she said.

"You want rhymes?"

"That would be nice." She took a sip of champagne.

He stood and tossed the guitar strap around his neck.

He strummed. He strummed again. She watched his face as he worked out what he was about to sing, and she leaned back on the bed with her champagne glass.

"Claire, Claire, you got me hangin' by my hair."

He strummed harder, mariachi-style, and Claire laughed.

"Claire, Claire, you got my heart in disrepair."

She raised an eyebrow.

"Claire, Claire, don't . . . give me your . . . questionnaire. And I won't give you my . . . hot air."

She laughed.

"Or my—or my Voltaire." He struck a dissonant chord and

smiled crookedly, crossing one eye, and Claire laughed champagne into her nose.

At that moment the door swung open, and Holly stood in it, grinning. "This looks cozy," she said.

Eli took a bow.

• • •

Back downstairs, Claire spent a few frantic minutes looking through the crowd until her eyes landed on Zoe's freshly dyed hair, and she relaxed.

She was sitting in the backyard with about six other kids, and they were laughing and eating hot dogs, and one boy was making rude noises with his armpit. Zoe looked like she wasn't contributing much to the conversation, but she didn't look unhappy, either.

Next up, find Dan. While she looked from kitchen to living room, Eli was making his way through the crowd, straight toward her, slow and sure.

He reached her. "Where's your date?"

"I'm looking for him."

"Have a beer with me. Then look for him."

She looked at his face and felt his kiss all over again. She nodded.

• • •

"You're not into him," Eli announced, handing her a beer.

"What's that supposed to mean?"

He snapped the top off his IPA. "Just an observation."

"I don't need to be into him. I need a stable marriage and some healthy sperm and to give the feelings time to grow. And I've sort of discovered I might want good sex to be part of the package."

"You've discovered?"

"Recently."

He grinned. "Let's sit side by side on the living room sofa and torment each other."

He took her hand and she followed him toward the living room.

"Hang on," he said. "Quick detour." He pulled her into the quiet and relative dark of the hallway leading toward the back of the house. His arms slid around her waist, and his eyes found hers, and then he made her wait for what seemed like a full five minutes before his lips brushed hers.

Her limbs turned liquid in his embrace.

"Just a little preview of our deal," he said against her lips, and she smiled into his lips.

They broke apart, both of them smiling, and turned to head back toward the living room.

Just ahead of them, crossing the hall from the study, was Dan. He hadn't seen them, thank goodness.

Wait. It took Claire a few seconds to register what was happening. Dan's arm—it was around the waist of a man she didn't know. Just as the two men approached the public space of the party, Dan withdrew his arm, and the other man looked at him and smiled a private smile, the meaning of which couldn't be mistaken.

Claire stopped, and once the shock wore off, she became aware Eli had done the same. They looked at each other, their eyes flashing with what they'd just witnessed.

"Oh, my," Claire said, sinking against the wall.

• • •

"Don't say a word," Claire said, glaring at Eli.

He lounged on one of the patio chairs, looking gorgeous, and held up both hands, all mock innocence.

She took in a breath and held it, trying to take in what had just happened. And then it all hit her, and the laughter took over. It was a mirthless, body-wracking, I-can't-stop laughter. For years she'd been telling herself Dan was the only man left in Haven Springs who was her age and suitable. *Dan!* Who was *gay!*

"Are you okay?" Eli asked, eyeing her.

She stopped laughing as suddenly as she'd started. "Sure," she said, taking a swig of beer.

"Really?"

She nodded.

"You seem a little . . . weird."

"You tried to tell me," she said.

"Uh, yup."

"I didn't believe you. How did you know? Why didn't I know?"

"Medium to good gaydar—me." He pointed at himself, then at her. "Didn't want to know—you."

"True. True. I didn't want to know. I didn't want it to be true." She cleared her throat, twice. She felt like such an idiot.

He reached forward and tucked a strand of hair behind her ear.

She looked up at him. His gaze was warm, kind. "Looks like we have our deal," she said.

"Do we?" He leaned back in his chair and studied her.

"A three-month, no strings . . . fling," Claire said.

"Have you ever said the word *fling* out loud before?"

"I—"

"Hi, guys."

They both turned their heads toward the interruption.

It was Dave, in a Led Zeppelin world tour T-shirt, one hand in his jeans pocket, the other holding a bottle of beer.

"Dave!" Holly called, following on his heels, her arm reaching out and grasping his bicep. "I've been looking everywhere for you. We have to do plan B now."

Dave cast a nervous glance at Eli and Claire. "Plan B?"

"Plan B! In which I hook you up with your perfect woman."

Dave turned a whitish-green, but he did follow her. Actually, Holly was pretty much dragging him, but he didn't fight it.

Once they were gone, Claire turned back to Eli. "Of course I've said *fling* out loud."

Eli took a swig of beer and grinned at her. "I cannot wait to get you alone."

CHAPTER 17

So the Haven Springs Kazoo Band was a real thing.

Right up until this moment, Eli had thought it had to be a joke. But now he was looking at a rainbow- and wig-clad group of Havenites, marching around at the Partying for Paws Festival, and, sure enough, they were playing kazoos. Badly. The kazoo players ranged in age from twentysomething to seventysomething, and the only thing they all seemed to have in common was that they were having a grand old time.

He was glad someone was. With Zoe spending the night, he and Claire hadn't been alone last night after striking their deal, and it was hard to focus on kazoos. Claire— He glanced around and his eyes landed on her. She was whispering something in Zoe's ear that made Zoe smile.

God, what was wrong with him? He craved Claire like his bandmates craved cigarettes.

He tore his eyes away and watched the kazoo players make their way up the block.

The Partying for Paws Festival, he'd been told, was one of the better festivals that took place each year in Haven Springs. One of the better—of approximately nineteen. Claire, of course, had counted them, and had them all preprogrammed into her calendar on HandleIt.

He felt like he was back in high school, with a sex drive the size of Russia and the chances of getting laid the size of Blue Eye, Arkansas. That was a sign he'd seen on the way to Haven Springs. That is to say, so small, it seemed almost nonexistent.

Almost nonexistent, but not quite. Claire looked up and gave him a little wave. He felt it in his solar plexus, and he smiled at her.

Throngs of people in weird outfits milled about on the street, cheering on the kazoo band. Some people gave him a longer than normal looking-at, but all in all, he was able to fade into the background better here than he had been in his final months in Manhattan. He made his way through the crowd until he was standing next to the girls.

"Can I get cotton candy?" Zoe asked Claire.

"Sure," Claire said, reaching into her bag for her billfold.

Eli stopped her, whipping a ten from his money clip. "Enough?" he asked.

The girls looked at him strangely.

"This isn't *New York*," Zoe said.

"Right," he said.

"You want any?" he turned to Claire.

"Nah. Not worth blowing my monthly sugar ration. I save that for ice cream."

"You have a monthly sugar ration?"

She eyed him. "Of *course*. Sugar is toxic. Consuming it can lower your immune function for five hours. Plus, you know, cancer."

Eli inclined his head toward Zoe, who was purchasing an enormous plastic bag of lavender-colored fluff. "What about her? Is that sugar-free cotton candy?"

"Extremist parents are more toxic than sugar. I'm thinking she'll live through one cotton candy. Besides, it's not like I'm feeding her microwave popcorn."

Eli looked at her. "No. No, of course not. Not microwave popcorn. Because that would be . . ."

"Cancer in a bag."

"Cancer in a bag," he repeated.

She nodded as though they were having a normal conversation, and he found himself fighting back a laugh. Claire's face was completely earnest.

God, she was beautiful. She was like a whole ripe peach compared to a life of street pizza and take-out Chinese. Or, heaven forbid, microwave popcorn.

Zoe returned, bag of fluff tucked under one arm, her hand

already purple and sticky.

"You're sharing, right?" Eli asked.

Zoe grinned a slow big grin and shook her head no.

"Man! I want my ten bucks back."

Her hand froze before it reached her mouth, tuft of lavender midair, looking at him. But then she laughed.

A group of men and women with rainbow-colored clothes and linked arms marched by, chanting, "Keep our rivers clean! No more pesticides!"

Another group followed, this one carrying coffee cans for donations for a something. Unfortunately, they were rattling the coffee cans for attention amidst the cacophony of the parade. *Parade* could only be applied to this gathering in the loosest sense of the word. It was more like the weirdest outdoor party he'd ever been to, and that was saying something, since he was from New York.

Claire and Zoe moved to the side.

A man, this one clad head-to-toe in bright leaf-green and wearing a mustard-yellow beehive wig, jostled against Eli, and Eli instinctively looked for Claire and Zoe. Claire was separated by about three cheering humans now, but Zoe was still within reach. To his surprise, her little hand shot out and inserted itself into his.

It was warm, small, and sticky with cotton candy. She looked up at him, her face an equal mixture of trepidation, awe, and happiness.

His heart gave an unexpected squeeze. Damn, this kid got under his skin. He wasn't a kid kind of person, either. He'd always known he wouldn't have kids, and he'd never been sorry about it. They were just a bunch of alien parasites who took over your life and ruined it with indignities like snot (or worse than snot), public crying episodes, and whining.

But Zoe, Zoe was cool. She was a soulful little wisp of a thing. Vocabulary like a twenty-five-year-old. This morning she'd been reading some book thick enough to make a college professor pause.

Zoe's hand in his felt familiar, like his own childhood. Like Saturday morning cartoons with his favorite cereal and his favorite blanket.

Despite himself, he thought about his mother, all her voice mails, each one growing more plaintive. They weren't exactly unreturned calls; he just made sure to call back and leave messages when he knew she was rehearsing with the orchestra. He was sure she was wise to it, but he wasn't ready to talk about any of it yet: the fact that he'd embarrassed her publicly with all the tabloid attention; his swirling-around-the-toilet-bowl music career; Coco. The entire last two years. And now, the crowning glory, the mug shot on the newsstands. Alec assured him the story was still alive and well in New York.

He gave Zoe's hand a little squeeze, and her sweet small face looked up at him adoringly. Not the typical music-fan sort of adoration, either. This was more of the looking-for-a-dad-and-you-look-pretty-good variety. His heart froze. Damn. He couldn't let her get too attached to him, not when he was leaving in June. He couldn't hurt this girl. Hell, he'd probably never see her again. He couldn't pretend otherwise. He withdrew his hand and put it in his pocket.

Claire looked over at him and smiled.

At that moment, an attractive young family landed in the crowd and chaos next to Claire. The man was tall with a sideways flop of wavy brown hair, and the woman was a petite and elegant brunette with a pretty face and a sheer blue scarf tied around her neck. On the chest of the man a blonde baby with enormous blue eyes dangled in a baby carrier, chewing its fist, dripping with slobber.

The family was saying hello to Claire. Eli's glance traveled from the family to Claire.

Claire? Her face was an odd shade of whitish gray, and she looked like she might go down. Eli snatched Zoe's hand and pushed his way through the crowd toward Claire.

"Good to see you," the man was saying to Claire. "I believe

you've met my wife. Marie."

Claire swayed a little in the crowd, saying nothing, her face the color of dirty dishwater.

Eli shot one hand behind her back to bolster her up, and extended his other hand out toward the man, who looked harmless enough, if a little full of himself.

The man's grip was a tight pissing-contest of a handshake, and pain shot through Eli's still-sore hand, but he didn't wince. "Hello," he said.

The couple both turned to him, and he saw their barely there double take of recognition, quickly replaced by neutrality. Eli tried to catch Claire's eye, to silently ask her if she was okay, but she was staring at the baby, transfixed.

"Cliff Jenkins," the man was saying, shaking Eli's hand. Cliff. Cliff. Why did that name ring a bell? *Cliff*. The broken engagement.

Oh, boy.

"Eli Archer."

"Gah!" the baby shouted, kicking her legs in rapid-fire motion.

"And this," the man said, his voice full of pride, "is Margot." He took the baby's fat little wrists and gave them an affectionate squeeze.

"Daddy's girl," Marie said proudly, her voice holding the faintest hint of a French accent.

Zoe made a silly face at the baby, who giggled and bounced in the baby carrier.

"And who are you?" Marie asked Zoe, smiling.

"Zoe." Zoe offered no further explanation, and Marie was gracious enough to let it drop.

"Nice to meet you," Marie said, and gave Zoe a little wink.

Claire sank into Eli's arm a little, and he moved a couple of inches closer to her, until her body was resting against his.

"So . . . how do you know Claire?" Cliff asked. "I mean, we heard you were in town. Are you a . . . patient? I mean, why—" He stopped himself.

Claire stiffened against Eli.

"I mean—" Cliff looked from Eli to Claire and back again. "What . . .?"

Was this guy for real? Was he really saying, *out loud*, that he couldn't imagine what Eli would be doing out with Claire? "I'm her date," Eli said, bristling.

"Really?" Cliff looked dubious.

Eli wanted to use his jacket sleeve to wipe the look off the guy's face.

"Well, actually. No, not really." Eli paused for dramatic effect, then lowered his voice. "We haven't told many people this yet, because Claire's so private, but actually, I'm her boyfriend. It was a love-at-first sight thing."

Cliff's bottom lip lowered and hung there.

Good. Put that in your pipe and smoke it, Cliff. It was a stupid name.

"Love at first sight!" Marie lilted, beaming. "I love it."

How had *this* dude managed to get two such classy women? Eli eyed Cliff's too-young-for-him faux-vintage sneakers, and realized his hair, which at first had appeared casually slung to one side, was actually artfully mussed and, he was pretty sure, hair-sprayed.

Claire still had not spoken.

"Gah!" the baby called again, this time with a less happy edge to it, her plump little legs pumping the air.

"Oh, my darling!" Marie said, reaching for the baby carrier clips. "You are getting hungry?" The baby fussed and reached toward her mother. Marie smiled at the impossibly perfect-looking Margot. The baby's blonde fuzzy head bobbed toward her mother as Marie lifted her from the carrier.

"I'll just find a quiet place to nurse her," she said.

"Okay," Claire mumbled, sounding even weirder than her silence had been.

Eli tightened his arm around her.

This asshole had done some kind of number on her. He

looked at the guy again. He failed to see what his power was.

"Good to see you, Claire. Nice to meet you, man," Cliff said, giving Eli a nod.

"Bye," Claire croaked.

"Are you all right?" Zoe asked her. "You look funny."

Claire's skin began to lose its deathly hue when she looked at Zoe. She cleared her throat. "Yes, yes, fine."

"That was a cute baby," Zoe said.

"*Mm-hm*," Claire said. She turned to Eli. "Thanks for doing that," she said, her voice quiet in the crowd and her face serious.

"Anytime."

"Claire?" Zoe said.

They both turned to her.

"I feel sick."

They all three looked at the half-eaten bag of cotton candy.

• • •

Back in her kitchen, Claire accepted a mug of tea from Eli with shaking hands. Her hands *never* shook. Shaking hands was not in her job description.

But seeing Cliff again, with his family—damn. Of course she'd run into him from time to time. They'd nodded or said a brief hello, but they didn't *talk*. Not really. And, of course, Claire had spied a pregnant Marie here and there around town, from a distance, always impossibly elegant with her endless collection of scarves and perfect empire-waist maternity dresses with wedge heels. That had been hard enough. But she'd never seen the baby, or all three of them together.

The baby. The baby. She was . . . luscious. Perfect. A baby from a mail-order catalogue for angelic, half-French, splendidly healthy, stunningly gorgeous babies.

She slurped some herbal tea and burned her upper lip.

"You okay?" Eli asked.

"Oh. *Mmm-hmm*. Tea's still too hot."

"I'm not talking about the tea."

She waved him off, but a lump formed in her throat. "That

was a really cute baby," she whispered. "Margot. A stylish name."

"I thought she was kind of ugly."

Claire snorted and swiped the beginnings of tears from beneath her glasses. "No, you didn't."

They stood silently for a minute.

"I was supposed to have a baby by now. I'm thirty-five. We were going to start trying right away."

"He's an idiot, and his shoes were stupid."

"He was the salutatorian."

Eli raised an eyebrow.

"He was!"

"Who was the valedictorian?"

She looked away and took a slurp of tea.

"You?"

She shrugged.

"I see. Hot."

"Exactly. I am not hot. I am smart. And I just thought . . ." She felt the tears coming, damn them. "I just thought smart and fairly cute"—she tried to sniff the tears back into herself—"would be good enough."

"I think you're hot."

"No, you don't."

"I don't?" he said.

"I'm passable. Somewhat cute. I know what I am."

He closed the distance between them, only casting a fleeting glance toward the back of the house toward where Zoe had disappeared into her room.

And he kissed her like she was way more than cute.

• • •

Monday morning marked Claire's first dose of reality with a child to take care of. She was supposed to be at work in twelve minutes, and Zoe seemed to be practicing some sort of mindfulness shoe-putting-on meditation. Slooowwly put on one shoe, paying attention to the feeling of the shoe sliding up the skin of your foot as you do. Then breathe into the shoe, letting yourself fully experience the shoe. Now, with your second foot, see if you can slow the process down even more. Really be present in your body. Feel your foot.

Claire was not breathing into her shoes. Every breath felt like it might explode her lungs. They had to get to Haven Springs Middle School, get through that horrendous parental traffic, then she had to get all the way back to the hospital and get parked and get to the locker room. Eleven minutes.

Claire had been late for work exactly once before—the day the hundred-year-old tree fell across the road in front of the hospital. She'd finally abandoned her car and climbed over the tree, putting only one minor snag in her scrubs, so, come to think of it, she'd only been about ninety seconds late that day.

Zoe tied the second shoe and started walking toward the back of the house.

"Zo! Wrong way. The front door is right here."

"I forgot my social studies homework."

Claire laced her fingers together and touched them to her forehead. "Look for it!" she called as she walked toward Zoe's bedroom.

Zoe was staring at her bed.

"What!

"I'm *looking*."

A hot bubble of irritation expanded in Claire's chest. She snatched the homework from beneath a half-eaten banana on the bedside table and shoved it at Zoe.

Zoe flinched, her face paling.

Claire apologized, feeling like an excellent candidate for worst human of the day, and they got in the car with no further conversation. Ten minutes after her scheduled arrival time, Claire finally arrived at work.

• • •

Eli watched Joyce scrubbing Claire's already-clean refrigerator and wished Claire would tell her to stop. He was on the verge of telling Joyce himself, but he could see by the look on

Claire's face they were about one minute away from meltdown, and besides, this was the first time Joyce had been back since The Building of the Fence.

So he shut his trap and kept it that way.

Zoe was hiding behind one of the closed doors in the back of the house.

Every once in a while, Claire would catch his eye, and he'd make a funny face, but it wasn't helping much.

When the doorbell rang, he was relieved to get out of the kitchen, and went to the door himself. A youngish-looking cop stood in the doorway.

"Help you ?" Eli asked.

The guy just stood there looking sweaty and like he might throw up.

"Kevin?" Claire asked, emerging from the kitchen. "What's wrong?

It took him a minute to answer, during which time he rocked back and forth on the balls of his feet. "Carolyn Stamper sent me over here."

Claire's face fell, and Eli felt his adrenaline kick in.

"Is everything okay? Did something happen?" Claire asked.

He nodded. "She's fine. Was just getting released from the hospital. Said she'd call you. But that's not why I'm here."

"Okay . . ."

Eli went to stand behind Claire, put his hand on her shoulder.

"I'm here to . . . To, uh, offer my condolences," Kevin said. "To, uh, inform the family that one Amber Anderton was found dead last night."

Eli heard a small noise from behind him, a kind of whimper, and he turned to see Zoe standing in the doorway from the hall. *Shit.* Claire should have been the one to tell her, or he could have told her. But she shouldn't have heard it from a stranger.

"Is that her mother?" Joyce asked.

Eli wondered if he'd be allowed to gag Joyce. Just for a few minutes.

"What are you going to do *now*?" Joyce asked Claire.

"*Shh*," Claire told her. She went to Zoe and wrapped both arms around her.

"What is she supposed to do *now*?" Joyce turned on the cop.

Kevin looked down at his hat. "I was just sent to tell you. I don't know anything."

"It's fine, Kevin. We'll figure it out," Claire said. She squeezed Zoe's shoulder. "Let's get you some warm tea."

"I'll get it," Eli said.

"I knew something like this would happen," Joyce said.

Zoe's tears were starting now, and Eli tried to steel himself and stay neutral, so he could be useful.

"This is quite the news," Joyce said. "Obviously we need to find another . . . *situation* . . . for the *situation* in question."

"Mom!" Claire said. "Zoe, would you like to lie down in your room for just a minute, while Eli makes you a cup of tea and puts a muzzle on my mother?"

"I'm just saying," Joyce said.

"Mom!"

"All I was doing was talking about the *situation*."

"That's it, Mom. Seriously. That. Is. It." Claire was really mad now.

Joyce threw her hands up in the air.

"All righty," Eli said, and they all stopped and turned to look at him. "I'm walking you home now," he said to Joyce.

"I need to finish up in the kitchen," Joyce protested.

"I'm walking you home now," he said again. "It'll be fine."

"Call you later," he said to Claire, and took Joyce by the elbow.

CHAPTER 18

The day they buried Amber Anderton was too bright for the occasion. The unusually clear April sun was an aggressor, beating on them, blinding them, pricking Claire's armpits with heat and fury.

How could Zoe's mother have left her like this?

Her death seemed to Claire like a choice. Abandoning your child to party with a man you'd just met? Why? How? Who could do such a thing? An overdose seemed like the logical next step in that dangerous game, and Claire blamed the woman in the coffin for that.

Claire had paid for the burial, since there was no one else to do it. The funeral director had offered cremation as an option, but Claire had thought it would be good for Zoe to have a grave to visit, a place where she knew where her mother was. Finally.

Claire and Eli flanked Zoe now, since there'd been no one else—no one Claire could find, anyway—to invite to a memorial service at ten o'clock on a quiet Wednesday morning. But Zoe needed this closure, even if the near-zero attendance was sad in its own way.

Pastor Flynn had taken her place in front of the casket, and Claire, Zoe, and Eli stood on the opposite side of the ugly gaping hole in the ground.

Zoe was unnaturally still between them. Claire held Zoe's right hand and Eli held her left. Zoe's hair was brushed, and she was showered, with brushed teeth, but she'd been lethargic this morning, and when she'd emerged in the kitchen wearing jeans and a knit top instead of the dress they'd bought, Claire had opened her mouth to say something, but then closed it. Why shouldn't Zoe wear jeans to the burial? There was no reason to dress up.

"Dearly beloved," Pastor Flynn said. "We are here today to

commemorate the life of Amber Paige Anderton. We turn to our heavenly father for comfort, and we turn to each other as well to extend and receive comfort. In Philippians four, verse seven, the scripture says, 'And the peace of God, which passeth all understanding . . .'"

Claire glanced over at Zoe, who remained motionless. Zoe did not cry.

After the speech, Pastor Flynn asked Zoe to shovel the first dirt over the casket. Zoe stepped forward and picked up the shovel. The dirt hit the casket with the faintest sound, and Claire swallowed back tears.

Zoe stood for a moment, staring at the casket, then turned back toward Eli and Claire with wooden movements and dull eyes.

Eli reached out and took Zoe under his arm, and Claire put her arm around him in gratitude, and for comfort.

"May the peace of God be with you," Pastor Flynn said.

Back in Eli's rental car, the air conditioner chilling their sun-hot skin, they sat in silence.

"Where do we go now?" Claire knew she was voicing everyone's question.

"Let me take you girls to lunch," Eli said.

Claire nodded.

"Then let's do what anyone who knows about hard times does on a bright sunny day," he said.

"What's that?" Claire asked.

"Draw all the curtains and sleep."

• • •

Claire called in sick for a second time so Zoe could stay home from school another day. The hospital staff were probably talking. Claire had *never* called in sick to work. Not ever. Not once. She had countless sick days built up, but it always felt wrong to use them, even if she really was under the weather—she'd have been letting too many people down. She figured it was part of what you signed on for as a doctor—you just had to buck up and get the job done. But really, it wasn't just about being a doctor. She'd always dragged herself to class in college, no matter how late she'd been up the night before.

She'd always done exactly what she was supposed to do.

But when she looked down at Zoe's sweet sleeping face, she felt fine about taking an illicit day off. Pippa was curled in the crook of Zoe's arm, snoring softly, her little dog belly exposed like a pale pink water balloon, rising and falling.

At ten a.m., Zoe was still sleeping, which Claire thought was a small mercy from heaven, for Zoe's own sake.

Another mercy—Holly was bringing dinner over that night, and they'd have some cheerful company and some good food, something other than spaghetti or eggs. It would be a big relief, because gloom had been hanging in the air like dust.

Zoe living here wasn't real life, wasn't sustainable, and they both knew it, and it was the unspoken thing between them. It wasn't like Claire could keep calling in sick indefinitely, but she didn't know how to talk to Zoe about it. Heck, she didn't know how to talk to herself about it.

And what was she going to do, call the social worker and return Zoe like a wrong-size sweater?

She'd have to. She just didn't know how. Couldn't imagine it. Couldn't let herself imagine it.

What did single mothers do? Was there after-school daycare for twelve-year-olds? Band practice that stretched until the parents picked the kids up? Or did the kids come home, ramble around the house alone, unsupervised? Was twelve old enough for that? It was official. She knew nothing about mothering a twelve-year-old.

She sighed and pressed the button on the electric teakettle.

One of Zoe's library books—Tolkien—sat tattered and bookmarked on the island. Evidence of Zoe was everywhere.

When Claire was a real mother, things would be much more organized and clear-cut. She would plan in advance for maternity leave. She would figure out what she needed to do to create a family-compatible schedule.

"Hi."

Claire jumped at Zoe's small voice behind her.

"Good morning," Claire said. "Does Pippa need to go out?"

"She's still asleep."

Claire smiled at that. "You hungry?"

Zoe shrugged and chewed a nail.

"Zo. Nails."

"Sorry." Zoe dropped the hand to her side.

They stood silently for a moment. It was going to be a *long* day until Holly and Ryan got there. What were you supposed to do with a newly orphaned child? Offer to talk about it? Play Monopoly? Claire was in over her head.

The doorbell rang, and Claire felt a palpable relief, thinking that it might be Eli. Eli always seemed to know how to be easy around Zoe, even when Claire was stiff with uncertainty.

The front door opened before Claire could get to it.

"Girls?" Eli's sonorous voice wafted toward her like music. "I'm taking you to the movies."

Claire exhaled her relief.

Before the matinee, they had giant mounds of pancakes at Maude's diner, and Claire didn't say one word about sugar.

Eli told Zoe a story about the time his bassist set his drummer's suitcase on fire over a dispute about a song. Zoe had laughed a real laugh, and Claire felt her worry ease a little.

After they ate, Claire found herself, in the middle of a bright weekday, sunk into the dark hush of a cinema, sandwiched between Eli and Zoe. The matinee rerun of the day was *Shrek*, and when it began, a baby wailed nearby. The mother stood and jiggled the baby, trying to shush him, while her two toddlers sat rapt, staring up at the screen.

Claire smiled and took put her arm around Zoe, and her hand on Eli's thigh, realizing she'd smiled at the sounds of a baby without feeling that familiar stab of pain.

• • •

After the matinee, they drove the half hour back from the

cinema in Springfield.

Claire watched as Eli stared into her refrigerator. "It's bunny food. Carrots and lettuce. How are you not hungry all the time?"

"We have eggs."

"True." He snapped his fingers.

Ten minutes later, they were having a very passable stir fry Eli had concocted out of spaghetti noodles, the bunny food, eggs, and a few of packets of leftover take-out soy sauce he found in one of the drawers.

Claire had been so frightened she wouldn't be able to get Zoe through these days of early grief. And she hadn't gotten her through them, not really—Eli had. Eli had gotten them both through, always knowing when to show up, what to say, what they needed right then.

She watched him washing dishes in her lavender floral apron and bit her lip in a wistful smile. Next to him, Zoe dried dishes, and they both laughed over something he whispered to her. For a guy who was so certain he wasn't playing for keeps, he was definitely a keeper. He'd be a great dad.

Claire returned her attention to her iPad, to HandleIt, to her looming work schedule, to the real life she had to go back to.

Tomorrow morning she'd ease back into work with a ten-hour shift. And in a couple nights, Zoe would spend the night with Holly while Claire pulled an all-nighter. Sooner or later, Claire would have to call Barbara, to find out about Mrs. Stamper, and the next steps. Reality would have to be faced, returned to.

"You can't like Stephanie Kelly just because Claire does," Eli was saying to Zoe. "I won't allow it."

"You can't *disallow* it," Zoe said, rolling her eyes, but smiling.

"It's too much for the karmic balance, for two people in one house to like her," he said.

"Karmic balance?" Zoe said, laughing.

It was so good to see her laugh.

"Whatever," Eli said. "It's not actual music."

"What is it, then?" Claire said.

Eli thought for a split second. "Electronics in a tin can with auto-tuned caterwauling."

"What about that . . . that . . . Radiohead you made me listen to?" Claire asked, pushing aside HandleIt and resolving to forget real life for another few hours.

He gave her a pained look. "As in, Radiohead, the most important band since the Beatles? How can someone have to *make* you listen to that?"

"I don't really get how it's important."

Eli turned toward Claire, a soapy wooden spoon in his hand, his long dark hair hanging down over the straps of the lavender apron. He pretended to stab himself with the spoon. "You're killing me. The child cannot grow up like this. She has to have exposure to something other than Stephanie Kelly. It's like trying to grow up without vegetables."

"We like Stephanie Kelly," Claire said innocently, taking a dainty sip from her water glass.

He groaned, waving the soapy spoon around. "She does it on purpose, Zoe."

"I know," Zoe said happily.

Claire's phone rang, and she glanced down at it. Barbara. She felt her face darken and turned away so Zoe wouldn't see it, and clicked her phone to silent.

But Eli and Zoe had both seen her face, and the good mood in the room deflated.

"What?" Zoe asked.

"Nothing," Claire said. "I let it go to voice mail."

Another long beat of silence followed. They all knew they were living on borrowed time. Reality loomed, ready to snatch it away.

"Zo—" Eli said, "finish drying these while Claire plans out the rest of her life on the iPad, and I'll make you a playlist that'll make you cool in high school."

"Cool?" Zoe laughed, snapping out of her concern over the phone call. "Never gonna happen."

"Trust me," Eli told her.

• • •

Holly and Ryan arrived a little after six with a roast chicken, some mashed potatoes, and a broccoli casserole.

Pippa stared up at the counters with one round brown eye, one icy pale blue one. Her nose twitched and her tail circled in a slow hopeful wag.

"Oh, Holl. This all looks so good. How do you do it?"

Holly shook her head. "It's easy."

"That's what you think."

"Where's Eli?" Holly asked.

Claire shrugged.

Holly put her hands on her hips.

"What? He doesn't live here. I assume he's at home. Doing whatever musicians do when they're at home. Listening to music that makes people want to kill themselves?"

"How's Zoe?" Holly lowered her voice.

Claire peeked into the living room to make sure Ryan and Zoe were fully occupied with their chess game.

It was a little too quiet to risk talking about Zoe, so Claire shook her head.

"How are things with Eli, then?" Holly asked.

"He's been really great." Claire paused. "He's gotten us through this week like he had some kind of psychic powers to know exactly what Zoe needed at every turn."

Holly grinned. "I wonder how those psychic powers play out in other venues?"

Claire choked a little on her wine. She felt herself flush, glanced toward the living room where the kids played.

Holly tapped her foot, grinning.

"Nothing to report. We've been a little busy parenting." Claire paused. "I mean, not parenting, but, you know."

"I believe I do," Holly said, grin widening.

"Honestly, as beautiful as he is, I haven't had time to think about it." And it was true, she hadn't been thinking about sex . . . much. Everything else had taken over, these last few days. But, now that she did think of it, she felt her flush deepen.

"Don't forget, Zoe's spending the night with me Sunday night." Holly waggled her eyebrows.

Claire's wine glass froze halfway to her mouth. Holly was right. And Claire must have been *mega* preoccupied not to remember this. Her insides did a slow somersault, waking up after a few days off.

"And I'm taking Zoe to school Monday morning. That means she won't be back with you until the afternoon. I *know* you can find an hour or two in there somewhere."

"I think . . . you're right," Claire whispered, awed at the possibility. And frightened. And thrilled. His touch last week, the way he looked at her, his skin, his smell, it all came back to her in a rush. She was actually going to let herself have something she hadn't planned five years in advance. Something just for herself, just for the pleasure of it.

"*Mmm hmm,*" Holly said, studying Claire's face, eyes twinkling, taking a grape from the bowl on the counter and popping it into her mouth.

After dinner, Claire loaded the dishwasher while Holly sat at the table with a glass of wine and a piece of dark chocolate. "Zoe looks good. She doesn't seem as upset about her mom as I thought she would."

Claire inclined her head toward the bedroom, where they could close the door to talk.

She clicked the bedroom door closed behind them, then listened for the sound of the Zoe and Ryan's muffled conversation from the living room.

They both sat on the edge of the bed.

"Barbara called."

"And?"

"She left a voice mail. I didn't want to pick it up in front of Zoe. She wants to know what I want to do. Mrs. Stamper is still pretty weak, so she's going to Little Rock to stay with her daughter for a few weeks. Barbara says she needs a decision by Monday, since I'm not technically approved and Mrs. Stamper won't be available. I mean, I could get approved, but she needs to know."

"Shit," Holly said.

"Yup." Claire let out a breath, pushed her glasses up on her head, and squeezed her eyes.

"Zoe's pretty cheerful, all things considered. Really cheerful, actually, but when the phone rang I think she knew. It's like she's waiting for something like this—she gets kind of anxious when my phone rings. Plus I have a terrible poker face."

"That you do. What did you tell her?"

"I've been avoiding the whole subject," Claire said. "I don't know what to say."

"What *are* you going to do?"

Claire looked at her. "What do you mean? I don't have a choice here. You know that."

"I just thought there must be some way—I mean, it just seems like she belongs with you. Like it was fate, or something. I don't know."

"Holl . . ."

"I'm sorry, but I believe in that stuff. I do. I know it's not scientific. I know it's superstitious of me. But I do, I believe in destiny. And you and Zoe, well . . ."

"There's just no way. I can't quit my job and take her to live in a box down by the river."

"Oh, come on. It wouldn't be like that."

"You know that's not true. Haven, two thousand people. Two thousand people and seven private practices. *Seven!* There's not room for one more. I'm lucky to have this job in the E.R."

"But you can't just send her away, either."

"I can't *not*. I'm trapped. The whole box down by the river? Not really a joke. It would be the only way I could keep her—if I didn't have the job I have. And I'm pretty sure I'm in a little deep for a career change." Claire set her wineglass on the bed-side table and straightened her glasses. "Not to mention that whole business I keep reminding you of—*I have no idea how to parent a twelve-year-old.*"

"Sure you do."

"I assure you, I don't. These last few days—it's all been Eli—not me."

"Babe . . ." Holly reached for Claire's hand. "I have to tell you something."

"Will I like it?"

"I don't know, and that's the damn truth. But the thing is, I *know* I'm right about this."

"What is it?"

"You'll regret it forever if you let Zoe go."

Holly's words hit her like a punch. She hung her head.

"I have a sense, Claire. You know when I get a feeling like that it's never wrong."

Claire wouldn't go quite that far, but the reason she couldn't answer, and her eyes were full of tears, was that she had that sense too. But she had no choice. All this time, she'd thought she so desperately wanted children, and now that she had one, she realized there was no room in her life for one. But if she had a child the regular way, there would be time to plan for that, to make her career fit with motherhood.

"I would help you," Holly said.

They heard footsteps shuffling in the living room, and real-ized simultaneously the kids were no longer engaged in their chess game. They both fell silent.

"Let's have a little more wine," Holly said, patting Claire's hand again. "This will all get worked out. Oh, Operation Dan and Marla was a big success, by the way. Lord that woman can get loud."

"Loud?"

Holly gave Claire a look. "Yep. Like *that.*" She kept on talk-ing as they walked back to the kitchen, but Claire barely heard what she was saying. She cast a glance toward the living room to check on Zoe, who looked content and blissfully unaware of what was coming.

"Are you listening to me?" Holly asked.

"Sorry," Claire said.

"Sheesh," she said. "Might as well be talking to myself. I *said*, don't forget the Douse Haven benefit is in a week. For the library fire." She made a hand microphone and sang into it, waggling her eyebrows. "*Eli.*"

• • •

Late that night, Claire was flopped on her couch going over her list for the next day when she heard a soft rap at her front door.

She padded over in her socks so as not to wake Zoe.

"I saw your lamp on," Eli said. He leaned against the doorjamb looking impossibly beautiful, and Claire's heart leapt to see him. To be alone with him, after all these days of prioritizing Zoe, it was . . . scary. It was thrilling.

"Can I come in?"

She nodded, biting her lip, smiling.

They sat on the couch together, and Eli took her hand. Claire had thought she was exhausted, but now that she sat here with him, thighs resting next to each other, her small hand in his large one, she felt wide awake.

"What have you been up to? I haven't seen you in seven whole hours," Claire said.

He grinned at her, and brushed a soft kiss across her lips.

"Song six," he said.

"Really?"

He nodded, took her face in his hand, and ran his finger along her jawbone.

"How many do you need?" she asked, trying to stay focused despite his touch.

"Ten. Eleven. Something like that." He studied her eyes and continued his tour of her jawbone.

"How is this one?"

"The best one yet."

"At the rate you're going, you'll be finished long before June."

He nodded. "Fine with me. More time for you."

She smiled, returning his gaze, and he kissed her. They needed to keep it tame, with Zoe asleep two rooms away, but their fully clothed kiss felt far from tame. It was slow and thorough and delicious. Claire felt herself melting into his chest, wrapping her hands through his hair, pulling him as close as he could be.

She loved him.

It was so clear to her now.

He'd been their hero this week, always knowing how to make Zoe feel better. He would be a wonderful father. He was a wonderful man. He was the best man she knew—kind and strong and honest, and creative and funny and sweet. She loved him.

While he kissed her like the way he was kissing her, like he loved her, too, the knowledge of how good this was, how real it was, began to grow in her chest, a glowing heat that expanded bit by bit. Her chest grew so full it felt it might burst with joy.

She found herself smiling into the kiss, and he pulled back for a moment, still holding her face in his hands, and looked at her.

Their eyes met, and there it was. Love. She'd never been more certain of anything in her life. It was undeniable. Wonderful. The best thing that had ever happened to her. And she wanted to say it out loud.

Her joy deflated a tiny bit when Joyce's voice inserted itself into her head. *Men only love you if they have to pursue you. You can't make it too easy for them.*

She sighed. She didn't want to play games.

"What is it?" he asked, still gazing at her.

"Can we get back to the kissing? Sometimes my mother's voice haunts me at inappropriate moments, but I'm sure you can exorcise her."

"Oh, I can handle that job."

And he did. After a few minutes, she was so lost in the kiss she couldn't have told him her mother's name.

CHAPTER 19

Of course Claire was at work when the call came from the school. When she didn't answer her cell, they called the main number of the hospital.

"Dr. Taylor, line three," scratched over the loudspeaker. When she got to the desk, Fox was standing there watching her. She ignored him and picked up the call.

It was the school. Zoe was fine, but she had thrown up during school hours, and it was policy that she remain out of school for twenty-four hours after vomiting.

Claire's eyes slid to Fox, who was vibrating with interest in her conversation.

She'd call Holly to see if she could pick Zoe up.

"Thank you, Mr. Howard," Claire said. She pulled out her cell phone.

Fox was staring her down. He could smell a family crisis like a drug dog.

"What's going on?" he asked.

"Nothing. I just need to arrange pickup for—" she stopped. "I just need to make a quick phone call, then I'll be finished."

She dialed Holly's number before he could protest.

"I was just about to call you," Holly said. "Can you pick up Ryan up after school? I drove up to Springfield to visit Mom for a few hours—she was stressed out about her Medicare paperwork."

Claire squeezed her forehead.

Fox watched her.

"Sure," she said. "I'll make sure he gets home."

Claire turned her back on Fox and called Eli. Voice mail.

Which left one person to call.

"Mom? I really need a favor."

• • •

When Claire got home from work, Ryan was sweeping her front porch.

"You're sweeping."

He nodded and kept at it.

"Couldn't pay for your meal? Broke my Mizzou coffee mug?"

"You're mom's kinda interesting."

Claire sighed.

Zoe was polishing furniture in the living room.

"I thought you were sick?"

"I'm not sick. I just made the mistake of eating the cafeteria chicken."

"Did Mom *think* you were sick?" Zoe shot Claire a look— would it have mattered?

"Mom?" Claire called.

"In the kitchen!" Joyce's voice rang out.

Her hands were in a large bowl full of soapy water. The sleeves of her yellow tracksuit were pushed up past her elbows.

"What's going on?" Claire asked.

"Oh, just washing the chandelier."

"*Washing the chandelier?*"

"Oh, it really needed it. I bet it hadn't been done in fifteen years."

Claire glanced toward the kitchen table. Sure enough, there was a stepladder and a naked chandelier. "I bet you're right about that."

"I already did the dog."

"The *dog?*"

"When was the last time you bathed that thing?"

It was then that Claire noticed Pippa sitting at Joyce's feet, slightly damp and shivering, but at least not hiding under the bed.

"We'll need to get these crystals good and dry before we hang them back on the fixture," Joyce said. "Otherwise they'll spot."

"Of course." She stared at her mother. "I see the children are earning their keep."

"Oh, yes," Joyce said proudly. "I have to say, I'm still not happy about staring out my back window at your privacy fence, but I am glad you called me today."

"Thank you, Mom. I appreciate your bailing us out. It was really nice of you." Claire sat down at the kitchen table, folded her arms on its surface, and planted her face.

"Oh, now. What's wrong? Bad day?"

Claire nodded into her arms.

She didn't look up as she heard Joyce sit on the stepstool beside her.

"What is it?" Joyce asked again.

Claire finally looked up. "The social worker wants an answer on Zoe. By Monday. And I can't figure out how to handle things like—like *this*."

"Well, it seems obvious—"

"Mom. Don't."

Joyce took the purple latex gloves from her hands and laid them across her aproned lap.

To Claire's utter amazement, she didn't say anything for a long while.

They sat like that, the weight of the thing hanging between them, for several minutes, until Zoe appeared back in the kitchen.

"Ryan got a text from his mother and made a run for it," she said.

"Wimp." Joyce put the purple latex gloves back on. "Did you finish dusting?"

Zoe nodded. Her face looked odd—mostly scared of Joyce (understandable), but also maybe a tiny bit proud.

"Okay, so now it's time—"

"To finish your homework," Claire interrupted.

"Girls?" Eli's voice echoed from the front door, stopping them all. "I brought takeout," he called.

Joyce made a little sniffing noise but said nothing.

His tall frame filled the doorway, reassuring and strong.

He set the takeout bags on the counter, gave Zoe a bear-hug-from behind, and said to Joyce, "I see you're turning the children proper."

Joyce flushed with pleasure.

"Proper as a sweatshop," Zoe muttered.

Eli laughed his rich laugh; Claire smiled; and Joyce turned pale. Then, to Claire's amazement, she smiled. "Well. Somebody had to do it," she said.

And then they were all smiling.

Just for a minute, like everything was going to be okay.

• • •

Two days later, Claire stood at Holly's kitchen door, poking her head in, calling out. "Holly? You home? Zoe left her suitcase."

"She's in the shower," Marla said, entering the kitchen with her ever-present enormous handmade tea mug. Dave followed close on her heels.

"Oh! I didn't know y'all were here. I would have knocked."

"It's all right," Marla said, smiling beatifically.

"Dr. T," Dave said.

He looked different. More self-assured, maybe? He wore a small but distinctly self-satisfied smile. And the hair was gone!

"Dave," Claire said, "you look great! You got a haircut?"

His hand flew to the back of his neck, now naked of its long waves of fuzz. "Yeah."

"You lost some weight too?"

His hand moved from neck to gut and rested there. "There've been some dietary changes."

"Hot dogs are not supposed to be a major food group," Marla said.

"But the ketchup—that's healthy, right?"

"Did you know raising animals for food takes up half of all water used in the United States?" Marla asked, setting her mug in front of the electric kettle and pressing the button.

"I didn't," Claire said.

"Plus the source for a lot of the hot dogs in the United States is factory farming."

They stood silently for a moment, until, mercifully, Holly appeared in the entryway in damp blonde curls and an ecru cotton spa robe.

"Did you hear the news?" she asked Claire.

"I'm not sure. Is it about hot dogs?" Claire said.

"No!" Holly rolled her eyes. "Hot dogs? No. Dave and Marla are *getting married!*"

"Oh!" Claire said. "Wow! Congratulations!"

Marla held out her hand. "It's an amethyst. The stone of St. Valentine and faithful love. Dave had it custom-made." She looked up at Dave adoringly, and he wrapped his arm around her, pulling her close, and kissed her full on the mouth.

"Wow," Claire said, more quietly. "I'm really happy for y'all."

"You're next," Holly announced.

Claire gave a small rueful laugh. "We'll see."

"Well. We need to get going," Marla said, taking Dave's hand in hers, smiling.

After the door closed behind them, Holly wasted no time. "Well?"

"Well, what?"

"*Well what?*" Holly put her hands on her hips. "Did you have sex?"

Claire plunked down in a kitchen chair. "No."

"Why *not?*" Holly howled. "Zoe was here all night! Then she was at school all day."

"I *just* left the hospital, and school will be out in less than forty-five minutes. We were short-staffed."

"Oh. Well. Shit."

"I'm starting to think it wasn't meant to be."

"You and your superstitious streak."

"Oh, like you don't have one."

"It's very small," Holly said. "No bigger than, say, Florida.

Want some tea?"

"Always."

Holly pulled a box of loose tea from a cabinet above the counter.

"So—Dave and Marla?"

"Dave and Marla." Holly grinned.

"You really are the master."

Holly huffed on her fingernails and buffed them on her robe.

"Who's next?"

Holly shrugged.

"Ah. Taking a break?" Claire asked.

"Nope. Just not telling."

"Holly!"

Holly bobbed her eyebrows and smiled a secretive little smile.

Claire's phone rang inside her purse. "I'll answer this, but then I'll weasel it out of you. Hello?" Claire said, the edges of laughter still in her voice.

"Oh. Barbara. Hello. I didn't recognize this number for you."

Holly set down the kettle and kept her eyes on Claire.

"Have you come to a decision?" Barbara asked.

Claire looked at Holly, who was watching her expectantly.

"No," she said. It was almost true.

"We'll need to decide something today. Give them our decision tomorrow."

Claire let out a pent-up breath.

"There's no way to get a few more days?"

"Not now that Mrs. Stamper is not in the state, and Zoe's mother is dead. We've pushed the limits already."

Claire thanked her and hung up.

"What was that?" Holly asked.

"They need a decision by tomorrow."

"Claire—"

"I need to go. I told Zoe I'd pick her up from school and get her vision tested. She thinks she might need glasses."

"You can't just give her back!"

Claire turned to Holly. Holly—all optimism and curls and huge brown eyes.

"Holl, I have to go," Claire said on a sigh. "I don't want to be late for school pickup. I don't want to disappoint Zoe."

• • •

Coco stared at the picture on her phone. Her stomach hurt, and not because of the innumerable nineteen-dollar cocktails she'd imbibed last night after the photo was texted to her.

She stared at the picture, the gnawing in her stomach amping up.

Apparently private investigators in slow-as-molasses Missouri had zero competition to hurry themselves along, but once they ambled their way around to doing their job, they managed to do it adequately.

Eli was at some kind of festival, and he was with a woman and a child. The girl had a bag of cotton candy, and they looked like a happy little family. Eli's arm was around the woman and he was laughing at something the little girl was saying.

The woman wasn't very pretty—certainly not model-quality. And those *glasses*. The glasses definitely would not be making an appearance in *InStyle*. And had she ever heard of *lipstick*? Blunt cuts? The twenty-first century?

But in the next picture, Eli was bent over to her, whispering in her hear, and the woman was smiling this smile, and Eli was looking this look, and they looked . . . intimate. Not in a way that Coco recognized. She'd never seen that look on Eli's face. She would remember.

At first she felt this sickening feeling she was pretty sure was jealousy, and it did not feel good. Not at all. It felt like the worst thing on earth, in fact. Unbearable. But luckily that was pretty quickly replaced by good old-fashioned, royally *pissed off*.

Pissed off, she knew how to handle.

Glasses Girl did *not* look like Eli's type. In fact, she looked like a total fucking goodie-two-shoes. Coco would obliterate her.

She stared at the photos. The woman had thick hair. Wavy. Sort of a caramel-color. Her face was all clean and girl-next-door. Was that what Eli wanted? God, she had to get ahold of herself. She was becoming some whiny insecure nobody over this *geek*?

She felt that horrible sick feeling again, and she'd do anything to make it go away.

She'd given Eli a chance to miss her. He'd had his little dalliance with the country girl.

Now it was time to get serious.

• • •

In the hush after Zoe went to bed, Claire and Eli sat in the living room by the light of a single lamp.

Her legs were tucked under her, and he sat on a chair flanking her, his face and hair half-lit by the small lamp.

"What are you going to do?" he asked quietly.

"I don't have a choice," Claire said.

He let out a breath. "I see your point. It's just . . . there's nothing?"

"I get the feeling Barbara thinks it would be better for Zoe to be elsewhere."

"*Why*?"

Claire shrugged. "I'm not permanent enough. Too busy. Single. Lots of reasons."

They sat silently for a moment.

"Zoe idolizes you," Eli said, his voice low and quiet in the mostly dark living room.

"Oh, I don't think so."

"Yes," he said.

Claire took off her glasses and rubbed her eyes with the palms of her hands. "That's kind of scary."

"No, you've been great for her. You *are* great for her."

"But it's not that simple. I have to do the right thing *for her.*

Take that afternoon when Zoe got sick—she needed to be picked up early from school. Routine school-mom thing, and I couldn't make it happen. That's why I had to call my mother. Because I couldn't leave work. Because Holly wasn't home. I—I didn't know what to *do*."

Claire shook her head.

"Maybe she'd better with a fresh start. Somewhere she's not known as the kid with the alcoholic mother who ran off and overdosed. Somewhere she never had to root around in the cafeteria garbage cans to make sure she had a few bites to take home for dinner."

"Haven Springs doesn't seem like that to me," Eli said.

"What do you mean?"

"I mean, it doesn't seem like anyone would hold a grudge against Zoe. It's more like the Island of Misfit Toys."

She threw a pillow at him. "Hey!"

"I meant that in a good way."

She shrugged. "I'm surprised what a hard time she's had."

"I am too. I mean, I guess the preteen years are tough any- where, but Haven Springs—it's not rigid, like I imagine a lot of small towns are. People are free to be who they are, and that's celebrated. By everyone other than your mother, or course."

"Yeah, true. You know, I think maybe she was trying so hard to hide her home situation, it probably prevented her from letting herself be known. She's such a good kid, but may- be a lot of people don't know it."

He nodded.

"I want what's best for her. I picture her with some blonde cookie-baking mother who's home every day at three o'clock who will plan slumber parties complete with mani-pedis."

"You could teach them to do biopsies. Like a party trick."

"You think I should keep her, don't you?"

He was quiet for a long time.

"Yes."

• • •

The next morning around nine, Claire was pulling a carton

of eggs from the fridge when the doorbell rang.

"I'll get it," Zoe called from the hallway.

Claire got up and met her in the living room, and they both stopped still when they saw Barbara standing in the doorway.

"I . . . ah, you're not at school?" Barbara asked Zoe.

Claire wrapped an arm around Zoe. "They don't go in until noon today. Half-day of in-service."

"I can come back another time," Barbara said.

"Why is she here?" Zoe asked, alert and suspicious. "Why are you here?" She turned on Barbara.

"I just came by to talk to Claire."

"You can talk in front of me," Zoe said, crossing her too-thin arms over her chest. "It's *about* me. I know something's going on. I have a right to know."

"I think Claire and I need to discuss everything before we present it to you, Zoe."

"I'm not stupid."

"Of course you're not. Nobody's implying that."

Claire stood there, helpless, not knowing what to say, feeling like the worst human on earth.

Pippa chose that moment to trot out of Zoe's bedroom, and when she spotted Barbara, commenced with the usual jetpack blast-off, adrenaline-spiked hair, and human-style shrieking.

Barbara took two steps back in alarm, colliding with the front door. "Oh my. *Oh my.* I forgot about . . . that."

Zoe didn't seem inclined to quiet Pippa, as she usually did, so Claire scooped her up, which Pippa tolerated, but she continued to whimper and strain toward Zoe.

"So you're here to take me away, right?" Zoe said.

"Why don't we all just have a seat?" Barbara said. "Zoe, it's important you understand no one is *trying* to take you away from Claire. It's just that the state requires action, now that your mother has passed away, and—" She turned to Claire. "The reason I stopped by today was to tell you that there's been some good news."

"Good news?"

"Yes. Very. There's a small group home for girls—only ten girls at a time—and they have a rare spot open. Openings don't come up often, so it's hard not to think of this as providential. I can't imagine a better situation for Zoe. The catch is, we would have to move quickly to get the spot."

"A group home?" Zoe asked. "Like Little Orphan Annie and Miss Hannigan?"

"Where is it?" Claire asked at the same time.

"It's in Overland Park. Right outside Kansas City."

"I don't understand. How is this better than a regular family home?" Claire asked.

"We have to consider the options that are actually available," Barbara said, and folded her hands in her lap.

Claire grew quiet.

"I can't stay here," Zoe said, her voice heavy with realization and resignation. "I should have known."

Claire felt the tears coming, but she knew she *had* to choke them back. She fought them so hard she couldn't speak. Finally, she managed, with her voice only shaking the tiniest bit, "Zoe, I want you to stay here. I just don't know how to work that out."

"Yeah," Zoe said. She kicked the floor.

Pippa was still whimpering and straining in Claire's arms, wanting to be in her rightful place on Zoe's lap, so Claire carried her over and deposited her there. She put her hand on Zoe's head, then under Zoe's chin. When Zoe looked up at her, she caught her eyes. "I don't want to let you go. It's not like that."

Claire could see that Zoe was fighting back tears, too, so she sat next to her on the couch, as close as she could, and put her arm around her.

"So, this group home." She turned to Barbara.

"Eileen Lawrence Home for Girls."

"Who's Eileen Lawrence?" Zoe asked.

"Was. She was an heiress who lost her own daughter to a

drug overdose, and she dedicated her life to helping girls who might not otherwise have the opportunity achieve stability and the academic success necessary to stand on their own two feet. She was passionate about what she did. When she was living, she even used her own home as sort of a halfway house and dormitory after the girls turned eighteen and left the group home. It's a very good organization."

"And Zoe's in?"

"It's not official, but we if we act, it can be. I have a friend there, and I pulled a few strings to get them to hold this for us. But we can't delay."

Claire let out a breath through pursed lips.

"I don't want to move away. I don't want to start another new school. I don't want to live with strangers." Zoe said.

"Can you excuse us for a moment?" Claire asked Barbara.

Claire led Zoe back to her bedroom, and patted the bed for her to sit down. They sat together, side by side, and Claire put her arm around Zoe.

"I think it's the right thing."

"I'll never get adopted."

"Zo. I don't know if that's exactly the point. If we can prevent you from being tossed around from foster home to foster home—and some of those homes might not be great—I think we should jump on the chance."

Zoe stroked Pippa's head for a long while until the little dog started to snore. "But it's just that . . ."

Claire waited.

"Why can't you keep me?" It came out on a strangled sob.

That did Claire in, and she couldn't fight back her tears. "I want to, baby. It's not that I don't want to. It's just that I'm trying to do the right thing for you and I have this job that eats my life and I can't be here for you and I don't want you to miss out on something great because of me." The last words came out sounding choked.

"Can't you get a different job?"

"No," Claire said. "Not right now."

"So that's it? I'll just never see you again? Or Eli?"

"Of course you will. It's only a few hours away. I'll come visit. And I'm sure Eli will . . . write you letters."

"And Holly and Ryan and Joyce?"

"Joyce?"

Zoe shrugged and bit her nail. "She's not so bad once you learn to stand up to her. And I heard Joyce telling some lady on the phone about me."

You don't say. Joyce was always a pill, but she was also always loyal, once she made up her mind. Claire wondered what had made her turn the corner.

"Joyce can ride with me to come visit you. If you really want her to." Claire pulled a couple of tissues from the bedside table, handed one to Zoe, and wiped her own nose and eyes.

Zoe just sat and cried silently, and Claire had never felt like such a failure, or so trapped.

"We need to tell Barbara yes so you don't lose your place. A chance like this won't come along again."

Zoe didn't look at Claire. She just stared down and continued petting Pippa.

When they returned to the living room, Barbara was waiting for them.

"We'll take the slot at Eileen Lawrence," Claire said.

"Wonderful," Barbara said. "It's the right decision."

Claire nodded. "What kind of dates are we looking at here?" she asked.

"Well, I was hoping for a little flexibility on that. I have to drive to Kansas City this afternoon anyway, and I need to get this paperwork filed with the state saying that Zoe is in legal custody."

"*This afternoon?*" Claire asked, horrified.

"You'll have several hours to prepare."

"*Hours?*"

"You could bring her yourself within the next forty-eight hours."

Claire let out a defeated breath. "I go in tonight for a thirty-six–hour shift."

Barbara raised her eyebrows disapprovingly. She might as well have said aloud, *See, your lifestyle isn't fit for parenting.* "I can come back in an hour or two," she said. "Give her some time to get packed, give the two of you time to say good-bye."

"No," Zoe said. "Let's just get it over with." She turned and went into her bedroom. Claire watched from the bedroom doorway as Zoe shoved her things into her duffel bag. She slung the bag over one shoulder and handed her backpack to Barbara. She scooped Pippa off the bed and held her in the crook of her other arm. "I'm ready," she said, her voice dead.

Claire pressed down a roiling mess of emotions and resolved to keep her face neutral.

Then Barbara said, "Zoe, I'm sorry so sorry, sweetheart. But there are no dogs allowed at the Eileen Lawrence home."

Zoe didn't make a sound. She didn't flinch. She didn't cry.

But something happened to her eyes in that moment.

They blanked out as though she'd just been drugged. They just went dead.

Zoe handed Pippa to Claire without looking at either of the adults or the dog, then turned and walked out the front door.

• • •

Pippa looked up at Claire. When Claire looked back down at her, her tail gave a hopeful little wave.

"This is not a good thing," Claire told Pippa. "You think she's gone to school for the day, but she hasn't."

Pippa's tail wagged at the eye contact and attention, even though she couldn't hear Claire.

Claire looked at the front door, which had just closed behind Zoe and Barbara.

She needed to put this behind her as quickly as she could. The pain was too much. She'd done the right thing, but sometimes the right thing to do was so painful it seemed wrong.

She went to Zoe's room and looked in, and the tears started

to flow in earnest. There was a library book on the nightstand, one she'd seen in Zoe's hands all week.

Weeping, she stripped the bed and took the sheets to the wash. She would just wash all this away.

Pippa used her sharp little teeth to latch onto the sheets, dragging behind Claire to the laundry room on her toenails, thinking it was all a grand game.

Pippa. She had to do something about Pippa. She couldn't keep her. You couldn't leave a dog alone for days on end just because you were at work.

Eli would watch her. He wouldn't mind.

But then Claire would come home, and she would see Pippa, and it would open the wound all over again. And Eli was leaving, and she'd still be working the schedule she worked, and Pippa would still need a home. It was better just to get it over with. Rip off the whole damn bandage, all at once.

She called Terri at the animal shelter and explained the situation.

"Little dog like that, they're the lucky ones. Get adopted right away."

"Oh, good." Claire said. "That's good news."

"She's deaf, you said?" Terri asked.

"Hard of hearing, yes. But very cute. With, uh, personality, too."

"Bring 'er on over. We can keep her in a crate behind the front desk until a kennel opens up, since it's you, Dr. T."

Claire thanked her, hung up, then tossed Pippa's squeaky bee, food and water dishes, crazy-rope (so named because of the head-shaking vengeance with which Pippa attacked it), and her donut bed, all into a couple of paper grocery bags.

Her heart felt like it had a lead vice locked around it, squeezing, but she knew she had to keep moving forward.

• • •

The Haven Springs animal shelter did not smell good. There was a teenage boy hosing everything down, but Claire doubted it would help all that much. Still, she knew Terri was good-hearted, and they were doing all they could with the funding they had.

Pippa was lolling sleepily in Claire's arms when they walked up to the door of the shelter. Only once they were inside and Pippa caught a whiff of the place did she start to stir, mistrustful, in Claire's arms. Her nose sniffed the air and her eyes darted to and fro.

"Hello, there, little one," Terri said, a big smile on her face, approaching Claire and Pippa.

Pippa reared her head back and let forth a series of staccato screams.

"Well," Terri said, halting, then taking half a step backward. "Well."

"I'm sorry about this, Terri. It all happened really quickly. Her owner, uh, her adult owner, died."

Pippa growled half-heartedly but allowed Terri to pet her.

"Think she'll come to me?" Terri asked.

Claire handed Pippa to her, and Pippa, the little slut, settled right against Terri's ample bosom just as easily as she had Claire's. Well, at least this was one less thing to feel guilty about.

"Our kennels are full, like I said, but I'll keep her right up here at the desk with me. Like I said, little one like this, she'll go right away."

• • •

Claire slammed her bag into her locker.

Anita, from behind her, said, "Somebody's grouchy today."

"What is it?" Claire snapped.

"Jimmy Beasley's back in Room 2 then Fox wants to see you."

"What is this, *Groundhog Day*?"

"Not 'til February."

"I meant the movie. Where you have to live the same thing over and over again."

Anita tapped a Dansko and raised an eyebrow.

Claire slammed the locker door shut. "Do I have time to urinate?"

Anita shrugged. "Depends how you want it to go with Fox. He's in a mood too."

"Great." Claire pulled the toggles tight on her Nikes. "Tell his majesty I'll hold it."

Anita stood there for a long moment, and Claire finally looked up at her. Anita was staring at her. "What?"

Anita cleared her throat. "Oh, nothing. Nothing at all." She gave the tiniest head shake and disappeared.

Fine, so Claire was usually little more polite at work. But most days she didn't surrender a dog and a child to homeless shelters before noon.

The three cups of tea she'd had on an empty stomach sloshed and threatened with heated menace.

Whatever. Everyone was entitled to a bad mood once in a while. She'd definitely earned it this morning.

Jimmy Beasley's wails were quiet today compared to his daughter's usual shouted pronouncements. "*Nobody* wants to fight you, Dad!"

Claire felt her jaw clench, and she averted her eyes as she walked past the daughter to find Mr. Beasley in room two. His ruddy face was tear-streaked, and as ever, his shirt struggled to hold in his massive, drum-taut, brick red midsection.

Claire patted his arm and made shushing noises, trying to comfort him.

Holly swished the dividing curtain back on its metal casters, surprising Claire.

"I didn't know you were on today," Claire said.

"I wasn't. Gloria needed off and I'm covering for her."

Claire kept patting Mr. Beasley's arm, and he was quieter. His daughter looked through the curtains, her face aggressive and hungry for more fighting, and she deflated a bit when she saw her father's calmer state. Claire inclined her head toward the hall, letting her know that's where she should stay.

"What's up at your house? Zo? Eli?" Holly asked.

Claire looked down and didn't answer.

"*What?*" Holly asked. "What happened?"

"Zoe's gone."

Holly stopped her IV preparations. Her mouth hung open and she stared at Claire.

Claire shrugged helplessly.

"What do you mean, she's *gone?*"

"There was a spot open for her at this really great place in Kansas City. It was a say yes right then or lose the spot sort of thing."

"What kind of really great place?"

"A home for girls."

"Oh, Claire." Holly's face was so full of disappointment, Claire didn't want to look at her.

"What was I supposed to do? Even the social worker thought she'd be better off there than with me as a single mom."

"Then she's wrong. Are you saying Ryan isn't okay because he has a single mother?"

"Of course not! You're a great mother."

"Damn straight. And so are millions of other single mothers. It's not like you're suggesting raising her with no food and a few beatings here and there. Single mothers can be great if they decide to be, better than being in a bad marriage. I'm doing it, and you can do it too."

Holly's words sounded so certain, so final, but Claire didn't feel certain of anything right now.

"Can you get her back?" Holly asked.

"I hear you on the single mom, thing. I do. But I'm not set up to take care of a foster child. I have a monster job and no family other than Joyce. This just isn't my plan. I've always said I didn't want to put another kid in the same situation I grew up in—no support network when the shit hits the fan. Only one parent, and if that one gets sick, you're screwed."

Holly said nothing, and her face was stony. Claire had tried to be diplomatic, but she could see she'd offended Holly. Irritation flared, sudden and hot in Claire's chest. Holly was supposed to be supportive, not judgmental. She was supposed to be making this easier for Claire, not harder.

Anita poked her head in. "Fox," she reminded Claire.

"Fine," Claire said through clenched teeth.

Claire looked at Holly, but Holly avoided her gaze, and Claire turned and left, following Anita toward the administrative offices.

• • •

By the time Claire got to Fox's office, her scrubs were itching, her hair was uncomfortable, and her heart felt like a fingernail bent backward. She was mad at Mr. Beasley's daughter; she was mad at Fox; she was mad at Holly; she was mad at herself. She was irritability incarnate.

She was, as Holly would say, cruising for a bruising.

She sat in the chair opposite Fox and tried to shut up and put a normal look on her face.

"Good news," Fox said. "I've come up with the perfect solution to our little problem."

"Little problem?" Claire repeated, barely able to whitewash the mocking from her voice. She looked at his stupid gold and diamond watch and his stupid golf shirt and his stupid smug face.

"Under-coding. Under-billing."

Claire sat back in her chair.

The gaudy gold watch glinted at her.

"Peer review," he announced. "We'll all check each other at the end of every shift."

"By *we*, do you mean the six already overworked physicians we have on staff? The six physicians we have to cover *all* the hours at the hospital?"

"Ah," he waved a hand. "It won't be much extra time."

"Extra time?"

"Just at the end of your shift, before you leave. It'll just be a brief meeting at the end of each shift. Coworkers can point out areas for improvement."

"Areas for improvement in getting money, not whether the procedures were actually medically called for?"

"The hospital needs to improve its margins, Dr. Taylor. Anyway, the best part. We'll have a little contest every month. Whoever comes up with the most missed opportunities—or missed codes, if you will—will be employee of the month. We'll have a framed photo."

Seven years of medical school for this. She felt like she might as well be wearing a Burger Derby apron. "A framed photo," she repeated.

"Yes. For just a few extra hours month—it should be a very good return on our investment."

Claire sat quietly for just a moment. She thought about why she'd gone into medicine. It was after her mother's illness. She'd wanted to help families in frightening situations, like Joyce and Claire had experienced when Joyce had cancer. She'd also wanted to make sure she wasn't vulnerable to another person's whims—that she would always have job security. She thought about what she'd given up that morning for the sake of this job. Zoe.

She looked into Fox's small, expectant gray eyes. She looked at his gold watch and his man-breasts under his golf shirt.

"I quit," she said.

• • •

"You did what?" Joyce said, bumping her head on the top of Claire's freezer as she turned to look at Claire in astonishment.

"I gave her back," Claire said.

"*Why?*" Joyce asked.

"Oh, Mom. Not now. I know, I know, I never do anything right, but just this once, give me a small break. You don't even *like* Zoe." Claire hadn't even told her mother about quitting her job.

"Sure I do," Joyce sniffed.

"Uh. No. We're not rewriting history on this one. You were

awful to her. And to me about her."

"I didn't *dislike* her. It's just that, I thought . . . she might be trouble for you. And I was sure she was going to interfere with your finding a husband and having a *real* family."

Claire raised her eyebrows and just stared at her mother.

"She's . . . Zoe is . . . not as bad as I thought she was."

"Gee. Great."

"Oh, Claire!" Joyce said, setting the casserole dish she'd been trying to squeeze into the freezer on the countertop. "Don't you see it?"

"See *what*?"

"Eli loves her."

Claire took her glasses off and squeezed her face.

"Oh, don't play all exasperated with me."

"Not playing, Mom. Assure you, not playing."

"You know what I mean."

"Really and truly, I don't."

"Well, if, at one point, I thought Zoe was going to hold you back from finding a husband, I don't anymore."

Realization dawned on Claire.

"You want me to marry Eli?"

"It's not a terrible idea. If he cuts his hair."

Claire shook her head in disbelief.

"Don't you like him?" Joyce asked.

"Of course I do."

"But he needs to stop wearing that ghost T-shirt. I don't understand it."

Claire shook her head, and on any other day, she might have laughed. "I'll be sure to tell him," she said.

• • •

Claire felt like crap. She stared at her DVD collection and wondered which movie might help her feel like anything slightly better than crap. Like maybe dirt. Or maybe just help her escape reality for a couple of hours. She eyed her choices—romantic comedies and science documentaries. Nothing looked good right now.

She could clean the bathrooms—that always made her feel better. And if it didn't, she'd clean the kitchen, which was already clean. And if that didn't work, she'd do something Joyce-like and find a chandelier to wash.

She took her cleaning bucket into the hall bathroom and started with the toilet. Then she moved on to the shower, scrubbing the white subway tiles to a wicked chemical shine.

She could not *believe* she'd quit her job with no plan. She didn't do *anything* without a plan!

She scoured the bathtub faucet with her green no-scratch abrasive pad.

Job . . . scrub. Zoe . . . scrub, scrub. Pippa . . . scrub.

The doorbell rang, and Claire cursed aloud. She pushed her hair back with the clean wrist cuff of her cleaning glove, and went to the door.

"Who is it?" she said, unwilling to take off the cleaning gloves to open the door herself.

"Me," Eli said.

"You open it," she said, and went back to the bathroom. She could hear him opening the door and following her, but she didn't turn around. That grout could really use a good going-over with a toothbrush.

She found the stiff toothbrush in her cleaning kit, opened the bathroom window, and sprayed down the seam between tile and bathtub. Then she moved to the top seam, where the tile met the wall above it.

"*Hmmm*," Eli said from the bathroom doorway.

"*Hmmm?*"

"I see your bathroom must have been very dirty. Flesh-eating bacteria?"

Claire stood over the bathtub, one Nike on the edge of the tub, and the other on the opposite corner. She turned her head over her shoulder to shoot him a look.

"What happened?"

"I gave away Zoe and Pippa and I quit my job."

The silence behind her went on for so long, curiosity finally got the better of her and she turned her head to look at him, grasping onto the towel bar for balance.

His mouth hung open in a way she'd never seen it do, and she could only surmise he was actually speechless.

"What?" she said, sounding surly even to her own ears.

He cleared his throat. "Uh, nothing."

"Don't judge me."

He held up both hands in innocence.

"Yeah, right."

"Where's the dog?"

"The pound."

"Shit. And you really quit your job?"

"I really quit my job."

"As in two weeks' notice?"

"No."

He whistled a low whistle.

"Hey, listen. I've gotta run. I'm in the middle of a good song. Don't want to lose my way."

"See ya," she said, and started in on the grout. Of course he didn't want to be around her right now. She was a despicable human and anyone in his right mind would flee.

• • •

Eli and Joyce pulled up to the animal shelter to wait for Terri.

Eli had called the friends he'd made in town—Dave, Holly, and Marla—to ask about who ran the shelter, but Dave and Marla didn't know, and Holly didn't pick up the phone.

But Eli had to reach someone, it couldn't wait, and he'd known his best bet, even if it was a little unpleasant, was Ms. Town Busybody herself, Joyce Taylor.

Sure enough, Joyce had a woman named Terri on the horn within ninety seconds, and after several minutes of Joyce bossing Terri around, she and Eli were now waiting outside the shelter, in the rain, in Eli's rental car.

"You're going to adopt the dog?" Joyce asked him for the

third time.

"No," Eli said, watching the driveway for Terri's approaching headlights.

"I still don't know why we have to come over here at night like we're robbing a bank." Joyce sniffed indignantly and shot him a sidelong glance.

"Because if someone else gets Pippa, it will be bad," Eli said.

"But you don't want her?"

"No."

"This does not make good sense. It's your hair, messing with your good sense. Don't even get me started on the ghost T-shirt."

Eli said nothing and watched for Terri's car.

"But you made me tell poor Terri it's an emergency to do with Claire. Are you planning to make a liar out of me?"

"Not planning to."

"Good," Joyce sniffed.

Finally, two headlights swung into shelter parking lot.

Terri got out in her red rain poncho and waved for them to come in. She extracted a heavy wad of keys from her pocket and unlocked the door.

A cacophony of awakened dogs protested the sound of the door, and the smell of the place hit Eli's nostrils like a fist.

"Did Dr. T change her mind about Pippa?"

"Yes," Eli said.

While Joyce said, "No."

Eli looked at Pippa, who was in a crate near the front desk, and his relief upon seeing her was nearly all-consuming.

Joyce whipped around on Eli. "Claire changed her mind?" Joyce asked. "But she doesn't have time to take care of that dog!"

"May I speak with you for a moment?" Eli said to Terri. "In private?"

Joyce huffed loudly, but didn't say anything, and Terri led him to her office and shut the door. That muffled the overall chorus of barking, but Pippa's distinctive shriek carried over all of it.

After Eli had explained the situation to Terri, she slowly nodded.

"I'd have to adopt her to you, officially, for the release papers," she said.

"That's fine. I just don't want her to go to anyone else."

"She almost did, today." Terri said. "Those little ones, they go fast. And she's cute to look at. We had two people interested in her, but I have to say, that little thing has a bark on her. I mean, all little dogs can be yippy, but this'un could audition for a horror movie soundtrack."

For the first time, Eli felt a little glad about that bark. He'd have to remind himself of that the next time she was actually doing it.

"I'm sorry, but it'll be ninety-two dollars. I have to charge you."

"It's fine," Eli said.

"Come on over here and fill out the papers, then."

He did so, then gave her an extra two hundred as a donation for the shelter.

He emerged with the dog, shoving some folded paperwork into his back pocket.

"Took long enough," Joyce said.

And then, God help him, he drove away from the shelter, back into Haven Springs, Missouri, in the dark, in the rain, with a bossy old bat and a crazy deaf dog.

• • •

Claire didn't knock on his door until the next morning, which surprised him. He would've bet on about three or four hours.

He opened his front door.

She looked better now, or at least not insane, and there was no bathroom cleaner in her hair.

She wore the jeans of hers that were his favorite, with just the right amount of cling, and the cardigan that always slayed him. She also wore, just as he'd known she would, a look of resolve. And peace.

"I have to go get Zoe," she said.

He nodded.

"You knew?"

He nodded again.

He watched her swallow her tears, then stepped onto the porch and pulled her in for a hug.

"You want to come with me?" she asked.

"Wouldn't miss it."

She smiled up at him, and he brushed a quick kiss across her mouth.

"Just let me get my wallet and keys."

CHAPTER 20

Claire stepped just inside Eli's door to wait for him, and when she did, she heard it. The nerve-assaulting, ear-insulting, hideous, horrible shrieking. Pippa!

Claire ran to her and scooped her up. She kissed her all over her crazy little head and started to laugh. Her whole body loosened with the relief of it. She'd planned to call Terri before they left, but she'd been dreading it so thoroughly, she'd allowed herself to put it off a few more minutes. She was so sure Pippa would have been adopted already, and she'd have to face Zoe without her.

She buried her face in the soft clean fur. "Oh, Pippa. I'm so sorry," she said.

"Ready?" Eli said.

"You got Pippa," Claire said.

He nodded.

"How . . . when?"

"When I saw you trying to remove your bathroom grout with an Oral-B, I knew you'd be going to get Zoe soon."

"I love you," she said through her tears.

For a split second, the words hung there between them, a spectacle, like a kinetic Calder mobile. Claire wanted to take them back, to say she'd meant to say thank you, or you're great, or . . . anything else. But she was frozen like someone had cast a spell on her, and she just stood there, unable to move or speak.

He came forward and wrapped his arms around her, and they stayed that way for a long time. "Let's go get our girl," he whispered.

Claire pulled back, laughed, and brushed at her eyes. "Yes," she said. "I can't wait to see her."

"Bring the devil dog," Eli said, and took his keys from his pocket.

• • •

Zoe couldn't have been happier to see Claire, Eli, and Pippa—in reverse order of importance, Claire suspected, but she was just fine with that. Zoe squeezed Pippa to her chest and Pippa's tail circled in a continual contented wag, like they'd never been apart. Zoe's eyes, unlike the last time Claire had seen them, were alight with life and happiness.

When Claire told Zoe she wanted to adopt her, Zoe had cried and cried, soaking Pippa's back, and then needing a tissue to blow her nose.

"Is that . . . okay?" Claire asked, hesitant.

Zoe nodded, tears still streaming down her face.

"Are you sure, Zoe? You don't seem to be."

"I'm just"—sob—"so"—sob—"relieved."

And then, Claire started to cry, too, and they held each other for a long time that way, a full body hug with Pippa sandwiched between them. They stayed that way for a long time—their first moment as a real family. After a few moments, Claire felt Eli's long, strong arms wrap around them both, and everything in the world felt right.

Janet Blankenship, the director of the home, called Claire and Eli into her office, and they left Zoe to sit with Pippa in the receiving room.

"The problem is," Janet explained, donning her reading glasses and looking at the paperwork in front of her on the desk. "Zoe is now in the legal custody of the Eileen Lawrence Home."

"I want to adopt her," Claire said.

"That's wonderful," Janet said, and set the reading glasses aside. Her face was kind but world-weary beneath her wave of grayish-brown hair. "But not quick."

"How long will it take?"

"It's not entirely predictable. Some cases sail through, others take longer for a variety of reasons—red tape, formalities, issues more serious than formalities, holidays. I can't give you an exact time frame. You should start filing immediately, and after that it's just a process. And a lot of waiting."

"Can't she come with me in the meantime?"

"It depends on the situation. And I understand she was staying with you before. But Barbara told me that wasn't an entirely legal situation—no paperwork."

Claire nodded.

"Unfortunately, we do need paperwork. But you could go through the system to become a legal foster parent. But since you're sure you want a permanent adoption, I wouldn't delay going forward with that paperwork concurrently."

Claire nodded again, and Eli squeezed her hand.

"Will she be living with both of you?" Barbara asked.

A long pause stretched out in silence.

"Yes," Claire finally said, not daring to glance at Eli.

"You'll both need to go through background checks and the whole nine yards. You're better off finding a local attorney in . . . where did you say you live?" She whipped the glasses back on and looked at the paperwork again.

"Haven Springs," Claire filled in.

"Haven Springs. Someone local will be much easier. So when you get home, you can get started," she said, giving them a smile and tapping her palms to her desk.

"Thank you for everything," Claire said. "Will you help me explain all of this to Zoe, so she knows I'm really coming back?"

• • •

On the ride home, neither of them said anything about Claire's answer to the social worker, her very brazen lie about their living situation. It had been a lie, right?

For a long time, Eli was so quiet, she was starting to wonder if she'd overstepped the line in some irreparable way.

But then Eli reached over, took her hand, and gave her a little wink, and Claire relaxed, so much so, that she fell asleep for the rest of the drive home.

Late that night, when they finally pulled up in front of their houses, he'd followed her into her house instead of his own. He hadn't asked, or discussed, or said anything at all. He'd just come home with her. Like that was where he belonged. She loved that they didn't talk about it. She loved that it was a given. She loved *him*.

She'd accidentally told him so, and that nagged at her, and it bothered her that he hadn't said it back, but in the days that followed, she could feel his love for her so strongly, it just stopped mattering whether he said it out loud or not.

They also didn't talk about it when they got in bed together for the first time. That, also, was a given, and Claire loved that too.

Finally, not because of any bargain they'd struck, or any kind of convenience, but because it was a love thing, Eli made love to her.

It was the sweetest moment of her life.

They were together now. A couple.

• • •

The next few days were everything Claire could have hoped for.

Eli left her house only to return to his rental for a forgotten book or some fresh clothes, and the days passed in a haze of sex and talking and laughing and movies and candlelit dinners in pajamas.

She loved the way, when they slept, Eli held her and didn't let go.

She loved the way he gazed at her when they made love, like she was the only person in the world for him.

He hadn't told her he loved her, but he didn't need to. He *did* tell her, all the time, but with his eyes. He just hadn't spoken the words.

But Claire knew it deep in her bones. She knew it like she knew her name or her own heartbeat.

"Order in or hit the grocery?" Eli asked, poking his head into the laundry room, where Claire was putting clothes in the dryer.

She was wearing one of his T-shirts and nothing else, and she looked down at herself. "Delivery," she said.

His eyes followed hers down to her bare legs, and his eyes lit up with that familiar look, and the next thing she knew, his hands were traveling up her legs and underneath the T-shirt.

And then she was on top of the dryer, and he was between her legs.

"Claire, I . . ." he stopped kissing her for a moment.

She waited.

He looked at her with such intensity, but no words came.

"What is it?"

"I think this is the happiest I've ever been," he said.

She felt his words as a physical ache in her heart, an ache from being so full of joy, it was almost more than she could hold.

• • •

Claire dressed for the Douse Haven benefit in khaki capris and a lightweight white linen blouse.

Eli was acting weird—drumming on any hard surface his fingers could reach, whistling, and just generally *noisy*.

"You nervous?" she asked.

He briefly paused the drumming on the kitchen counter in front of the coffee pot. "No. No, why?"

"You're fidgety."

"Just stage prep. A mental thing," he said.

"Ah."

For someone who made his living performing, he didn't seem even a little at ease with it.

He retreated to the corner of her living room he'd turned into his makeshift music area. Then he began the incessant guitar tuning and paper shuffling.

"We need to be there at five-thirty," he told her for the eighth time.

"Five-thirty," she called back from the bathroom, blotting her freshly applied lip gloss.

"Dave's picking us up in the van at five-twenty," he repeated for the twelfth time.

"Dave. Van. Five-twenty," she called back. She ran a brush through her hair and put her glasses back on.

He didn't relax much after they got to the festival. Bodies packed Basin Park, and people milled about drinking beer or herding toddlers or eating food truck burritos.

And, of course, Eli was the closing act, not the opening one, so they had a long time to go. He stood still amidst the moving crowd, stone-faced, his only movement his fingers drumming on his jeans.

A bluegrass act, Jenny and the Banjos, hit the stage first.

"Hello, Haven Springs!" Jenny called out, hoisting her mandolin into the air.

"Hello," the crowd shouted back. People whistled and clapped.

"We're here today to raise money to repair our library, so it's a very good cause," Jenny continued, beginning to strum her mandolin.

People cheered again.

"So every one of you who purchased a ticket to be here today is helping."

More cheering and whistling.

"But the fire department needs our help too. If you're here today because you love Haven Springs—"

She was interrupted by the cheers.

"Stop by the pledge table to go above and beyond your ticket. Murray Atkinson . . ." She pointed at Murray, bearded and tie-dye clad behind a fold-out table, and he waved. "Murray Atkinson will take your pledge."

People clapped and cheered and a few people wandered over to Murray's table.

"Now, Haven, are you ready to rock out?" Jenny called.

Three more bands followed Jenny's, and finally, it was Eli's turn.

Claire found she'd caught his case of nerves like a virus.

But then he took the stage.

Dusk had fallen, and the stage was now lit with a few spotlights. The crowd was hushed and waiting for Eli to speak. You could feel the taut energy of expectation.

He stood in the middle of the stage, surrounded by instruments, but with only Dave at his side with a bass strapped around his neck.

Another moment passed in silence.

And then it happened. He sang.

He left all the instruments silent, and just sang a cappella. His voice pierced the evening, and Claire was pretty sure, every soul in the place. She knew it pierced her own.

Grab your coat, love
The tarmac glows in the dark
It's that house you remember
The one
Where the birds sleep
The one
Where you fed me an apple

Everyone stood awed and silent.

Claire thought about the first time she'd heard those lyrics, how they'd seemed like nonsense to her, but now, they seemed like the truest thing she'd ever heard, and it was like Eli was singing them just for her.

Eli's eyes were closed and he held the microphone close to his mouth, grasping it in both hands on its stand. His dark hair framed his face, which looked otherworldy in the stage lighting.

His voice rang so clear and true, it was enough to crack Claire's heart in half.

And then he stopped singing. "This is for Haven Springs, which has been *my haven*, and for Claire, who has as well."

Claire's throat ached and her eyes welled with tears. She pressed her hand to her heart, and joined the crowd in giving an expectant cheer.

Eli picked up his guitar and strummed a couple of chords.

"I'm going to get to a couple of your favorites," he said, and everyone cheered. "But first I'm going to make you suffer through something new. You're my guinea pigs, Haven Springs."

Everyone went wild.

He played a song Claire had heard snippets of countless times, in her living room, these past few days. But the whole thing together, with Dave accompanying him on bass, was better than she could ever have imagined. Better than anything Eli had ever written.

"Here's another one for Claire," Eli said, and several people turned around to look at her, knowing smiles on their faces. Eli sang about finally finding home, and it was tough to tell whether he was singing about a woman or a place, with his enigmatic lyrics, but Claire was pretty sure it was both. Her heart swelled, remembering being in Eli's arms, the way he looked at her, the way they were one in those moments, and she knew exactly what he was singing about.

She let the tears stream down her face without embarrassment. It was far too beautiful not to cry.

The song ended to an avalanche of applause. Haven had had a lot of festivals and concerts, but never one like this. Eli's voice was majestic.

Eli waited for the applause to die down. "Okay. We got that done. Now what's that saying? Shut up and play the hits?" Eli asked.

The crowd around her laughed and waited.

Eli's stage presence was humble, almost reluctant, and it was impossible to take her eyes off him. It was impossible for anyone to take their eyes off him. "So I'm shutting up and playing the hits now," he said, and he gave his guitar a powerful strum, an opening chord apparently some people recognized, because half the people in the crowd went wild.

After a few more songs and two encores, he finally wrapped

up, to the protests of the crowd.

Claire was so proud of him, she felt she could almost burst.

When, a few minutes later, Eli found her in the crowd and kissed her on the lips, she didn't even care how sweaty he was.

"You were incredible," she said.

"You really were," a voice said from beside them, and they both turned.

Claire froze.

If it was possible, Coco Sky was even more superhumanly beautiful in person than she was in photographs.

Her skin was luminous, glossy, impossibly perfect, as was her white-blonde hair, which fell in a sleek, expensive-looking bob around her famous pink cheekbones. She had the face of an angel. Her flesh-colored silk tank top suggested—not subtly—nudity, and her perfect breasts were generous and braless beneath it. Claire's eyes traveled downward. Coco wore skin-tight waxed black pants with thigh-high black boots, the heels of which made her as tall as Eli. She slid her arm around Eli's waist. "Hello, lover," she said in a voice like silk.

Claire's stomach cramped painfully at the sight of Coco's closeness to him, the familiarity, his lack of protest. To give him credit, he appeared to be in a state of shock, but Claire still wished he would make some sort of grand proclamation right now. *Claire is the only woman for me!* That would do.

Claire realized gradually that you could hear Coco's name, repeated through the crowd as everyone talked about her: Coco Skye. Coco Skye.

Claire's cheeks burned as she looked at that arm around Eli's waist, knowing that all eyes were on them, talking about them.

Coco whispered something in Eli's ear, which she was tall enough to do, but rather than push her away, Eli just stood there looking like a deer in headlights.

"I'm Claire Taylor, by the way."

"Hi." Coco looked amused.

Eli still said nothing. Coco must really have some kind of

hold on him to upset his equlibrium like that. A wave of fore-
boding slid through Claire, ugly and nauseating.

"Are you ready to go home?" Claire asked him.

"Actually," Coco turned on Claire. "Eli and I need to have a
little chat, Chloe."

"Claire."

Claire looked at Eli, raising her eyebrows in an unpsoken
question.

He said nothing, still looking shell-shocked.

"I did come all the way from New York," Coco said.

After a moment, Eli finally spoke. "She's probably right. I'm
sorry, Claire. I'll call you later."

Clarie stood there, gaping, feeling like she'd been punched,
as they walked away from her.

That's how Holly found her.

"Are you okay?" Holly panted, breathless and worried, having pushed her way through the crowd.

Claire looked at her and let her face give the answer.

"Oh, Claire." Holly wrapped her arm around Claire's shoulders. "Let me walk you home, get you a cup of tea. Or a shot of
whiskey. Or something."

They hiked the steep streets from downtown back to Crescent Drive, and Claire found herself in her house, surrounded
by Eli's things, which had, over the last several days, managed
to insinuate themselves everywhere. He'd pretty much moved
in.

And Claire realized she felt better. Eli wasn't involved with
Coco. That was silly. He was living with *her*, with Claire. He
didn't want Coco. He loved *her*, Claire. He had very nearly told
her so—very nearly told half the town tonight, from the stage—
and she could see it in his eyes, and she could feel it in the reverence of his touch, in the way he gave himself to her so
completely. In the way he loved Zoe because Claire loved Zoe.
This was where Eli belonged, with her and with Zoe.

It was stupid and pointless to worry. Eli hadn't talked about

Coco much, but when he had, it was tight-lipped, terse, in a way that made it clear he viewed it all as a big mistake.

Coco's impossibly beautiful face, her almost inhumanly beautiful body, presented itself in an unwelcome mental picture. Her arm around Eli's waist. The way it rested there as if it were a familiar spot. How could any man resist beauty like that?

Claire let out a big sigh. "It's probably nothing," she said, taking the mug of tea Holly handed her.

"It's definitely nothing," Holly agreed. "Eli loves you. Anyone can see it."

• • •

They waited for Eli for an hour.

"Babe, Ryan is texting me," Holly said, breaking Claire's reverie of misery. "He needs homework help and it's his bedtime, and you know he'll stay up playing chess if I'm not there to force his skinny ass into bed. Then I won't be able to wake him up in the morning and I'll have to get him to the bus in a wheelbarrow."

Claire looked up at her, slack and barely listening.

"I'm rambling," Holly said. "I just hate to leave you."

"It's okay," Claire said.

"Please call me if you need me. Or if you want to talk."

Claire nodded, and set down the mug that had grown cold in her hands.

"Are the lights on next door?" Claire asked.

Holly poked her head out the front door. She turned back to Claire, biting her lip, and nodded.

"I'm going to bed," Claire said.

"Do you want to sleep at my house?" Holly asked.

Claire shook her head. Her heart felt like lead in her chest.

But he would be coming back. He would come back to their bed tonight, as soon as he could. Of course he would. They hadn't slept apart, not even for naps, since the first time they'd made love. There would be some logical explanation for why he hadn't contacted her immediately.

"Let's get you to bed," Holly said, putting her arm around Claire.

Once they were in the bedroom, Claire laid on top of her bedspread with her shoes on.

Holly slipped the shoes off. "Call me after he calls you. Or comes back, or whatever."

Claire nodded her head against the pillow, staring at the ceiling.

• • •

She woke at 2:12 a.m. to a silent and dark house. Her hand automatically reached to the left side of the bed for Eli.

The cotton bedspread was cold and flat and empty.

At the realization that she was alone, the burn of shame and rejection heated the inside of her skin, scalding her, sickening her.

In devastating seconds of rolling-in visual memories, it all came back.

Her chest constricted and would not let go.

She reached for her phone on the nightstand and pressed the button to wake it up.

An empty screen. No messages. No calls.

Her heart went from constricted to cracking open.

She lay that way for a long time, for the first time in her life in too much pain to cry. She could scarcely breathe, much less cry.

Then, finally, the rage took over.

She sat up in bed and swung her legs over the side.

She put on her shoes.

And she stormed out the front door and into the front yard, staring down Eli's house with a lethal rage.

All was dark. A shiny black Lexus convertible was parked outside Eli's house.

Apparently, he was inside that house, sleeping, *sleeping*, with Coco Skye. Claire wished she could remember Coco's long and unbeautiful Scandinavian name, the one Zoe had re-

cited, that first day they'd met Eli. But even if she could remember, it wouldn't turn Coco Skye unbeautiful.

Of course Claire couldn't compete with that. Coco Skye was
probably the most beautiful woman in the world. What had
Claire been thinking? She was a Grade A, colossal *idiot*. Her
fists itched to pound on the front door, pound out her rage and
shame, demand answers.

Then something worse happened. Her imagination kicked
in. Eli's naked body, so familiar to her, curled around the perfect supermodel body. Every nerve in her body sscreamed at
the thought of it.

The rage fizzled out and turned into a much deadlier ache,
so all-encompassing it was hard not to be afraid she'd have to
live with it forever. She turned and went back to her own
house.

It was 2:57 a.m. now, and she knew for sure there was no
way she'd be able to coax her eyelids into closing. She looked at
his corner of her living room, at his cello and notebooks and
music stand and headphones, and the pain eased a tiny bit.
He'd be back. There'd been some sort of misunderstanding.
Coco had drugged him. Or he'd been knocked unconscious.
That was it. He was in a deep sleep, but he would be fine, and
he would call her tomorrow, and they would laugh about all the
crazy thoughts that had gone through her head.

She retrieved her orange plastic cleaning caddy from the
laundry room and started on the kitchen.

• • •

It was eleven the next morning before he showed up.

By then, she had fallen asleep sitting up in the living room,
woken again, and generally reached a state of mental disrepair
she hadn't known she was capable of.

She was eating a cracker, trying to fight back the vicious bile
in her stomach, when he finally knocked on her front door.

She tried to arrange her face properly before she looked at
him, but she couldn't seem to make her facial muscles cooperate.

His hair was damp from the shower, and she hated him for that. She'd been trying not to vomit by eating half an ounce of cracker, and he'd taken the time to shower, like everything was ordinary.

"Can I come in?" His face was unsmiling, grave.

She shrugged and moved out of his way.

She walked toward the kitchen without looking at him. She couldn't turn him away, but she couldn't just stand there in the same room with him, either.

When he followed, she was standing aimlessly behind the kitchen island, not sure what to pretend to be doing.

"Can we talk?"

She shrugged again, then nodded.

"In the living room, where we can sit together?"

She followed him there, shame and humiliation scorching her as she prepared to be dumped. She had to somehow keep any trace of hopefulness from her face while she waited for him to say what he was going to say. She had to tell him he was exactly right, he belonged with Coco, not with her, and in New York, not here. She agreed with him. It was what she wanted too. They just had to be rational about this. She could still escape with her dignity intact. He didn't need to know how hurt she was.

He sat on the couch, patting the seat next to him, but she took the armchair flanking it, just as she had that first night they'd talked.

"I'm sorry about last night," Eli began.

Claire waited.

"I didn't know she was coming."

Silence.

"Claire, say something."

"This feels awful," she said, finally stealing a quick glance at him. At the sight of him, his unaltered beauty, his fresh-from-the-shower dampness, she nearly went numb. She'd been home, alone, scrubbing, weeping, waiting, and her eyes were surely as puffy and red as pink cotton candy. He looked rested. Handsome. She hated him a little for that in the moment, but then her heart wouldn't even let her have that and went straight back to heartbreak. All her plans to act like she didn't care seemed far away, like an echo.

"I know how this must look," Eli said, searching her face. "I'm sorry. I feel like such a jerk."

"How it looks," Claire said, and she could hear the venom in her voice, "is it looks like you slept with Coco Skye last night."

He sounded genuinely surprised when he said, "What? Wait, no. Claire, *of course not*." He scooted over on the couch so he was closer to her, and he took her hands. "I did *not* sleep with her."

A rivulet of hope. She looked up at him.

His face was open and honest and looking right at her with concern, and she believed him. He was a good man, and she believed him.

She fought back a relieved smile. "Then why didn't you call? Or sleep here?"

He sighed, put his hand over his eyes, and leaned back on the couch, releasing her hand. "Rough night," he said. "It wasn't the kind of situation where I could say excuse me while I make a quick phone call."

"What happened?"

"Apparently sometimes breakups don't . . . *take*, and they have to be done a second time."

"Oh. Ouch."

"There was a lot of crying. I didn't know Coco had working tear ducts before last night," he said. "She does. And they are definitely in working order."

Claire sat and waited for him to resume, a butterfly of hope beginning to flap inside her chest, slowly and rhythmically, increasing its speed bit by bit. He *hadn't been with* Coco. Not that way. He'd just been trying to be sensitive because Coco was hurt, because he was a good guy. And because he really loved her, Claire Taylor, M.D., ordinary five-foot-six-inch human with regular cheekbones, small breasts, and glasses.

"I don't know how I could have miscommunicated with her so badly," he said. "I really messed up."

"What do you mean?"

"She wanted a commitment. I can't commit to anything other than exactly the kind of relationship we had, which was casual. And I thought I had been very clear about that. This seems to be an ongoing problem for me. I'm not sure how I'm getting it so wrong."

The hopeful butterfly stopped flapping.

It had happened to her too. Exactly the same thing. He'd been clear with her, too, but she'd been so sure she was different. She'd rewritten what he said because of how *she* felt. Was that it? She felt as if she were swimming in a river, murky vision and dragged along by undertow, unable to see what was in front of her. She had to get clarity. Right now. Her heart couldn't take any more of this, and she knew that, no matter how much it hurt to deal with it, to hear the truth, she was about to be a mother, and she had to face up to the facts, whatever they were. And maybe the news would be better than what her battered heart was telling her it would be. The butterfly wings flapped their hopeful little wings again, just once, twice.

"I did it too," Claire said quietly.

Eli stopped massaging the stubble on his face. "Did what?"

"Thought I'd be the one you'd really commit to."

His hand dropped to his lap and he just looked at her.

It wasn't open incredulity or anything, but there was zero reassurance on his face.

Her stomach sank and she forced herself to plough ahead.

"I was an idiot. I let myself believe we'd be a family. You, me, and Zoe."

"Claire, I—"

His face said it all.

"You don't need to say anything. This was all my fault. You

were clear with me. You have been clear with me. Crystal. You're going back to New York in June. This is a temporary arrangement. Marriage and children are not in the cards for you because of your job. Et cetera. I've got it. I've got it all. I just let myself get carried away. Like any other Eli groupie." She gave a shaky laugh.

"Claire, no," Eli said, taking both of her hands in his. "Nothing like a groupie. Claire you *were* different. You *are* different."

She snorted before she could stop herself.

He squeezed her hands. "Please, let's part as friends. I've loved—" He stopped. They sat in silence for a moment. "I've loved this time with you."

"This *time*," she said.

"Claire."

She looked at him in disbelief. But of course she should have known. She *had* known, on some level, that this was exactly what would happen. When mere mortals got involved with celebrity gods, they got crushed. Obliterated.

"Claire, if there were ever anyone I could imagine having a family with, it would be you. But that's not in the cards for me. You know that. I won't repeat Gage Archer's choices. I won't be that guy. And my life, my career, is in New York." His face flinched, as if in pain, and he looked away.

Claire wanted to let out of her body a deep, feral scream, which was trapped in her like knives in her lungs. But this was a very dignified breakup they were having, after all. They were speaking calmly. And now Eli was looking at her with compassion and kindness. She reigned herself in, forced herself to sound normal. "I'm spent. If there's any more to say, we can talk about it tomorrow, after Coco leaves. She *is* leaving today, right?"

Eli nodded.

"I'm tired and sad and I need to be done with this for now," she said. She could let the scream out into her pillow once he was gone. "Just call me tomorrow by nine. Zoe is expecting us to visit tomorrow afternoon, so we'll need to get our act together and act normal for the couple of hours we're around her. I don't want to disappoint her, or give her any more to deal with right now."

Eli said nothing to this, and a pregnant silence began to grow larger and longer.

"*What?*" Claire asked, not bothering to keep the dread from her voice.

"Coco *is* leaving today," he paused, his face a stiff mask. "And I need to go with her."

Claire felt like she'd been slapped. Her mouth went dry. She was so sure she'd cried all she had in her during the night. She was so sure she could hold it in, in front of him. But she hadn't seen this coming. Somehow his broken promise to Zoe felt like the worst part of it, worse than Coco, worse than the breakup.

Worse than the fact that he didn't love her.

"I need to pack up the things I have around here."

A horrible little noise came out of her.

"I'm sorry, Claire."

CHAPTER 21

"*Dr. Taylor,*" Zoe said with exaggerated patience. "Did you sanitize my shoes again?" Zoe hadn't quite settled comfortably into the word *Mom*, so she'd taken to making jokes out of what she called Claire.

Claire bit back a smile. "They looked like they could walk on their own," she said. "Just not quite far enough away from here. I think they'd be happy in Australia."

"They're all weird and dark-looking when you do that to them," Zoe said.

"If you'll give me those shoes, I'll buy you any shoes in the world you want. Gucci. Prada. Louis Vuitton." She paused. "But not high heels."

"But I love *these* shoes." They were checkered Vans that Claire was certain would be rejected by the Goodwill.

Claire sighed and slid Zoe her breakfast plate. She'd actually managed to bake a zucchini bread that had not come out like a sticky brick, her first successful attempt.

Zoe eyed it suspiciously.

"It's good," Claire assured her. "I tasted it first this time."

Zoe took a tentative bite, her lips curled away from the potentially unacceptable bread.

Claire rolled her eyes, not bothering to hide it from Zoe.

"Well, I can't help it! You know what that last one was like! Even Pippa wouldn't eat it." Pippa's tail gave a half-wag when Claire looked at her. She waited right by Zoe's feet in case of food droppage. Zoe's face changed as she chewed. She swallowed. "Wow," she said, an amazed look on her face. "It's pretty good."

"*See.*" Claire swatted her with a dish towel.

"Hey, so. After school, can Emma and Emily come over? We're doing Emily's campaign for student council."

"I still don't see why you didn't run. You have just as good a chance of winning as anyone."

"Me," Zoe pointed to herself dramatically. "Public speaking? Nuh-uh. Never gonna happen."

Claire wanted to argue Zoe out of that viewpoint, or at least tell her to tone down the drama, but she was beginning to get the hang of picking her battles after a year of parenting Zoe—four months of it as her actual parent.

"How much homework do you have this week?"

"Not too much. So can they come over?"

Claire nodded.

"Awesome. And don't forget it's cross country practice today, so we won't be here until four-thirty."

"Need me to pick you up?"

"Emily's mom is driving. They can walk home from here."

Claire glanced at the clock. "Eat up and let's go. I don't want to get there after the drop-off line is all the way out to Gentry Road."

Zoe tucked in to her breakfast, and Claire's heart gave a satisfied maternal clutch watching her eat.

• • •

After the carpool line was completed, Claire turned her car toward Springfield in preparation for her twenty-five–minute drive to work.

Claire smiled a little to herself as she pressed the button to turn the radio on.

After a year, she could finally turn the radio on.

For a long time, she'd lived in fear of hearing *his* voice if she turned it on. And sometimes, any music at all had been too painful a reminder.

After Eli had left, it had been worse than just not turning on a car radio. There was a time—thank goodness it was before Zoe had come to live with her for good—that Claire hadn't been okay. She'd managed to rally, mostly, while she was at work, but the rest of her time passed in a fog of grief and sleeping too much, crying too much.

Looking at Eli's empty house next door was like a slap in the face every time she saw it. He hadn't even stayed until his lease was up.

The worst day was the day the piano movers came.

Watching the piano carried across the yard, she'd known then he wasn't changing his mind. He wasn't ever coming back.

He'd called people in Haven, people who weren't her, and made these arrangements. Somehow, the thought of other people in town having talked to Eli, knowing he was moving out for good, when she herself hadn't known, hadn't heard from him—she felt acid-burned with humiliation.

And then the pictures had been published, the ones of him and Coco, back in New York, *together*, and it had felt like more than she could bear.

But soon after that, she'd found out Zoe's arrival was imminent, and that had saved her. She'd managed to pull herself together, at least on the surface. She wanted to be the rock of a mom who could handle anything, so she slapped a smile on her face and started forcing herself to stay in bed only regular hours and pretending she was a fully functioning human.

Once Zoe was with her, she never even told her to stop talking about Eli, even though the little snippets of news from his life knifed Claire straight in the heart. She always made sure to keep her face neutral, so Zoe wouldn't know.

She was better now. She was very nearly over it. Over him. Just, sometimes, when she remembered how she'd admitted to him that she'd thought they'd wind up together, she still wanted to crawl back in bed and escape the world. Really, how stupid could a person be? She should win some kind of stupidity contest. He'd been photographed with Coco Skye within days of leaving Haven.

The most humiliating part of all was, as much as she tried to tell herself she was over it, and as much as she *was* over it seventy percent of the time, sometimes she still missed him. And that wasn't abating. It was like an arthritic shoulder that nagged at a person, only it was her heart.

She worked really hard at not thinking about him, for Zoe's sake, as well as her own. Zoe deserved a happy and stable mother, one who wasn't crumpled in a heap on the bed crying.

She had a good life now. It wasn't exactly the life she'd planned for. She'd still never known the magic of being pregnant. And she was a single mother, something she'd always said she'd never be. But she was a *mother*. And she loved it every bit as much as she'd thought she would.

And she loved the morning clinics at Springfield Whole Family Health. Sure, it was a half hour commute, but she was back in Haven in time to see Zoe after school, and she was able to carpool two days a week. And she loved the experience of treating the whole family—pregnant mothers, toddlers, tiny babies, sullen teenagers, the whole thing.

So she had a nagging heartbreak underneath? Who didn't? She still had so much to be grateful for.

Eli *had* sent her a text message about a week after he'd left Haven.

I miss you.

Claire had felt a wild, euphoric hope when she saw it.

She'd been driving when the text came through, and by the time she'd parked her car and started, with trembling fingers, to answer, something else had come through on her phone screen: a picture from her mother of the latest cover of *Stargazer Magazine*. Featuring none other than Eli and Coco, both wearing black sunglasses and black clothes and striding down a Manhattan sidewalk, Eli's arm around Coco's shoulders.

So, yeah, Claire hadn't answered Eli's text.

And he hadn't sent another.

Eventually, her heart would heal the rest of the way. It had to, right? And she didn't even want a man who would drop out of Zoe's life like that.

Joyce wanted Claire to get back into online dating, and Holly had offered to help her with her profile, but Claire wasn't ready to start bringing strange men around her daughter. Plus, she just wasn't ready.

Joyce had actually been pretty good with Zoe, once she'd come around. Zoe seemed to have a unique ability to give Joyce as good as she got, and Joyce, oddly, respected Zoe for it. In fact, she seemed to enjoy it. Watching Zoe get to have a grandmother meant Claire could forgive her mother nearly anything.

It might not have been the family Claire had always dreamed of, but it was her family, and it was enough.

• • •

Eli sat in his office and fingered the valves of his trumpet without making sound, then set it on top of his piano.

"One of the best decisions you made was to keep things under wraps, so there were no leaks," his assistant, Erin, was saying. Erin, as ever, was competent, organized, and anticipated problems like a fortune teller, but at the moment she was also driving him crazy.

He made a noncommittal noise and picked the trumpet back up.

He'd created the best record he would ever make. He'd created his own label. He'd released the record himself, and achieved commercial and critical success in one fell swoop. *Rolling Stone* had called it "a record that managed to be both singable and heartrending in the same note."

Now Eli had no idea what the hell to do with himself.

And Erin wouldn't let up that they needed to promote this record, just because that was how it was done.

But *Clarity*, the new record, didn't need any more promotion. It had just gone platinum—a million in sales. Eli fingered the trumpet valves again.

Erin was still talking. "Now that the initial buzz of the release is wearing off, I really think you should reconsider a tour. P.R. tells me the sales are leveling, and will begin to decline without one."

"I know," Eli said, and looked up at his immaculately

groomed assistant, who wore a seventies-looking secretary dress Eli guessed was supposed to be ironic.

"So?" Erin said. "Is this something I can get started on? We've had so many phone calls."

"No." Eli looked back down at the trumpet.

"No?"

"No."

"I don't understand," Erin said.

"There's not going to be a tour for *Clarity*. Ever." Eli thought of the eleven songs on *Clarity*. Claire-ity. He'd written half of the record in Haven before he'd left Claire, and half of it, afterward, in New York. He'd bled those songs out, sure as if he'd an ax in his chest, and he couldn't do it again. He sure as hell couldn't get up on a stage and repeat them over and over again while women he didn't know cried and tried to grab his pants.

While Claire stood far away in her kitchen, beautiful, serene and content in her life without him.

These songs were not just personal. These songs were everything. He'd only released the record to the public because . . . well, he'd thought he'd done it to get his career back, but in the end, he'd done it for Claire. He didn't know what he wanted her to do about it, but he knew he wanted her to hear the record, to understand it, and to figure out how in the hell to fix this mess he'd made. Claire could fix anything, couldn't she?

After he'd released *Clarity*, he'd turned into one of those compulsive phone-checkers. He'd thought he was going to have to put some kind of software on the phone to lock him out, or he was gonna go crazy, checking his e-mail every twenty-nine seconds. He was surprised he hadn't gotten a warning from Google saying he was going to bring the mail server down if he didn't cool it.

"But—" Erin said.

"Listen. I'm picking up House of Chow. I have to be back here by two to meet with the accountant, make sure I don't piss off the I.R.S. with any of this. Want some chicken chow mein?"

"You won't even talk about a tour?"

"Chicken chow mein?"

Erin sighed. "Ma po tofu. Please."

• • •

Later that evening, Eli poured his mother a glass of sherry and handed it to her.

"You just seem unhappy, that's all," his mother said again. Her sleek dark hair was swept in its ever-present chignon, and her black linen dress was indistinguishable from any of her other clothing. He'd find it comforting if she weren't busting his balls at present.

"Oh, is that all?" he asked, trying to look and sound amused, and, he was pretty sure, failing.

"This is important."

"Mom, I made your dinner. I bought your sherry. Why you gotta bust my chops now?" His mother would not approve of the word *balls*.

She arched an elegant eyebrow in his direction and took a delicate sip from the little sherry glass he kept in the cabinet for her. "I happen to have known you all your life," she announced. "And I happen not to be an idiot."

He sighed. "I know you're not an idiot."

"Then why have you been lying to me for six months?"

"Lying? What? Mom—"

She held up the hand that wasn't holding the sherry glass. "Now just stop right there. The time has come that we're going to talk about this. No more male avoidance tactics."

"I think that's a little sexist."

"Fine. I'm a sexist. Why are you still in New York?"

"I live in New York."

"Why?"

"Because I was born here and it's the greatest city on earth?"

"Okay, let's try a different avenue. What's her name?"

"*Whose* name?"

"The woman in Haven Springs."

Eli's beer lodged in his throat like a solid. He set the bottle down on the kitchen counter. He looked into his mother's eyes, so like his—intensely brown—but somehow gentle. Kind. And scary wicked smart.

"Mom, don't."

"I already told you, we're talking about this."

"Why?" he asked, trying to keep the growl from his voice. "Really. *Why*? There's no point. I'm in New York. She's there." He waved his hand in a southerly direction. "She has her life. I have mine. And mine doesn't involve moving to Smalltown, Missouri, and it doesn't involve . . ."

"What?"

"All that entails."

"But you love her?"

He shrugged and looked away. God, he loved her. He couldn't stop. He'd thought it would go away if he cut off all contact.

It hadn't stopped.

When he'd released *Clarity*, at first he'd thought it would help him get him over the whole thing, put him behind him. Like it would be cathartic or something. That illusion had quickly evaporated.

He was more hollowed out than he'd ever been. He'd achieved the pinnacle of his career, and he was miserable.

Once, right after he'd left Claire, he'd sent her a message. Just once. But when she hadn't responded, and he'd been off his game for four entire days afterward, he knew he had to throw himself into work. Stop thinking about her. Get over it.

"You hate performing," his mother announced, apropos of nothing.

"What? Mom—"

"If you want to be a record label owner, fine." She took another tiny sip of her drink. "Wait. I take that back. Not fine. You are *not* a record label owner."

"The I.R.S. says different."

She sighed and walked into the living room, expecting him to follow. He stood in the kitchen for a moment, annoyed, but then he picked up his beer bottle and followed her.

He sat across from her and picked up the stereo remote, ready to put on one of her favorites—Debussy or Schubert.

She held up a finger, requesting he wait. "I know I'm getting on your nerves, making you talk about subjects you'd rather avoid."

She was right about that. It was unlike her to be pushy. He'd have to make her sign a waiver before she came to dinner next time—small talk only. Or music talk. Safe subjects. Not Claire. Not his hatred of performing. How did she even know that? How did she know either of those things?

"But the thing is, son . . ." She paused for a long moment. "You're on the wrong path."

Eli fought the urge to tell her it was time to call it a night. He was doing exactly what he wanted to do. He was writing music he was proud of and he was maintaining creative control. He was putting something of value into the world. Something the critics respected, but more importantly, something people loved, and that made their lives a little more tolerable. He was proud of it. He'd achieved everything he'd set out to, and he was happy with it. Well, almost. Was it really possible to be happy in this world? This world where there were fleas and Nazis and global warming and hungry children? He shut his eyes against a flashback of Zoe, shoveling his food into her mouth as fast as she could that first night at Capers.

"Son, please listen."

"Do I have to?"

She went ahead like he hadn't said anything. "Do you know that poem, it's by Mary Oliver? The one where she says—*what is it you plan to do with your one wild and precious life?*"

Eli took a swig of beer. He nodded. He knew the quote, if not the poem.

"You're fucking up."

He gasped before he could stop himself. His mother had

never, to his knowledge, said the F-word aloud. Certainly not in front of him, and he really doubted even to herself in the bathroom mirror. His mother used the word *fanny* because *butt* was too vulgar.

"Yes, I said it. Now that I have your attention." She paused. "Some people only fall in love once in their life. You should have that, Eli. And if whatever constraints you've invented for yourself about your career keep you from having it, you need to reinvent your thinking."

"It's not all in my head. I can't be a professional musician in Gnatspeck, Flyover."

"Nonsense. I'm a cellist, and I make a living, despite the fact that my mother told me I was destined for homelessness."

"Yexactly," Eli said, inclining his beer bottle toward her. "You make a living. *In New York.*"

"There's always composing."

"Yes, there's been a real stampede on composing careers lately. The opportunities are so abundant, it's what all the college kids are studying these days."

His mother just sat and looked at him. Finally, she spoke. It was even quieter than her usual voice, so he knew she was deadly serious. "You just ditched DMG and made a platinum record on your own. You could do that from anywhere in the world, and you very well know it. You're being a chicken."

He put the beer bottle down on the side table. "A chicken? What is this? You think I'm going to go all Marty McFly on you and freak out? Some kind of reverse psychology? Well, I'm not."

"Yet," she said.

She obviously thought Eli was a lot smarter than he was. Or at least a lot less stubborn. He had made his life plan, and he was living it. He was doing exactly what he wanted to do, and that was that.

• • •

Eli looked at the clock next to his bed: 4:04 a.m. In another twenty-six minutes, he'd just give up and get up for the day. He'd already been awake since one.

And he had an interview this morning. For *Vanity Fair*. The journalist was an acquaintance of his, Wes, a friend of Eli's drummer. Wes had once filled in for a trumpet player with a broken arm on one of their tours, and Eli had even seen him cry once, over election results, so it wasn't like they were strangers, but still, this was Vanity Freakin' Fair. The cover. It didn't get much bigger than that, for a musician. And it was widely read enough, the opportunity for making a jackass of himself was much larger than usual. But both his P.R. lady and his assistant had basically told him they'd quit if he didn't say yes, and he knew they were right.

All night long, his whacked-out conversation with his mother wouldn't stop replaying in his head. The next time he had a big interview, he'd make a mental note *not* to have dinner with his mother the night before. Obviously, his former and lifelong belief that she could be counted on not to be *insane* had been erroneous.

He swore as he swung his legs over the side of the bed. He'd promised himself he'd stay in bed until four-thirty, on the off chance sleep managed to hit him over the head and take him, but he knew it was pointless.

Really, his mother had a lot of nerve lecturing him on relationships. Her own track record was solely comprised of Gage Archer, libertine. Wait, make that Gage Archer, *absentee* libertine.

Eli pressed the button on his single-cup Bunn, but he didn't take his usual pleasure at the whir or the coffee aroma that followed a few seconds later.

What if he just called Claire? Just once? Just to see how she was. See how Zoe was doing?

He removed the coffee cup and took a slug. He couldn't call Claire. She hated him. With good reason. He'd walked out on her a year ago, after they'd had soul-melding, once-in-a-lifetime sex. She'd told him she loved him, and he'd left her.

She'd be a fool not to hate him. And Claire wasn't a fool. His chest cracked a little when he thought of her face, that day he'd left.

He tried not to think of it—all the time he tried—but sometimes, it just came anyway.

• • •

Wes Conrad was one of those guys you could tell was sporting a hefty intellect just by looking at him.

He always wore little Ben Franklin style glasses just in case his reputation as a top-notch journalist left any room for doubt. But really, it was the crystal-blue hawk-eyes behind the glasses. They didn't miss much. He was a pretty mean trumpet player, too, for an amateur.

Eli walked through the crowd gathered at the door of Cookshop, the ever-crowded Chelsea brunch restaurant Wes had chosen, and spotted his friend at a table near the window. Heads turned as Eli made his way through the crowded restaurant, followed by a wake of whispers, but no one approached him.

"Ajax," Eli said.

"Are you ever going to stop calling me that?" Wes stood, smiling, when Eli approached.

"Probably not."

"You clean one sink—"

"It wasn't just the sink. It was the fridge too."

"There was a complex protozoan society living in that fridge."

"How you been, man?"

"Working for a living," Wes said. A waitress approached and set some kind of froo-froo coffee drink in a soup bowl in front of him.

"Espresso," Eli said. "Two. Please."

She turned to him and her mouth opened and hung there.

"Oh my God," she said. "My boyfriend is going to *die*. You're, like, his idol, not even kidding. Can I—"

Wes interrupted her. "I believe my friend here needs a menu," he said. His voice was calm and not unkind, his face placid, but somehow there was an authority and a firmness that made the waitress close her mouth and take a miniscule step backward.

"A menu. Of course."

"The frittata is good," Wes said, and Eli found himself ease back in his chair, glad to be in the presence of someone he knew to be a decent guy.

"So, man, I haven't seen you since the tour. What was that, two years ago?" Eli said.

"Yeah, about that. I heard you ran away from home for a while," Wes said.

"Yeah. It was good to get away."

Wes studied him for a moment, then took a sip of the froo-froo drink. "The reviews on the new record, are—let's go for understatement here—effusive."

"Are we starting that already?"

"We can talk about the Yankees or your sex life for a few minutes first."

The waitress came back with the espresso drinks and set them in front of Eli, casting a wary glance at Wes.

"Thanks," Eli said to her. "Fine. Let's get it over with," he said to Wes.

"Max Cohen, over at Acceso, said, "This record is brilliant because it mixes the absurd and the mundane with the—"

"I read it."

"So you usually read your reviews?"

"Not usually. My mother sent me that one. She was impressed because it was Max Cohen, and he noticed me, even though I'm still an amateur because I've never played Carnegie Hall."

"But you could. Play Carnegie Hall."

"Not likely."

"I know they asked, man."

"Maybe I'll do it some year, to make my mother happy. Not

this year."

"*Clarity* is a very personal record. I can see how it would be a difficult one to perform."

Eli finished off the first espresso in front of him and moved the second cup into its place.

They sat in silence for a few more seconds.

"Help me out here," Wes said.

"I think the record speaks for itself."

"It does. But that sentence is going to make for an awfully short article."

"Can't you just talk about how it was to be on tour with us, without making anyone look too terrible? I know the other guys signed releases."

"Sure. Of course, and I will do that. But you know what everyone really wants to know about is *Clarity*. The lyrics—and the tone, really—have the unmistakable ring of truth that gets people's curiosity whetted to fever pitch. They want to know what happened."

Eli glanced around the room, let the clang of steel against stoneware turn into a song in his head.

"Who was she?" Wes asked.

"Nobody." Eli's gaze whipped back to meet Wes's. He felt his breath and pulse warring for speed. "She was nobody."

They stared at each other, suddenly not friends but journalist and subject, until Eli broke the stare. "Don't print that."

Wes shook his head. "Of course not."

Another awkward pause hung between them.

Wes finally spoke. "It's a brutally sad record, but, of course, that's its power. I guess people are responding to that sadness—I counted four Internet memes, just in a few minutes of looking, about listening to it too many times and going insane. But people love it. Did you know it would come across that way when you were making it, that it would affect people that way?"

"I really wasn't thinking about it like that. I wanted to make something in a vacuum, something where I didn't think about the critics, or the sales, or anyone, while I was making it." *Except Claire*. The record was a love letter to her, but he couldn't say that. And if he talked about music, they wouldn't have to veer back into the personal, and talking about music was something he could do. "I didn't listen to anything written after the nineteenth century while I was writing it. Except Satie. He was my modern allowance."

"Satie. You were partying."

"Yes. A party animal."

"On the tour I did with you guys, there was a surprising lack of drugs and womanizing. Not much like the stereotypical rock stars. I confess to a small amount of disappointment. I thought there were going to bras on the chandeliers."

"Yeah, you know, I think people do the drugs and stuff not because they're partying rock stars, and having so much fun, but because life on the road can be hard, lonely. So boring, really, at times. Relentless at others."

"Most of the guys in your band at that time were married."

"Right. And they aren't into the after-parties and the drugs and all that crap." Eli thought for a moment. "Because really, they'd rather be at home in their own backyard, having a glass of wine with their wives, and they're just trying to make it through until they can get back to that, with enough money in the bank to make it until next time. And then it starts all over again."

A familiar weight pressed against Eli's chest. No one was waiting at home for him, no glass of wine in the backyard. He'd done everything he'd set out to do. He'd made the best record he could make, probably the best record he would ever make. He'd achieved the critical success he'd craved. He had more than enough money.

And he felt like hell. Pretty much all the time now, he felt like hell. Making that record hadn't been able to exorcise the feeling. Achieving every last one of his goals, like checking off a grocery list of the unattainable, hadn't even made a dent in it.

Was this it? Was this how he was going to keep going? Could he, even?

"You're known as a reluctant performer, a private person. Are those public perceptions accurate, in your opinion? I mean, of course I have my opinion about that, but I'm asking you."

The waitress came back and asked if they'd like to order.

"Frittata, please," Wes said.

The clang and whoosh of the restaurant, Wes's perceptive gaze, the waitress standing, waiting to hear Eli's order—suddenly it all seemed like an alternate reality.

Everything around him, it was all just scenery in a fake-world amusement park he'd built for himself, trying to get away from real life.

Because his real life was 1,181 miles south, and if he didn't go live in it, he was nothing but a giant Mickey Mouse suit, waving at people, but never real.

Was he brave enough to go there? To get messy and crowded and bored and angry, along with happy and peaceful and inspired and . . . loved?

Wes and the waitress were both staring at him now.

And it finally seemed so obvious he didn't have an answer to the question, the question of whether he was brave enough. Because he didn't have a choice. He had to go there. He had to dive in and get messy and get real and make a real promise to Claire, one he would keep. He was not his father. He was a musician, but he was a man, too, and he wanted to be a good one.

He looked back at the waitress, then back at Wes.

"I have to go," he said. "I'm sorry. I just don't live here anymore."

• • •

"When grandparents emoji," Zoe said, rolling her eyes, and holding up her phone screen for Claire to see.

"I like the emojis," Joyce sniffed. "Besides, you should be grateful you have a grandmother who knows how to text. And who is willing to text you, despite your uppity attitude."

"Uppity is considered to have negative racial connotations. I think you meant *impertinent*," Zoe said.

"I'm going to burn your vocabulary book while you sleep," Joyce said.

"You two, knock it off. I like this song." Claire turned up the volume on the kitchen radio for a Stephanie Kelly song.

It was the song that had come on the radio when she'd been in the car with Eli, the one he'd teased her about. Usually, the song made her feel like her chest was going to split right down the middle, but not now. Now, for the first time, she didn't change the station—she turned it up.

She'd turned a corner, all thanks to a picture.

Holly had texted it, accompanied by the message:

I feel funny about sending this, but it felt like the right thing to do, and I know you don't read Stargazer.

It was a picture of Eli, sitting in a New York restaurant, sitting in a New York restaurant with none other than Julianna Wakefield, the top-grossing box office star in the country. Not the top-grossing *female* box office star. Just the top. Period.

They were in a window seat of a restaurant, and the photo had been taken from outside the window, but the gloss of her thick mane was clearly visible, along with her open mouth, head thrown back in laughter, over something Eli was saying. She was impossibly beautiful.

Holly had been right to send her the picture. When Claire saw it, something broke loose inside her. She didn't *want* Eli. She didn't want a man for whose attention she had to compete with either the most beautiful model in the world or the most successful actress in the world.

She wanted a comfortable life, surrounded by warmth and love and family—even if the two people comprising the family were currently bickering over whether political correctness had gone too far.

It was time to be free of this, and she could feel the vice around her heart begin to loosen. She hummed along with the radio.

It was time to move on with her life, not just on the outside, but all the way through.

Eli's heart was pounding like he was calling a girl to ask her to the ninth grade dance.

He stood two feet from Claire's front door, staring at the fresh glossy paint, the color of a roasted chestnut.

Nothing happened. The living room curtains were open, and everything looked still and quiet.

"She's at the wedding!" a voice shouted from behind him.

He turned. Phyllis Neuman was getting out of her Cadillac, hair first. He was pretty sure none of the hairs had moved since he'd first rented the house next door from her, and he wondered if they made some kind of cement hair spray.

"Hello, Ms. Neuman," Eli said.

"Phyllis," she said, exasperated. "I'm not *that* old."

"Of course not. Not a day over twenty-five."

She sniffed.

"What wedding?"

She waved a dismissive hand toward downtown. "Oh, you know. The music store owner."

"Really?" Dave hadn't been completely out of touch in the time Eli had been gone—there'd been a few e-mails, Facebook—but Dave had said nothing about getting married.

"Shotgun, I hear. Somebody new in town. Martha?"

Eli often thought Phyllis Neuman would have been wearing hot pants and smoking and smacking gum at the same time if it had just been a few decades earlier. "Ah," he said. Well, shotgun explained the lack of invitation. Ol' Dave had been busy. "Where's the blessed event?"

"Basin Park."

Eli nodded.

"Say, you don't wanna rent the house again, do you? These last people like to've driven me nuts. Only here a week and the kitchen needs paintin'."

"I'll let you know."

"Painter'll be by tomorrow. My George ain't good for nothin' but sittin' around with his finger where the sun don't shine. If you get my meaning."

"I do." Eli imagined the gum popping here.

"Well. I reckon you got my number."

"I do."

"See ya," she said, waving behind her and walking toward the house he'd lived in for five short weeks.

Eli slid into his rental car and sat drumming the steering wheel, restless from the anticlimax.

He didn't want to upstage Dave and Marla's big event, but he had to see Claire. And she couldn't kill him in front of half the town. The plan had its upsides.

He left the Escalade parked behind Claire's car—still the same old white Honda, which made him smile—and headed down Crescent Drive on foot. He wished briefly for a hat and some dark glasses, maybe a scarf to hide his hair, but then he remembered this was Haven Springs, not New York, and he felt his shoulders unclench. He took a deep breath of the spring mountain air, and felt his muscles ease, relax.

He felt good here. He belonged here. Here, with Claire. He had a lot to make up to her, but he was ready to spend the rest of his life doing it.

• • •

Eli felt his tension return as he approached Basin Park. Would Claire be glad to see him? At all? Or would she look at him like she hated him?

What about Zoe? Would Zoe forgive him? He'd just have to stick it out until she did. He was, after all, going to be her dad. And he'd do whatever it took to be a good one.

He felt the telltale cold, sweaty hands he always got before he went on stage. Claire had to say yes.

The wedding ceremony was still going when Eli approached

the back of the crowd. Probably two hundred people stood in Basin Park, all eyes on Dave and Marla, fond smiles on everyone's faces. People held hands and passed tissues and Dave was speaking.

"—mainly, I just want to be there for you through the dark times, and laugh with you in the happy times, and I want to thank you for making me a father." His voice broke on the last word, and he placed his hands on her round belly. Marla's radiant face glistened with tears.

Eli tried to make himself invisible near the back of the crowd, and his eyes scanned the crowd for Claire.

He finally spotted her near the front, her arm around Zoe, Holly and Ryan by her side.

Marla was speaking now. "Dave, since you've come into my life I'm the happiest I've ever been. I didn't even know how much I needed more fun in my life until you showed me. And now, we're going to be a family." Marla sniffed, Dave handed her a handkerchief, and everyone in the audience laughed softly and wiped their own tears.

Once the ceremony was over, people began to mill about and the hum of conversation filled the park.

Claire's beauty was like a beacon in the crowd. Her face, the sweetest face on earth, was lit up with a huge smile. She was still standing with Holly and Ryan, and Ryan was saying something the women thought was very funny.

Zoe was a few feet away, talking to another girl about her age. Zoe was starting to look more like a young woman, less like a little girl. She'd gained weight. She looked healthy, and her hair was clean and glossy and hung to her shoulders now. She appeared to be wearing some makeup, which Eli wasn't so sure about, but it was probably premature for him to say anything about that.

Claire laughed again, and Holly hugged her son fondly. Claire's laugh slowed, and she looked just as he remembered her—her glossy chestnut hair flowing around her shoulders, her tortoise-shell glasses, her rosy cheeks, her beautiful body, and most of all, her radiant smile.

Until she looked up and saw him.

Her face fell.

Her smile was so gone it was like it would never happen again.

It was like watching the sun get sucked into a black hole.

His heart physically dipped lower in his chest, he was sure of it. He stood motionless, his eyes locked with hers.

He had no choice now but to approach, but he wasn't sure how to make his feet move.

Holly, aware of Claire's sudden change in demeanor, was scanning the crowd for the cause, and her eyes landed on him. She did not look glad to see him.

He forced himself to walk forward.

"Hi," he said to the group.

"Eli," Zoe said, rushing toward him and throwing her arms around his waist.

He petted her hair, looking over Zoe's head at Claire, whose expression had become murderous.

"This is a surprise," Holly said, deadpan.

"I, uh—" Eli began.

"Follow me," Claire said, her voice low, and Eli's heart gave a hopeful little kick, even though she sounded angrier than Satan. At least she wanted to speak privately with him. That had to be a good sign. He knew she'd forgive him eventually, because he was prepared to spend the rest of his life making sure she did—but maybe she'd go ahead and forgive him *now*. That would be really, really nice. "Be right back," he said to Zoe, disentangling himself.

He followed Claire to one of the stone staircases leading to a higher street above the park. "Step inside so we don't get interrupted," she said. He followed her onto the staircase, and she took a seat on the step a few steps above where he stood.

"A phone call would have been good," she said.

"I'm sorry. I wanted to call. So many times. I just . . .

thought I could get over it. You know, if I didn't—"

"No. I meant a phone call rather than just showing up here. How do you think this looks to Zoe?"

He wasn't forgiven. Not even close. She was really, really angry. And he couldn't blame her. "Claire. Please don't." Even he could hear how lame he sounded.

"Don't? Don't what?"

"Don't hate me."

She let out a sigh, put her glasses on top of her head, and squeezed her eyelids with her hand. "I don't hate you, Eli."

"I want to move here. I want to be with you. I want to get married and give you the babies you want. I want to be a good dad to Zoe. I'll even suck up to your mother. I'm sorry it took me so long to realize it. I've been an idiot."

She replaced her glasses and looked up at him, mouth ajar a little. "*What?*" she asked. It came out in an almost-whisper.

He knelt in front of her on the stairs and took her hands in his. "I do. I want all those things with you. Everything you needed from me, and I was too stupid to offer it to you right that minute, when I should have."

She shook her head.

He looked at her, saw the real *no* on her face. First, his heart burned with the rejection of it, but then his jaw clenched.

"You met someone else?"

She shook her head again.

"Then what? I don't have anything else to offer you. I'm offering you everything I have. Me. My word."

She sighed again, and the sadness on her face was lacerating him. "Oh, Eli," she said, her voice so gentle and full of kindness, he knew it was going to bad news. "It *is* everything I want. I just . . . this is hard to say." She paused. "I just don't believe you."

CHAPTER 23

"What do you mean, you don't believe me?" Eli asked.

Claire could see the pain on his face, and it killed her, but she had to say what she had to say. She took a deep breath and forged ahead. "You didn't come home. You were with someone else while we were together, that last night before you left."

"It wasn't like that. You know it wasn't like that. Claire, I love you. I loved you then, and I was too stupid to do anything about it, but now I'm here, and I'm all in."

"I saw the pictures, Eli. Last year, after you left. You and Coco, together, just days after you were practically living with me. I've already been cheated on once, when Cliff left me. I don't need that. Ever again. I *can't* go through it again. I have a daughter to consider now."

"It wasn't like that, Claire," he said. "Coco is unstable. I couldn't leave her alone in that state, that night I didn't come home. I admit, I shouldn't have left Haven Springs like I did. I was freaked. I knew you and I were getting too close, closer than we'd agreed we would, and I didn't want to go through some big bad breakup."

"I saw the pictures. I'm not an idiot."

"When I got back to New York, Coco showed up a few places when she knew I'd probably be there, and the paparazzi was waiting. They do that. *She* does that."

Claire paused. For a split second, her heart felt a little wobbly, but she forced herself to recover. "What about Julianna Wakefield?"

"Juli—what?" He looked genuinely confused, and some small part of her felt gratified, against her will, but she forged ahead.

"I saw that picture too," Claire said. "People send me this stuff."

"I'm not sure what picture you're talking about, but I've only met Julianna Wakefield *twice*—once to discuss her investment in my record label, and once to tell her in person that I'd decided not to take on investors."

She nodded. She could see that he was telling the truth. She could also see, with fierce clarity, that they lived in two different worlds, and she needed to stick with the regular mortals from now on.

One thing that had been crystal clear when he'd left, even in the haze of heartbreak, was that she'd been right all along—she'd needed a stable guy, a boring guy, a guy who wanted backyard barbeques and strollers. Not a rock star. Look where going against her own plan had landed her. She couldn't do it again. It would be colossal foolishness to repeat that mistake.

"I adopted Zoe," she said.

He nodded. "I'm glad it's official now."

"So even if my trust hadn't taken a beating with the Coco thing, and then not hearing from you, and then not hearing from you some more, I still couldn't say yes. I know you're a decent guy, Eli. I just can't get involved with someone with your . . . lifestyle. I need stability. Trust. For Zoe. Hell, for *me*. I don't *ever* want to watch the man I love walk away with a supermodel."

• • •

Eli wanted to punch things. He wanted to punch things and spit on things and break things.

Of all the things Claire could have said to him, she'd really gone below the belt. *I don't believe you.* A simple *I don't love you anymore* would have sufficed. But if there was one thing he wanted in his life more than he wanted to be a good and respected musician, it was to be a man of honor. He *was* a man of honor. And if Claire couldn't see that, she didn't deserve to be with him.

He allowed himself a couple of hard punches to the hotel bed pillow.

Then he decided to do something he hadn't done since he was a freshman in college—he decided to get very, very drunk.

And he was in luck. The Grand Hotel, at the top of the highest point in Haven Springs, had a bar. The bartender, a young guy, no more than twenty-five, spotted Eli and his eyes lit up.

"What may I get for you this evening?" He placed a cocktail napkin in front of Eli. His voice was overly solicitous and his eyes greedy, but at least he wasn't making a fuss. Yet.

"Glenfiddich. Please. Neat."

"Yes, *sir*."

• • •

Claire was doing something she thought she'd never do.

She was listening to Eli's new record and crying her eyes out. She'd sent Zoe to Joyce's house for a sleepover, and now she lay on her living room sofa, weeping. She cried until her face hurt, until she had nothing left, like she was a wrung-out towel.

Somehow, although she'd known the name of the album was *Clarity*, she hadn't caught on that it had anything to with *her*. She'd been so steeled against anything Eli Archer that she just hadn't let it penetrate.

But listening to it, there could be no mistake. It was *all* about her. Her certainty that the record was about her—it wasn't like when they were together, the wishful thinking of a stupid, naïve girl. This was the hollowed-out, deeply sad, certain knowledge of a woman who'd had her heart broken.

She turned off the album and lay there, staring at the ceiling.

So. Eli loved her. The record made it clear in a way she couldn't even begin to doubt. He'd told her this at the wedding this afternoon, but she hadn't believed him.

She believed him now. She just couldn't think of a way that it could change anything.

• • •

Eli woke the next morning with the worst hangover he'd

had in many years. He reached for his phone reflexively.

He looked at the screen, sat up, and spewed a fountain of profanity worthy of ten rock stars.

On his phone screen was a photograph of him with the blonde woman from the bar last night. He'd barely talked to the woman. Hell, he didn't even know her name, but you wouldn't know that to look at the picture. She was smiling broadly and flirtatiously at him, her hand on his arm, and he was, of course, drinking. It was not a pretty picture.

Holly had sent it. Thought you should know, the caption read. Joyce will send this to her.

How? How had this happened? He was in Missouri, for crying out loud. Who *cared* if he was seated next to a noncelebrity at a bar?

Claire.

He clicked on the picture, only to be led to the Haven Springs Town Talk Facebook page. Well, that explained who cared about the picture.

His phone dinged again. Holly.

She saw it.

Eli sank back onto his pillow and stared at the ceiling for a long, long time.

• • •

Claire was working hard to be as normal as she could with Zoe—picking her up from Joyce's house; packing her a little breakfast, making sure she got to school before the bell. But Claire knew her own face looked like a broken version of itself. Even she could see it in the mirror.

Zoe was eyeing her with a disquiet that squeezed Claire's heart. Claire didn't want Zoe to go through any more instability or uncertainty in her life. She wanted to protect her from it all.

She wanted to kill Eli. She wanted to run to Eli. She wanted to hate Eli. She wanted to love Eli. But she couldn't do any of that.

Once she got through the carpool line and said good-bye to

Zoe, she pulled over to a spot on a side street and rested her head on the steering wheel, hands shaking and heart hollowed out.

She pulled her phone from her purse.

"Holly?"

"Hey, babe. How you doing?"

"I'm a terrible mother."

"Not even close. You're doing great. *Really* great, Claire."

"I wasn't able to look normal this morning. Zoe was scared. I want her to have *security*, not a crazy mother who gets her heart broken and can't make breakfast."

"Did you make breakfast?"

Claire didn't say anything.

"Of course you did," Holly said. "Was it Pop-Tarts?"

"No."

"Then you're fine."

"I'm not talking about the food."

"Oh, honey. I know. Here's the thing, though. No, we don't want to be an unstable presence in our kids' lives. But here, listen up, I'm about to tell you a big secret—" She paused for dramatic effect.

"What?"

"Our kids need for us to be authentic with them, even more than they need to think we're perfect. They already *know* we aren't perfect—whatever we may think—and if we can be real, and 'fess up when we mess up, then, you know, everything will be okay. And it's so much less scary for them when we talk to them about it."

"So just tell her I'm all screwed in the head over a man?"

"How about, you tell her you're sad about Eli, but you still love her, and you'll be back to normal in a few days?"

"Will I? Be back to normal? I feel like I'll never be normal again. And now I have to do four hours of clinic with my face intact. I swear I look like I've had a stroke since yesterday. My smile muscles will not cooperate, no matter how hard I try."

"Can you take a day off?"

"Full clinic. Overbooked, in fact."

"Okay," Holly said, sounding like she was getting down to business, about to fix everything. *If only.* "I have a crazy idea. First, everything is gonna be fine with Zoe. She loves you, and she'll understand if you just talk to her. Second. Do you think you could get through clinic with your regular face if you . . ."

Silence.

"If I what?"

"Well . . . If you let yourself think about saying yes to Eli? He *proposed.* He offered to move here. You can't get much more serious than that. It's everything you could have ever wanted."

"*Holly!*" Against her will, Claire felt the tears come. "How can you *say* that?"

"I don't mean to upset you, honey. But I say that because, well, because he loves you and you love him. And that's not a small thing."

"I know it's not. A lifestyle where women throw panties at your head is not a small thing either. And a husband gone half the time, constantly resisting those panties? That is not the life I want for myself—nervous all the time. Alone with the kids."

"Okay, okay, I hear you," Holly said.

But Claire heard the reluctance in her voice.

"I have to go to work," Claire said. "Do you think I should stop at Walmart for a mask?"

• • •

Eli had been so angry with Claire the day before, he could have spit nails.

Today, he could kinda see where she was coming from.

As much as he hated to admit it.

He could take out his anger on the bartender who'd set him up, but he found he didn't care enough to do it. People would always be doing stuff like that, and it wasn't worth fighting.

His phone rang. Again. His mother. Twelfth time this morning. He'd been letting it go to voice mail.

"Mom."

"Well?" she said.

"Well, what?"

Eli had always thought of his mother as the most serene, dignified woman of his acquaintance. Her life was the cello, the orchestra, tiny sips of sherry—only beautiful things allowed for Leah. He didn't know what to make of this spitfire who kept calling him and telling him to get married. It was like some weird menopausal personality transplant, only he was pretty sure she was old enough to be past that.

"Well, did you talk to her?"

"She said no," Eli said, sinking into the hotel room chair and sighing.

"She said *no*?"

"She did indeed."

"How? Why?"

"Are you really going to make me do this with you?"

She waited.

Finally the silence grew long enough that he answered. "Because of Coco and all the bad press and lifestyle differences."

"Sensible girl."

"*Mom!* Damn, that's brutal."

"Now, now. I don't mean it like that."

"*Hmm.*"

"Listen. I'm coming down there."

Eli snorted. His mother hadn't left Manhattan since before he was born.

"Where do I go? Hold on, I'm getting a pen."

"You can't be serious."

"Why not?"

He sat there, speechless, staring at the white popcorn hotel ceiling. Where had he taken a wrong turn and wound up in *hell*?

"If you don't tell me, I'll call your assistant and find out. I know it's somewhere in Arkansas."

"Missouri," Eli sighed.

"Great. I have a pen. I'm ready."

Eli knew the futility of argument, knew it like he knew the taste of her pot roast or the smell of her apartment—lemon Pledge and books. Leah was dignified, and (usually) quiet. She was also inflexible as titanium once she'd really made up her mind.

"Fayetteville." He sighed again. "XNA."

"XNA. Great. I'll let you know when I have my itinerary."

• • •

Claire followed Holly's parenting advice and told Zoe the truth.

Zoe wanted to make her dinner, to help her feel better, but Claire thought that would taste about as good as a bowl of steaming hot guilt. Zoe had clocked way too much time taking care of herself and a dysfunctional mother already.

Claire stared into the cold air of the refrigerator. It was a far cry from the old days—she still had the ever-present bag of celery and bag of carrots—but now she had chicken breasts and green beans and cheese and beets and other things that required cooking. But tonight, the food just sat there staring back at her without offering any suggestions.

"I know how to make macaroni and cheese."

"We don't have it."

Zoe vanished to her room and returned a minute later.

She held up a slender box of store brand, neon orange macaroni and cheese. "Sorry. I smuggled it in with allowance money. I mean, I like the healthy cooking and all, don't get me wrong . . ." She gave the box a tempting little shake, smiling a you-know-you-want-it look.

Claire, for the first time since yesterday, felt a smile creep over her face, and it was the real thing. "Zoe, you know what? I would *love* a bowl of neon orange macaroni and cheese."

Zoe grinned.

She tied on Claire's apron and got to work, looking pleased and proud of herself.

• • •

Claire looked down at the beautiful newborn with his tawny skin and curly brown hair. He was nursing at his mother's round brown breast, his eyes droopy with sleep, and Claire put a hand on his tiny, curly head. "How are things going, Mama?" she asked quietly.

Nicole beamed up at her with a joy so radiant it squeezed Claire's heart. "Wonderful. Thank you, Dr. Taylor. He's wonderful. Nursing really well."

"Have you named him yet?"

"Charles."

"Charles," Claire repeated, smiling. "A good strong name. Let's have a look at him, shall we? Want to wait until he finishes eating?'

"That pretty much never happens. Is that normal?"

"Yes, for the first few months."

Nicole pulled her baby from her breast and he gave a sleepy pucker of a protest but then seemed to doze off almost immediately.

Claire set him on the examining table and went over his tiny, perfect, incredibly luscious baby body.

And suddenly she knew she would never have this. She wasn't getting any younger and she didn't have a man in her life. She'd tried, halfheartedly, in recent months, to talk herself into using a sperm bank. A little brother or sister for Zoe. The pregnancy experience. But every time she tried to get serious about it, she would remember her own fatherless childhood, and she couldn't stomach the thought of making that happen on purpose.

"Charles looks great, Nicole."

Nicole beamed at her.

Claire smiled a real smile at her, one with no tears in it, and put her hand on Nicole's shoulder. "Call me if you need anything," she said.

• • •

Several days had passed since Eli had shown up at Dave and

Marla's wedding, and although Claire hadn't seen him, the rumor mill—complete with photos—had him staying in the Grand Hotel. She found the photos were becoming less painful—they were the uncontrollable detritus of Eli's life—but they did give her the unwelcome knowledge of his exact whereabouts. Knowing he was just a few blocks away had been like a new permanent ache in her body.

Claire focused on the carrots she was slicing and tried to place herself in the here and now, which did not include Eli.

"Helloooo," Joyce yodeled, entering the kitchen. She hung her purse on the back of a chair.

"Hi, Mrs. Taylor," Holly said.

Claire's mother looked around, presumably for something to give advice about, but Claire hadn't committed any obvious grievances.

"Is that Zoe's famous salad?"

"It is," Claire said.

The doorbell rang again.

"I'll get it," Zoe shouted from the living room.

"Expecting anyone else?" Holly asked.

Claire wiped her hands on a dish towel, and looked up. "No one." She walked toward the living room, towel still in her hand, to find Zoe with her arms wrapped around Eli's waist. A woman Claire had never seen before was alternating between watching Eli and Zoe, and checking out Claire's living room.

She was a tall woman, dressed in simple black linen pants and a black linen blouse. Her dark hair, streaked with gray, was swept back from her face, and not a strand of it dared defy her by coming loose from the updo. Her fiercely intelligent, luminous brown eyes left no question as to her identity—Eli's mother.

"Hello," Claire said.

"Claire. This is my mother, Leah Archer. Mom, this is Claire Taylor."

Leah Archer seemed to float toward Claire without doing

anything so ungraceful as moving her feet. When she spoke, it was in a dignified tone. "Hello, Claire. It's a pleasure to meet you."

Claire had the distinct impression, looking in Leah's eyes, that Leah already knew everything about her, but she knew Eli too well to think that was true.

Joyce chose that moment to burst into the living room, freeze in her tracks, and give Eli the stink-eye.

Leah eyed Joyce's magenta Chico's track suit from top to bottom, her eyes dragging slowly down, and back up. Apparently she wasn't snobby unless you gave her son the stink-eye, and then all bets were off.

"I," Joyce announced imperiously, "am Joyce Taylor, mother of Claire."

"And I," Leah echoed back, but without bite, "am Leah Blum Archer, mother of Eli."

"Well," Claire said. "Well." She wrung the dish towel.

"Can I get anyone a glass of wine?" Holly asked.

"*Yes*," Claire said.

Eli raised his hand.

Leah raised hers, too, and Claire found herself liking the woman.

Claire had almost forgotten about Zoe's friend, Emily, whom she now realized was frantically texting people. Claire bent close to her and whispered, "No pictures."

Emily just nodded, her face awestruck, but not looking up from her phone except to glance at Eli, her thumbs flying.

And then everyone was in Claire's kitchen: Joyce, Leah, Holly, Emily, Ryan, and Eli. Claire took a slug of wine, but she knew there wasn't enough wine in the world.

"What brings you to Haven Springs, Mrs. Archer?" Claire asked, trying her best to sound casual and friendly.

"Leah, please. And—I'm just here visiting my son. He lives here."

The mouthful of wine sat in Claire's mouth with nowhere to go. She couldn't swallow it, that was for sure. She couldn't spit it out. She just stood there, frozen.

She finally got the wine down and managed to speak. "I'm sorry. Lives here?"

"Yes. I'm here to see his new house. He just bought his first house. It seemed like an occasion worthy of a visit."

Claire turned. Eli stood there, looking calm, like the whole world was not collapsing. His eyes were on hers. It was the first time they'd looked in each other's eyes in what felt like an eternity, and Claire had almost forgotten that it felt like everything, like the whole world in a glance. She knew, also, that he understood exactly what she was thinking.

"You what?" she whispered.

"I didn't mean for it to come out quite like this. I wanted to start by introducing you to my mother. But she refused to wait until tomorrow." He shot his mother a sidelong glance. "But since everyone is gathered now, I'll just go ahead and tell you all."

Claire braced herself against the kitchen counter.

"Some of you may know I asked Claire to marry me."

Joyce gasped and Zoe made a small squealing noise.

"She did not say yes."

Everyone looked at Claire, then at the floor.

He held up a hand. "Now, wait. She had her reasons. Good reasons."

Holly was full-on grinning now.

Claire watched him in horror. What was he *doing*? Was he going to tell everyone the entirety of their conversation? Had he recently suffered a head injury? Eaten some bad mushrooms?

Eli saw the look on her face. "Stick with me," he said to her. "I have a point."

Claire nodded. What else could she do?

"So the reason I'm choosing this moment to say what I have to say is we're unexpectedly all in one room together."

Everyone waited.

"And marriage is a whole-family affair."

"But—" Claire said.

"Claire and I love each other."

Claire heard a strangled sound come out of her own throat.

"But she doesn't know yet that she can trust me, and she's got reasons for that, so we're all going to give her all the time she needs with no pressure. Everyone hear that? No pressure." He eyed Joyce.

"Awwww," Holly said, beaming.

"And that's why I've moved here. So Claire can have all the time she needs to see that I'm serious about this. Serious about being a good, stable husband to her, and a good dad to Zoe."

Claire stared at him. She couldn't even allow herself to understand what he was saying.

"I'm not going anywhere, Claire." Eli turned and spoke directly to her. "I've signed on to do the score for the new Jacob Cohn film. It's only a six-month project, but it's high profile, so it should lead to a lot more work like it. I can work from here. In fact, it's *better* if I work from here."

"But . . ." Claire finally found her voice. "New York. Your career. Your whole life."' She choked the thoughts out in fragments, unable to form sentences.

"My life started when I came here. We can figure this out. I work for myself, and I can do what I want, and this is what I want. This, this life with you, is the life I want. I want you to be my wife."

Claire felt the knot in her throat dissolve, and she felt the tears come.

"I bought the house next door, Claire."

Claire couldn't speak. She held up her hand—*stop*—and shook her head.

Eli fell silent. No one moved for a long minute. Eli looked like he was waiting for Claire to say something, but she found she had no words. Finally, Eli cleared his throat and spoke. "Okay. I've said what I came to say. You folks have a good night." He took Leah's elbow.

"It was so nice to meet you all," Leah said. She lowered her eyes then, and she and Eli walked out of the kitchen and out of the house.

When the front door clicked shut, the kitchen was still quiet. Everyone looked at Claire.

"Wait ... Claire?" Zoe's eyes were like saucers. "Are you just going to let Eli Archer walk out of here?"

Claire looked at Zoe. Her heart began to beat faster, and an uncontrollable smile took over her face. "No. No, I'm not. But he hasn't gone far." She ran across the living room and threw open the front door.

Eli stood just on the other side, eyes closed. "Claire!" He raised his arms and Claire stepped into them..

Acknowledgements

Thank you to Jane, Jim, and Alicia for three years of tireless cheerleading. You always believed in me, even when I wrote books that went on to live in the sock drawer.

And thank you to editor Jamie Chavez, who, with kindness and good humor made Yours for a Song a better book.

Thank you to my writing group—Abby, Amy, Debra, Rexanna, and Robin--you help me get to the good stuff.

ABOUT THE AUTHOR

Amy James is a fiction writer living in the middle of
Missouri with her daughter, her husband, and their two
lunatic dogs, Cookie and Rose. She has owned two
bookstores, painted a lot of paintings, and cooked a lot of
food. She wrote her first book in the third grade, but the
critics panned it.

Made in the USA
Columbia, SC
02 August 2017